Sylph or Satan

Lee Cockburn

Clink
Street

Published by Clink Street Publishing 2024

Copyright © 2024

First edition.

The author asserts the moral right under the Copyright, Designs and Patents Act 1988 to be identified as the author of this work.

ISBN: 978-1-915785-45-9 paperback
978-1-915785-46-6 - ebook

Acknowledgements

To my steadfast and hardworking proof reader and editor, Lynn McGregor, nee Duke, a journalist, Photographer and most important of all a good friend since childhood. She has spent a lot of time sorting out my grammatical mistakes and putting my writing into some semblance of order, a task not for the faint hearted. I unfortunately write as fast as I speak, without stopping to look back and check.

To Gordon Adam – a fellow quizzer that saw potential in my books and has assisted in the financing and marketing of book for and the much-loved crime series. He is a friend that has chosen to back my writing and support me in getting my books out to a wider audience. His kindness and belief in my work is greatly appreciated.

To Christine Hoopy Collins a friend for over 30 years. She kindly and selflessly sponsored part of the publishing costs all because she loved my books so much. This assisted me in get-ting the latest novel published. A big thank you to her and to show my appreciation to her, I have written her into book four as a thank you.

Chapter 1

Not Just a Pretty Face

Limbs numb, static, but supple, fully aware but unable to move, his heart pounding, eyes wide open, watery, as his tears filled the corners of his eyes, realising the futility of the situation he was now in. How did this happen? Everything seemed fine, desperate kisses, clothes being pulled off, drinks flowing, then, here. Why?

Helpless, alone, with desperation now overwhelming his thoughts, fear now building inside as the panic was set in, a terror twisting in his gut. Was he alone?

His bath tub was large, very deep, an old stainless steel one, free standing and awkward to get out of. The water in it was shallow enough for the back of his head to lie on the bottom and keep his face above water. He could see the tiled walls still covered in condensation, but the water was now cooling, as he had lain there for nearly two hours, or so he thought.

Muscles unable to move, his head swirling with confusion, fearing the worst, as he started coming to his senses a little more, but his body was still paralysed and ignoring the signals screaming out from his brain to act, to move, to try and escape, his thoughts now running wild, like being left there to die. Was the bathroom empty? Could there still be someone there? Fucking bitch! She must have left him there to humiliate him, he thought, the young female he had been with the night before. He hoped it would just be a matter of waiting it out, and if it was just debilitating drugs, the effect should be wearing off soon and then he could just get up, get dressed and put it down to a bad experience, and certainly not be so careless in future. He was thankful his wife wouldn't be back for two days. He was worried she would find out what he did in his spare time, which he didn't want to happen. She would leave him in a heartbeat.

His eyes scanned around his bathroom, head unable to follow them, checking, searching, making absolutely sure she had left. Minutes passed, and he gave an internal sigh of relief, and comforted himself that everything was going to be okay. If his wife came back, he could say he had slipped and hurt his back.

Silently she stood up from the corner of the bathroom, her blouse torn, a bite mark on her neck and a bruise on her wrist, her memory of the evening before not quite the same as the male who lay there, still helpless in the bath. Her long blond hair lay limp over her shoulders, her tiny childlike frame looked a little sorrowful as she stood there meekly, small neat breasts, boyish hips, all of which made her look underage, even though she was nearly 18, which she now knew was the reason for his choice.

She looked at the man in the bath. His large frame seemed cramped in there, everything limp and still, not quite as intimidating as he was the night before – heavy handed, demanding, uncaring and selfish. She knew she looked very young, maybe 12 to 14, no older. There was a certain type of man that wanted her for that depraved desire. She knew she had to suffer a bit before she could control them and show them, she was not just a pretty face, and teach them that what they do is wrong, disturbingly wrong, and that they must face the consequences for it.

She moved slowly over to the bath, just out of sight, his

eyes unable to see her over the rim of the bath. She looked at his body, strong shoulders, and arms, his tummy a little softer than it used to be judging by his frame. His gold wedding ring, sitting boldly on one of his thick fingers, there on full display on his left hand, fingers that she recalled from the night before, stabbing as they entered, violating her with his neediness, groping her as they transgressed upon her, defiling her most intimate areas, taking her as if it was his right, not caring the pain and discomfort his clumsy desires felt to the receiver.

She moved closer. This time he caught sight of her and his eyes bulged, his pupils reacting with the fear he felt inside. He had thought she had gone, leaving him there as punishment, but her face made him realise that she had a little more in store for him. His mind raced back to the evening before, what he did, how he had acted, what he took, with no consent, without boundaries, with force and cruelty, dominance and selfish wanton desires. Now she stood above him, tiny and vulnerable, watching him in silence, his morality being silently judged and her eyes empty and unfeeling, dark pools leading to her soul, or lack of it as he was soon to find out.

Unnerved by her presence, he tried to move with every nerve and muscle in his body, but nothing was working, apart from his eyes and brain. He could see her expression, her eyes focussed on his, enjoying his fear and the power she was now holding over him, this now emasculated, naked lump of flesh.

She moved closer to him, staring down at him, her face mannequin-like, still and void of any emotion. There was an uneasy standoff, silence for several minutes, his eyes searching deep into hers, looking for emotion, any emotion, good or bad, but there was nothing, only an empty stare. Finally, she spoke quietly to him, her soft innocent voice, the same one that had excited him so much the night before, now sending alarm bells shooting down his spine, but his body could not react in protection of himself, his brain screaming out for help as he tried to shout out, but nothing came. His mouth managed to open, but his tongue muscle failed to respond and only a low-pitched incoherent mumble escaped.

Eventually she smiled down at him as she bent forward, her bare skin in full view, the bite mark clear and raw on her neck, the flesh cut with the force used, the bruised wrist now visible as she brought her arm forward just above his face. His eyes widened even more as he witnessed the evidence of his foul and brutal behaviour, his depravity, his animalistic lust-filled, self-satisfying desires. He had taken everything from her without consent or permission, with force and violence, and the injuries consistent with that were in full view, a realisation in his stare that his actions may have come back to haunt him this time.

He looked up at her. This time it was his turn to be submissive, and he pleaded to her with his gaze. Her eyes met his, but she did not blink, or pay any attention to the false sorrow in them. This tiny sylph-like female was now starting to make him feel really uncomfortable. His vulnerability, never more obvious as she moved round the bath, finger trailing the edge, and slowly turned on the taps. His heart pounded fiercely within, his intense trepidation spiralling out of control, twisting inside his gut, and he could not respond physically, as his nonfunctioning body just lay there, motionless in the water, naked and exposed, his flaccid penis floating, enhancing his vulnerability.

The power of the water filled the bath quickly and his head was no longer supported beneath, but it remained floating just above the surface naturally, which he was relieved about, but his relief was short lived. She leaned into him, whispered, "Are you sorry?"

Her voice rising. "Are you fucking sorry now, you pitiful, posh twat, an unfaithful, married, perverted wanker?" Her face twisted into a contorted childlike smile, a mixture of sweetness and evil as her neck seemed to stretch awkwardly, her expression doll-like, as she lifted her arm over the rim of the bath, placing a single finger on his forehead. Her smile never wavered or altered, not even a tiny bit, her eyes remaining fully focussed on his, hate and resentment shining from her eyes, as it kept building inside her. There was nothing within her to control her urge to harm him.

No pressure was used at first, as his eyes pleaded one last time. Silently, he begged for her to show him mercy and forgiveness for what he had done to her. His regret and sorrow were too late, and now he had to pay.

She smiled, a smile so sickly and sweet, her head tilted to the side as she spoke gently to him, "I like hurting people!" She twisted her hair in her fingers as she spoke again. "You've made this so much easier than the last one. He didn't deserve it, but you certainly do!" Anger and resentment spread all over her face, no sweetness or innocence on display now, just the look of the devil, pure, unadulterated evil.

Her finger gently pushed down on his head again, his eyes screaming out silently as they slipped beneath the surface, and then his nostrils, which sprayed water outward as they too became submerged. Water streamed down the back of his throat from his nose, and he started to choke. He was panicking inside, trying desperately to hold his breath, but he couldn't stop the water pouring in and slowly drowning him. His size and strength, which he had used to overcome her before, could not save him against the pressure of a tiny slim feminine finger.

She smiled openly as she pulled his hair tightly to bring him back up to the surface, mucus and snot flying out from his mouth and nose, as he desperately tried to clear space to breathe. She gave him long enough to cough up enough water to steal a breath before she leaned over him seductively, her breasts held over his face, just like he demanded she did the night before. He had bitten hard down on her nipples, repeatedly, and did not stop, no matter how much she cried out.

"What's wrong with you? Do you not want them anymore?" she rasped girlishly in his face. "Hold your breath now, or you'll choke." A sinister smile covered her face.

Letting go of his hair, this time she pushed his head right back with intent, extending his neck, taking away any chance to hold his breath, nostrils now full, and water free flowing into the back of his throat. He couldn't stop himself breathing in a desperate attempt to get a lungful of air, and he tried in his mind to get up to the surface, willing his limbs to move, hoping the drugs would wear off and give him a chance. Terror filled his eyes, panic making them bulge out, wide and bulbous, pleading for some mercy from the young woman above him, but there was none coming, and he didn't deserve any, as his mind raced back to the night before, and everything he had done to her, using her like a piece of nonhuman trash. He had failed to show the mercy that he was now so desperate to receive. Finally, he felt remorse for his actions, but for him it was too late.

Forgiveness didn't come, all she felt was revulsion, the need for vengeance as she pushed down on his head with the weight of her body, all seven stones of it, two hands close together on his forehead, creating a debilitating angle, to make sure there was no chance he could get his head back up to the surface, if some miracle recovery was to happen.

His body started to convulse as the lack of oxygen was now killing him slowly, cruelly, in the most helpless and terrifying way possible, fully aware of what was happening to him, with no hope or ability to save himself.

She was still smiling, then giggling, her heart pounding with the excitement of what she was doing, the power she held over him, as his once precious life dwindled away from him, his evil actions, deserving of his fate.

Finally, she let him go, when she thought he had been under long enough to die. His head remained below the surface, his eyes wide open, staring upward, his gaze fixed and remaining in sheer terror, his expression now etched on his face for eternity. Small air bubbles escaped from his nostrils, which looked like mercury bubbles beneath the surface. This amused her as she reached under to free one, to watch it rise to the surface and burst. She smiled once more at the finality of the last morsels of air rising up from him.

The young woman walked round and round the bathroom, laughing, holding herself tightly round the waist, as her eyes darkened from within, her pupils so wide they nearly covered the whites of her eyes, the madness within now contorting her whole expression, demon-like features now visible, her innocent little face now completely gone and the evil within on full show, and an unimaginable force lurking within her.

She snarled a deep guttural growl, an unnatural sound from someone of her frame and stature, her vocal-chords unlikely to have been able to produce this type of sound, not one so deep and masculine, from one so slight and feminine.

She fell to her knees, growling, rocking back and forward, repeating incoherent words, over and over.

She dug her finger nails into her own skin. Deep scratches appeared, oozing blood, as she continued to rock back and forth, her heart rate slowly dropping back to normal, before she was able to stand up and stare at the man in the bath. No remorse was felt as she went about sorting out the mess.

He had mentioned his wife wouldn't be back for a couple of days, plenty of time to clean up, wash the bed clothes and leave the place spotless.

She looked at the body. He was a really big man, but not too big to manage. She pulled his head up and out of the water, and freely poured as much gin and vodka down his throat, pulling his head up and down, letting it run down his throat, hoping it would reach the stomach and not his lungs.

Another suicide, unexplained, but the stress of work and guilt can do funny things to people, sex-enhancing drugs and alcohol in his system, kinky for many, used to heighten orgasms and other deviances, and also to dull the fear of taking that final step to escape their sins.

Those left behind would wonder why, but she knew exactly why – you reap what you sow was now her motivation to hurt others.

Chapter 2

Good Morning

Taylor rose up majestically from her bed, her nude form smooth like marble, her taut frame with curves where they should be. Kay smiled adoringly at her as she pulled her back down on top of her, her weight heavy and unbalanced as she slumped back, practically squashing Kay. She too was naked, still warm from her slumber.

"Wow, careful, you'll hurt yourself. I'm pretty heavy!" Taylor laughed.

"Pretty, definitely; heavy no. Just heavy enough to know that you're there."

Taylor laughed as she had to manoeuvre herself up a little and held her weight up, moving over a bit, to avoid squashing Kay again. This time her weight was placed skilfully, to allow her to engulf Kay in a fond embrace, her thigh placed high up between Kay's thighs, gently touching her firmly and intimately, Kay already waiting with apprehension of what was to come. Their soft tender kisses fell upon one another, entwined as one, skin on skin, their breasts gently touching, as Taylor lowered herself down, pushing her thigh more firmly up between Kay's legs this time, Taylor enjoying Kay's obvious pleasure.

Kay looked into Taylor's eyes. "I'm so lucky to have you here with me. I really thought this would never happen like this again. I love you so much Taylor; you know that, don't you?"

"I know you are sooo lucky," Taylor said, with mirth in her eyes and a broad smile across her face. "I'm the lucky one here. You're beautiful inside and out, and I wouldn't have it any other way."

Kay leaned in to Taylor and kissed her softly on the lips, then again, and again, their mouths opening to share a deep, passionate, love-filled kiss, a kiss which just got deeper and deeper, their tongues dancing together as their bodies moved against one another, the warmth and moisture enticing. Taylor pushed up against Kay's intimacy, the pressure making Kay moan a little. She reciprocated by opening her legs wider and raising up to meet Taylor's thigh, hand and fingers. Taylor loved when Kay moaned lightly into her mouth. It sent tingling sensations through her, and the desire to make love to Kay was now unstoppable. Taylor's hand slipped over her more vigorously, repeatedly, Kay's moans willing Taylor to make her cum. Kay responded feverishly, kissing her deeply as she held Taylor's face, willing her to fuck her. Kay paused momentarily; her desire overwhelming. She pulled Taylor over her and pushed her firmly onto her back, moving herself over her and up above her face, letting Taylor's mouth continue loving her, Taylor clearly obliging and willing as she finally thrust her fingers deep into Kay's smooth silk, her mouth continuing the onslaught of pleasure upon Kay's exposed haven. Kay's thighs trembled and gave way a little as the sensation of Taylor's tongue and fingers weakened her, tongue and fingers working in harmony offering feverish sensations to reach that climax, Kay's orgasm so close to the edge, but she didn't want to let go yet. It was too soon, so she lifted herself up off Taylor's desperate mouth to let the swirling tingles subside a little before she couldn't resist anymore and moved back down, close enough to let Taylor fuck her again, her hand moving with strength up inside her, Taylor's mouth finally taking her into it, one more time, her tongue rhythmically licking and fingers fucking deeply into her. This time Kay couldn't stop herself. Her orgasm was all-consuming, with provocative moans of pleasure, back arching, breasts protruding, her nipples taut with pleasure and her release physically obvious to both of them. Taylor's fingers pushed deep inside, fast and deep, not stopping, her thrusts relentless and welcome as Kay's orgasm continued to spiral deep inside her, until it was released again, even more intense than before, finally raising up and pulling away as Taylor's touch became too intense to bear, letting her know that she was finally ready to stop and couldn't take any more.

Taylor kissed Kay deeply as she began reaching out to touch Taylor intimately, stopping her gently. "Kay! I was late the first time I got out of bed, now I'm really late. You'll have to join me later to finish what we started here. You know Findlay doesn't need excuses to have a go at me, especially if my neck is flushed from making love to you. I love you, but now I need to get there for seven. I'll see you when you get in at nine, and you can love me later, I promise."

Kay pulled a sad face as she caressed Taylor, licking gently over one of her nipples. "I'll hold you to that. I want to savour your pleasure, not just a quickie in the morning." She took her nipple into her mouth once again, sucking it firmly, sending a twist of pleasure through Taylor, her fingers deliberately slipping across her intimacy, making Taylor jump a little.

"What's wrong with a quickie?" Taylor said, breathing in hard, and looking into Kay's eyes. "I like quickies." Taylor smiled at her mischievously, fighting the thoughts of letting Kay's hand do a little more, but she was late for work, too late, and was up and out of bed in a flash and now heading to the shower, perfect breasts, neat, firm bottom and definition all over, her olive skin and long wavy brown hair setting the rest of her off nicely.

Kay sighed deeply. "I wish you could stay with me. I want more; you know what I'm like," she said as she turned over onto her back, her silky skin glowing with her recent pleasure. She kept her eyes on Taylor's as she seductively allowed her legs to open, teasing her, Kay's intimate pleasure, a hand placed there, moving over herself, beckoning Taylor back to love her more.

Taylor knew she needed to leave soon, or she was going to be late, but the view before her was too inviting and irresistible, the glistening haven, inviting breasts, taut nipples and a beautiful face, the face of her lover and trusted companion, the person she loved, and she could not help herself from crawling back on the bed. She kissed feverishly as she delved her fingers into her once again. Kay screamed out aloud. Taylor made love to her, kissing her with such intensity that Kay gripped the sides of the bed. She could not hold back, toes curling, as Taylor's hand thrusted relentlessly. Kay whimpered loudly as her climax was mesmerising and desperate, and very quick to Taylor's delight. There was still a chance she could get to work in time, but Kay knew Taylor was on the verge of her own orgasm. Kay knew that making love to her turned Taylor on, and she knew the pleasure her hand could give, so she took her chance and slipped into Taylor. To her surprise, and pleasure, Taylor felt the surge of desire and need as she too was entered. Kay's perfect motion over her and deep into her sent spasms swirling in her, and in less than a minute, Taylor's orgasm was gripping Kay's fingers, silky wetness revealing just how much she too was needing this intense pleasure. With numerous final thrusts inside her, Kay, knowing Taylor needed more to be satisfied, continued until Taylor moved away and motioned to get off her, only now realising the time.

They kissed, smiling, Kay moaning loudly, curling the duvet between her legs as this time she finally let Taylor go.

Taylor rushed through to the shower, still totally aroused herself, her needs not quite fulfilled. She smiled again as she licked her lips, enjoying the taste, before letting the water flow forcefully over her face.

Her shower was the quickest ever, her hair towel dried as she threw on decent underwear, a little lace, her suit, fitted and dark, smart and businesslike. She sprayed some scent all over, pulled on her heeled boots, and shook her hair out, then tied it up as it was still soaking wet.

She went back through to Kay less than ten minutes after she had left, kissing her, deliberately keeping her at arm's length to try and avoid any further nonsense before work.

Kay kissed her back and turned her around, holding her with one hand. She opened the front of Taylor's trousers with the other, just enough for her hand to slip over her. She stroked her, moisture still awaiting further promise, and slipped over and into her again, her firm and gentle feminine hand heightened the pleasure with her ability to please. Her skilled adept hands swept Taylor to a swirling release. Taylor had tried to resist, but she knew she had wanted more. Still standing, and leaning slightly back on Kay, she moaned in delight, her nipple now gripped tightly between Kay's fingers, her legs giving way a little as her orgasm came, twisting luxuriously inside her. Kay supported her and leaned forward to kiss her intimately again, her fingers wet and still moving deep inside her beautiful partner.

Taylor pushed a strong kiss into Kay and said, "No more. I have to leave!" This time Kay let her go. Light kisses, a little adjustment of Taylor's clothing, and she was gone.

Taylor, a detective sergeant in the Major Investigation Team, had to get to work in time to avoid the wrath of Detective Inspector Findlay, a rotund man who didn't appreciate strong women, especially those that were gay, popular and good looking!

Meanwhile, Marcus Black, a detective constable in the same unit as Taylor, had already kissed his wife Maria, his young son David, and Maria's tummy to say goodbye to the baby growing within her, Maria now showing a large bump. He had been up early enough to shave, shower, eat and prepare some nice healthy food to take to work with him. Marcus was tall, dark, strong, attractive, kind, caring and very professional, as well as punctual, the polar opposite of Taylor. Taylor was the boss that he looked up to, because she had a great mind, was a good leader, fair, experienced, would not be beaten down and would make sure her point of view was heard and explained.

Marcus had already arrived at the office. He said farewell to the skeleton nightshift crew and put the pot of coffee on for all the troops to share when they got in. He was the one many relied on. Findlay had not appeared yet. He was always a little late, usually to collect some carry-out unhealthy junk food snack to devour grotesquely in full view of the others on his way in, much of it landing on the front of his shirt or tie.

Thirty minutes later, and just on time, Taylor swept into the office, flung her jacket over her swivel chair and rushed over to Marcus to squeeze his ribs in a friendly but rough way, nearly knocking him onto his desk, playful mirth on her face, and clearly still on a high after her morning of passion.

"How's Maria? How's that bump coming on, and Wee Davy, of course, all good I hope?" Taylor chirped cheerfully.

"You're in a good mood. Any particular reason?" Marcus smiled, knowing full well why Taylor was happy. He had seen the telltale flush on her neck when she arrived, and that meant only one thing.

"Things going well with Kay then, I take it?" This time he had a cheeky smile on his face.

Taylor turned with her coffee cup in hand, smiling from ear to ear. "Better than I could ever have imagined. I thought that it wouldn't go back to anything nearly like it was before, but Kay is doing well, really well!" She smiled at Marcus.

He smiled back as other detectives filed into the kitchen to get their life-giving caffeine too, before Findlay blustered into the office, late as usual, to darken everyone's spirits, everyone wishing that DCI Sommerville could come back to put him in his place, as she had done before.

They had all been sharing some chat, office banter and coffee before Findlay came in and burst their bubble, his appearance enough to turn heads, not in a good way, in the opposite direction. He was dishevelled and unkempt, stains on his clothing from food, recently devoured, the look certainly not of a leader, not one to be respected anyway.

"Right, folks, we have a new body, recently washed up at Silverknowes beach near to Gypsy Brae. Another suicide, probably a jumper off the bridge," he said with no emotion or feeling.

He didn't stop for breath or comment, because he just wasn't interested in what others had to say. He was an auto-cratic ruler, certainly not willing to listen to others. He carried straight on with a completely different subject. "We also have a new detective joining us tomorrow. He's from PPU (Public Protection Unit, who deal with sexual crimes). His name is Christopher Steele and he'll be coming next week, so welcome him, please!" He clearly couldn't care two hoots if the new detective was welcomed or not, but he knew he had to say things like that to conform.

Taylor looked round, getting back to the original message about the body. "At Gypsy Brae? That's another one out with the normal placement; the tide usually takes them further up to Niddrie Bents, East Lothian, or over the water to Fife. There must have been some freaky tide or something."

"Or something!" Findlay just glared at her, totally unaware and not interested that a body had turned up where it shouldn't for the second time in less than a month, as if it was not significant at all.

"We'll take it. We had the last one a month back!" Taylor said enthusiastically.

"Nope, you won't. You take the Nathan case, the vehicle collision you attended a while back. The press are all over it now because some daft bastard has leaked the link to his sister Amy to the press, and the fact he ran over a paedo doesn't read too well, so you're going to go over every last detail, as the public are clearly insinuating it was deliberate, and not the accident you wrote it off as!" He smirked at her, knowing she would rather deal with the body. He was intentionally keeping her from a more interesting case. He liked dominating her, deliberately pissing on her leg like a dog, a control measure she hated and resented.

Taylor's face showed visible rage. His continual control, putdowns and redirection of tasks were wearing thin. The body was something Taylor would usually take the lead in, and rightly so, to check there was nothing more sinister, but Findlay was being his usual disruptive and antagonistic self, deliberately taking control away from Taylor to suppress her spirit.

Taylor looked at Marcus. They had both had their suspicions that Nathan may have been slow to brake on the day of the accident and may have known about the guy's murky past. But they couldn't prove it then, and they wouldn't be able to prove it now. They had gone over everything they could, but Findlay seemed to think they could dig a little deeper, in case they had missed something.

Taylor leaned into Marcus, in full view of Findlay, but covered her mouth, deliberately wanting Findlay to react. "We'll keep an eye on the washed-up body too. I've worked here a long time, and it's not normal for a body to be washed up there, unless it's been dumped by someone who doesn't know how the tide works. I'll make a point of emailing the ocean-ographer first thing."

Findlay looked like he was going to blow a gasket, but all eyes were on him, and their loyalty was with Taylor, so red-faced and livid, he left, already plotting his next move to put her in her place, maybe for good this time.

Taylor led the way out of the office, Marcus hot on her heels as they walked through the open plan office and through to the rear door, just as Kay was walking in. Taylor stopped to greet her and openly kissed her cheek as their hands met. Findlay turned and watched, jealous as he too had eyes for Kay, and in his narrowminded, narcissistic, chauvinistic world, could not see why she would choose a toned, athletic, smart and intelligent woman over him. He was unaware that his fists had clenched into tight little balls, his temper start-ing to spill over into something more uncontrollable, vengeful and more dangerous than before. Findlay's bigotry and hatred were now manifesting themselves as a hostile game of control and dominance, without the restraint he once had.

Kay looked at Taylor. She could see that she was annoyed, and it didn't take a genius to work out why when she saw Findlay waddle out of the kitchen after the rest of the troops had filed out, his eyes fixed on them, cheeks flushed and angry.

"Don't let him get to you. He's loving this. Just do your job. He'll screw up in his own time!" Unbeknown to them, he was planning Taylor's demise.

Kay's words were said softly but with venomous hatred towards the despicable man that deliberately set about under-mining Taylor and who openly demoralised the officers he was in charge of. She could not understand how a man like that could keep his position, although, deep down, she knew the boys' club looked after their own.

Findlay kept looking and met Kay's stare, and what Kay saw was not healthy. It made her skin crawl. He kept his eyes on hers, then they dropped and trailed sleazily over her breasts, then over her whole body, lingering, and then slowly back up to meet her eyes, before he smiled an ominous, creepy smile right at her and turned away.

Kay nudged Taylor to look at him. "Eeeuuch, did you see that? The letchy creep, he just blatantly stripped me with his eyes. He's gone too far now. I actually think he's dangerous!"

Taylor spun her head around, but she was too late to witness Findlay's vile stare. She was boiling inside. She knew that he had her over a barrel, but without proof, she was totally unable to stop this ingrained, misogynistic and previously accepted chauvinistic behaviour, especially in a rank-driven organisation.

"Don't worry about him. Even if he was up to something, he's shown time and time again that he's a useless lazy wee prick. He really needs taking down a peg or two though."

Kay held Taylor's arm. "I'm not so sure, you know. He frightens me now. It's gone too far; I think it's more than the joke we make of him. He's not right in the head, old school and untethered!"

Taylor listened and reassured her, not wanting to give that fat little creep any kudos. He could be dangerous.

Taylor and Marcus left the office and moved out into the car park at Fettes, the old police HQ. They took the best of a bad bunch of vehicles, the usual reek of stale chips and a healthy dose of litter left inside to meet them. This infuriated Taylor, as there was no need. It was pure laziness and slobbery, but she had an idea who had been in the car last, and there was certainly no love lost there.

She looked at Marcus as she flipped a wrapper up at him, hitting off his perfect hair, and his face was a picture as he flicked it right back at Taylor, showing his disgust at being touched by unclean wrappers, the wrapper now skidding off her brow. "Beat it you!" Taylor smiled as she rolled it into a ball and took it out of the car and threw it into the bin.

Chapter 3

Nathan

It was chilly outside. Neither of them were wearing anything that would keep out the cold, and the heater in the dilapidated Peugeot offered very little warmth. They were cold in their thin but fashionable dress suits as they headed to Silverknowes to speak to Nathan about the vehicular accident he had been involved in recently.

Nathan's sister, Amy, had been convicted of multiple murders the year before. She had taken the law into her own hands when she had infiltrated a paedophile ring and carried out a string of brutal assaults and murders as she reaped her revenge for the abuse and cruelty she and Nathan had endured in their younger years. Both suffered at the hands of her parents, but only Nathan seemed to have come through his troubles and made a good life for himself, with a wife and young daughter. To his surprise, Amy had left Nathan an unwanted parting gift when she was given a life sentence in a psychiatric institution. It was a list, a detailed list of despicable men that were suspected of being involved in cruel and vile acts against children. Those men had never been convicted (beyond reasonable doubt had not been secured) as there had been insufficient evidence at the time, although they remained under suspicion. Nathan had swithered about what to do with the list, whether to take it to the police, destroy it, or keep it. In the end he had decided to keep the list, because of the effort his sister had gone to get the information and the price she had paid to out these people, to make them pay for their crimes. Nathan's intention was never to act upon it though. He had looked through it, taken a mental note of the names contained within the sordid pages, noting who was suspected of the horrendous crimes. He made a decision that he would not take the law into his own hands as his sister had. He had more to lose, his beautiful wife and beloved daughter, to whom he was devoted. This decision was easy to keep until a name he recognised from the list appeared, too close to home to ignore. The name had also appeared on a list of newly appointed teachers at the nursery school his daughter now attended. His past came rushing back to him at full force, a dreaded fear that history would repeat itself. Nathan's face had prickled with pain and his stomach churned violently, causing instant nausea and discomfort, as the memories of the brutal, cruel violations that he and his sister had suffered at the hands of his depraved mother and her partner, when they were the same age as his daughter, returned. He had become overwhelmed with rage and panic. He was not going to sit back and risk letting anything happen to his precious little girl. He was going to make sure she was never going to experience anything that he had been put through. He would stop at nothing to keep her safe and away from that man. He was prepared to do anything to keep her innocence intact.

Nathan had made his mind up. He had reread the file and the teacher's attraction was exactly that of pre-school-age females, but unfortunately there was no conviction, no record, nothing to stop him taking his perversion further, except for Amy and Nathan. Nathan knew offenders tried to try and secure occupations that allowed them to be close to their desired prey, and positions of trust were favoured too. He had made the decision to do something, although he wasn't sure what he could do. He couldn't go to the authorities, he would have to give up the list, so he decided to follow the teacher home from school multiple times, watching, waiting for a chance to take action, his patience wearing thin. Eventually, after several days, the opportunity arose. He was handed the perfect scenario as the teacher decided to cross the road right in front of him. He felt the electricity course through his veins, pins and needles stabbing all over him, an animal instinct taking over him as his foot jolted into action. Decision made, he pressed the accelerator down hard and watched, almost in shock, as he knocked the man clean off of his feet. The teacher landed heavily on the road, his body grazed and contorted. His injuries were obvious to Nathan, a possible broken pelvis, a femur protruding from his trousers, the deformity clear as well as a nasty bang to the head. Nathan had got out of his car straight away, his face a picture of believable shock and innocence as he offered assistance to the injured man. He was the one who had called an ambulance and was the most caring and apologetic person he could be. There were numerous bystanders and witnesses that came to help after seeing the accident happen. They saw Nathan's actions, and he had made sure his emotions looked genuine, filled with sorrow and apology.

Taylor pulled their vehicle into a residential street in Silverknowes. Nathan's home was a modest semi-detached property in a popular area on the North side of Edinburgh. Once stopped, Marcus turned to Taylor with a look she was used to, a look of conflict and undecided opinion. Both of them had dealt with Nathan before, and he seemed a really decent guy. He had been wrongly accused of the assaults Amy had orchestrated and had served time for crimes he did not commit. His innocence was finally proven after the crimes continued even though he was incarcerated.

"What is it, Marcus? What are you thinking, apart from

hating Findlay?" Taylor said in an attempt to draw his thoughts out of him.

"This just feels wrong. It feels really shitty. It's already been dealt with, investigated with more effort than normal. It's almost victimisation because of his association with his sister Amy and her crimes, which he was proved to be completely innocent of!" Marcus's face looked pained with his furrowed brow and sorrowful eyes. He actually liked Nathan and thought he was a decent human being.

"Listen, even if he did run him over deliberately, there's no proof of what was going on in his mind. The guy didn't die, and he made sure he received medical attention straight away, with a lot of witnesses speaking up out of concern for the man, and his genuine sorrow and his multiple apologies. He's either a great actor, or he didn't mean it. People get knocked over all the time!" Taylor exclaimed.

"What do you think, genuinely?" Marcus asked, knowing she was saying all the right things.

"I think he knocked the bastard over deliberately. He's a new teacher at the school, who has access to his daughter, and, if you check him out, he was part of an investigation into the distribution and viewing of pornographic child images: no conviction, no restrictions put in place."

Amy had given Nathan her list of those who had been involved in child pornography, but not yet convicted, unbeknown to Marcus and Taylor.

"I believe Nathan chose to take him out, and rather than waiting on that deviant little creep to act, he took early action. Very drastic action, I'll give you that, but everything was to protect his daughter. Try proving it though, just like the charges that should have been brought against the teacher!" Taylor said in a totally serious voice, with her all-knowing eyes.

Marcus was taken aback. "You're serious, aren't you?"

"One hundred percent I am. That's why I applied for a warrant for the house, to search for any documentation that would link him to the crime, and a review of CCTV from a couple of weeks before, although we've done all this before. Even if he's followed him a couple of times, there's nothing to say that's not just coincidence. Everything rides on the search. If it's negative, then end of enquiry into the accident." She paused, and said, "I'll definitely be reopening the enquiry into the nursery teacher though. There must be more to that, something missed due to other pressures and heavy workloads. They were aiming for the ringleaders and sacrificed the capture of the Minnows on the sidelines, until now!"

Both of them knew they had to dig deeper into Nathan and whether he had knowledge or the motive that the two detectives were now aware existed, but they both secretly hoped they wouldn't find anything.

"C'mon, let's do this." Taylor strode towards the front door, with Marcus right behind her, both smart in appearance and a picture or professionalism.

Nathan answered, hearing the very stern police knock on the door.

He opened the door and looked at the two smart officers standing on his doorstep.

There was recognition, and a smile was offered to them both, with genuine respect. Nathan was a cool customer, and he was realistic enough to know the police would try and uncover every piece of evidence, but he was happy in the knowledge the paperwork was stored in a safe place away from here. There was nothing that could prove the crash wasn't an accident.

Taylor and Marcus provided ID and introduced themselves again with an explanation of their visit. They showed Nathan a copy of the warrant, giving them and the other specialised officers the right to search the premises, curtilage, vehicles and outbuildings. Nathan did not show any emotion, just polite affirmation of what needed to take place, and acknowledged their need. Inside, he was a little worried he might have left something, but he assured himself he hadn't, and his motive was to protect his precious daughter. He knew he would destroy the files at some point, but only when it was safe to do so.

Chapter 4

New Arrival to the Team

Chris Steele looked in the mirror. His kind eyes gazed back at him. He was in his late twenties, tall, with dark hair, well-groomed facial hair, and a lean but wiry physique. He wore a fitted suit and bright coloured shirt, with tie to match. He turned around and looked at his rear, checking that his tailored trousers fitted him perfectly. As he turned back to the mirror, another face appeared and a strong masculine arm reached around his waist. His partner's rugged features smiled at him, eyes meeting in the mirror.

"Good luck today. You've worked hard for this. You'll be fine; just be yourself."

Chris turned to Phil and kissed him tenderly.

"Thank you. I can't wait to get started," he said proudly.

He freed himself from the embrace and made his way to the underground car park. He clicked his key and his sporty little Audi came to life, black with a white roof, a little flamboyant, but it suited his character perfectly. Chris was not camp in any way and had not come out at work yet. He was glad about this, as he had heard that the inspector in the unit was a complete ballbreaker and a raging homophobe.

He arrived at Fettes in plenty of time. He wanted to make a good impression. Once there, he had to wait at the door, as there was a number-locked keypad entry system and he had not yet been given the code. He pulled his jacket straight and adjusted himself again, making sure he looked his best. Marcus bounced his way through the office and headed for the door, as there weren't many of them in the office yet. He peeked through the glass, smiling at the guy on the other side. He opened the door and checked for ID being worn. Chris was a bit embarrassed that he still had his lanyard in his pocket, and had forgotten to put it on. He managed to get it out just as Marcus was about to ask for it.

"Hi, Chris Steele, sorry about the ID. I never drive with it around my neck, just in case, oh, and I'm the new guy." He smiled at Marcus, taking in the good-looking detective standing in front of him.

"Hi, Marcus Black, one of the many detectives here in the MIT, which is the best team, of course!" He smiled with his hand out to greet him, the rivalry between the teams still very much alive within the force.

"Come through, I'd invite you to meet the others, but there are only one or two in just now. They're not quite as keen as us!"

Marcus showed Chris around the office. As Taylor arrived, Chris looked up to see the statuesque figure of a woman walk in, striking features, smartly dressed and pretty good looking for a woman, he thought.

Marcus called her over, and she turned and made her way over to meet the new arrival. She smiled at Chris. They both recognised each other, but not from work, somewhere more sociable, both knowing well The Street, a gay bar and club.

Chris felt his insides twist, as he wasn't ready to be outed at work.

"Taylor, Taylor Nicks, detective sergeant, nice to meet you, and welcome to the mad house, well, of late anyway!" She smiled at him, aware of their mutual recognition, Taylor completely unfazed by it.

More officers arrived and Chris was introduced to them all, and Kay too, as she had also come in, her flexi time allowing her to start slightly later than the cops. They headed to the kitchen to sort out some coffee when the door to the open plan office swung open with force as Findlay made his clumsy entrance, coffee and bacon butty in hand, having used his foot to kick the door. He hadn't meant it to swing so hard, but it had clattered off the filing cabinet, making an embarrassing noise and an entrance that couldn't be ignored.

Chris and the others looked up at him, and Taylor took pleasure in introducing him to his new boss. Chris couldn't help having a little smirk at the state of Findlay, a shiver going down his spine as he thought of the type of man he would be, and he'd met plenty of them in his time, reaffirming the need to stay in the closet and avoid any unwanted attention from his boss.

"Inspector Findlay, come and meet our new recruit, Chris Steele," Taylor called over, fully aware that Findlay was an antisocial ignoramus and would hate being put on the spot, especially by her and also when he had his breakfast to eat.

He muttered under his breath, something along the lines of another jumped-up pretty boy, here to make their mark, but unaware he was a pretty boy that likes boys, that pleasure was still to come.

He waddled over to where they stood. Chris tried his best not to stare as this dishevelled, overweight man came bumbling towards them. His thoughts filled with what the public would think if Findlay turned up at an incident, he was a fucking disgrace, and he was his new boss!

Chris disguised his thoughts and gave his best effort to smile genuinely as he reached out to shake Findlay's hand, something he regretted the minute he felt the moist clammy hand touch his. He felt repulsion, and the desire to pull away, but didn't. Chris was immaculate in his appearance and hygiene was uppermost in his repertoire of what was important for people.

"Hello, welcome to the team. I'm sure you'll fit in nicely." Findlay shuffled closer, and added, "We were getting a bit outnumbered lately!" He nudged Chris and gave a little wink as he looked over at Taylor and Kay.

Chris couldn't believe his ears, and although he hadn't said the words, Findlay's insinuation that there were too many females, or worse, too many gays, was felt loud and clear. Chris felt his stomach knot as his fear of being outed to this man became even more terrifying.

The moment Findlay turned away, Chris couldn't wait to wipe his hand and clean every piece of him from himself, and he was already regretting his decision to come to the MIT (Major Investigation Team) if this type of man was going to be his boss. His friendly words towards Chris were only there because he was male, and as far as Findlay knew, a straight one. Chris could only imagine what it would be like when Findlay found out that he batted for the other side.

Taylor had watched the meeting, fully aware that Findlay couldn't give a toss about the new guy, but was just happy it was a guy, a straight guy. Taylor knew Chris would be even lower down the food chain if Findlay found out he had a shirtlifter in his team.

She came over to a slightly more awkward-looking Chris than the one she had met moments before. She was smiling right at him as she closed the gap and put a hand on his shoulder and gave it a squeeze. "Don't worry too much; I won't tell, and he really doesn't care what the fuck we do, as long as he comes out smelling of roses, but don't get me wrong, he'll fuck you over in a second if he doesn't like you, or you're gay, or fair, or if you're not a misogynistic arsehole like him.

"Stick with Marcus and you should be alright, but don't come out just yet if you want to be here more than a week!

Coffee?" Taylor smiled and moved towards the kitchen and Chris followed, a little sheepishly, but happier now that his first-line supervisor was switched on and clearly bold and fair.

Marcus had made several brews for those that were in the office. He smiled at Chris. "It's alright you know. The team's good, and pretty normal, just a little oppressed at times, but he seems to be untouchable, almost bulletproof. He must have some shit on someone! How the hell he hasn't been emptied before now is pretty unbelievable really, but I'm a believer in karma and it must be about time to be found out and sorted!"

Marcus didn't normally speak out of turn about anybody, but he couldn't hold his tongue any longer about Findlay, as he had watched him try and destroy Taylor more than once. He was a disgrace to the uniform and didn't deserve his silent subservience.

Kay came into the kitchen. Taylor looked up and her face flushed a little. Kay moved closer to Taylor, deliberately brushing against her hand that was resting on the counter.

"Excuse me!" She smiled; aware Chris was watching.

"Did you meet the boss then?" Kay made a face of unease and shivered uncontrollably, as if something nasty had crawled up her spine.

Chris smiled uneasily. "Yes, I did. What a nice guy," he said in a sarcastic voice.

His mouth froze mid-speech as Findlay pushed open the door to the kitchen, hunting for some sauce for his bacon roll. Fortunately, he had not heard the conversation preceding his unwelcome entry.

Those in the kitchen shifted uneasily, knowing what would come next.

Findlay pushed past to the fridge, deliberately brushing against Kay to get there, and then turned to those brave enough to remain. "Does nobody have any work to do?" The sarcasm was obvious to hear.

Kay moved herself out of his way to avoid further deliberate accidental contact with him. It had only been minutes since everyone had come to their work, and nobody was slacking, just getting their fix of coffee before the day ahead, unlike that slovenly pig, who would sit and munch his breakfast and read the paper for over an hour before he even switched on his computer.

Taylor was fuming at his double standards and continual negative comments about the team. They were never given a minute to kick back a little, no praise or encouragement, nothing positive. She noticed Kay looked a bit off, not seeing that Findlay had brushed against her, and how it had made her feel, her skin visibly crawling.

Findlay almost barged his way back out of a kitchen, which was too small to avoid the pressure and sensation of claustrophobia when such a big man was in there with several others.

Kay gently gripped Taylor's arm as she was about to leave and asked for a word with her.

"What is it?" Taylor looked right at her, aware something was up.

"Did you see that, him leaning in to me deliberately? He's always doing that, touching, hovering, coming too close too often, and it's happening a lot more lately. It's making me even more uncomfortable, and it's escalating and he's loving it!".

Taylor turned as if to go towards Findlay's office, but Kay stopped her. "Don't, that's what he wants. Don't give him reason to focus on you," she said, smiling, and gestured, adding, "not more than he does already anyway!"

Taylor pulled closer into Kay's ear. "He's treading on thin ice. I'll have him before he destroys everything we have here, filthy lecherous pig!"

Taylor knew she was right, and that they had to pick their battles wisely. "Use your phone, Kay. Keep it with you at all times, record him, film him, get evidence. This can't go on.

We need proof. This can't keep happening, especially given you're the one that's always left alone in here with him when we're all out at jobs."

Taylor kissed her ear gently and let her get back to her desk. Chris watched this, now knowing that Taylor and Kay were together, and realising just how bad things were in this office.

"C'mon, Chris. We've got a corpse to look at, inside and out!" Taylor smiled, knowing that autopsies were not everyone's bag and certainly were a test of one's stomach as every piece of the person that once was, was dissected, studied, weighed, details noted and anomalies analysed and detailed as evidence, in an attempt to establish the possible cause of death, and the smells were not pleasant.

Chapter 5
Wandering

She walked innocently along Princes Street, unnoticed by all that passed, hidden in plain sight, a wolf in sheep's clothing. Slight slim features, high cheek bones, neat frame, a woman that still had the features of an adolescent girl, naturally blonde hair, fair, pale skin, dark eyes, the opposite of what you'd expect of someone so fair. She was beautiful to look at, appearing defenceless to those that thought they could take her, but deceptively wiry and capable. She was dressed casually and inconspicuously to avoid anyone remembering her, her desire to remain unnoticed already proving very positive, as nobody had even looked her way, the dark beanie hiding her hair, and stopping the usual unhealthy interest in her. Secreted inside her was a wild animal, tethered and desperate to break free, ferocious like a Tasmanian devil, evil lurking within, evil stirring and controlling her twisted path. She was broken beyond repair and hell-bent on sharing her torturous terror, and cruel intent, with as many others as she could.

She looked up to her right and looked up at Edinburgh Castle standing proudly high up on the rocks, the city's history watching over her, protecting her. In front of her were the art galleries at the bottom of the Mound on Princes Street, the Royal Scottish Academy, the frontage very grand with pillars like that of a colosseum, the city steeped in glorious history.

She wandered further, unmoved by the splendour she had just passed by. She could now see the Scott Monument ahead of her, the second largest monument to a writer in the world, a Victorian Gothic structure to Scottish author Sir Walter Scott, built between 1840 and 1844, standing tall and proud in Princes Street opposite what was once the luxurious and popular Jenners Store. The towering Scott Monument was a popular tourist attraction for those brave enough to climb its narrow spiral staircase and withstand the lowered balconies and tight spaces at the top. With a 200-foot drop, it was not a climb for the faint hearted.

As she got closer, she couldn't help but start to skip towards the monument. She was going to be a tourist for the day. Her appetite for death had grown of late. The recent events over the year had changed her forever, her hatred festering inside, and she now wanted to hurt people and take her desires to another level. The thrill she felt as she killed was like intravenous drugs, leaving her in a euphoric state for days afterwards as she relived the final moments of suffering prior to her victim's death. Up until now, in her mind, they had wronged her and they had deserved it, but she now no longer wanted to wait for someone to annoy her; she wanted that fix once again, and she didn't care who gave her it.

She paid cash to enter, deliberately lowering her head as she went in, her face fully hidden, chin down, hat low down on her eyebrows. She entered and started up the long and winding stairs. On her climb to the first platform, she smirked at those that were too scared to go any higher than the first level. When she came out onto the balcony and looked down, even here she felt her stomach lurch at the height and the thought of falling. She shuddered, never wanting to experience falling, but she quickly shook off the feeling. Her own fear was not what she wanted to feel here today. She wanted to feel her power, inhale her chosen victim's fear as they looked into her eyes in disbelief, begging for their life as she callously shoved them to their death, or so she hoped.

She sat inconspicuously, at level two of four, and waited for her next victim. Children skipped by and she knew they would be the easiest, but even she couldn't do that. It just wasn't right. Cruelty, yes, but there are unwritten rules. She sat and thought of her own childhood and considered, for a moment, the thought of any other child having to go through what she had and possibly saving them from abuse and unnatural desires, but dismissed the idea as soon as it arose. She was right the first time; children would always be a no-no, but any adult that harmed them was a definite yes.

Lots of people came and went, most heading further up, the braver ones anyway. Some were big men, and countless ladies of weight passed her by. She knew she could never get any of them over the edge, not without a very noticeable attention-drawing struggle. Cameras were clicking all around her, but she made sure her image was never captured. Her heart raced as she waited, and waited and waited, something she was happy to do, as she had time, too much time. Nobody looked the road she was on. She probably looked a little rough today and the type of person that others would choose to pass by and avoid eye contact with, which, of course, was perfect and exactly want she wanted. She sat there and sighed heavily with frustration and growing impatience, but just as she was about to give up hope for an opportunity, there they were, a young couple, early 20s, having a furious row, both shouting and screaming at one another, causing others to leave the platform in embarrassment or fear of having to get involved if it got physical. The two rowing individuals continued their raging argument, totally unaware of their very interested audience, singular.

It appeared that he had been caught out two-timing her, as she had just seen a text that contained more than he would have wanted her to see, and enough for her to know that the person sending it was more than just a friend. She giggled inwardly at the tears and grief the female was showing for this wretch of a guy. She would just have poisoned him, she thought to herself, suffocated him in his sleep after drugging him, certainly not belittle herself, or make a fool of herself trying to right his wrongs, already reasoning with herself, that this young woman was deserving of what was to come. She watched in awe at how much emotion they both shared. The male was clearly getting fed up with his partner ranting openly at him. "I can't do this anymore," he finally said. "No wonder I cheated on you. You're a fucking psycho bitch. We're done, over, finished. Now fuck off out of my face and get a grip of yourself. Look at the way you're acting."

The female stood there dumbstruck and open-mouthed, ingesting what he had just said. She could not believe he was dumping her just like that after two years, and she could feel the desperation build in her stomach, terror that this might be it, and she went into panic mode, grabbing frantically at his arm, tugging at it almost madly in an attempt to stop him leaving. She had lost it and wasn't going to let him go that easily. At this point, a group of American tourists arrived, drawling their words about the amazing city, taking very little notice of the warring pair. One or two of them became aware and deliberately tried to keep their distance, some looking over in amusement, more than concern, at the shameless scene the female was now making, trying to get the male to stay.

She herself just watched. She looked with intent at the screaming female, slight in frame, light in weight and, to her, a perfect size to be assisted out of her troubles by helping her over the edge, a quick and final way to stop her making more of a fool of herself. She looked on, but at this point there was no opportunity to do anything. There was no way she could act if the couple were together. That was, until she saw him shove her away, this time with enough force to move her back several feet, and turn abruptly to leave.

The female then knelt down on the ground, tears running down her face as she screamed at the male, who was already making his way to the stairs in haste to get away from her. "If you leave, that's it, I'll bloody kill myself, I will. I'll do it, you'll never see me again!"

He turned, with a 'yeah right' expression on his face. "Don't be so fucking stupid. You're all drama, you, attention-seeking and needy. Why did I not see it before? I'll get my stuff later this week, and don't call. I'll be out." He turned and walked purposefully down the steps, making it clear it was over. He did not look back and certainly didn't believe she would act on her words.

"FUCK YOU, YOU TWO-TIMING BASTARD. YOU WERE SHIT IN BED ANYWAY. SHE CAN FUCKING HAVE YOU, THE SLAG BITCH." The niceties now over, the true colours on full show, and the female shouted again, "You'll be fucking sorry; I'll make sure of that!"

The woman turned and headed up the stairs, taking them two at a time, wincing a little at the claustrophobic tightness of the walls, but her rage kept her moving up, up to the romantic spot she had been about to share minutes ago with her boyfriend, a sight he said she would never forget. She reached the third level and looked over, shuddering at the height and how it made her feel, an uneasiness coming over her as she saw the sheer drop, but she was determined and wasn't going to give up. She wanted to get to the top as he got to the bottom, and shout to the whole street what a useless lowlife he was. Decision made, the watcher went into the stairway and moved swiftly up, closing in behind the woman, only to come face to face with her when the woman turned as she neared the top. Their eyes met, she with the girl in the beanie hat, and shared an uncomfortable, slightly embarrassing smile.

"Oops, sorry, clumsy me," she said. "I didn't think anyone else was up here."

"Don't worry. I'm going up another level; it's all yours!" replied the woman, with a little dismissive venom, which only fed the reasoning of the girl's choice of victim. The female marched on and up the final set of stairs, one way up and one way down at this level, or so she thought.

The girl looked over the edge, the thrill of the fear of the height sending unhealthy feelings through her body, which she channelled into her plan. She glared at the woman before quickly following her up to the top level, a small parapet, like that of a princess's palace, but not pink and sparkly. Once there, she watched the female slightly in front of her step up to get a better view. There was not a lot of space up there, and the female had not realised she wasn't alone.

The girl smiled. "Perfect," she thought. "Thanks for making this easier." Things couldn't be going better for remaining undetected, or even suspected.

She moved up next to the woman and spoke to her, her voice soft and kind, and putting an arm around her in offer of support, genuinely appearing to care. The female jumped initially, a little startled at her presence, but not unnerved, she was so consumed with vengeance and the imminent pleasure of embarrassing her boyfriend.

She was about to shrug off the arm of the young girl, but human kindness made her accept the offer of comfort, the finality of her position now very clear, but she was still angry. Still wanting to vent at her boyfriend, now ex.

"You're better off without him you know. If he's done it once, he'll do it again!" The words shared were genuine, but with false kindness and reassurance, all showing support, designed to gain her trust.

The female sniffled weakly, and that's when the girl in the beanie hat felt the revulsion, the hate for her, the other's weakness and desperation made her angry, her skin crawling with hatred. Her face warmed with the sensation she was feeling. It crept through her like deadly poison. Her face curled like a rabid dog, her eyes narrowed with her breathing rate altered, it changed enough for the whimpering female to feel it, causing her to turn and face her maker.

The eyes that she now looked at had changed from kind and caring to sinister, like pools of darkness, shark-like, dead of any emotion and totally focussed on her. She slowly tried to pull away from the girl, her spine tingling with terror, but her comforting hand was now tight around her waist and holding on to her waistband, the grip not equating to her size and perceived strength. Before she could utter a word, her face was forced down and forwards, overbalancing, her face now against the wall below the small railing, her cheek scuffing violently against it before she felt her hips rise up, with her whole body teetering unevenly over the top of the railing. She twisted her neck around and screamed at the girl who was holding her forward by her head and waist and pushing her over the edge, "Please, don't do this, don't let me fall. Please, I beg you, why would you do this to me?"

The girl felt her heart surge with a heavenly sensation of pleasure as she heaved the female's legs over the side. No feelings of remorse, just a cruel satisfaction as she watched for a moment as an innocent young woman plummeted to her death, her body hitting off the lower floor sending her spinning brutally around. A guttural scream alerted those below to get out of the way, with someone not making it. An old man was too slow to move out of the way quickly enough. He was hit full force by the falling woman, leaving them both in a crumpled heap of deformity.

The girl skipped down the first two floors as quickly as she could. There was no one else at the top, and only when she reached the busier second floor, did she slow down, take her time to innocently go onto the balcony and stare over the edge at the carnage she had caused below. She gave a little squeal of delight as she saw that there were actually two bodies lying there, damaged limbs, contorted and clearly broken. She felt her stomach twist in fear as she saw the female move, clearly still alive, her unbroken arm outstretched. Her forehead was severely injured, the other arm crushed beneath her crumpled body. The man, on the other hand, was still, his neck at a disgusting angle. He was clearly dead, his severe injuries not conducive with life.

She joined a group heading for the stairs, walked slowly down with them, and even looked out at the first level, watching as the first police car arrived. This made her hair stand on end.

"Bloody hell," she thought, "the feds are quick today." An unhealthy feeling was circling around her body, tingling, excitement, from the fear of capture. Fortunately, the cops headed straight to the injured people, before considering locking down the monument and securing witnesses. Sirens rang out from all sides of the city, distant for now, but she knew it was time to leave or face being stopped along with the others and her details and statement being taken. That was not an option. She must ensure her anonymity.

She followed a family that were leaving, but they were slow, and she got increasingly impatient as she finally reached the bottom, her frustration directed at the very slow children in front, their speed causing her to consider shoving them out of the way to get past quicker, but she had to keep calm and not show her fear and certainly not a guilty presence.

Finally, she reached the bottom and went out of the exit door. She breathed in the fresh air and saw several officers heading towards the monument, so turned quickly and unobtrusively away, deliberately moving calmly in the opposite direction to make good her escape. Her motion was slow and uncaring, but inside she was screaming at herself to run, but she refrained, quashing that desire. Hesitating momentarily, she looked over at the bodies lying on the ground, officers kneeling down beside the female she had just thrown off the edge of the famous monument and the contorted corpse of the unfortunate male. She was fearful that the woman would tell them what had actually happened up there, but smiled to herself. "Oh well, collateral damage," she thought, as she looked at the poor old guy crumpled underneath her intended victim.

She joined the mass of onlookers; macabre scenes being ingested by those who craned their necks to catch a glimpse of the sight that they would never be able to unsee. Ghouls, nosey parkers, not offering help, phones out filming, the casual watcher and compulsive sharer, about to put the faces of the two injured people out there for all to see.

Mingling in, she pushed through the crowd and squeezed right up to the fence, the female's disfigured body on the other side, lying there for all to see and still partially on top of the dead male. An officer was holding her hand, leaning in towards her as she tried to say something, but her jaw looked out of place and badly broken, the bone sticking through her chin, making it very difficult to speak.

She watched and smiled at the female on the ground, her eyes focussed on her mouth. She smiled at the damage caused by the fall, the officers trying desperately to hear what was being said. Her eyes bored into the female's face, as if she felt it, the woman turned her head around, trancelike, to see the cause of the sensation. Paramedics were on scene and trying to stabilise her, treating the worst of her many injuries. She managed to turn her head to the side and caught sight of the evil girl staring right at her, the terror of recognition causing her to panic, fear of her coming to finish her off. Her movements became violent and desperate, damaging her already ravaged body, in an attempt to escape her evil foe. She lifted her arm, the crepitus audible as the broken bones' ragged edges rubbed cruelly and noisily together, but she managed to point towards the young female. "Her," was all she managed to say as her ribs ripped into the wall of her heart. Her breathing changed and her body started to convulse violently, her failing heart finally giving in, a quandary for those trying to save her as they needed to carry out CPR. To do that would push her ribs deeper into her heart and internal organs, but to do nothing was certain death too.

The officers helping the paramedics turned and looked up to where the female had pointed, but they were met with a sea of faces, most of them staring, some jostling for a better position to view the macabre scene and record the gruesome course of events with their phones, sharing it online before the police could even get close to letting loved ones know of their relative's cruel fate. There was nobody standing there that stood out to them; the girl was already gone.

"Move, move please, let me through. OH MY GOD, that's my girlfriend. Let me through!" A young male came rushing forward. He had heard the sirens blaring and the horns of the unknowing and impatient, and seen the swathes of people move towards the base of the Scott Monument. His heart was thumping, fearing the worst as he remembered his girl-friend's last words, an idle threat, he had thought. Never for a moment had he believed she would carry it out.

He got so far and was stopped by the officers now forming a loose cordon around the female, the medics still desperately trying to save her.

He gave a bit of a physical and verbal challenge to the offi-cers stopping him, which was short lived when he caught a glimpse of his ex's twisted and bleeding body, deformed beyond recognition, and his efforts to get closer ended at the realisation they were futile. She already looked pretty dead.

He bent over and vomited at the feet of an officer spattering the shiny front of his boots. Nonplussed about his boots, the officer leaned forward, put a comforting arm on his back and took hold of his arm to steady him. He was now a person of interest and no longer allowed to go on his way.

More police arrived. The road was fully closed and traffic being redirected. The swathes of onlookers were ushered further away from where the medics were still trying to save the young woman's life, but their efforts were in vain. They had tried everything they could to save her, but had failed. There were no longer visible signs of life, the injuries suffered so catastrophic, they had not been survivable.

Lead paramedic Ms Parker pronounced life extinct there on the street below the monument and looked towards the officers to make a decision regarding the body, whether it was to remain in situ or be instantly removed. The other paramedic, still young in service, Scott Casement, looked a little green about the gills, as he had had to administer CPR, something not out of the norm for the job, but he had felt the damage that his hands were causing to the female's ribs, the brutal crunching, damaging the vital organs beneath and, on top of that, copious amounts of blood had poured and spurted out of the poor girl as he tried in vain to save her. He had had to use enough force to save her, in an attempt to get the heart pumping again, but this had just destroyed the already damaged ribcage. Ms Parker had placed the automated CPR machine on her, to save Scott from suffering any longer; the stress of what he was having to do was clearly affecting him. She had continued to bag the woman as the machine went to work, this specialised equipment, looking like a torture machine, the woman's body just jolting violently up and down, as the machine ravaged what was left of her severely damaged chest to keep the oxygenated blood circulating, but to no avail.

The sergeant on duty, an older officer, quite long in the tooth, Brad Laurence, an old sweat, bearded and not a fool, wasn't happy with how the incident was looking, the proximity of the partner to the scene. He believed there might be more to it. He instructed the officers with the woman's partner to remove him from the scene, and either get his statement or interview him, along with gathering evidential DNA and swabs. He then lifted his radio up to his mouth and contacted CID to attend the scene. This was a given, as all suicides and deaths outdoors were to be attended and dealt with by CID. He spoke with them at length and shared his thoughts of possible foul play. It was decided that the body would remain there in situ. CID were already en route with the tent to cover the corpse, as they had been given the heads-up when the call originally came in.

Taylor was sitting at her desk, looking at the computer and perusing the jobs before she went about her business for the day. As a matter of course, she looked through the high-risk incidents, and all of the deaths in the city and surrounding areas. She opened up the text to the incident titled, "female fallen from the Scott Monument." Her heart skipped a little, her own fear of heights making her question how anyone could even go up there, far less throw themselves off it. She read the details, and that CID were dealing with it, but never gave it much more thought, other than the shivers that the height forced her to imagine.

The girl moved away at pace, her steps light and quick, but not enough to draw attention to her haste to leave the area. Head down, beanie hat pulled low, her genderless frame making ground away from the monument, and once at the West End, she allowed herself to slow down and savour what she had just done. She questioned why she now wanted to do such hideous things; with the pain she would cause their families. She searched herself for kind emotions, and remorse, but none came, just a sinister and cruel smile, eyes transfixed as she remembered meeting the eyes of the woman's before she let her fall to her agonising death, the despair and disbelief, pure terror in them as she fell. This made the girl feel more powerful than ever, untouchable and totally in control, no sadness, regret or empathy, only exhilaration, nothing more human than that and certainly no remorse. The woman had been weak and unhappy. She had saved her from her miserable destiny, which in her mind was a life of subserviency to guys like that.

Chapter 6

Analysis

"Fresh water, fucking fresh water, what the fuck are you telling me, Sergeant Nicks?" Findlay rasped. It was as if it was her fault that the male washed up on the shore was not just another tragic suicide. This new evidence made this a suspicious death, or worse a murder.

"Yes, definitely fresh water, and traces of soap too, sir," Taylor added with a little mirth and sarcasm in her tone, knowing that steam would be coming out of Findlay's ears shortly, as this meant work, lots of it, and heat from above, because it appeared someone had gone the extra mile to cover up the true facts regarding the nature of this death, and this indicated he had not drowned by taking his own life.

Findlay noticed the twinkle in Taylor's eyes, her amusement at his anger, and he could barely hide his rage. Controlling it was becoming even harder these days, although he knew he was being watched by his colleagues outside the office, all was on show for them to see through the glass walls.

Audience in mind, he leaned menacingly closer to her, his lips tight as he snarled words through gritted teeth, enough to avoid others reading them. "What the fuck are you so smug about? This isn't a laughing matter, and for that, this one lies with you and Marcus. Oh, and take the new boy too. He's making the office untidy!" Taylor saw that he was starting to lose it a bit, the control he usually held was faltering, and he was actually frightening her, as he looked like he was ready to assault her. There was a visible madness about him.

He was now openly raging, and what he really wanted to do was slap her in the face, bring her down a peg or two, control her, dominate her, stamp out her air of confidence. He wished her to fail, but this would only reflect badly on him on this occasion, and he wasn't prepared to let that happen either. Her expression was annoying him. There was certainly no love lost between them, but there was nothing he could do about her disdain for him, or was there? He started to smile back at Taylor, which was a first. He watched as her slightly unnerved face flushed a little. His smile was not a kind one. He was smiling at her because he knew he couldn't beat her fairly. She was too professional for that, but he could arrange for her to be moved and disguise it as some sort of developmental shift, and that way he wouldn't have to watch her smug gay face any longer. He knew she would hate that. She was the lynch pin of this team, but he knew Marcus could step up to the plate, and, at last, he would have some normality back in the office and a male in charge again, emphasising that he was straight, in his narrow little mind.

Taylor shifted uncomfortably and could not wait to get out of the office. She didn't like what she was feeling. She could see by his piggy little self-satisfied face that he was up to something, and that was never good where she was concerned, knowing she would be at the brunt of it.

He could see that he had finally managed to rattle her, make her a little worried and, for him, that felt good.

"Well! What are you waiting for? Get digging on the dead guy. See what his friends have to say about him: a wife, his associates, places he has been, people he has met, get online and see what other stuff he's been up to. There must be something about him that led him to this!" Findlay's tone was scathing and resentful, impatient to be rid of her.

"Really! What about Nathan?" she quizzed, never thinking that he would let her take this enquiry, as it was going to be a big one.

He took this as insolence, rather than the genuine question it was meant to be. "Fuck Nathan! This is far more important. Get that tidied up and get on this case, and don't think you can play the fucking daft wee lassie with me!"

Taylor was taken aback. Even for Findlay, his response was unhinged and she could see he was losing control and going to blow.

She hadn't meant to create this reaction from him. She had thought he would deliberately keep her on the other case, to annoy her, so the reaction was both troubling and gratifying at the same time. She hadn't wanted to create any more animosity than was already there.

Taylor tried to remain professional and did not rise or react to his anger, but all she wanted was to get out of his office. She was starting to think that things could get physical between them one day, unaware how accurate her thoughts actually were.

He moved abruptly towards her, aggressively, and she instinctively shifted to the side, but all he did was smile and thrust his hand to the handle of the door, right in front of her face, deliberately menacing, before slowing his hand to open the door for her, dismissing her silently as he did so.

She left the office quickly, and went straight towards Marcus, signalling with a nod for him to follow her into the kitchen. He instantly noticed her flushed cheeks and a familiar rage on her face, but this time her look to him was different. She looked scared, unnerved at the behaviour she had just witnessed. He had been watching from afar and could see from the body language behind the glass that things were not going well in there.

Taylor waited for Marcus to join her and closed the door

behind them. She could not wait to tell him about Findlay, the change in him, and that she sensed danger this time, the shift in his ability to control himself and to stay within the rules, albeit, the rules that Findlay had already twisted far beyond that of what was normally acceptable. Marcus's face was a picture of disbelief and anger. He hated the way Findlay spoke to Taylor, his open bigotry, his disdain and lecherous behaviour towards the women in the office, which Findlay classed as fair game, but never enough to evidence any wrongdoing. Findlay was not a fool and had played this game a long time, his old school buddies higher up the tree always backing him. Once she had got that off her chest, and calmed down a bit, she went on to explain to Marcus about the lab results and that they were to take on the suspicious death, which surprised him a little too.

"What, no more Nathan?" he quizzed.

"Nope, we've to wrap that up. There was nothing from the search or the CCTV anyway, just all pretty normal, so whatever happened or why, we'll never know what he was thinking at the time of the accident unless he chooses to tell us. He's offered his version of events, and we can't scan his mind," she said, quite happy that Nathan would not have to go through any more police intrusion. The case was now deemed an accident. That was the official finding and the enquiry could be closed, a vehicle accident with injury and nothing more than that.

Kay had been sitting at her desk, watching it all as usual, wishing things could be different. She had tried not to look towards Findlay's office if she could help it, because she did not want him to think she was looking at him, ever, not even for a second, but she had to watch, because of his open dislike for Taylor. She too was fearful he would do something to her, and this really bothered her. She had always believed he was dangerous and there was no filter, no control switch. He was vile and nasty, but even to his standards, there was a definite escalation in his behaviour, no sense of control, and Taylor the chosen target.

Chapter 7

Kerri

Curtains closed, darkness surrounding her, just the way she liked it, the slender, childlike young woman sat on her single bed, arms wrapped around her legs, her head lying on her knees, her thoughts swirling silently in her head. Confusion, hatred, sadness, and the need to right the wrongs she felt inside, welled up within her, as she rocked herself back and forth trying to reason with what she had done that afternoon and for the other incidents in the months before. Why was she now able to do things like this, when before it had just been thoughts and nightmares? She rubbed her scalp roughly as she thought of the exhilaration she had felt when she carried out these atrocious crimes to these people, the last one completely innocent, but it had exhilarated her, made her feel in command, an executioner, with the powers of the devil.

She had been in care for nearly a year after her parents had disowned her, and refused to offer any explanation for this to social work and other child services, not a word or a reason or any further engagement with the authorities. Kerri had arrived there at 16, her family giving very little away in explanation. They appeared troubled and secretive. One social worker stated they looked haunted and traumatised themselves and took the time to mark that in her notes but did not investigate further at the time. They did not discuss why their daughter was being placed there and point-blank refused to take any further interest or responsibility from that moment onwards. Categorised as a young person and now a cared-for child, the local authorities had a duty of care until she turned 18, which was only a few months away. This frightened her as she would have to fend for herself in every respect. Even though she was capable of carrying out heinous crimes, and was evil in her actions, she was still a very troubled little girl inside.

A knock came at the door. It was one of the carers checking that she was okay, as they did several times every day. On entering the room, the darkness was all-consuming, and they could barely make out the petite frame of the girl sitting still on the bed, head raised now, a feral glare fixed on the intruder, vexed at being disturbed.

"Kerri, why do you always sit there in the dark? It can't be good for you. Surely if you added a little light, that would help with your mood," Inga said in a caring voice, genuinely trying her best with this awkward young woman. She took note of the look in the girl's eyes. Inga had tried to get through to her since she had arrived and thought she was making headway until more recently, but something seemed to have snapped inside her and the girl had been consumed by something, becoming even more morose, insular and inwardly damaged. Inga had been a social worker for years, caring and kind, but frank and honest when required and wanted the best for all of her charges, and she was certainly able to hold her own if things got volatile.

"We've got a new worker assigned to you. He's lovely and I know you'll like him."

Kerri looked up, her blond hair, tousled from being under her beanie hat all day, looked a little worse for wear and a little sweaty, as she had walked pretty quickly to get out of the area where she had just killed an innocent young woman.

She stared at Inga, her expression irked and questioning, and spoke with an insolent tone. "Why would I like him? He'll be just like the other weirdo paedo creeps that you send me to, and that other fat conceited bitch too. They're all the same, bored in their jobs and fucking useless. Tell him to get to fuck! What's the point, anyway? I'll be out of your hair in a few months, and don't give me that crap that these people actually give an actual shit about anybody. It's just money in their pockets!"

Inga tried hard not to show that this type of negative attitude angered her and made her want to give the girl a shake, a wake-up call. She knew Kerri was troubled, but the girl had included her in that collective dig. She also had to bite her tongue in relation to the expectation for others to sort out their residents' problems, residents who frequently took no ownership of anything they did themselves and blamed their problems on everybody else.

"We do care, you know we do, and Phil is genuinely lovely. Give him a chance. He'll be here tomorrow after lunch, and this is one of the meetings you're required to attend. Missing it is not an option without consequence!"

The frown marks grew deeper on Kerri's forehead as she looked up at Inga with a visible snarl on her face. "What do you mean without consequence? Is that a threat?" Kerri's eyes narrowed and her stomach twisted. To her, this type of language was antagonistic and made her angry, and that was something she found difficult to control lately.

Inga sighed. Even her relaxed demeanour was cracking a little, but she managed to remain calm as she explained, "What I mean is, it's obligatory, not optional, and the consequence would be a review of your status here, nothing more than that, albeit you may have to move on if you don't try and comply with us!"

Kerri glared at her, but felt herself relax a bit more inside.

Even though she hated being told what to do, she knew she had to toe the line a bit, or her coat would be on a shaky peg. This place was the best of a bad bunch. Although she'd never admit to it. She liked it here. She felt safe, unlike those around her.

"Fine! I'll meet him, but if he's a condescending prick, or another chubby-fingered lechy pervert, I'm out of there and I won't do it again, consequence or not!" Her words cut into Inga, and Kerri's stare made her feel uncomfortable, eyes wide and boring into her. The hair on Inga's neck bristled as she shivered inside. She tried to hold the stare and not give in, but she could have sworn she saw Kerri's eyes visibly darken and her lips tighten as she struggled with something inside. It almost felt like she was being hunted.

Little did Inga know how close she was to being attacked at that moment, the urge to attack was consuming Kerri, her rage rising to a level she struggled to control.

Inga felt uncomfortable and decided it was time to leave it there. It was rare that she felt uneasy like that, and Inga was a strong-willed, confident, physically able woman, but she was unnerved by this girl's aura, a presence that left her feeling a little shaky, with a crawling sensation under her skin. She felt her step quicken, shuddered, as she rid herself from the evil she felt emanating from this girl, and she even looked back along the corridor a couple of times, making sure she wasn't being chased.

Chapter 8

Second Autopsy

Taylor drove through the city with Marcus and Chris, one in the front, one in the back, chatting away as if they had known each other for years. They weren't too dissimilar in looks either, although Marcus was a bit more rugged, and Chris immaculately groomed. Chris kept himself well. He too was muscular, but in a trimmer and lithe way, with good pecs and biceps, and a nice bum, which on the gay scene were like the clothes on your back. Without them, the attention received would be less. Marcus was a little bulkier, more solid, heavier, but trim too. Both men were keen gym users and cared about their physique and appearance and the need to be physically able when the shit hit the fan. They cared how they looked, and both wanted to be able to deal with whatever their work threw at them. Taylor was a formidable force, physically fit and able to handle herself. She was impatient and hated being late, so she headed up towards Queen Street to make progress, but not quite blue-light speed and glad that the cobbles had ended. She liked the noise they made driving up from Stockbridge, but they made the vehicle they were in rattle in places it shouldn't, another of Police Scotland's finest ramshackle buckets of steel. Queen Street was busy, the hustle and bustle of the city centre the norm, pedestrians everywhere, the throng of people heading out from their offices to catch a bite to eat, a walk, a break from the monotony of their daily dirge at work. They moved closer towards the junction with Princes Street, the traffic heavier than normal, and only after crossing the junction did they look left and see that the road was still closed at the East End, beneath the Scott Monument.

"Hey, guys, look, another sorry soul has chosen to take their life!" Taylor said with concern and sadness, but also a little dismay that they couldn't just reach out and ask for help, tell someone what they were feeling, although she understood life when you're living it is never that simple.

Marcus turned and managed to look around and catch a glimpse of the circus taking place along the road, numerous police cars and officers still present at the scene from earlier, the tent still in situ, with the usual gathering of people wanting to see what had happened.

Chris was too late to see. "I saw that on the computer earlier in the city centre incidents, and it wasn't just one dead. The woman landed on an old man when she fell. When I read it, they were still working on the woman. She didn't die straight away, but he was apparently dead on the spot, his neck snapped!" Chris made a choking noise simulating instant death.

Taylor looked at Marcus and grimaced at the thought. "God, it's bad enough when one decides to do it, but to kill another in the process is fucking hideous, and tragically sad too. He was just minding his own business, poor old sod!"

"Who's dealing with that one? I take it uniform will need a bit of help with it. Two dead, and the press will have a field day. What a spectacle for the ghouls too!" Taylor asked with genuine curiosity, as she thought they should have been given a heads-up about it, even though this type of incident would lie firmly in the CID's bag.

Chris was a bright young man and had taken the time to read the full incident report, because of the nature of it.

"Taylor, I read that DS Mac Andrews CID, had marked himself off at the scene, along with Mags Karen and Sammy Smithers, a couple of DCs I used to work with, hoddit and doddit, a couple of cheeky fun-loving lassies, always looking for the funny side. Their dark humour is a source of great amusement and their saviour in the job which they are bloody good at!"

"Oh, okay then. I'll give Mac a ring later and see if there's any more to it, but he's sound and perfectly capable of managing this. I've actually worked with all of them at some point in my illustrious career!" Taylor said, with a hint of sarcasm, but she still wished she had had a call. She may have even attended, or given it a little more interest, but they still had a gruesome task of their own, attending their second autopsy of the week, which was never a favourite task for her.

Happy to be through the worst of the traffic, they headed down past the rear of the old Bank of Scotland building, grand in stature in a commanding position, sitting at a vantage point above the city, with the art gallery below, although neither as grand as Edinburgh Castle, a sight that many locals took for granted. If they took the time to look at it with the eyes of a tourist, they would be in awe of its setting, sat upon an extinct volcano. Sheer rock faces on all but one side, canons still in situ, with one that fired at 1300hrs every single day, the famous one o'clock gun. Taylor drove at pace now, safely, but the delay had made them late for their appointment at the mortuary with the pathologist who was working on behalf of the coroner. She hurried past the Waverly Station and under the North Bridge, a bit of a long way for a shortcut, but needs must to try and get through the traffic, and couldn't help but glance up to the underside of the bridge, a place where so many had chosen to take their lives. They headed over the junction of the Royal Mile, the famous street a mile long between Holyrood Palace and the Castle, another historic feature of

Edinburgh, and, to Taylor's dislike, more cobbles rumbling beneath her as they headed down to the less salubrious area of the Cowgate, speeding tyres slipping slightly as they struggled to grip in the damp. The Cowgate, steeped in history, was currently filled with lives less fortunate. The Salvation Army building dominated the foot of the Pleasance. A few of its customers sat outside, men and women, all a little the worse for wear even for the time of day, although it was now after two, a row of purple cans of super lager lined up in front of them. Recognising the fed car passing, a man raised his can up to the officers inside. Smiling a nearly toothless grin at them, his three brown stubs of teeth like gravestones in his mouth, he was barely in his forties, but the methadone had taken its toll. The thick green sugary heroin replacement taken on a daily basis rotted his teeth. Taylor raised her hand to acknowledge the man with the can, always willing to recognise others, whether they had gestured in half fun or whole earnest. Taylor believed that everyone was a human being, deserving of respect, no matter how bad a deal life had given them.

She cursed as they turned into the mortuary, a hundred yards further down into the Cowgate. They were now ten minutes late for their appointment, a pet hate of hers. They had left in plenty of time to make the appointment, but the unforeseen traffic, due to the events in town, had scuppered plans.

She headed around the side stairs from the car park and to the entrance where they were buzzed in and met by the pathologist, Dr Marie H McKay. It was clear she wasn't happy. Taylor was quick to introduce herself and her new colleague, gently offering her hand in a peace-type gesture, with a firm shake, she offered their apologies and the reason for their lateness, putting it down to the unfortunate death of two people at the Scott Monument and the road closures that were still in place causing havoc across the city.

The pathologist's face softened and Dr McKay met Taylor's eyes. The pathologist liked to pretend to be more formidable than she actually was, and saw that Taylor appeared to be genuinely sorry and a little embarrassed at her lack of punctuality. She smiled. "I'm Dr McKay, I carried out the autopsy on the other body found on the coastline last month. I believe this one was found down at Silverknowes beach. Hmmm, that's a first, well a first for me anyway!" she said quizzically, knowing the pattern of the sea and where the bodies would usually be washed up.

Taylor acknowledged the comment with a smile of her own. "Yes, a first for me too, as well as the factor with the fresh water and a hint of soap found in the other suicide last month. The bodies were also found in an area never yet documented as a place for a body being washed up, so this may turn out to be a little more than a coincidence and maybe not how it was meant to seem. Whoever dumped these bodies didn't do their tidal homework. I wish I'd been present at the last one too but, unfortunately, I was off. It would certainly have helped with the continuity in evidence, because if this one turns out to be the same, and we hadn't considered any foul play or any link of sorts up until now, it won't go down too well. Not that I want to jump the gun with this one, but everything so far seems to be pointing that way!"

Dr McKay just raised her eyebrows in a humorous, cartoonlike gesture. "I take it from what you're saying that you might be expecting this to be the same?"

Taylor shrugged her shoulders. "I certainly don't want it to be, but where the body was found is suspicious enough, and pretty naïve of the person choosing to put it there. The tides have never deposited a body there in my service, and I've got 15 years!"

Taylor stared at the doctor with a look of regretful expectation, almost resigned to the fact that the lungs of this body would also be filled with fresh water and not sea water. She suspected that this person was already dead before they reached the sea, just like the last one, and that meant only one thing, foul play, a double murder, and a hell of a lot of work to come for the Major Investigation Team if they were to bring the murderer to justice.

They suited up, masks on, goggles, the lot, as there was now a very important need to be forensically careful. Any fibre or deposit that still remained on the corpse was a vital clue to who was present at the time of death, and potentially the same person that caused it.

Dr McKay was very thorough with the initial examination, looking for external injuries, no matter how small and unobtrusive. They all took notes on everything, marks, scars, tattoos, hair colour, eye colour, ethnicity, weight, the use of ultraviolet to illuminate substances, an x-ray to locate foreign bodies and breaks, fractures or previous injuries. Written notes and voice notes recorded everything on the body and a detailed diagram was drawn up. Taylor glanced at the doctor's notes. She could barely understand some of the words used; she felt she needed a thesaurus to work out what it all meant. Taylor made comment and could see the pathologist's eyebrows raise above her mask. She could tell just by her eyes that this amused her. Dr McKay was aware that her vast vocabulary regularly made many people wonder what the words she used actually meant but continued to fill her paperwork with them. Those who wanted to know would have to look them up, albeit Taylor was sure there were a few made-up ones in there.

Prior to the first cut, the pathologist heaved the torso onto a rubber block with a slight thump. She didn't mean to be so heavy handed, but the weight she had to shift required some force. This extended the body's arch, which gave greater access to the chest and abdomen. Then she carefully performed the

Y incision, the scalpel slicing through the cold lifeless flesh. Chris and Marcus looked on, a little uncomfortable at the process. It was a person lying there, one about to be dissected like a slab of meat. They knew it was a necessary process, but it never got any easier, especially once the rib cutters were brought out. They were like small pruning shears, very sharp and capable of crunching through bone. The doctor was used to the response they created among the audience when she worked with great effort to cut her way through the bones and remove the front part of the ribcage. This exposed the internal organs, allowing her to examine them in situ, taking time to have a good look prior to their removal. She was systematic in her order of removal, carefully weighing, cutting, examining them all individually. The process she was using is called the Virchow technique. She chose to examine some of the organs fully, there and then, and save certain organs for further investigation if required, ensuring they were preserved in formalin.

The lungs were removed, inflated and samples and tissues taken from within them, especially the fluid, which was visible in reasonable quantity for them all to see. Other samples taken included fluids, such as urine, blood, vitreous gel from the eyes and bile from the gall bladder to check for drugs, infection, chemical composition or genetic factors that could have contributed to an untimely death.

On this occasion Dr McKay wanted to examine the brain too, much to the dismay of DC Steele. He was already having trouble holding it together. The doctor looked over at the officers as she pulled out the equipment, smiling at them before she turned it on. She knew how uncomfortable they would soon be feeling. The special saw squealed out as it cut into the cranium. Everyone flinched except the doctor. Wincing at the sound, they cringed as she continued, watching on through slightly closed eyes. The saw was designed to ensure the tissue below was left unharmed, with the skin already peeled back, the person lying before them now looked nonhuman.

Samples taken, documented, and other organs preserved, Dr McKay set about the reconstitution of the body, replacing the top of the skull, folding the skin back over and recreating the face. Some organs were returned and stitched back inside; others were preserved for further examination.

Chris looked white, with a little greenish tint. Taylor could see he was close to vomiting. She had noticed the change in him when the cutters crunched through the ribs. He had got even worse as the doctor sawed into the brain. Taylor elbowed Marcus, and they both enjoyed a little mirth at the new boy's expense, typical police humour.

The doctor also took a moment to smile over at Taylor, she too aware of the less fortunate member of the team, suffering after viewing the most macabre scene and experiencing the rancid smells that came from inside the torso. Some of the dissected organs also gave off a very unpleasant odour, especially the bowel, intestines and stomach contents, all of which had unique and quite hideous smells.

Once the autopsy was concluded, there was visible relief in Chris's frame, his shoulders relaxed, the tension gone. Taylor, Marcus, Chris and the pathologist compared notes, ensuring the important details observed matched the notes taken. The doctor popped the kettle on and got out the biscuits, totally nonplussed and unaffected by the gruesome task she had just carried out. Speaking in her soft infectious Geordie accent, she offered round the biscuits. Smelling the sickly sweetness, Chris stood up and left the room, much to the amusement of the others, who had been unfazed with the sights and smells encountered. They saw his hand rise to his mouth as he struggled to keep the contents of his stomach in. The thought of eating after that had been the last straw. The noise that emanated from the toilet was evidence that he did not have the stomach for autopsies. Meanwhile, the others carried on as usual, sharing a laugh at Chris's expense. Selecting several biscuits each, they enjoyed the sugary treat with a nice cup of tea, their stomach contents still very much in place.

Chris appeared ten minutes later, looking a little sheepish and aware that the others were laughing at him. They giggled as they offered him a biscuit, shoulders rising up and down when he declined. He sat down, hoping that the nausea would leave him, but the smell of the place was reactivating his desire to vomit again, and the scent of the biscuits was certainly not doing it for him.

At last, Taylor got up from her seat and thanked the doctor for her services, taking the opportunity to apologise once more for being late.

"Call me Marie." The doctor smiled. "You're forgiven. You were clearly genuinely held up, unlike so many others that are just late as part of their normal day. It's the same cops every time, coffees in hand, sauce on their face. They're the bane of my life to be honest. They just hold up the day!" They shared a knowing look, agreeing about those less professional than them with exasperation and annoyance. Dr McKay offered timescales for the results, aware of the importance of the enquiry, and acknowledged Taylor's priority request for the fluid from the lungs.

As they left the building, the smells that had infiltrated every inch of their being were finally gone, the stench of death, foul and unforgiving for those that breathed it in. Taylor and Marcus followed behind Chris, who was clearly desperate to get out of the stuffy building, their amusement at his discomfort still being enjoyed. He was clearly still suffering.

"Fresh air at last." Chris took in a massive gulp of the fresh unscented air, and it was clear he had been holding his breath for the last few steps to their exit, the sensory pleasure he felt from this made him smile at last, and he began to feel a little better, the colour returning to his pasty face.

Taylor laughed at him, with kindness and a hint of cruel satisfaction at the suffering the job regularly gave, all part and parcel of a normal day in the police. It was the small pleasures that kept everyone sane.

Marcus poked her in the ribs and gave her a look, but he too was enjoying winding up the new guy.

"Whhaaattt! He'll get used to it," Taylor said, smiling at Chris. "Won't you?" But he was bent double again as the memory of what he had seen emerged at the forefront of his mind causing him to leave another pavement pizza for the pedestrians to avoid.

"WOOOWW!" Taylor mouthed to Marcus, giggling once again at the expense of poor Chris, turning away from the sounds of vomit splattering the pavement, this time spattering up onto Chris's perfect tailored suit.

Taylor was downwind of Chris and unfortunate enough to catch a whiff of the vomity scent, and after all she had seen and smelt earlier, she finally felt her stomach lurch and had to subdue the need to vomit herself. This time Marcus was in stitches, a real belly laugh, at Taylor's expense. He poked her in the ribs again. "You deserved that!"

Taylor managed to stop herself being sick. She straightened up, adjusted her suit jacket and stared at the two of them, who were now staring at her laughing. Her face looked angry, and they both thought they were going to get it tight, but her eyes softened and her mouth turned up at the edges, before she too was in fits of laughter. "Wankers!" she said, smiling. "Coffees on me then! Where do you want to go? I want to sit in." Taylor liked a laugh and knew she had been unkind to Chris and deserved her comeuppance.

"I like the Elephant House, great cakes!" Marcus suggested, eyes lighting up at the thought of filling his tummy.

The Elephant House was a long-standing coffee house on the famous George IV Bridge, laid back and popular with students, and where author JK Rowling was believed to have written parts of her famous Harry Potter novels. It lies a stone's throw away from the Central Library.

"You can eat now?" Chris looked at Marcus in amazement, traces of sick still visible at the side of his face.

"Yup, you'll learn, young one!" Marcus said, smiling and rubbing his stomach.

Taylor squeezed Chris's shoulder. "Marcus should be the fattest man on earth with the amount of food he shovels in that face of his, lucky git. Oh, and wipe your face; there's a little vom still there!"

Chris wiped frantically, mortified he had ming on his face.

Marcus, meanwhile, made a 'who me' face, and shrugged.

"I train very hard you know, and I must have a good metabolism!"

They got to their vehicle and climbed in. The gathering of the homeless at the Salvation Army building were still there, forever vocal, and drinking their super lagers. Comedic jeers and laughter rang out as they mocked the trio driving by once again.

Chapter 9

A Trusted Individual

Kerri fiddled with the paperwork from the social work department. She knew she had to abide by certain rules or she would be out on her ear. She had a hatred for her previous social workers. In her mind they were all condescending and uncaring. Reality being that they had all tried their best to help her, but she had been so intimidating, abrasive and difficult that the social workers eventually became despondent with her. Kerri had a misplaced negative perception of their failure. Their tolerance, patience and empathy, should have continued indefinitely in her mind. When it ended, she blamed them for giving up on her, instead of realising it was down to her. Their reason in the end was burnout at the lack of progress they made with her, and fear!

Philip Chancellor, a social worker for over ten years, experienced in his field, 32 years of age, tall, strong, with well-groomed facial hair, handsome, and very gay, although you couldn't tell by looking, sat in his office reading the case notes for Kerri Sweeney. He felt his skin prickle a little as he read the details: her stare; the constant darkness she craved; the insular mutterings she made when they had tried to speak to her, almost like spells and incantations; her morose moods; and the way her eyes never wavered from theirs as they spoke to her and she gritted her teeth. All mentioned how unnerved they felt in her presence. Her demeanour made them feel threatened, although she was not violent with them, and never said she would harm them. Many mentioned that they did not feel safe with her, that there was an underlying tension, something sinister and evil, like she was holding herself back from doing something to them. Reading between the lines, the other key workers appeared relieved to have been reassigned to somebody else.

Phil liked a challenge and never liked to prejudge anybody, always giving everyone a fair chance. He himself had experienced discrimination and was not prepared to offer the same to another person. He did take note of how his natural reaction to the content of her file had made his body respond and made a note to remain wary and vigilant of her. She did appear odd from her behaviour. Not a standard case of neglect, or poor behaviour, this was very different and not yet explained.

Their first meeting was tomorrow, and then regular contact was to be biweekly, initially, in an effort to build trust and attempt to get to the bottom of her issues.

Chapter 10

Back at the Office

Kay was typing away furiously at her desk, the backlog of paperwork never-ending. A pile of files rose high up in front of her, and there were also many tapes to be transcribed for the detectives in the team. The pile was so big that she hadn't seen Findlay waddling over towards her in his grotesquely casual manner. The office was empty and she had thought she was alone. Assuming that the inspector was in meetings for the rest of the day, she had foolishly relaxed and was enjoying the peace and quiet.

Kay was an attractive woman, mid-thirties, fit, lithe, with long light auburn hair, and currently in a relationship with Taylor, Findlay's least favourite person. He was homophobic sexist, and intolerant of anything that he wasn't. He had been appalled when Kay turned to what he called the dark side, away from being straight and liking men, being normal, to being a queer like Taylor. He had always leched over her, watching her every move and having many inappropriate thoughts about her and what he would like to do to her. In his small but hopeful mind, he believed he had a chance, unaware of how his appearance and behaviour was received by others. In reality he was a complete turn-off for everybody that met him, almost to the point of repulsion and total disregard. His actions abhorrent and unacceptable.

Kay got a fright when he appeared in front of her, visibly jumping. Findlay was too close for comfort as usual, and he carelessly shoved her pile of files over so he could perch his rather large and wide backside onto the edge of the desk. Kay was taken aback and felt very vulnerable with this new and even more disconcerting forwardness towards her. She felt even more uncomfortable than she normally did when he was around. On this occasion, she was right to feel that way; today was different. Findlay was different.

He handed her a folder and asked her to create an index for it, and put the sections into Poly Pockets, but instead of putting it on the desk like he usually would, he handed it to her, making her have to reach out to take it, leaning even further into her personal space. As she took it from him, his fat sausage-like, damp piggy little fingers deliberately stroked her hand, and not by accident. The gesture wasn't even disguised as a mistake. Kay froze, needles stabbing into her senses as she became very aware of her own vulnerability. They were alone in the office. Fear rushed through her, because she knew the inspector was a vile person. He strongly disliked Taylor, who had always believed he was capable of bad things but wasn't fully aware of his intentions. The empty office loomed in front of her. Almost movie-like, her surroundings zoomed in on her, and a vertigo-like sensation engulfed her. She was frightened and very alone, the stress building up inside her, which soon changed to terror as her memories of the trauma she had previously suffered at the hands of a violent sexual predator came rushing back, something she hoped she would never feel again and certainly not at her supposedly safe place of employment. Terror crept up her spine and everything within was telling her to run and scream.

Findlay watched, enjoying seeing her squirm. He was enjoying the obvious discomfort he was causing her. His eyes narrowed with resentment as Kay pulled her hand away quickly in repulsion at his touch, and he, the opposite. He had savoured the touch, how it made him feel, the power he had over her and the sexual gratification he got, just from that slight touch. He knew he was frightening her, although not to the extent she was actually feeling. He was unaware of the real terror she felt, the panic inside her, but he was attracted to her. She was eye candy for most red-blooded males, and he wanted to provoke Taylor, who already clearly despised him. He knew she was a passionate and very reactive person, and that she was highly likely to do something in response to what he was doing to Kay. He wanted Taylor to step over the line, so he could then ruin her. He just needed the ammunition.

Kay didn't know what to do. She had to use everything she had not to show the fear she was experiencing and not to vomit. She was frozen to the spot, with no idea what he was going to do next, hoping he would just sleaze away back to his office. Unfortunately, his eyes were focussed and menacing, and he stared right at her, his eyes moving slowly downwards to her breasts, a visible lick of his lips. Her instinct, "I must create distance", her legs were like jelly, she managed to force herself to move. She pushed back her wheely chair in haste and made her excuses, still treating him with respect, as he was still the boss, saying she needed a drink, even though her bottle was on her desk. She made off quickly towards the kitchen area, when she should have made a run for it, but that thought was still an irrational response. She didn't want to look like a fool.

Findlay watched her, her haste to get away from him, and it excited him all the more. He saw her hand tremble as she reached for the handle of the door to the kitchen, her long legs, strong calves, fitted skirt and blouse giving a glimpse of the outline of her bra, and he let his eyes wander up to her buttocks, firm and inviting. He knew what he was doing and would quite easily get away with it, his hand having only accidentally touched hers, a genuine mistake if ever asked, even possible denial. They weren't going to swab for DNA for something trivial like that and a genuine mistake.

He swithered on going back to his office, but he was enjoying this too much. It exhilarated him, and he chose to stay. The office was empty, no cameras, no witnesses, and he wasn't finished yet. His behaviour recently had become a little unhinged and desperate. He was becoming out of control. He stood up and the desk creaked with the shift of his weight. Kay turned around like she had been struck by a bolt of lightning. As she passed through the door, she looked back at him and saw him coming in her direction, his eyes focussed on her, with intent and purpose.

Once in the kitchen, she instantly regretted her decision. Her heart was pounding fast at the realisation she was now trapped. There was only one way in and a window with a drop outside. She reached up for the biggest mug she could find, knowing if she had to strike him, it would do some damage. She stepped back to the window, facing towards the door. Sweat beads had formed on her forehead. Her hands continued to shake, and her stomach was twisting inside of her, fear gripping her, the unknown consuming her. She felt dizzy, and then everything went black. She fell forwards, full force, face down on the floor.

Findlay heard the noise just as he reached the kitchen door, opening it to see Kay lying on the floor, with blood coming from her head. It was his turn to feel scared and sick to the pit of his stomach, only now comprehending the terror he had made her feel.

He stood back, hands on his head, his shirt becoming more untucked, exposing his fat apron below. He muttered to himself, expletives flowing at the situation he had caused. He wasn't remorseful, he was angry with her for being so weak, halting his depraved plan and causing him no end of grief. How would he explain this fiasco?

Coming back to his senses, he hurried to the phone to call an ambulance and started thinking about what he was going to say about what had happened. He was well aware of the fear he had caused Kay, but he hadn't really done anything, he convinced himself, and due to her untimely faint, he couldn't do any more, or could he?

Once the ambulance was called, he smiled to himself and went back to Kay. He shook her shoulders to see if she would come round and, when she didn't, he knelt down beside her, put something under her head, licked his lips as he stroked her hair, before moving down to her legs. Her skirt was hitched up and, from where he was, he could see her underwear. He felt unnatural stirrings of strong desire and was tempted to touch her there, but refrained initially. Leaving his DNA there would be virtually unexplainable. He knew first aid and enjoyed touching her legs more than necessary to raise them up, deliberately touching the inside of her thighs, opening her legs, imagining what was beneath her panties, unnecessarily exposing her even more. Taking in the vision, he leaned in close and breathed in her scent. He enjoyed the view very much, his fear gone, his deviance taking over. Every touch could now be explained as necessary to see to her medical needs. He had moved the bin to prop up her legs and went back to her head to sit beside her, her blouse askew, the top of one of her breasts now on show. He leaned forward and stroked the hair off of her face and continued to stroke it. He could smell her perfume, and that excited him. His desire for her was growing with every touch, her heady scent, and the fact that he was actually touching her brought out a deviant sexual predator, the realisation of what made him tick emerging, the cases he had dealt with in the past, and why he had reread so many statements from victims, especially the ones with a sexual element to them. Instead of focussing on just solving the crimes, he had been enjoying the fear oozing from the pages, terror and fear from within the women that were being assaulted and violated, raped and abused. He wanted to visualise the events and savour them. Rather than punish the perpetrator, he wanted to be them. And now, he wanted Kay. He imagined gripping her breasts roughly, pushing his hands up between her thighs, taking her. Aroused and out of control, he opened her legs one more time and this time he stroked over her panties, pushing them upwards and to the side, enough to feel her intimately, just for a second. In his mind, it was just a brush against her as he was raising her legs. His intent could never be proven beyond reasonable doubt.

He snapped out of his unnatural thoughts, finally remembering where he was and the consequence of what he was doing if found out, but why would he be? Why would they check? He moved quickly away from Kay, making sure he appeared like a caring boss, the good Samaritan, not the controlling deviant he really was. Within seconds of standing up, security from reception had brought the ambulance crew into their open plan office, and he went to the door to show them where help was needed.

To the new arrivals, everything seemed normal. A woman had had an episode in the kitchen area and was now in the recovery position. The boss had come to her aid. Nothing seemed untoward, and they got on with their jobs, none the wiser as they treated the head wound and took her vital signs. She had not regained consciousness, and for that Findlay was glad. The floor was his to set his innocent picture of the events that had taken place. He could give the heroic version for the crew to take down, the possible mechanism of the injury, that what may have been a faint had resulted in further injury as she fell heavily.

The ambulance crew had worked efficiently and were wheeling Kay out of the office on a stretcher just as Taylor, Marcus and Chris came breezing in, laughter still ongoing at the expense of the new guy. Taylor stopped dead in her tracks as she saw the ambulance crew with Kay. Her heart screamed out as she recognised her lover, bandages to her head and clearly unconscious. She went straight to her, before noticing Findlay further behind. She looked around the office in panicked rage, quickly realising it had been empty except for Findlay and Kay. She knew instantly that something had gone on here, something not right, but what?

Anger boiled up within her, and she flew over to Findlay, and in full view of the others, ambulance crew and all, she yelled into his face, challenging him aggressively, swearing at him, her face contorted and confrontational. She looked like she was going to strike him, and the others watched in astonishment, unknowing of their previous history.

"What the fuck did you do? You vile bastard, tell me! Tell me or so help me I'll rip your fucking fat head right off of your sloped little shoulders!"

Taylor was barely holding herself back from assaulting him, her chest puffed out in a challenging manner, her face very close to his, her words rasping through between her gritted teeth, saliva dotting Findlay's face. He took a step back and innocently put his hands up in false fear in an attempt to show a pacifying manner, for the witnesses to see who was the aggressor, and for him to fake that he was the victim.

Marcus had already started to run towards them. All he could do now was damage limitation for Taylor. She had already overstepped the mark; he wanted to stop her going any further, fearing she might not be able to contain herself this time.

Marcus got to them just in time and took hold of Taylor by her shoulders, gently but firmly pulling her back and around to face him, trying to get control of her.

Taylor looked like she was about to hit him too when their eyes met. She relaxed when she realised who had hold of her, and as she turned back to Findlay, he smiled, just long enough for her to see, and for Marcus to catch the end of it, lighting a fire to her hatred for him once again.

Marcus felt her tense up even more and knew she was about to attempt to hit Findlay. He gripped her for all his worth, dropping his arms down to initiate a bear hug, holding her arms into her sides, preventing her from doing anything else wrong. He lifted her off her feet and carried her away from her triumphant boss.

"Taylor, calm down! Don't do this. It's what he wants. He'll win if you hit him. You're playing right into his hands!"

The words were out before Marcus realised the boss was still there and glad to hear his thoughts, and where his loyalty lay, as he had always been pleasant and respectful to the inspector.

"Get her out of here! She's suspended indefinitely. Tell her not to return. We'll let her know when the disciplinary hearing will be!" Findlay shouted, ushering Marcus away.

Taylor jolted towards him, nearly breaking free, to the surprise of Findlay, who winced backward in a cowardly fashion, to her delight and to Marcus's disbelief.

"For fuck's sake, Taylor! Let it go! Kay needs you. C'mon, leave him!" Marcus growled at her, and pulled her away having to use a fair amount of strength to do so, but without aggression, as she was still pulling with all her might to get a pop at Findlay, and she was a strong woman.

Eventually, she relaxed and gave in to where Marcus was directing her, her head still turned towards Findlay, their eyes fixed on one another, Taylor's eyes rage-filled and his full of smug contentment. This had turned out better than he had thought it might, and quicker too.

At last, he had finally won, and he could now get rid of her!

Everything had happened so fast. The security officer was still standing there, his mouth agape, and the ambulance crew had stopped to watch the scene unfold too, their casualty still unconscious and unknowing of the trouble her love was now in.

Taylor accompanied Kay to the exit. She turned to Findlay, shouting very loudly, "You won't get away with this. I'll make sure you don't!"

"We'll see about that," Findlay muttered as he closed the door to his office with a loud slam. He smiled, a mixture of thoughts rushing around his head, a little fear, with a lot of pleasure, one dominating the other. He would relive his actions once home with a beer.

Chapter 11

Next

Kerri was filled with anger. She hated being told what to do, who to meet, who to like, who to respect. It filled her with fear and huge discomfort, it brought back memories of feeling trapped and controlled, and she had vowed that this would never happen again. She walked quickly along George Street, in the city, her pace quickening as she thought back to the sadness and disappointment she felt in relation to her family. She bumped into an older woman, who had accidentally got in her way as she shuffled along the road. This irked Kerri and she swore rudely into the woman's face, her words vicious and unkind, and totally unnecessary. The woman was astonished, with disgust following shortly after.

The woman tried to challenge Kerri. Frail and tiny in stature, but brave with her actions, she was quickly shot down in flames with a tirade of verbal abuse filled with expletives and even more vile, nefarious and insulting words. Kerri was consumed with spite and hatred, but her face remained calm and sweetly innocent. Her eyes were vexed. Pools of darkness stared back threateningly at the little woman, angry because she knew there was no more she could do to the woman, not without the law being involved, and that was not an option just now. She gave one last growl, spittle spraying from her lips, and then she smiled at the woman. The woman shivered deeply inside with a discomfort that frightened her to the core. The unbridled hideousness of this girl unnerved her, and she was glad to have walked away unharmed.

Kerri walked at pace through the historic George Street. She cut over Hanover Street and then Castle Street and turned onto Charlotte Square, before heading towards Princes Street, the junction bustling with tourists and other pedestrians. She could no longer progress as quickly as she wanted and this added to her irritation, which was growing into uncontrollable anger. She felt pins and needles prickle all over her face, and she knew she needed to get back to the unit before she did something she regretted, but it was too late. Incensed by the tiniest thing, her inner fury needed an escape, to vent, a release she only felt through dominating another, some unwitting soul, harming herself was not enough anymore. She looked down at her arms, the healing wounds telling their story.

When she got to the junction and the throng of people waiting for their turn to cross the road, she watched as a tourist stepped out carelessly in front of the traffic, totally unaware of the direction the vehicles were coming from. Kerri smirked at the person's stupidity and how close they had come to meeting their end. Her hands squeezed tightly to her ears at the sound of the blaring horns which were making her heart beat faster. She began to shake as she stood in the swarm of people, their presence causing her to panic. She could feel the person behind breathing on her, her thoughts haunting her. Squirming inside, she tried to calm herself. She stood still as a statue, her fists balled, taking deep breaths. She was losing control and didn't like feeling like this. She needed to take control, banish her fears. Her mood now heightened, a cruel smile crawled across her face, like creeping ivy. Her mood darkened. The traffic had started again, at greater pace this time after the delay caused by the naïve tourist, drivers now more desperate to get through the lights and get on their way. There were now numerous cars waiting impatiently to come through the busy junction onto Princes Street, impatience a common theme.

She watched as the lights turned to amber, her pulse racing, the pressure building in her temples. The throng of people waiting had increased, almost doubling as they waited, they too becoming impatient for their turn to cross. Kerri felt claustrophobic. A three-and-a-half-tonne truck increased its speed to get through the lights, with no consideration to the build-up of pedestrians only feet away. With an innocuous single-handed push to give her space in front, the woman who had had one lucky escape was jolted harshly forward onto the roadway once again, straight into the path of the speeding truck. Brakes screeched loudly, but with the weight of the truck in motion, it had no chance to stop. Pedestrians at the front of the throng saw the most hideous scene unfold before them, every gruesome detail on display, the events played out in slow motion as the truck hit the tourist, only for her to then slip beneath it. It bounced over the poor woman, her stomach splitting grotesquely as she screamed out, still fully conscious. Those at the front winced at the sight before them and turned away quickly and covered their faces. No one seemed to suspect that the woman had been pushed, and those who were still looking watched as the rear wheels silenced her screams forever, the truck only managing to stop a couple of metres further past her.

Those closest, who were brave enough, ran to her aid, but their efforts or hopes to save her were short lived, as her very obvious injuries were not survivable, her insides exposed and her body destroyed by the weight of the truck, traces of her visible on the tyres. To their horror, the woman's hand was still moving and there was a faint groan. A man knelt down beside her and took the hand in his, offering words of comfort, telling her she was alright, but knowing it was impossible, and she was most definitely not.

Kerri looked on with the others that had not moved. The woman had been in her space, crowding her. She deserved this, in Kerri's mind. They all stood motionless, staring at the poor woman. She knew she had to move off soon, and did so with a few other people that just wanted to get on with their business, she herself walking deliberately slowly, not wanting to get caught up with the police and their enquiries, wanting no part of what they had just witnessed. She moved along with the portion of society that were often too scared or simply unwilling to assist others, Kerri nonchalantly joining them. Elated at the devastation she had caused, triumphant at the macabre way the woman had met her demise, only now was she calmer, her odd fix appeasing her previous vexation and venomous desire to harm an innocent soul and rid her of the creeping discomfort she had been feeling inside. Kerri had killed her fear with demonic hatred and harm.

Smiling from under her hood, she walked in a controlled manner, no longer marching, her anger eased with the soothing sensation that the pain and torture of another gave her. It seemed to right the wrongs that had been done to her in the past, almost like retribution, but misplaced and misdirected at the innocent strangers who were unfortunate enough to cross her path.

She could hear the sirens approaching, police coming from stations and all over the city, an ambulance hurtling down Lothian Road at pace, all the way from the Edinburgh Royal Infirmary, unknowing that they were already too late to save the woman. She had just breathed her last breath, her head now resting on the stranger's lap, his hand never leaving hers, his gentle kind words giving her hope and some comfort right to the end as her life's blood emptied from inside her.

Chapter 12

Time for Action

Taylor seethed as she sped through the town centre, the ambulance already out of sight as it had sailed through the red lights, which she legally could not, although she did so where it was safe, her need to progress was more important than the punishment she might face. Her mind raced as she played out what could have happened to Kay in the office. She knew from the sensation in the pit of her stomach that whatever had taken place, it wasn't right, and Findlay was to blame.

Findlay had gone too far this time but, unfortunately for her, so had she. With her reactive temper, she had been unable to act calmly, and that smirk on the deviant fat little prick was just too much for her. She hadn't been able to stop herself, and it had felt good, because when she had headed straight for him, she had seen a glimmer of fear flit across his eyes, but not knowing what she was capable of. He was actually a coward and feared her ability.

She drove through the Meadows. Spring flowers in abundance blanketed the grass there, beautiful to see, and normally they would make Taylor smile, but not this time. Her mind worried for Kay, and a little for herself too, wondering how she could get herself out of this mess. She travelled up past the Commonwealth Pool, glancing up at the imposing sight of Arthur's Seat, an extinct volcano sitting high above Edinburgh, its red volcanic Salisbury Crags cutting the sky with their jagged line at the top, making her way to the hospital to join countless others also struggling to find somewhere to park.

Taylor's fingers tapped impatiently on the steering wheel, more vigorously the longer she waited, but she had seen a car move out of the parking bay furthest away, and once through the gate headed straight there, accepting she would be quicker walking further than waiting for a closer space.

Once parked, she made her way quickly around to the A & E department and spoke kindly to the receptionists. They recognised her straight away, but she did not have time to chat today and they pointed her through to the receiving unit where Kay lay, a doctor and nurse by her side. She remained unconscious. Taylor moved towards her, only to be directed to the waiting area. Annoyed, she protested, but knew they had their jobs to do for the benefit of Kay, and she couldn't help right now.

Taylor's posture expressed defeat as she went reluctantly to the waiting area. She slumped heavily onto the uncomfortable seating. Only now did she have time to think, thoughts racing around in her head with no answers coming. She needed help. She had friends, but not many in power to sort this. She thought of Temporary Superintendent Brooke Sommerville, recently moved up a rank to oversee a project in the Central Region of Scotland. Her fingers hesitated before she dialled the number. She could be opening up another can or worms, but she had to risk it. Brooke was strong and fair, and well aware of Findlay's indiscretions. She dialled the number, but to her annoyance it was engaged, and she didn't really want to leave a message. There wouldn't be enough space for what she had to say, so she hung up and chose to phone back later.

She didn't have to wait long. A doctor came through and told her that Kay had regained consciousness and was chatting to staff, a little disorientated but fine.

Taylor made her way to see her, and she was happy to see that Kay was awake, albeit looking a little groggy, but pretty well considering how she looked before.

Taylor hugged her where she lay, and they were both silent initially, but she had to address the elephant in the room. She took a deep breath.

"Kay, I need to ask, do you remember what happened?" Taylor wondered whether Kay would have a full recollection of what had happened after that bang to her head.

Kay looked at her. Their eyes locked. Kay had tears building up in hers. "Findlay!"

"Yes, Findlay, but what did he do to you? Are you okay? Did he hurt you? Did he touch you? What did that fucked-up fat little creep do to you?"

Kay's face was troubled as she tried to explain, knowing he had not done a lot, but his intentions not been good. She knew, from the depraved look on his face, that he had wanted more. She had sensed the obvious enjoyment of the terror he had created inside her, revelling in it as he came towards her, looking like he was getting off on it, but she could not remember anything after seeing his corrupt face as he approached. She must have fainted, her body hitting the floor like a dead weight, her head clattering off the tiles, knocking her clean out cold.

Taylor's heart sank. She knew that you could not prove guilt with thoughts about somebody's intention. It wasn't Minority Report, what ifs and what he might have been going to do, certainly not without another witness, would not wash in court.

Taylor was a little impatient with Kay and worried for herself now too, after her reaction and her witnessed aggressive outburst at Findlay. "What did he actually do?"

Kay's face saddened as she explained. "He sat on my desk, stared at me and touched my hand, very deliberately, holding his touch on my hand, eyes never faltering apart from to look down at my breasts. He licked his lips while his eyes deliberately wandered, not caring how I felt, practically salivating at the time. He was close; I could smell his breath he was that close, and he made me feel very uncomfortable. I got up immediately, pulled my hand firmly away and started walking quickly, straight to the kitchen. That bastard knew he was scaring me. He followed me. I could barely breathe when I saw him heading towards me. I was so scared. His eyes were cold and nasty and he never broke his stare. He wasn't acting normally; he looked angry and vengeful. I shut the door, and realised my mistake. There was no way out. I knew he was going to hurt me, and then nothing. I can't remember anything after that!"

Taylor's face was red with anger, fury gripping her. She knew that unscrupulous creepy little bastard had looked at Kay like that for a long time, and on this occasion an opportunity had arisen and he had acted on it. She too believed that he was capable of badness, and he was old school in his opinion about women and their place. How far would he have gone?

"Do you think he knew how much he was scaring you?" Taylor quizzed.

"Absolutely! He switched, he was no longer playing by any rules, he was clearly getting off on it. I'm sure of it. He was adjusting himself in the trouser area as he walked towards the kitchen, bloody disgusting even to think of him wanting me like that. I was frightened at just how far he was going to go. That might explain the flashback and my body's response to shut down to protect me, to stop me experiencing that again!"

Kay's eyes filled with tears once again, "I couldn't help thinking back to Brennan." Brennan was the male that had raped and murdered several women and Kay had been a victim. She was only alive because another brave woman saved her life by killing him. "I couldn't breathe. I was terrified."

Kay looked at Taylor. "Who was with me when the paramedics came to help? Who called them? He must have been alone with me when I was out of it! He must have got a fright when I collapsed."

"Or a hard-on more like!" Taylor couldn't help her natural misplaced thoughts and outbursts.

She continued, "Or had free rein to do what he wanted to you, when he was alone, with no witnesses!"

Taylor raged, as her mind ran through the scenario. She knew that piggy-eyed, fat-fingered, chubby little bastard wouldn't have been able to control himself.

Taylor explained what she had come into, how scared she had been for Kay and how angry she was when she looked at Findlay, quizzing him with her eyes as to what had gone on there, with only her own picture of what might have happened, and that was not good.

"Oh no, what did you do?" Kay looked worriedly at Taylor, knowing how angry she could get, and her reactionary behaviour.

"I reacted like anyone else would have done; I called him out on what I thought had happened. I threatened him and swore right in the fat little fucker's face. I only managed to stop short at hitting the fucking smug little bastard because Marcus put me in a blinking bear hug, the job saving, sensible, brilliant little dickhead, and I will thank him for that, as his quick thinking saved me from a sacking rather than just a suspension!"

"Suspension, have you been bloody suspended? What about him, what about Findlay? He was the one that caused this!" Kay was as angry as Taylor now, and had virtually forgotten why she was there, all the pain gone as the unfairness of the situation became clear. How it might play out for Taylor was heartbreaking, because this is what Findlay had always wanted. He had been on her back unfairly for years.

"Do you think he did it deliberately, Kay, or was it just the depraved little fucker's desire to have you?" Taylor's face contorted, and she put her head in her hands as the realisation hit of the severity of the situation, she was now in.

"Who knows? He's a sly little bastard, and I wouldn't put anything past him, but if this was his plan, then we've played right into his hands!"

They were still in the cubicle when the paramedics that brought in Kay came past. Taylor knew one of them, Debbie Parker, so she got up to speak to her.

"Have you calmed down a bit then? I thought you were going to rip his head off back there!" Debbie smiled at her long-term friend. "My money was on you!" she said with mirth.

"Actually, I was about to hit him, headbutt him, poke his eyes out, bite his face off, anything to hurt him, but good old Marcus saved the day. Thank God, really. I don't know if I would have been able to stop myself if I'd started. I hate that little fucker so much!"

"I need to ask you a question, nothing you can't tell me, anyway. Who was there when you arrived in the office? Who was with Kay?" Taylor asked with apprehension in her eyes.

"It was just the short plump, sweaty wee guy that you were about to knock out. The security guys brought us down to the office, and he was there with Kay in the kitchen, alone. I didn't see anyone else. Why?" Her brows furrowed, quizzing Taylor.

"You're fucking kidding? You mean that fat little creep was with her incapacitated and alone? For fuck's sake, you couldn't make that up!" Taylor's eyes watered with sadness and failure to protect her love.

She tried to smile. "Thanks for letting me know."

She gave her friend a hug as Debs left to find her young colleague, Scotty Casement, and was quick to get on the phone to Marcus to let him know what she had discovered.

Her heart was racing as she explained everything to her friend and trusted colleague. "Marcus! I need you to get hold of Michelle at the Public Protection Unit. I need her here. Kay wants to report what happened to her, and I will need her clothing forensically recovered. I think that depraved little bastard has fucking touched her and I'm going to prove it! I'll have the misogynistic, depraved little bastard if he has. There's no way he's been alone with her and been fucking able to keep his grubby little hands off. I know it and he's going to pay for it! You'll need to get the incident restricted and make sure he doesn't have access to the job. I don't want him to get a whiff of what's coming to him."

Chapter 13

Infatuation

A day had passed since her last episode of rage, with no conscience or consequence. Kerri arrived back at the home and was met with a stern-faced, foot-tapping Inga, normally kind and patient, but she was now being pushed to her limits. Kerri was late for her first meeting with her new social worker Phil Chancellor. Kerri had told Inga she was just going out to the shops to get fags, but she had been away for ages, which had infuriated Inga. It was the latest thing on a long list of excuses, blatant disregard for the rules, just bad manners and stinking attitude.

Inga was a tolerant woman, but this girl was pushing her to her limits. She deliberately wound people up, pushed their buttons to get a reaction, always angst with her, a darkness surrounding her. There was an absence within, ever since she had arrived there. Inga hoped that the new social worker was going to be the change in her behaviour, but she wasn't going to hold her breath. Many others had tried and failed before him.

"What? What are you looking at, you'd think I'd killed someone?" Her words brought a wry smile to her face at the irony of what she had said. Not today though, she thought, remembering everything she had done in the last month or so, with not an ounce of remorse for her victims, the last ones completely innocent. The rules for Kerri had changed. The lives of those people were gone forever, leaving an odd satisfaction within her.

Kerri stood there. Her appearance was impish, slim and delicate, weak looking and vulnerable, the exact opposite of what she actually was. She was feminine beneath her nondescript clothing, looking much younger than her years, but cruelty and unnatural desire to harm others ran through her veins, secreted beneath a false unassuming exterior. Her self-asserted sense of vengeance driving her to take it out on anyone who crossed her path. She felt justified because she had been harmed, then abandoned.

"You're late, where have you been? Have you forgotten your new care worker's here?" Inga's frustration showed in every word she uttered.

"This appointment can't be missed. I explained this to you, many times, and if you don't comply this time, you'll have to move on. It will be the end here and, without support this time, you'll be on your own. I bloody warned you! Why do you never listen? We're here to help you, so let us." Inga was almost begging, her voice now raised as she knew the girl was deliberately ruining her own life, but why? What was wrong with her?

Kerri actually felt a surge of regret. She heard what Inga was saying and knew the magnitude of it. For once, fear of losing her security blanket worried her. Even though she treated those that cared for her like shit, she had genuinely got caught up in her own thoughts, deep and dark, and had forgotten the meeting was that afternoon, so her lateness on this occasion was not even deliberate.

An exasperated Inga escorted Kerri through to the meeting room to ensure she wouldn't abscond again, thinking her lateness was another act of defiance. As they entered, Inga apologised to Phil as he looked up from the paperwork in front of him.

"Don't worry, these things happen." His words were kind and unfazed, his voice smooth and deep, his look, masculine and strong, his facial hair immaculate and his sexual orientation carefully hidden beneath an outer exterior of straightness, a choice he had made in his profession, to keep his private life very private and not allow perceptions and biases to change how things went for him.

He couldn't believe how young and vulnerable Kerri looked. Her notes painted a totally different picture, aggression, violence, hatred, evil, unpredictability, empty, and void of emotion and an uncontrollable temper, nothing like what stood before him.

"Have a seat." He beckoned to her and pulled out a chair, his gaze focussed on her and watching every motion.

She appeared flustered and embarrassed, bristling with something. He just couldn't put his finger on what her issue was.

She was angry that she was late. It had been unintentional. She was actually embarrassed and couldn't help noticing how kind and genuine he seemed. He was also very good looking, something she had never bothered about before. This unnerved her. It was so much easier to hate the lumpy men and frumpy overweight women. She felt at ease putting them down. In her sick mind they deserved it. All the men were labelled paedos and the women were fat, lazy slags or dykes, and she was never slow in letting them know with her constant abuse, day or night. The more anyone showed kindness, affection or care, the more she would let fly with vile abuse, filthy and vulgar obscenities, belittling them in the cruellest ways. When they were nice it made her feel uncomfortable. She didn't believe them, didn't trust them. Why would they like her? Nobody but her brother had so far, so she would systematically wear them down until they became more hostile and unkinder, less tolerant of her, and then she had proven to herself that they never cared. Once they changed towards her, she felt her abuse was deserved as they were all liars, and she no longer felt bad anymore, the odd sensation of remorse gone. She was broken and twisted. She had become a danger to everyone.

Kerri tugged the chair forcefully and petulantly from his hand, scraped it along the floor deliberately and slumped down hard on her bottom like a huffy child. She was about to speak and abuse him, her brows down and lips curled, but she was beaten to it. Phil spoke first. His manner was calm, his words soft and caring, his face kind and understanding, and she couldn't speak. Her foul words seemed to get stuck in her throat, a little taken aback by this man in front of her and, for the first time in a long time, she couldn't bring herself to be unkind to him.

"Hello, I'm Phil, a senior social worker, now assigned to your care." He smiled at her, his arms open in a welcoming gesture.

She was silent, despair and sadness overwhelming her. She couldn't understand her unexpected reaction, but it was there, and everything she had buried so deeply within herself was bubbling just beneath the surface, a volcanic eruption simmering below and now ready to erupt, full of emotion. Nothing made sense and it was bursting to get free.

Phil had no idea what was going on, her inner turmoil simmering. He had never met her before and had no preconceptions about her. He did not know if this behaviour was normal or not.

"Are you okay, Kerri? Can I get you something to drink? Do you want to take a minute? Are you okay?" he asked kindly in his deep and genuinely sincere voice.

A feral growl came from deep within this petite-framed young woman, a noise that wouldn't be out of place from a wild animal and certainly not natural or expected.

Phil stood still as a statue, eyes fixed on the young woman, a little disturbed at the reaction from within her. He didn't believe in possession, but he didn't think her vocal-chords could create a noise like that and feared for his safety, something he rarely felt.

Tears poured from her eyes, her shoulders heaved up and down from genuine emotion, but not a single word came from her mouth. Lips sealed, her inner anguish tormented her, her past, the things she'd done. A flood of despair overwhelmed her, and then her face hit the floor, the noise deafening as her head landed heavily with a sickening crunch.

Chapter 14

Fran – Welcome Back

Glasses clinked together. Pink fizz for a wee celebratory drink before she returned to the shift. Her long recovery finally over and her injuries healed as much as they ever could. Her scars, burns and patches of hair missing all on show for all to see. Fran didn't care. Her eyes remained bright and full of vitality. She had an insatiable zest for life untainted by her near-death experience last year and other challenging events. Her fate had brought her to a new future with a new partner, Lana, who was kind, strong, caring, honest, faithful and loving, everything she could ever want. Fran fought hard to ignore a little niggle inside. She knew Lana was perfect for her, both committed and safe, but her mind kept wandering back to Taylor! The exact opposite of Lana, exciting, dangerous, flirtatious, thrilling and certainly not safe and very hard to be with. Unfortunately for her, Taylor made her tummy flip, her insides tingle, and sadly she felt herself still thinking about her and wanted her.

Taylor was elusive, a strikingly attractive, confident and alluring human being. She had been unfaithful and was currently unavailable. She had tried to get her out of her mind and shake her from her thoughts and hoped that she had done so once and for all. Her new life with Lana had been amazing, secure and filled with passion and good times. Now that she was due to be going back to work, her mind was a haze of memories both good and bad. They were filled with lust, passion, sadness, heartbreak and despair. All were thrilling and eventful, with mind-blowing, toe-curling sex, a breathless torture as her mind carelessly took her back there. Imagining her body willingly beneath Taylor's, wanting her touch and needing to be taken.

Lana moved closer. She was aware there was a layer of water over Fran's eyes and kissed her head softly. She wanted to ask a penny for her thoughts, but chose not to. She allowed Fran to have her time with her private thoughts. She had felt a shift of emotion this week, although she didn't think too much of it. It was normal to be apprehensive about returning to work after such a long period off. She also had her recovery and the fact she had nearly died to cope with too.

Lana gently kissed her lips. Her mouth soft and tender as she pulled Fran towards her and held her in their kiss. Fran was still and unresponsive until her mouth opened, her kiss feverish and needy, her petite hands reaching round, holding the back of Lana's head to pull her face closer into hers. Lana was taken aback by the passion she was displaying. She was totally unaware that Fran's mind had just floated back to the past. Back to her tumultuous past with Taylor, and it may not have been Lana she wanted to take her this evening.

Fran couldn't hold back another second and pulled Lana onto her. She pushed her hand between her legs. There was no doubt she was turned on. She was soaking wet and there was no holding her back. The minute Lana's hand touched her, Fran pushed down forcefully onto her fingers, full weight, her need to be taken very clear.

"Fuck me! Oh God! Please just fuck me! I need to feel you inside me. Fuck me hard, now!" It was as if she wanted Lana to fuck her thoughts of Taylor out of her head. Over and over the thrusts came, Fran's breathless pants loud and desperate as she just kept going. Lana, a physically powerful and fit woman, struggled to keep up with her insatiable desire to be taken, long fingers fucked her over and over again. Lana was taken aback with the change in Fran, but she wasn't complaining.

Lana flipped her over, keeping her there pinned down with her arm while her mouth delved into Fran's glistening pleasure, adoring her, her silky warm haven inviting her, the heavenly scent of her intimacy and the taste of her love soon driving them both into a frenzy.

Fran closed her eyes tightly, her thoughts betraying her, but her animal desire taking what she needed, Lana loving her, unaware of the silent betrayal, as Fran came hard.

Chapter 15

Suspension Works Both Ways

Findlay's face was a picture of fury. His face twisted into a mask of pure hatred as he read the formal letter before him. The words knotted inside his stomach, like a burning pit of rage.

"Suspension of duty pending further enquiry."

He read on; his heart was pounding inside him like a hammer hitting an anvil. He was bright red, sweat beads forming. If anyone had seen him, they would have called for medical assistance as he looked like he was about to have a heart attack, his colour so unnatural.

"Allegation of inappropriate conduct is now being investigated."

He couldn't contain himself any longer and he let out a guttural roar of pure anger. His mind was racing, not at his wrongdoing, but of how to make these venomous women pay for what they had done to him, retribution uppermost on his mind, his vile behaviour not even registering as the cause of his possible demise.

"Please attend a formal meeting, 1100hrs, 10th of June, Fettes Police Station, to go over the allegations and confirmation of suspension on full pay, until this matter is resolved."

Findlay's pudgy hand crushed the papers he had just finished reading. He could barely catch his breath. The sensation engulfing his being was incredibly unpleasant, a creeping sense of vengeance and an overwhelming loss of control. His eyes narrowed and his unwholesome thoughts started plotting how he could rectify this situation, once and for all.

"BITCHES, DYKE BITCHES, YOU WON'T GET AWAY WITH FUCKING WITH ME. I'LL SHOW YOU HOW THINGS ARE MEANT TO BE!"

He looked at his watch. It was nearly 10am. "Nothing like giving me plenty of notice, you never cease to amaze me, you incompetent wankers!"

He walked through to the kitchen area, and started to make a coffee, when his thoughts raced back to the episode with Kay. Initially he was excited by his thoughts. He believed he was untouchable, but the realisation of where he had touched her stung him deep inside his gut. There was always trace evidence, but he didn't think for a moment that this would be considered and assumed it wouldn't have been preserved. But now his hate-filled face was picturing Taylor, in his eyes an arrogant self-confident and very capable officer, and although he loathed to think it, he knew she was an inspirational detective and very good at what she did, and her hatred for him matched his constant loathing of her. He didn't want to consider that her astute mind would have considered forensically recovering Kay's clothing to ensure evidence was captured if something untoward had happened.

"This is her doing. She's put a fucking complaint in. The grounds, who knows. There was nothing to suggest more than a medical emergency, unless Kay's embellished what really happened?"

Time seemed to take forever, and 11am was getting closer. He even went to the rest rooms and tucked his shirt in, straightened his tie and pulled on his suit jacket that lay dormant on the peg in the office. He had noticed a stain on his shirt and his virtually unused attire was needed to cover it up. He sorted his slightly greasy hair, the comb emphasising it even more, and wiped his mouth, removing the remnants of last night's tea and this morning's breakfast, a collection of grotesque savouries left on his unwashed face, a sleeve usually removed most.

He was ready, a final straightening of his clothing and he walked briskly through to the higher-ranking officers' corridor and he paused briefly, took a deep breath and knocked firmly on the door, arrogant to the last. He waited impatiently for nearly a minute and was about to knock again when the door swung open in front of him.

He saw a strawberry blonde female, light freckles on her face, kind but focussed eyes, slender, 5'5" tall, mid-thirties, sporting a crown on her shoulder, an officer he had never had the opportunity of meeting. Inside there were two others, Superintendent Paul Richardson a smart, well-presented man, early forties, that clearly looked after his physique and, to Findlay's utter dismay, Acting Superintendent Brooke Sommerville, the chief inspector that had lorded over him the year previously, another formidable female, and definitely on Taylor and Kay's side. He felt even more angst. He hated the woman, and he knew he didn't stand a chance. The Superintendent opening the door introduced herself as Lara Blantyre and motioned him to enter and take a seat.

The scene was ominous, their faces stern as each of them was introduced. Everything was very formal, and for the first time in his service, Findlay felt intimidated and thought that he might actually be in serious trouble.

Superintendent Blantyre spoke first, her words clear and concise, very matter of fact and to the point. There was no room for pleasantries as the allegations were read out. The matter would be treated as a criminal allegation until proven otherwise due to the sexual nature of the complaint.

Superintendent Richardson spoke next, explaining what

was to happen and the rules he was required to follow. There would be no return to the office, no contact with team members and specific restrictions in relation to those making the complaint.

Finally, Acting Superintendent Sommerville handed over the formal paperwork to Inspector Findlay. His hands were shaking, damp with sweat, but it wasn't with fear. It was utter resentment, thoughts of what the force had become, women everywhere, queers taking over and real men like him being pushed out in the cold. He looked up at her, their eyes meeting and his visibly altered, snakelike and demonic as he squinted at her, his stare sending a very clear, but silent, warning to the woman in front of him, threatening, a clear loss of control and pure hatred. She felt the power of his anger and was unnerved at how he was acting. She had seen this behaviour before, but this was in the criminals that she had helped put behind bars, not from her colleagues in the force.

He turned to leave, and Brooke Sommerville couldn't help but feel a little intimidated and unsure about what Findlay was capable of. He looked unhinged, out of control, and was certainly not acting normally. It was unclear how he would react and respond to the papers and restrictions served upon him.

Findlay pulled the office door open with force, just stopping it from hitting the wall, and turned ominously and spoke, "What happened to innocent until proven guilty? I've done nothing wrong! This is a bloody witch hunt and you all know it!"

He looked directly at Brooke, eyes fixed with intent and vengeance. "And you, I don't think you're neutral enough to be on this panel, and you know why!" His eyes never left Brooke's, her face turning red instantly. This did not go unnoticed by the two other panel members, leaving them questioning his attack on her.

Findlay left before he took his anger too far. He didn't want to give them reason for another disciplinary action or worse, to arrest him for assault.

The panel looked to Brooke to explain what Findlay had meant, but no answers came. She brushed off his accusatory words as the act of a desperate hate-filled man, who thought he could muddy the waters by throwing a spanner in the works.

Brooke was a fair person and, even though her path had crossed Taylor's, she would treat this matter as the facts presented themselves. She was well aware of what a vile man Findlay was and what he was capable of, or so she thought, not considering the reality now could be much worse.

Lara said her piece and went over the allegation made. The fact that they were sending clothing off for forensic analysis was a very serious matter. Lara knew of Taylor, that she was a professional, that she could be hot headed and fiercely loyal, and would always stand up for what was right, she believed that for her to be taking things this far, she must have grounds to do so.

Chapter 16

I Met This Girl Today

Phil thumped his bottom down hard on the sofa, glad to be home at last. He kicked off his shoes and put his feet up on the pouffe, stretching like a cat and beginning to relax.

His mind went over his day, everything he still needed to do; the list was pretty long. He was troubled by the young woman he had met earlier. A presence about her had made him feel uncomfortable and, for him, that was a first. He had met many lost souls and violent young offenders, but this girl was different, very much so.

He looked forward to his partner Chris coming home from work, as he was always a good listener and, with him being a detective in the MIT, he was no stranger to evil and what corrupted minds could do. He would definitely be letting his thoughts be known about this girl.

He took out his notes. He had already noticed there wasn't a lot of history with the girl, no back story, which he found a little strange. Usually there would be an explanation in the past that revealed many things that could cause such insular and disturbing behaviour, as well as deep-rooted issues, be it violence, sexual abuse, neglect, or all three of them, with many more heartbreaking reasons where adults have horrifically let those in their charge down. With Kerri's case, it seemed like abandonment was the issue, her parents all of a sudden refusing to look after her anymore and also willing to pay for her care, a very rare situation. It was all very odd. He made a mental note to look deeper into this and her past, because he believed there was more to it. He had never come across parents washing their hands of their children through choice rather than need.

He was aware that she had seemed to like him, and the last thing he wanted was her to like him a little too much, or become infatuated by him, because in his experience that only led to bad things. He did, however, feel that he had managed to get through to her a little, and have her listen to what he was saying. He had listened to everything she had said too and felt there was much more to this girl hidden deep inside, and he aimed to dig deeper through time and uncover what made her tick.

The door opened without the sound of a key. Chris was home at last. His day had also been filled with heartache, despair and a large spoonful of gossip.

"Phil, you never locked the bloody door again. Some wee housebreaking, lowlife bastard will just walk right in some day!" He said this with half fun, whole earnest, his cop head always at the forefront of their safety.

"Hello to you too," Phil said with humour and warmth. "I'm a big guy, I can handle myself and, anyway, I would hear someone come in, and I always check it at night!" he answered in a nonchalant manner, nonplussed about whether some random would ever come in, as he clearly thought he would be able to deal with it. "Come through here anyway, and a cold beer would be nice!" He had been about to get up and get one for himself. Chris would save him a journey, he thought, with a smile.

Chris was in need of a cold beer too and brought them through. He leaned over and kissed Phil on his stubbled face, lingering for a while, enjoying the masculine scent of his lover.

His words went straight into Phil's mouth. "How was your day? I've missed you."

Phil responded without pulling away from Chris's kiss. "Very interesting. I've got a lot to tell you!" He stopped talking and kissed Chris properly, a full-on passionate kiss.

Both were in need of a bit of relaxation, or a bit of unbridled sex, to set them free from their days. Shirts pulled open, exposing defined muscular chests with clipped chest hair, Chris not sporting as much as Phil though. Jeans buttons pulled free, exposing their very obvious desire for one another. Chris dropped to his knees and took Phil into his mouth, and his groan was enough to let Chris know he needed his touch. His buttocks tightened and his release freed him at last. He pulled Chris up from his knees and took him through to the bedroom where Phil took Chris, pushed him over the edge of the bed and caressed his ass, lubing up, his hand reaching around to grip his cock firmly as he entered him. Both of them allowed themselves to let go, getting really physical, until their stress and frustration was over, and they could finally relax and continue their conversation without any further distraction.

Both lay back on their pillows, Phil joking about having a fag, as they were sweaty and out of breath. If they did smoke, this would be the time.

Chris got up to get more well-needed beers. His slight frame, wiry and muscled, with a perfect butt, strode through. Phil watched him and sighed deeply; his body worn out with the very physical lovemaking. He knew he was lucky to have someone as decent as Chris, strong-willed, caring, kind, and very capable. The gay scene sometimes provided the very opposite. They had been together for several years, and were very happy with what they had. Phil loved Chris.

Once Chris was through with the beers, they sat up, clicked on the TV and started to chat about their days. Chris went first, explaining about his boss getting suspended. Phil was pretty happy about this, as he had heard Findlay was a misogynistic prick, a total homophobe and a sleazy sexist pig, so he thought to himself, no loss there. He asked after Chris's other boss Taylor, knowing that she too had been suspended in relation to the same incident. Chris said he was worried at how everything would end but mentioned his handsome mentor Marcus, telling Phil he had been moved up to act as sergeant for the team in Taylor's absence, but his wife was heavily pregnant and he may have to take time away in the near future. He then went on to mention that Fran was back on the team and how nice a woman she was, especially after what she had been through. He was aware that there was a history between Fran and Taylor, so expected there may be a little trouble in the future. He told Phil that her personality was intact and seemingly undamaged from what he had heard about her. Before she had gone through her most recent near-death experience, she was an inspirational woman, and he was looking forward to getting to know her properly, as she seemed his type of person. He went on to mention the deaths they were remotely involved in and that the two drownings were looking more suspicious than previously thought. There may be more to these cases than the original belief of suicide.

Phil listened intently, always sad when someone took their own life, having lost a few friends in the past, unable to live their lives fully without feelings of guilt and rejection, and sadly choosing to end it, rather than fight on.

He was taken aback when Chris told him about the most recent death that had been passed to the MIT to cast their eye over, the woman crushed and half of her body de-gloved at the junction of Princes Street. He winced at the details of her injuries and questioned why a Road Traffic Incident would come anywhere near the reaches of the Major Investigation Team, as they were specifically used for murders by unknown persons. The MIT dealt with enquiries that were far-reaching, long-term and in-depth, all of which would be required to solve murders. When there was no known suspect, these cases were very time consuming and labour intensive, requiring the MIT's well-practised skills and coordinated teamwork, with numerous other officers drafted in to each squad for investigation.

It was Phil's turn to talk about his day, and he went over Kerri's case, no breach of data, protection as known partner agencies were allowed to share information with one another, even at home, so no secrets spilled, although Chris was not able to share everything the MIT were involved in, especially in cases where leaked information could affect the outcome of a trial.

Chris was intrigued by the sound of this petite young woman. He was always interested in the unknown, the damage that some people have suffered in their younger years, the consequences of it and how it manifests itself. Many of these damaged souls turned to criminality, their lack of nurture being the reason for the type of crimes they committed, sometimes coming to fall under his remit in the MIT due to their very nature.

Both men enjoyed winding down after their work, sharing their thoughts. As partners from other agencies, they could offer up their ideas to help resolve matters, each having different points of view for each of their problems at work.

They got dressed, headed through to the kitchen and started making a steak stir fry for dinner. Some nice red wine and their movie chosen; it was now time to relax. Glasses chinked loudly together as they smiled at one another, happy and content with their union.

Chapter 17

Reinstatement

Taylor was still deeply frustrated and angry at her suspension, but enthused by the fact that that fat sleazeball had finally been called out to answer for his despicable behaviour, after so many years of slipping beneath the radar, assisted by others from the same group of talentless, old school, boys club hierarchy.

Kay was home from hospital and her head was healing. Both she and Taylor were off work. They had time to relax, try and move on from what had happened and talk about what was still to come. Their time together wasn't going as smoothly as it could, however, because Taylor was letting the incident get the better of her. She was never happy at the aggressor winning over the oppressed, her moral fibre twitching at the unfairness at work. She had reacted to what she believed had happened and now she had to prove that something had happened between Findlay and Kay. She knew Kay had been terrified of something, but of what? Taylor knew she had a reactive personality. Thankfully, Marcus had stopped her going any further, and she loved him for that, for always being there for her. He was her rock and guardian angel at work. He was cool-headed, strong and would not see a friend step out of line.

She paced the floor, waiting and wondering why the police

had not yet been in touch with her about where she stood regarding her suspension, timescales and when the formal hearing would take place.

The phone rang loudly making her jump, almost spilling the cups of tea she was carrying. She quickly handed one over to Kay and put her own cup down, before slumping full weight down on the couch, almost sending Kay flying off the other end. She reached for her phone and saw that it was a withheld number, meaning only one thing in her world, the police were calling. Her wishes for finality had been answered, and she listened expectantly, covering the speaker, as she spoke to Kay. "Oh well, this is it. Fingers crossed they've made the right decision!" She looked over at Kay with a hopeful expression.

Kay smiled. "You'll be fine, you only shouted at him! It's hardly the crime of the century, and he bloody well deserved it, the vile, horrible little man!"

"Hello, Taylor speaking."

"Hello, have you got a few minutes? Are you free to speak?" an unfamiliar voice came over the phone. "It's Superintendent Lara Blantyre speaking, and if you're free to speak, I have some news for you, Sergeant Nicks, some good and some not so good!" she said in a calm but friendly voice.

Taylor went over what the bad could be, and she could feel a little bristle of temper rising. She knew there was more to what had happened and that her reaction would be proven to be justified.

Superintendent Blantyre went on to say, "Unfortunately you will be given a written warning for your verbal outburst to a senior officer, which is unavoidable, as your actions were witnessed and established to be unprovoked at this time, so it was proven that your conduct was unbecoming of a police officer, and you'll have to attend the station to sign the paperwork regarding this."

Taylor was about to argue the case, but knew there was no

way there would have been no consequences for her rage-filled and threatening outburst, but before she had time to say anything in her defence about it, the superintendent closed down her opportunity and, as if deliberately stopping her attempt to argue, she continued speaking calmly, "However, you are the most experienced sergeant within the MIT, time served and with several years of experience, and we need someone to take the place of the inspector while the enquiry runs its course. DC Black is currently filling your role as acting detective sergeant, and I need you to take on the responsibility for the unit as acting inspector for the duration of DI Findlay's suspension. Do you think this is a position you'd like to take on?"

Taylor could not believe what she was hearing but was also very aware that the other sergeant on the team was nowhere near as efficient as her, with very little experience, and she knew she was the best placed officer to lead their highly trained team to the best effect.

The superintendent spoke again, as there had been no response to the offer she had just made. She had expected a quicker reply, of a positive nature.

"Oh, my apologies, ma'am. I was taken aback a little with this offer, after just receiving my written warning, and, yes, of course I will happily take on this responsibility. Thank you very much for considering me for this role!"

Lara Blantyre was an astute woman. She knew Taylor had reacted to the situation like many a male colleague had done in the past, all without even raising an eyebrow or suffering any consequence. Her punishment was only because she had crossed the line in front of witnesses from another service, and this could not be ignored. It was unacceptable conduct, going on the facts they had to date, so it had to be dealt with more seriously. The paramedics were unaware of the background between the parties involved, and their statements were detailed and a little damning, but they were factual and not over-embellished, with no deliberate intent to get her in trouble.

Superintendent Blantyre explained that the written warning was fair, and that this would be the end of the matter in relation to her poor choice of action taken that day and that it did not reflect on her ability to carry out the temporary promotion being offered. They as a department would be making a big mistake to overlook her, as she was clearly the most experienced and qualified officer to take on the role and carry the responsibility for the enquiries that were already ongoing. She knew what was still required and the progress made on each of them.

"I know it's short notice, but are you able to start back on the team tomorrow? I'm sure DS Black will be happy to see you back and, I'm sure, from what I've heard, you owe him a debt of gratitude," Superintendent Blantyre said with an element of humour and relief. Newly appointed Superintendent Sommerville had filled her in about Findlay's unsavoury character and how he mismanaged the team.

Taylor's face flushed a little, aware of what she had been about to do to Findlay in the heat of the moment. She had been saved by friend and trusted colleague Marcus Black, who had prevented her assaulting the inspector and possibly losing her job.

"Yes, ma'am. I know DS Black is a good man, the best in fact, and I wish there were more like him! I will thank him, after I tease him about jumping into my shoes so quickly after I left!"

Superintendent Blantyre responded quickly, "Well, control that temper then, and we wouldn't be having to have had this conversation and the staff reshuffle, would we?" Taylor could hear the friendly tone of her voice. The superintendent had a job to do, but there was no necessity to be unkinder than the system dictated.

Taylor replied, "I understand what you're saying, and I apologise for my conduct on that day. It won't happen again, and hopefully when the full enquiry is complete, you will understand why I reacted how I did. That man has always been skirting the line of inappropriate behaviour, and now he's stepped over it. Although I can't yet prove that, his shifty demeanour let me know he had!"

"DI Nicks, you know I can't discuss an ongoing enquiry, and you shouldn't speak about it either. I understand your frustration, but you'll have to wait for the finalisation of the enquiry before you can lawfully make those accusations. Now, get on with your new role, and show me and any doubters that you're more than capable of stepping up and proving you're good enough for the job. Don't let me or Superintendent Sommerville down!" Superintendent Blantyre said this deliberately to see if there was a response or reaction now she had made Taylor aware Brooke Sommerville was involved in the panel.

Taylor paused, not for long, but it was noted. "Superintendent Sommerville, when did she get promoted? I wasn't aware she was involved in this enquiry." Taylor tried to remain calm and appear nonplussed, but her mind went back to the night they had shared. The thought was more than pleasant, exquisite in fact, and her tummy fluttered. However, her tone remained calm and non-reactionary when she responded again to her senior, realising she was clearly fishing for something, which was par for the course in this line of police work.

Superintendent Blantyre continued, unphased but aware of Taylor's pause, "She was promoted recently, actually; I take it you know her?"

"I do. She worked with us on the paedophile ring case. She was a good boss. Why?" Taylor responded without giving anything more away.

Superintendent Blantyre paused noticeably before proceeding,

"Just wondering with something Inspector Findlay had said at his meeting, that's all." Deliberately creating a curiosity within Taylor.

Taylor could imagine what that sly jealous fat little fucker would have said about them, but didn't ask what had been said. She had done nothing wrong and did not seek fortune or favour for the short and passionate interlude she thought may have been suggested. He could only have suspected there had been something between them. He could not know for sure, and neither could the curious super.

Taylor took a breath and spoke calmly, knowing she was fishing for more.

"I've no idea what he's on about, and I won't elaborate about him, as I've learned my lesson about reacting to things said without detail or explanation," she said with sarcasm in her voice.

"Ah, okay then. We'll have to see if he says any more then," Blantyre said with disappointment in her voice that Taylor had not elaborated, but she hadn't really expected her too. "Okay, I'll let you get yourself organised for going back to work tomorrow then."

"Thank you for the phone call, ma'am, and I appreciate your understanding and support. I won't let you down!"

The call ended and Taylor looked at Kay, who had been listening to what was being said, although she had missed bits here and there.

Taylor played it down at first and told her about the written warning and that it was a fact-based formality and their hands were tied, apparently, though many before had never been punished for their behaviour. It was usually put down to exuberant, misplaced aggression, but, with a handshake, nothing more was said and certainly no disciplinary action taken, unlike in her case.

Taylor smiled and told Kay about her temporary promotion,

deliberately missing out anything said about Brooke, and took Kay's hand gently, but firmly enough to pull her closer.

Kay leaned in, but Taylor continued to pull her hand with intent and strength to lead Kay to sit over her. Kay was happy to oblige. She liked when Taylor had that glint in her eye, and she hadn't seen it for a couple of weeks now. Kay knelt over her, knees on either side of Taylor's thighs. She could feel Taylor's strong hands stoke over her bottom, gripping it gently, and it felt nice. Kay was wearing loose thin cottons that allowed Taylor's touch to penetrate through and make it even softer, with an arousing sensation. Taylor knew this, and was deliberately stroking over Kay's erogenous zones, slipping over and under her bottom, down the middle of her cheeks, round and gently over the front. Kay jumped a little as Taylor deliberately pushed harder over her pleasure, teasing her, making her want to be touched a little more intimately.

Kay moaned as her mouth engulfed Taylor's, the tension that had been around since the incident in the office was gone. Her tongue pushed into Taylor's mouth. Her hips pushed forward onto Taylor, with Taylor's hands now gripping her ass, with her fingers pushing under her and pushing between her legs, the material not stopping her fingers from going into her slightly, and setting Kay's cheeks into a fevered flush. Her hips lifted and pushed back down onto her awaiting hands. She no longer wanted her clothes on, so she pulled her blouse open, exposing her breasts close to Taylor, her nipples taut with expectation, and leaned deliberately into Taylor's face, teasing her, knowing she would like what she saw. Taylor was quick to respond, her mouth surrounding one breast and sucking over it and down onto Kay's nipple, her tongue and lips skilled in giving just the right pressure to excite, not annoy. This time when Kay raised up from Taylor, Taylor gripped the top of her jogging bottoms and pulled them down enough to allow her to touch her intimately. As she lowered back down, Taylor glided her fingers inside her, pushing deep, Kay's wetness a sign of her pleasure and expectation. Taylor started to pleasure her slowly, as Kay moaned and willed her further into her, her kisses stealing Taylor away from her needy breasts. Kay pulled on Taylor's shoulder, moved her onto her back and lay on top of her kissing her feverishly, Taylor's hand still round her ass and fingers stroking her from behind. Kay's breathing was changing, and little whimpers of delight were escaping as she started to wriggle free from her cottons, leaving her naked from the waist down, her top half clothing open and dishevelled and even more of a turn-on for Taylor's eyes. Kay moved up further onto Taylor, and Taylor helped her, pushing and lifting her over her face. She paused and held herself there, looking at her glistening haven, inches away from her mouth, her heavenly scent intoxicating. Neither of them could wait. Taylor raised up and Kay came further down, causing Taylor to bump her nose off Kay's pelvis.

"Ouch!" came from beneath Kay, and laughter from above as they enjoyed the moment. Kay still wanted to be taken, and even though Taylor was suffering a little with her nose, Kay came closer again and this time she was met with a warm tongue and long, strong fingers sliding deep inside her, the caress of a well-practised lover. Taylor's mouth devoured Kay, her mouth working in harmony with her hands, Kay writhing at the intensity and her inability to stop herself from cumming straight away. She wanted to savour this sensation, the curling twists of the imminent orgasm, but she wanted it to last, because it just felt so gorgeous, the tongue and deep thrusts in time with each other. She could feel the flow of her cum and she had to let go. Gripping swirls began and grew stronger and stronger. Taylor could feel the pulses and tightening inside Kay as her thunderous release took full hold of a desperate and lust-hungry body, moaning as Taylor stopped with her mouth and started to fuck her, thrusts, deep and strong, keeping the swirl of the orgasm going, the sensation now deep inside her. Kay could barely breathe.

"Oh God, oh Taylor, ooo, don't stoppp, aahhh, ahh, mmmmm, shit, shit, I'm cumming again, keep going, please don't stop, ooo fuck me, fuck me harder, harder, oh God Taylor, fuck me, pleaaaasssssee."

Her words slurred into Taylor's needy mouth as their bodies slipped close to one another. Kay's release was warm and obvious, and Taylor was also in a frenzied state, fully aware of what was happening. Never before had Kay allowed herself to let go like that and by the level physically displayed by her body. Her ejaculation excited Taylor even more, a flush of satisfaction came over her at what she was able to do for this beautiful woman.

They were back to where they started, free of fear and interruption, free to love, free to be together. Their physicality to make love had no boundaries.

Chapter 18

Livid

His teeth ground together. The papers were crushed and soiled from being stuffed into his pocket. He was seething. His life had been turned upside down by these dyke bitches. In his mind, not a shred of blame lay at his feet. He had lazily coasted through for over 25 years of policing, barely lifting his fat useless fingers.

His wife Annette had tried to speak to him but made a hasty retreat when she saw his face was puce in colour, a large whisky in his hand, and that sight from a man who wasn't shy at lifting his hand to control her with a far smaller display of outward rage. She dared not ask what was wrong, and she was not stupid enough to stay either. Years of laziness, a raised hand, conjugal rights and a few savage beatings were enough for her to finally make her decision. She rushed up the stairs and packed a few things, fearful that her leaving would be discovered.

Findlay was too consumed in his internal desire to reap his revenge to notice. They would not get away with this witch hunt, the man-hating cunts. His anger was taking over his logical self-preserving thoughts. The decisions being made were out of control and all stopping him thinking straight. He had finally lost it; self-control was no longer a boundary that he had to worry about. His eyes narrowed. Hatred and revenge were all that filled his mind.

"Annette, hey Annette, ANNETTE!!! Where are you, you fucking lazy bitch? ANNETTE, get down here, will you?"

His wife would normally come running obediently, but no answer came. He was irked that she had not answered him and had the nerve to stay upstairs when he had called for her. He waddled up the stairs, with more haste than normal, gripping the banister as he went, already thinking of what punishment he would enforce.

He was just about to shout at her when he saw a couple of drawers were open, the clothes inside dishevelled.

"Messy fucking cow," he thought to himself, not yet realising the meaning of the untidiness caused by the haste in his wife's departure.

Only when he went through to the other rooms and shoved open the closed bathroom door, his last place unchecked, did he realise she was not hiding from him, and was actually not there.

He caught sight of his ruddy face in the mirror, sweat forming on his forehead and dripping down onto his face, his skin clammy and a general look of poor health staring back at him. He took time to look for longer, something he chose not to do too often for this reason.

He didn't like what was looking back at him, what he had become, how far he had gone down the path of greed and slovenliness. All of which just made him even more angry, more spiteful, and the people he chose to blame for it were Taylor and Kay. His own fault or responsibility was nowhere to be found in his remit of thought.

He turned away in anger, his mind flitting back to what he was doing and the disbelief that his wife was not there, the realisation that she had actually left him not yet crossing his mind. He assumed she was away to the shops, never thinking she had the strength, ability or funds to leave him.

Annette was already halfway across the city, heading for

Waverly Station, tickets bought for a train down south where she had two sisters she could stay with until she was sorted out, her phone switched off to prevent any sort of tracking, because he had done sneaky things like that before. She smiled. For her, a new life was on the horizon, and with a new phone!

Chapter 19

New Beginnings

Marcus continued stroking Maria's shoulders, Wee David off at his Grandparents' house. He liked his grandad Andrew and his granny Annie, and their big retriever, Kimmy.

They laughed together about the hot curry they had just eaten, allegedly a known way to spur on the birth of a baby, ever hopeful the old wife's tale may come true.

He reached his hands around her tummy gently, her skin taught with the now overdue baby inside her, clearly with no intention of coming out any time soon. He kissed the side of her head tenderly and breathed in her scent. He whispered, "I love you," then paused and smiled at her, adding, "both of you."

"Aww, Marcus, you're so sweet, kind and gentle and I love everything about you." Maria smiled at him with mischief in her eyes.

"You're up to something! What have you done? C'mon spill." Marcus laughed into her ear, wondering what it was.

"Maybe gentle isn't the way forward?" She paused and smiled again, the look a bit naughtier this time.

"No! No, no. We've not done anything like that for so long. We can't now, we shouldn't. No, no and no!" Marcus said in a definite tone.

"I've been reading these articles about sex and pregnancy,

and how it can assist with bringing the birth forward, albeit it seems like a myth!" There was another pause, and then she said, "But I miss it, I miss you and I want you, and that's it really, and we've already tried the curry." She smiled at him with intent.

Before he could say no, she had covered his mouth with hers and was kissing his masculine lips deliberately teasing him with her soft feminine lips and tongue.

"Nooo, we can't!" he mumbled into her mouth, "the baby."

"The baby will be fine. We'll be careful, and I need you, now! It's been too long!"

She held her hands over his and brought them up to her swollen breasts and let him hold her. She liked his hands, strong and kind, tender and loving and aware of what she liked and wanted. He had not seen her this way for a long time, and he tended not to get in her way when she wanted something.

"It's only been a month, Maria. It can wait, can't it?" Marcus said with worry in his voice.

She faked a sad face and asked, "Do you not want me anymore?" as she moved his hands lower down and between her legs.

Marcus took a deep breath as he allowed his hands to stroke the inside of her thighs, his firm touch even more enticing for Maria.

"I've been reading about it, and I say we can and we should. I'll show you how." A huge smile spread over her face. "Lie back with me, spoon me, and let me lead you." She pushed him gently back on the bed and leaned into him. The fit was perfect.

She could feel his need, although his need to do what was right for Maria and the baby was suppressing his desires.

She spooned into him even closer and pulled his hands around her and again helped him to where she wanted them.

She pushed down on his fingers, her skirt lifted up exposing her toned legs. Marcus felt her need as his hands gently slid over her silky pants, the moisture escaping through the material and inviting his touch.

He breathed in a heavy sigh. Her wetness had turned him on so much that he now wanted her any way they could have one another. Maria turned her head to allow their mouths to meet. She reached for his chin and pulled him into a beautiful heady kiss, and Marcus had no trouble responding. He gave a light groan as his tongue met hers and their kiss lingered and grew in strength.

His hands moved in a skilled caress as he gently slipped them beneath her pants and stroked gently over her, causing Maria to coil up a little as the sensation was so strong it tingled, halting her breath for a moment.

She kissed him more intensely as she wriggled at his touch. It was clear she wanted more, needed more, and he did as she wanted and gave her more, his fingers slipping inside her. She felt his body tense up in response to what he could feel. She was soaking wet, and it was clear her need to be loved was stronger than ever, almost primal. His fingers pushing gently over her and into her, and Maria pushed herself onto him, to allow more depth, as she knew he was holding back. Marcus loved what he felt and how it was making his wife feel. She moved with his fingers, and he could feel the grip of her climax, and the change in her body, the acceptance of him inside her. She reached back to him. He was ready for her but too caring to enter her, but she had something different in mind as she pulled at his buttons and pulled down the front of his pants, showing him where she wanted him and he gently followed her lead, entering her. There were moans of delight, pleasure to his ears as she let him push into her, firm and gentle. She allowed him inside her enough for what she needed, for her pleasure, and that was more than enough for Marcus. His thrusts were now controlled and shallow, but needy, their mutual dance leading them to a climax neither had experienced before, the desire heightened by the situation and restriction. Marcus liked Maria taking the lead as neither of them would ever risk harming the baby.

Marcus was thrilled at his pre-work lovemaking, leaning back enjoying the feelings and arousal he had missed for what seemed like an age, but Maria wasn't finished yet. She stealthily curled herself around and took him into her mouth, his erection not fully gone, and soon to stand once again. He looked into her beautiful eyes, her love for him clear, and his pleasure at what she wanted and was doing was obvious. This time there was vigour in her actions, allowing Marcus to let go more without fear of harming another. She knew what he liked, and how he liked it, and she never lost contact with his eyes until he came, taking all of him into her mouth. He knew he was a lucky man in every way possible, and he certainly wasn't a selfish one. As soon as he had orgasmed, he gently lay her down on her back, stopping to admire every inch of her, her body transformed by the baby, and he loved what he saw even more. He gently opened her legs, excited at what he could see. He could feel Maria breath in hard at the excitement of his touch, and how exposed she felt, completely vulnerable to his lust-filled desire. The anticipation was intense until she felt a smooth stroke of his tongue, from her bottom to her clitoris, ignite every tiny corner of her body. The touch was sublime, Marcus a master with his mouth and hands. He made love to her with his tongue and fingers, knowing what he was doing to her, when to be firm, when to be gentle and when she was at the point of no return and knowing not to stop until she practically pulled his head off. Her body loved every little thing he did to her, her fingers threaded through his hair as she pulled his face into her needy pussy. He pushed his fingers into her rhythmically and his tongue continued with its adept skills until every curl of her gripping climax was finished.

Once she was finished, she pulled him up to her and kissed him deeply – lusty, happy, fulfilled kisses – and she liked the taste of her love in his mouth, on his face. She found it a turn-on, and so did Marcus, the scent of love a natural aphrodisiac.

Both of them smiled and kept smiling. He moved up closer beside her and held her close to him. No words were needed as they kissed one another gently.

After a while Maria had to get up, and Marcus put on his sad dog face. She rubbed his chin and whispered, "Got to go. I need a pee!" She giggled as she ran through to the bathroom.

He watched her wiggle through to the loo, her soft curves, neat bottom, her beautiful hair, her baby bump. He loved every little thing about her. To him she was perfection.

He leaned up on his elbow once she was out of sight and shouted through to the bathroom, "How am I supposed to go to work after that, Maria? I'm a broken man. I want to stay with you all day!"

"You go to work for a rest, try being a housewife and working!" she teased, knowing fine well that, when he was at home, he certainly did his fair share, but sometimes his work seemed to take him away for days on end.

He sighed a happy sigh. His life at the moment could not be any better. A lovely family, nothing too harrowing at work, a baby girl on the way and he had just been loved into submission, a pleasure he had thought was out of reach for at least another month or two.

He walked through to the bathroom where Maria was still sitting on the loo.

"Are you alright?"

"Yes, I'm fine. Baby has just been kicking a fair bit. Your love has certainly been noticed."

Marcus smiled, knelt down beside her and gently put his hand on her tummy, as the biggest kick yet responded to his touch, the shape of her foot visible. His face lit up followed by a look of pure love for his wife and unborn child.

"That's why I don't like going to work. It takes me away from you and the children, well nearly plural. I miss you so much!"

"We all miss you too, but what you do is so important, and we need this house for the beautiful family we've made, and that means we need money!"

"I know, but it's hard sometimes, especially today. After that, I just want to be with you and not be apart." He smiled and looked up at her.

Maria cupped his face in her hands and kissed him full on the lips. "Love you. Now get that sweaty body in the shower and let me watch you!"

Marcus smiled and did as she asked, and she took in an eyeful of his firm buttocks, the defined indentations at the sides, his triangular, well-defined back, and his well-groomed hair and, when he stepped over the edge of the bath, she got another look as what she had just had.

He turned and caught her looking at him, mirth in her eyes, childish at the intimate sight she had just seen.

He too taking a look at her naked body as she sat there watching.

The shower powered loudly as the cascading flow of hot water spread over Marcus's taught frame, and Maria continued to watch as he washed every bit of himself, feeling another twinge of desire within, or so she thought.

Once clean, he pulled on well-fitted white briefs, highlighting his tan. His shirt fitted neatly to his chest, pastille pink with a bright and coordinated tie, and a tailored navy suit with smart light brown shoes.

Hair tidy, facial hair trimmed and a nice scent, and he was

ready to step into Taylor's shoes for a while, unaware that she would be back and sitting at Findlay's desk.

The office certainly wasn't the same without Taylor and Kay and, now Fran was back, it would have been back to the good old days, with a little less touching, he hoped, smiling to himself at his thoughts. He willed the other two back soon.

More kisses and a short embrace before he had to leave for his back shift. Marcus was always early for work. He was a little sad he always left home before Wee Davy got home from school, seeing him would make the best day ever. He smiled as he thought about his beautiful family.

He turned the key in the ignition of his sporty black VW Golf GTi and enjoyed the sound of the engine, still a young man at heart. He moved off slowly in the residential area and let her go a little bit on the bigger roads, getting to work in good time.

He pulled into the car park at Fettes at the same time as Taylor and was a bit taken aback at seeing her, one, because she was rarely early and two, he thought her suspension would have lasted longer.

They parked close to one another, as there were no spaces side by side, and when they got out, she just looked at him, with a knowing smile.

"Is it that obvious?" he said with a coy but happy look which spread to a Cheshire Cat grin all over his face.

He walked towards her, opened his arms wide and hugged her tightly, and she reciprocated. Theirs was a true friendship, a bonded trust.

"I've missed you. The team have missed, you, although I didn't know you were coming back today. I don't mind not acting up. The seat is yours!" he said humbly without resentment.

She didn't understand what he was talking about at first.

"Aww, I get it, you're me for a bit, Acting Sergeant. Well

done you, on the promotion." She smiled, holding something back.

Marcus thought she was taking the piss out of him, and that he would be back to DC again, which wasn't an issue.

"Ah, you've not heard then? You're keeping my job!"

Marcus's face sank immediately, thinking the worst.

However, a huge beaming smile came over Taylor's face. She paused and then blurted out the news. "I'm taking Findlay's slot, and you can have your time in mine, a great trade, I should say!"

Marcus stood there his mouth agape. "And Findlay?"

"There's a full criminal enquiry now taking place, as the allegations being made need investigated, and that all takes time!" She had a broad smile still fixed on her face.

"Sorry to ask, but what happened to you? Is everything sorted with your side of it?"

"C'mon, Marcus, get with the times, WRITTEN WARNING, and a wee mini promotion after my slap on the wrist. They believe there must have been provocation and some back story to the incident. It was out of character for me, apparently!" She said this with her eyebrows raised and a guilty smirk on her face.

Marcus laughed from his belly. "Out of character, do they not know you?" he said with humour in his voice, knowing fine well she had a temper, but still knowing it was always well placed and necessary wherever it showed.

"C'mon, ya cheeky beggar, get your arse into work before the new boss calls you in for being late!"

They both practically skipped into the office, delighted to be together again and to be able to lead the team with some professionalism at last, neither of them with stains on their clothes, and their shirts tucked in properly.

They opened the doors to the open plan office where the majority of the dayshift were still at work. A few of their back-shift team were also in and an audible comedic "wwh-hheeyyyy" greeted Taylor and Marcus, their colleagues glad that the dark lord had left the building forever, or so they hoped anyway.

Chapter 20

Murder or Not?

The children's unit in the Drylaw backed onto an old railway, leading to all ends of Edinburgh city. It had been made into a cycle path, safe from traffic, but also used by those who wanted to stay away from the main route to avoid detection. It was a thoroughfare for many people commuting for work or for leisure during the day, but it had a sinister, darker side once the sun went down. Then you needed to have your wits about you and be able to fight or run fast.

The route between Drylaw and Leith had long been used as a getaway. Assaults, robberies and thefts had become common place by groups of feral youths and those out to make a name for themselves. It also led to the golden arches of a McDonald's, the feeder of many less fortunate children on a daily basis, cheap filling meals with no sign of fruit or veg being selected by choice.

This day was like no other. Tensions between rival, serious organised criminal gangs, was hitting a new peak, the angst higher than normal. The level of violence had escalated to stabbings, machete attacks, hammer assaults, using cars to run over people and shootings. Although, unbelievably, until recently nobody had been murdered, but many seriously injured. The intention may have been to kill, but there seemed to be an unnatural ability of these individuals to survive from what many others would certainly have died from.

Kerri left the care home just before her tea, to the annoyance of the staff there. Inga called out to ask where she was going, to be met with an arrogant reply. "The food here's shit! Do you want me to bring you something back?" Sarcasm and disrespect oozed from every pore on Kerri's body.

Inga was beginning to lose her patience with this girl. Her attitude stank for someone so close to being the age to leave, and she was skating on thin ice. She was always on self-destruct. Inga had tried everything she could to get her on board and accept help and support, but to no avail.

"She may as well have said fuck you," Inga thought to herself. "That one will be the death of me," Inga groaned inwardly.

Kerri walked slowly towards the cycle path. There was a group of loitering teenagers there offering up the usual smart-mouthed welcoming comments and a jibe or two, trying to get a rise out of everyone that passed. But the look the loudest one got from Kerri was enough to make him swallow hard and shudder inside, her eyes dark and lifeless, shark-like in their appearance with no human emotion to show. She bared her teeth at him like a feral animal, before walking away, just able to stop herself going straight into attack. The others had not quite copped sight of the full hostile possessed look that the now not quite so gallous boy had, and they foolishly continued to goad her, his warning to them a little too late. She moved swiftly up to one of the boys and grabbed his hair full force, pulling him off of his bike with unnatural strength and shrieking maniacally in his face, before biting him hard on his head, drawing blood and cutting flesh. He yelled in pain and went to grab at her face, only for her to bite him again, this time his fingers were clamped brutally between her teeth. His mate's squeals were desperate for a wee hard guy as his bones loudly crunched. His mates watched in silence. Normally they would offer up more resistance and jump into the fight, but there was something about this strange girl that made them take off at speed rather than take the incident any further. Grassing to the Polis was not in their DNA, but this was the first time they fleetingly considered it.

Kerri carried on her way, passing the odd brave cyclist racing by, trying to avoid any unwanted attention themselves or the invisible garrotte line that was sometimes pulled tight across the track to unseat the unsuspecting riders so they could be robbed when they lay fallen and helpless. None of the evening commuters paid Kerri any attention, despite her outward appearance being that of a vulnerable young girl. No one felt compelled to check on her, in case she was a plant for a set-up.

She carried on up the lane, up onto Telford Road, and to the traffic lights assisting with crossing the road to the local McDonald's where more youths and numerous Just Eat delivery men stood outside waiting for orders.

One of the men in the queue was clearly ogling her, her neat frame, blonde hair and pert breasts, looking younger than legal, the choice of many a pervert. For most, too young to consider but not for the one with an unhealthy interest.

She hated this kind of attention. It made her feel sick to the stomach, so she walked up to him and punched him discreetly in the balls with enough force to cause him to double up and groan out loud, the others waiting unaware of how the man had come to double over. Kerri walked casually by and right into the store and ordered her food, nonplussed at what was happening outside, the male unwilling to explain what had happened and why, clearly not wanting any unwanted attention from the police if she reported it, his past and ill intentions a habit he was already known for.

She ordered a Big Mac meal and six chicken nuggets, diet Coke and ketchup, to take out. She did not want to sit in and have any more unwanted admirers.

The male on the receiving end of Kerri's punch was now

a little more upright as she strode back out. He kept his eyes down and did not try to get hold of her, clearly avoiding eye contact. It would look bad on him if he retaliated due to her size. He knew he was in the wrong, and now his gaze had allowed her to see his desire for her, his perversion visible in his eyes.

She, on the other hand, stopped, and sneered at him. "Look at my tits like that again, and the next time I'll gouge out your eyes, shove them down your throat and make you swallow them, you fucking creepy paedo pervert!" Her words rasped out of her mouth, causing the crowd to stare at them, their realisation of what may have happened coming to light, some clearly in support of her by the way they looked at the man still wincing from the physical pain and words cascading out of her mouth.

Kerri walked back in the direction of the cycle path, with the intention of eating her food on the swings near to the care home, deliberately staying out longer to avoid being there as long as possible. She liked being alone more and more, and it was safer for other people.

As she walked back towards the home on the path, both sides shielded by bushes and trees offering a place to hide, she became aware of how dark it had become. It felt a little creepy, even for her. She stopped as she heard sounds of male voices, shouting and screaming, the revving of engines. Motorbikes, she thought, probably stolen. The screams from a male sounded desperate, which drew her attention, and caused an urge to move closer to allow her to see what was going on and to watch, hopefully unseen. She liked watching people suffer. It made her feel alive, dominant and weirdly calm. She was evil inside, but not stupid, and she stopped short enough not to be noticed. The men were clearly not messing about, and the guy on the floor already looked badly injured, his head split wide open, with blood in his eyes, and his hand raised up to protect himself from blow after blow from a hammer. The sound was sickening as it struck bone, and Kerri smiled. The male was then struck heavily on the head and seemed to flop forward and offer up no further resistance or defence. His aggressors, done with their brutal assault, mounted their cross bikes, thinking their task was over, thinking he was dead, one of them deliberately riding over their victim's legs, ripping open his existing wounds. He lay still. Kerri watched and thought of the agony that would have caused if he had been alive, but then she noticed a slight movement. The riders missed it, believing they had killed him outright with the final hammer blow that caved in his skull, with brain matter visible.

Kerri walked over to where the assault had taken place and turned her phone torch on to look at the man on the ground. His head was a mess; there were visible shards of bone, and a lot of blood, thick globs matting his hair. The gashes in his skin on his arms and legs were deep and right down to the bone. The tyres had also caused hideous wounds and damage to his lower legs, where the skin already slashed had slid away from the bone, exposing it as the wheels spun around taking the flesh with them.

Kerri found a tree branch to sit on and eat her food, keeping her torch on to look at the man, still wondering if she had actually seen him move, and whether he was still alive. She hoped nobody would interrupt her meal.

As she bit into her burger, she heard a moan. The man's hand moved and he tried to raise his head, aware of the light in front of him, hoping there was a chance of some help.

The slurred words came, "Help me, please. Help me!" his breaths shallow and desperate.

Kerri took another bite of her burger, her eyes wide, enjoying the suffering before her, barely blinking, not wanting to miss the show. Her entrenchment in revenge and vile acts gave her a release that was strong and overpowering and addictive. Being cruel had become like a drug, driving her to do more bad things to fulfil this craving. She liked hurting people. It made her feel powerful. The feeling of invincibility like a protective shield, hidden beneath before the abuse and betrayal she had experienced.

"Why should I?" she said through a mouthful of food. "I bet you're a drug-dealing wanker, and you'll have done the same thing to others yourself, so why the fuck should I help a wee lowlife schemy cunt like you?" Kerri hissed the words callously towards him.

Even in his state of injury, with his life fading, he took in the harsh words, said in such a sadistic way by a female voice. He was cold and shivering with the severe blood loss, and was aware of the danger she now posed.

Kerri got to her feet and crouching near to him asked, "Where does it hurt the most?" She really only wanted a closer look, with no care for him at all.

"Pleeasse, help me. I need help. I'm dying here, you fucking deranged bitch!" His true colours now coming through, as his normal actions would be to smash her face in for being sarcastic. He had never taken shit like that from any fucking lassie, but he was at her mercy.

"OOO, manners, you. Abusive little arsehole, what a lovely fucking chap! Unfortunately, I have no mercy," she said with cruel honesty. "I'm going to watch you die, you feral little rat, then finish my tea and get home. I'm late, so you'll have to hurry it up a bit, you rude fucking prick!"

She stepped forward onto his fingers, scrunching them on the concrete, and he gave a desperate but weak yelp as she dragged her foot back, degloving the last two digits on his hand. The muffled screams were his last, as the strain of his voice forced a rush of blood to his head, his injuries now oozing more blood, his last to offer. His breathing quickened and started to rasp, and then his eyes dimmed as the tension left his frame when his heart finally gave out.

Kerri straightened her head up, then tilted it into an abnormal position, a pose she adopted as she watched others suffer in agony, her mouth agape as she enjoyed the life leave another, the thrill of death engulfing her being. A serenity flowed over her before she mouthed the words, "About time!" She then nonchalantly picked out some chips and stuffed them in her face, dropping a few from her mouth, regretting standing on his fingers, although she had enjoyed the outcome of her actions, knowing he would have died anyway.

Chapter 21

The Crime Scene from Hell

Taylor sat in her new office. The glass partition was a bonus; she hated being cooped up away from the others, missing being part of everything, but at least she could still see everyone and what was going on, but never in an intrusive way like Findlay, just curious and showing a healthy interest in what the team was doing.

Kay was back as well, feeling a lot better, but she was in the other smaller office today, collating some of the files in relation to the two drownings. They were getting ready for the Holmes team to get to work with the evidence and action creation, and there was a squad set up to identify similarities to the cases and whether there was any key evidence to link a possible true locus for the deaths so that crime scene investigations could be carried out.

It was well after six, and Kay was heading home as she did not follow the same shift pattern as Taylor. Her hours were core hours with a three-hour flexibility when required at either end of the shift. Kay came through in her usual manner, her frame statuesque, amazing considering the trauma and injury she had suffered not that long ago at the hands of the rapist and murderer Brennan. Her mental health was back on track, and she was back to the proud, confident and pleasant individual she had always been before, despite the incident with

Findlay which had rocked her and caused her to relive the fear and anguish she had suffered before, her body choosing to shut down that day rather than face Findlay's unhealthy desires and further trauma.

She looked up at Taylor and smiled, gave a jokey salute and squeeze of Marcus's shoulders, before she went to put on her coat. Taylor watched as she pulled it over her arms, her fitted blouse pulling tight on her body, a sight Taylor knew she would never tire of. A twist of desire twinged gently in her stomach. Kay made her way over to the office to say goodbye to Taylor and they offered a small kiss to one another, enough to show their love for each other, causing Taylor's cheeks to blush. Then Kay turned to leave, aware that Fran was back in the office. She wasn't too perturbed by the return of Taylor's ex-lover now that she had a new partner, Lana, and didn't seem to be interested in Taylor any longer. Kay said her good-byes to her colleagues. Then she was gone with her trademark swish of her long auburn hair.

Taylor watched until she left the office, her heart giving a flutter of love for Kay, a smile for Marcus, who was telling a story with full animated actions. Fran watched Marcus as he spoke, but quickly and deliberately glanced at Taylor. Fran was in the periphery of Taylor's vision, but she too dropped her eyes to look back at Fran. She thought she could feel her looking at her and she was right. Her eyes were staring right at Taylor, her stare intense and probing, almost searching her soul. Fran just kept looking right at Taylor, now that Kay was gone from the office, it was now safe, and she allowed herself a look without harming another, a lesson she was trying to learn. Taylor met her eyes, she too more respectful and loyal than before, but her eyes questioned Fran's gaze. Why was she looking at her like that, a look that seemed to be wanting more?

Taylor liked Fran a lot. Fran was lovely inside and out, but she believed Fran was over her and happy, which made things easier for Taylor. Fran was no longer available and had started a new chapter in her life so their relationship was now purely friends, wasn't it?

The uncomfortable moment was broken as a call came through to Marcus from the sergeant at Drylaw station. Gary Watson contacted them to say there had been a murder in their area, the culprits unknown. It had been called in by a cyclist on the old railway cycle path near to the park beside the young persons' unit.

Marcus pondered the best route to get them to the locus, which wasn't easily accessed by vehicles. He decided going past the YOU, which was the quickest and easiest way for them to get close to the crime scene by car.

He almost forgot he was the one responsible for organising everything now.

"Gary, are CID off at the scene yet? Do you know whether they brought the tent down from Gayfield to conceal the body from unwanted viewers?" Marcus enquired.

"They're there already, they're on scene and they've widened the initial cordon, no witnesses yet, and the body is in a proper mess apparently." Gary's colleague Kerr Thomas, ex CID prior to promotion, was on the ball and already on top of things.

"Okay, thanks for the heads-up. We'll get some evidence kit and head down. Are you calling SOCO, or has that already been requested? We'll need to get hold of the response inspector Caz Fletcher to get more resources, as that lane leading to the scene will become pretty busy with the local worthies when they hear what's happened, and they tend not to do as they're asked, so numbers of cordon officers will be needed to double up. We can start door to door initially, before we can set up a coordinator and a team for tomorrow to do it more systematically. We need to know who's seen what or what the word on the street is. Oh, and we'll need a set to go off to the

YPU. Some of the residents might have been around and may have seen or heard something, if they'll talk!"

Marcus put the phone down, nodded to Fran and Chris. "There's been a MURDERRRRR," he said in the voice of the TV cop show Taggart. Fran and Chris smiled at his shit impression, and the fact he was clearly excited as he walked through to the office to let Taylor know what was happening down at Drylaw.

By the time they arrived in two cars, Marcus and Taylor, Fran and Chris, the place was awash with youths, on electric scooters, bicycles and motocross bikes, and lots of hangers on. They were out in numbers, not just kids, adults too, and there was a lot of angst and hostility towards the police; many living in that area of the city did not like the police and what they stood for. Police were seen as an occupational hazard, regularly locking up their children, siblings, friends, husbands and family members. There was a deep-rooted hatred bred into them from birth, training them for a life of crime and mistrust of the authorities.

Taylor muttered, "For fuck's sake, it's like a bloody circus down here already. We need to get rid of these people, now, or they'll destroy all the fucking evidence!" The crowd was out with the cordon, but she recalled the time a man had been stabbed when she was in uniform. A gang had ridden motorbikes right through the cordon tape and the crime scene became a lawless mess.

Taylor let Marcus go over to the CID and speak with the crime scene manager Sandy Watt and offer assistance and guidance as to their needs. Taylor went to the uniform sergeant Pete Wilson at the crime scene cordon. He was doing his best with the officers he had to keep a sterile area and keep the groups of youths from marauding through it. She called up to the area control centre to offer a little clout to redirect more resources.

As she introduced herself to Gary Watson, who knew the area and the troubles they were likely to face, a woman was striding over towards where they stood, her face twisted with rage and tears flowing down her cheeks.

"Get the fuck oot o ma way. That's ma fuckin laddie lying over there, and none of yoose cunts are gonnae stop meh!" she rasped and spat as she growled at the cop on the cordon.

Taylor and Gary looked over from where they stood 20 metres away, disturbed by this raging female, wondering why she was so angry and upset.

The young officer on the cordon, Lizzie Johnstone, was taken aback by her approach, unaware of the reason for it. She wasn't a naïve officer and pre-empted an attack, raising her arm, motioning for her to stay back, and was punched square in the face and knocked to the floor. Taylor and Gary moved quickly to try and intercept the crazed woman. Taylor ran fast towards the fracas and managed to get hold of the female's arm, ducking just in time to avoid the next haymaker heading straight towards her face. She adeptly swept the woman's heavy legs from beneath her, still holding onto her arm to prevent her smacking her face off the pavement. She put her in a tight gooseneck hold. The woman squealed with the pressure as pain compliance was applied.

"What the fuck are you daen, ya fucking snotty-arsed boot? Get yer fuckin big lezzie hands oaf of me, ya cunt. Who the fuck dae ye think ye are, ya daft cow? Let me go or I'll fuckin have ye murdered, ya piggy black bastard!" The words flowed like well-rehearsed poetry from her foul mouth, clearly the usual kind and welcoming tact reserved for police officers.

Taylor tightened her grip on the woman's wrist, and Gary took hold of her other arm with an equally firm grip, preventing any further assault.

"Get your fucking scummy hands off of me or I'll tear your fucking face right off of ye, ya bitch!"

Taylor squeezed tighter and the female winced and dropped to her knees in pain in an attempt to try and free herself from Taylor's vice-like hold, but Taylor held on with all her might.

"Calm down and I'll let you go. Who are you? We can help you, if you let us!" Taylor remained composed. She was very capable, Gary too. He smiled at her calm but firm words.

"What are you fuckin smirkin at, ya daft wee prick?" The woman tried to kick out towards Gary's balls and struggled again with more effort, almost freeing her hand.

It was clear she wasn't going to cooperate, but they needed to know who she was and why she was so desperate to get into the cordon. They had not heard what she had said to the cop before she had decked her to get past.

Luckily, PC Lizzie Johnstone was back up on her feet. She came over to them, her eye already closing and an open cut bleeding heavily from where a large gold sovereign ring had connected with her face, but she was a hardy lass and not known to stay down for long.

The woman, now kneeling on the ground, looked up at the officer, and laughed. "How's yer face, hen? Ooo, that looks nasty!" Her smile was vile. She was proud of her efforts, her teeth stained with a few missing.

The officer leaned in to speak with Taylor. "Boss, before she hit me, she said that was her son over there."

"Did she say her name?" Taylor enquired.

"One of the cops says she's Sean Malcolm's mum, you know the one with all those kids? He's the oldest!" the officer stated while the pain in her face grew.

"Ah, I never realised who he was!" Gary exclaimed, realisation of how big a player had just been taken out and the repercussions to follow. He also thought to himself, "No wonder I didn't know who the stiff was, with his face so badly beaten."

Once Taylor was aware who the victim was, she tried to balance sympathy with understanding for the woman who had already assaulted an officer and was now a continuous breach. She needed her to talk, so false leniency could be the way forward.

Other officers, Lawrence Anthony and Ethan Hicks came over and Taylor tried one more time to get the woman to calm down, but her efforts were wasted. The cuffs were put on with another fierce struggle and she was arrested and removed from the scene. A van was driven over the grass to assist with taking her away, but this did not go down well with the locals. They began to throw things at the police, anything they could get their hands on to try and prevent her arrest. The loyalty of the locals to the dead man in open display. They had to show face or they would become the next victims of rage when the brothers arrived.

More officers came forward, Curt Collins, Soph Elder, Holly Mather, Evan Sinclair, Steve Deans, Sara Hart, Gogs Mac, Paul Guthrie and wee Scotty Douglas and even the Chief Inspector who had just arrived from the station close by, Will Neils, young in service, but rising quickly through the ranks, a kind and fair man, who was willing to get stuck in with the troops. They all created a physical cordon, drawing their batons to assist with the dispersal of the group, as more locals were arrested. Public order officers had also arrived and were authorised to wear code one dress, which meant riot kit and helmets due to the escalation in the level of violence being used against the officers.

Taylor was walking over to Marcus when a wee scrote launched a beer bottle towards her. It bounced off of her forehead as a loud cheer went up from the jeering crowd.

Taylor winced and held her head, blood seeping between her fingers. "Who the fuck was that? I'll fucking have that wee motherfucker!" she said, looking up, right at the wee arsehole that had thrown the bottle, now struggling to keep her cool. She wasn't wearing any protective equipment, as she had thought she would be walking the crime scene as an inspector. However, she did have on sensible flat boots, so was on equal pegging when it came to a foot chase.

Marcus had seen what happened to Taylor. She had been cut above the eye and it looked a sore one. He knew she quite liked her face, but he also saw that her poise was different and her facial expression was now that of the hunter rather than that of the hunted. She was going to throw caution to the wind and give chase.

Marcus watched her tear off in the direction of a breakaway group of teens, and she was moving at some pace, clearly forgetting she was now an inspector and shouldn't really be rampaging after wee neds.

Marcus followed and gave chase, knowing they would gather around her like feral dogs and attack.

The lads ran as fast as they could, but she was hot on their heels. Her target looked over his shoulder at her, stumbled and lost his footing. He went crashing to the ground, his face scratching into the dirt. He was scrambling to get back up when he felt the force of Taylor's shoulder as she launched herself off of her feet and slammed him back to the ground with a rib-crunching tackle, deliberately landing on him with her full weight. There was no finesse in the struggle that ensued. The lad was about 17, wiry and strong, and he was desperate to break free. Taylor wrapped her legs around him and had hold of one of his arms, but the lad was still pushing to get up and hitting her where he could reach, as she put her mouth to his ear. "You're under arrest for assault. You're not obliged to say anything, but anything you do say will be noted and may be used in evidence, do you understand, you fucking little prick?"

"You cannae arrest me, ya daft cow, nae corroboration, ya fuckin stupid radge, muppet bitch!" he sneered, even though he was beaten and couldn't break free from her grip.

"She can and she has," came a male voice, a little breathless after racing to keep up with them. Marcus came up beside them with several other officers in tow, Fran, Chris and a couple of response cops, all eager to assist, as the guy that Taylor was unceremoniously rolling on the ground with was another well-known worthy with a criminal record longer than the Forth Road Bridge.

Marcus took hold of the lad and unceremoniously heaved him up to his feet, and he was cuffed by the response officers. Taylor was now in a sitting position, her hair a total mess, tousled and over her face. Her cut eye looked atrocious as the blood was drying up and smeared over her face along with the dirt she had been rolling in. Her suit was ripped at the knees and some of her shirt buttons had popped off.

"Well help me up then!" she moaned to Marcus and her officers. Although she had been assaulted, she was clearly alright, despite looking a complete shambles, and would be the talk of the office for months to come, as Taylor was usually immaculate in her appearance, including her face.

Fran asked an officer with a body-worn camera to swing around and record as Marcus leaned down to help their boss up from the ground, making sure there was photographic evidence of the moment, for plenty of office jokes for the foreseeable future.

Taylor was no slouch, and certainly not stupid, and noticed what Fran was up to and she smiled. "Don't you fucking dare, young lady. Get that deleted," she said to the officer.

Fran mouthed to the officer at the same time, "Don't you dare. We'll buy you cakes forever!"

"Fuck's sake, Marcus, I'll need to go back to the office and get changed. I'm a total fucking mess!"

"The hospital more like! Your head's burst open, ma'am. You'll need it glued. It's a decent one and such a beautiful face too!" he said, smirking at her, knowing she was a little vain, and deliberately calling her ma'am too, which he knew she would hate.

"Fuck you too!" she retorted. "It's not funny. That wee tosser would have gotten away with it if I hadn't chased the little bastard down, and he wasn't getting away with ruining this face." She smiled back, displaying her face in a comedic manner, motioning her hands to highlight her face and batting her eyelashes humorously.

Taylor brushed herself down. "Marcus, get Fran and Chris to go to the unit and speak with the staff and residents there, and see if we can get some semblance of control here. I'll pop to the minor injuries unit at the Western General hospital, it's open for another 20 minutes. They'll glue my eye and clean it, and I'll get changed and sort things out from the office for the rest of the shift!"

Marcus agreed. "Yeah, you've done enough tonight, and just like being back on the street, eh?" He smiled at her, dug her gently in the ribs, said his goodbyes and turned back to the cordon. The rest of the group of lads had run from them had rejoined the throng of people still gathered at the blue and white cordon tape and continued the relentless tirade of abuse towards the officers.

Chapter 22

The Meeting

Kerri sat close to the window watching the mayhem unfold. She was smiling from ear to ear, until she looked down at her shoe. There was blood up the side of it and, on checking, there was some on the sole. And, to her horror, there was a smear on the carpet too, small, but it was there.

"Holy fuck!" She got a cloth from her sink, and soap, and got scrubbing. Within a few moments it was gone, and her trainers scrubbed too. There were no visible signs of blood anymore.

Her heart was pounding as she watched three plain-clothed feds coming towards the unit, crossing over the grass of the park, two tall men and a smaller petite woman.

She popped her head out of the room and was glad to see that the scabby dark carpet was not displaying any stains, although it must have been secreting DNA in her shoes and many other stains from its past history.

She went back to her room and sat waiting. It was only a matter of time before they would come to her room, as Inga knew she had been out.

She heard the staff downstairs speaking with the officers that had just entered the unit, their voices low and calm, asking how many residents lived there, what ages, were they able to speak to any of them, because they appreciated that it was late and the last question: "Are you aware if any of the residents have been out this evening, either by permission or absconding?"

Inga sighed. "What's happened? What have they done?"

"Oh, they haven't done anything. We just want to see if any of the residents were out and about and might have seen what happened earlier on the cycle track!" Chris explained apologetically, not wanting them to think there was any blame on the unit residents, not knowing how wrong he actually was.

Inga enquired, "Why, what's happened? I've not heard anything. I've been cooped up in here all evening, busy night, a few disruptions and tantrums tonight. I think there were two or three of the residents that went out after 5pm, but only Kerri's back. She's in room 10 up the stair here if you want me to take you to speak with her."

Kerri's stomach twisted tightly, an uncomfortable feeling, one she was not used to. For once she was now the hunted, not the hunter. She may have been evil, but she was still young and naïve. She felt sick but also knew they had no idea she had seen anything or been anywhere near the man in question. She could quite easily have walked home without any sight or involvement with the ongoing incident. She thought back to when she heard the commotion and how slowly she had walked prior to seeing the violent act, and knew that the timings would coincide with the CCTV at McDonald's, so she could quite easily be telling the truth, and that's how she would say it happened. She just had to play it cool and act like a daft wee lassie.

Chris and Fran headed up to her room, as Marcus stayed and took details of the other residents and staff on duty.

They gave a light knock on the door and waited for an answer.

"What!" She put on her usual aggressive and petulant tone, her outward nonchalant and abrasive attitude oozing from her.

"Can we come in? It's the police," Chris said in his gentle voice.

"Why, what do you want? Am in ma bed, fucking nosey tossers," she muttered under her breath.

"This won't take long. Just a wee word and a couple of questions, if that's alright? Please," Chris added.

"Fer fuck sake, okay then, but yoose better be quick, am tired!" Kerri moaned, but she knew she had to at least entertain them, or they would never stop coming around, and she didn't want that.

The door opened a tiny bit, and both Chris and Fran were taken aback at the size of her, not very tall, slim and very petite, with blond hair, aware of their unconscious bias from the mental pictures they had already created in their heads of what they thought this girl was going to look like from the way she had spoken to them blindly through a door, neither of them imagining this innocent-looking little thing.

They looked at one another, knowing they had thought the same and made a mental note not to judge a book by its cover, but Kerri, on the other hand, was hoping they would, by taking in the outward persona of a slightly pathetic-looking weakling, which was the opposite of what she was inside.

"You can close your mouth. What were you expecting, Godzilla?" Kerri could practically read their minds.

Chris and Fran both looked sheepish, as this young girl had the measure of them already and now had the upper hand. They were also a little embarrassed for being caught out as being judgemental.

Within the room there was a single bed beneath the window, looking out onto the field that led to the cycle path, a cupboard, a desk and chair and a smaller comfier chair in the corner with a TV on the desk, a wee Bluetooth speaker and not much else.

Fran was aware that the girl was eyeing them up and down,

absorbing every detail of each of them, and she felt a little unnerved by this. A slight shiver crawled slowly down her back as Kerri's eyes came up and stared right at her, both not dropping their gaze, a standoff, before even sitting down.

"Can we sit down, rather than stand at the doorway, if that's okay with you?" Chris asked politely.

"Aye, fill yer boots. I'll sit on the bed." Kerri finally dropped her gaze and sat waiting for the questions to come, and they did.

Chris explained why they were there, and that there had been a serious incident close to the unit and someone had died as a result.

"Were you out at all tonight, Kerri?" asked Chris, already knowing the answer, a wee tester of how truthful she was going to be, and if not, why not?

"Yep, I was out for a bit, why?" she answered, deliberately not giving more than was asked.

"What was the purpose of going out tonight, are you able to tell us that?" This time Fran asked, knowing exactly how this was going to go, as she had met many youngsters like this, smart and obstructive. Aware of this, she would try and circumvent it by asking multiple questions to get the information they needed quicker, and try her best to get Kerri to cooperate a little more quickly than she was clearly planning, as there were numerous residents to speak to.

"Aye, I was out getting ma tea at Miccy D's. The food here's shite! I was a wee bit longer because some pervy wanker was ogling ma tits, so I hit him in the balls!" Kerri also knew how to play the game and gave more information than she needed so that the cops would have to check that out too, and it would be verified, which would make her explanations appear more truthful.

Chris smiled. "Really! That couldn't have been nice for you, a little scary, no?" His voice was kind and enquiring and filled with genuine sympathy as he hated the way some men openly mistreated women and girls in an intrusively sexual manner.

"I wasn't scared. Folk like that rip ma knittin. They think they can undress you with their eyes, and they have the right to act that way, and given half a chance they'd do worse, much worse. They're all the bloody same, fuckin creepy bastards, but I showed him. I bet he hasn't reported it!" Kerri answered with defiance and confidence, the opposite of how she looked and must have looked to the male earlier, giving him a wee shock for his lecherous and unacceptable behaviour.

"Which way did you go, and come back? Did you use the cycle track, and did you see anybody or anything when you were out getting your food?" Fran asked, now more sympathetic, because she too, along with countless women and girls, was still having to put up with inappropriate sexualised shit on a daily basis, due to false entitlement to do so.

"Naw, I didn't see anything on the track. I just walked back. I sat on the swings and ate ma nuggets. I ate my chips and burger on the way; I was starving. I heard motorbikes though, but the bushes were in the way and I never bothered to go and look as there are always lads on stolen motorbikes around here, nothing special, and the less you see around here the better, eh? I don't want ma windows tanned in, or my face kicked in for grassing anyway!"

"So, you heard motorbikes. What time was this? How long did you sit on the swings for? Did you notice what way the bikes went when they left?" Fran hit her with more multiple questions, a tactic that seemed to be working, helping Kerri open up a bit.

"They must have headed to the red bridge. They never passed the gap in the trees, so I never actually saw them. It was about 7.30-ish I think. I sat there until I couldn't hear them anymore to finish my food and avoid coming back here early."

"Last questions then, just now anyway, where did you cut

through to the field? Which path did you take? Could this event have been ongoing when you were walking back and you just didn't notice it?" Chris asked with a tone of finality in his voice, and he put both of his hands on his knees, showing his chunky white gold ring with Celtic engravings on it.

"Nice ring by the way." Kerri paused, always curious about people. "I cut though at the main path bit, and I didn't hear anything until I was sitting down in the swings, so that's when it must have started, eh!" she answered with a little more determination than within any of the previous questions, asserting the untrue fact that she hadn't seen anything or heard more than the bikes, but she tried to make it sound truthful and genuine.

Chris twisted his ring on his wedding finger and smiled. "Nice isn't it? My partner gave me it!" He was aware of how observant she was, also aware that his partner worked with these kids, although he didn't realise that the girl was the one he had been talking about with Phil. He also knew Phil rarely wore his matching ring at work to avoid answering the 'are you married' questions, and then having to explain what sex he was married to, as he looked like a straight guy to most, on first meeting him.

"Oh, I thought you were a poof, with yer soft camp voice and all that?" Kerri quizzed, deliberately being smart and a little rude with her choice of words, hankering for a reaction, knowing fine well that Chris was gay, but she was just testing him, seeing if he would lie to hide it.

Chris was used to this. Life had a way of defining you. "You were right the first time, Kerri. I am gay, and I have a husband!" He was not bothered by what she had said, although he preferred not to be called a poof these days. That was old hat and now only used in a derogatory way.

"Anyway, Kerri, thanks for all your help. We might be back again if something new comes up, and we'll leave you to get to your bed now." Fran saw the conversation was digressing away from the original topic. They had asked what they had come to ask, and at present there was no reason not to believe Kerri's version of events, especially due to offering up the incident that could give them a more concrete timeline for CCTV and phones used in the area of the murder.

They left the room silently, waiting until they were downstairs to speak about what Kerri had said and whether it was truthful of not. Either way, it had not been a dead loss and there were two motorbikes or more to start trawling CCTV for to try and see where they came from and where they went. Hopefully they would find them before they were burned out.

Chapter 23

Watching

Findlay knew where Kay lived, and also where Taylor lived, but wasn't quite sure where they stayed at present, or if they actually lived together full time or not. Neither of them had changed their details on police systems, because he had checked, so he had to choose one house and see if either of them turned up, but he knew to be careful. Taylor was a switched-on lady. If he was seen once, she would not hesitate to get back up into his face.

He was nervous as he sat in his car, fearful of being spotted, his car a big gas guzzler, a vehicle chosen with enough room for his oversized belly, although his short fat legs didn't require the extra length it afforded.

The car had never been tidy, but now he was suspended, he seemed to spend more time in it going nowhere and eating, and failing even to tidy it as he had occasionally done before, when he had had to keep to a certain standard for work, albeit for him that standard was never too high. His wife used to get frustrated and tidy it for him, because she was embarrassed to have to get out of it when they went anywhere together in it.

He had become even more unkempt and chaotic since his bitch of a wife had up and left him. "Ungrateful cow, taking all my earnings and lounging about doing next to nothing," he thought to himself as he sat there. He had never had a high opinion of women, a man with his head back in the 1950s. A woman's place was in the home, in the kitchen, and there to look nice and serve him, in every way, willing or not. He was still a believer in conjugal rights, even though he was in the police and knew that nowadays this was classed as rape and punishable by law.

While he waited, he ate crisps, some chocolate and drank full fat Coke, all adding to his unhealthy frame, not caring about his body, albeit he still had a misplaced high opinion about himself.

His wait had been worth it, his choice of dwelling correct. Kay had returned home from work later than she normally would, due to working the flexi shift to help out with conjoining the two enquiries. Findlay was annoyed at this, never appreciating the extra effort that his team made to get things done in the busy times, because he never did, so couldn't know the effort of others. His eyes narrowed. He shifted uncomfortably in his seat, his heart racing, as he watched this lithe and feminine young woman stretch her leg out to leave the car, her skirt raised and her thigh exposed momentarily, and he felt his arousal and the unhealthy desire burn inside. He wanted her, and to hurt her, with the feeling of vengeance ignited once again.

She seemed to be in and out of the flat in no time. She came back out in a rush, a little flustered. She had changed and freshened up, looking like she was heading out again. He watched, licking his lips, and liked that she was alone, no Taylor to protect her.

Findlay thought about work and looked at his watch. Taylor would be at work. He had heard the news of the death of a male in Drylaw, so he assumed she would be pulling a late one to cover that enquiry, the beginning of it anyway, until ownership of the case was decided, CID or MIT. Findlay was unaware of her new role at work, which was just as well. Every ounce of his self-control would have been lost if he had known she had taken on his job.

He slumped down low, inconspicuous as the car was nothing to look at, and he had parked it well to avoid any unwanted attention, but in a good position to see without being seen, remembering back to when he did actual work in the police surveillance team.

He watched Kay head around the corner at pace, her stride wide and with purpose, as she made her way to the main thoroughfare of pedestrians. He drove cautiously around the corner, slowly and carefully, following her, hoping she didn't turn around and see him. The bus stop wasn't far away. He parked up behind a car, and watched her stand at the bus stop, his heart was thudding in his chest. This was thrilling, and he was liking what he felt, no longer caring how wrong it was. He could see why all these deviant criminals he had put away could get carried away with their badness, the rush it was giving him and the new freedom from constraint he was quickly getting used to.

"Must be going out for a wee drink then, day off tomorrow presumably, given the hour she's heading out. Her innocence, so pleasant and endearing. Why would that perfect specimen of a woman end up whoring herself out to that predatory big lez on the team? Fuck knows why us men are not good enough for her," Findlay raged to himself, almost speaking out loud, totally unaware of how repulsive he had become to the women he managed.

He had liked Kay since the moment she started working for him, and remembered when she was engaged to Tom and how normal she was, that was until that deviant Taylor had arrived on the scene and sprinkled gay fairy dust in her face, transforming her into a feminist lesbian. Findlay had never considered any wrong in the fact that Kay's fiancé had cheated on her months before the wedding. That had been the reason she was open and free once more to meet other people, probably never even considering a gay partner until she met Taylor. The timing of everything, the situation and a broken heart, had paved the way for a different kind of love, both Kay and Taylor single at the time. Kay had enjoyed the new venture, much to Findlay's disgust and jealousy! Findlay never saw any wrong in his behaviour. He was blinkered to what he thought should be, rather than what was right, and he always thought he had a chance with most women, oblivious of his current physique and unacceptably letchy manner towards them and how it made them feel.

He looked longingly at Kay, as she ruffled her hair, her fitted blouse tightening over her perfect breasts as she did so, her neat jeans on her slim toned legs and nimble feet in nice boots, her beauty natural, not forced, and very easy on the eye.

He watched, never taking his eyes off of her, and he licked his lips again at the thought of having her. He had got the taste for it when he touched her thighs at work. He had been so aroused then that he lost his senses and hadn't cared about what might happen. He had wanted to touch her for so long and now wished he had done more in that kitchen, gone inside her. Nobody would have known, just him. He sat there and allowed his mind to focus back on the sexual offence committed against her previously but, instead of sympathy for her, he put himself in the place of the rapist and allowed his mind to wander, virtual enjoyment of what he imagined took place, the taking of her sweet pleasure, and what he felt as he sat there was jealousy.

He watched as the bus arrived and she stepped high up to climb on, his eyes fixed between her legs. His mind was made up. "I'll make her regret teasing me all these years, reporting me, telling her big butch girlfriend on me. I'll have the last laugh, put that selfish cock-tease back in the looney bin forever this time. By the time I've finished with her, she won't want to live."

He had become delusional, believing he could get away with it. The enquiry was ongoing to prove he had touched her where he shouldn't have and, if proven, he'd be out anyway.

He had nothing to lose. These bitches would pay, every last one of them, and Taylor wasn't out of bounds either. He'd take her down too.

Chapter 24

Kerri's Adoptive Family

Kerri had been adopted at a very young age, her heroin-addict parents giving her up after a month. She had been on the child protection register from birth. She suffered from foetal alcohol syndrome, was born addicted to heroin and had been bounced off the floor a few times in her short time with her dysfunctional parents. The social worker had tried one last time to get the mother to switch on and care for Kerri, but the influence of her controlling drug-addict partner was too strong, and she chose him and drugs over their child. Baby Kerri had suffered attachment issues, never bonding with her mother, never feeling love or comfort in her earliest age, only angst, aggression and neglect, now deep rooted within her DNA, awaiting the trigger to release.

She was in care for over a year before they managed to make her as well as she could be, albeit she was an angry baby, crying for hours, and never settled, not wanting anyone to hold her, so young and already so damaged, only ever seeking loving arms, but none came.

The family that took her in, at 18 months, already had a five-year-old son with his own issues, learning difficulties and on the autistic spectrum, nonverbal. He brought his family many problems due to his outbursts of rage and destruction of their property with his unnatural strength.

The family had waited a long time, but now they were first in line to adopt this troubled girl, the mother hoping that she would bring balance to their family and make things easier. The husband just did as his wife asked, as it was less trouble, his inadequacies magnified by his silent agreement. Their wait to adopt was over, and they successfully took Kerri home into their family, hoping for a new beginning.

Years went by. The two children appeared to calm one another, Kerri able to suppress a lot of her brother's anger, and she possessed the ability to get him to do things for her. Any trouble at school, he sorted it out by planting one on the aggressor, his brawn assisting greatly with that, and Kerri did like him, big and docile with her and silently obedient, which for her was perfect.

Kerri became a very pretty young woman, still troubled and aggressive at school, but settled, clever and functioning, until one day she came home and her mum was out. Her dad was sitting watching the TV. He was slumped on the couch and hadn't noticed her coming in to the living room.

When he did, he was startled. He had a large whisky in his hand, something she hadn't seen him do too often, his wife rarely allowed it, and he seemed a little tainted, and different. He was slurring his words and acting strange.

He had just been laid off at work, let go, dumped, made redundant. His whole world had come crashing down, his last shred of masculinity and purpose gone, his ability to provide for his family shattered and he was fearful of telling his wife, which was why he was blind drunk.

He watched Kerri in her short school skirt, watched her in a different way than normal, only now realising how much she had matured and, until now, blind to the fact. Everything had changed. His self-esteem shattered, his self-control and decency shredded, he now looked at her and saw her differently. She was a young woman, and he was a man, an emasculated, downtrodden, useless man in the eyes of his wife, and he could not recall the last time they had had sex. He actually no longer wanted to be with her in that way; she was always making derogatory comments, constantly putting him down, mocking his soft frame, his size, anything that would have him shrink into himself, a despicable woman in every way, not the nurturing comfort-giving person you would want, and not a motherly person in the slightest.

He had watched porn secretly for years and had recently started on some of the darker sites, which moved into adolescence, school age females in uniform, and this is what he now saw right in front of him, the drink clouding his rational judgement. He had never looked at his daughter that way. He had been watching deviant films, but he had boundaries and there was a line not to cross.

He was blind drunk, normally a kind and supportive man to the children, never bad, or leery. He had seen something though. His guard was down, his moral fibre in tatters, as he called her over, patting the couch beside him. She obediently went to him, no reason not to trust him. Even though he was drunk, she still trusted him and his usual kindness. He was different today, but she was wise enough to know why and sat on the couch. He cruelly mocked her short skirt by putting his hand up it and suddenly pulled at her blouse, popping two buttons, before tugging at her bra strap, hard enough to pull it down, allowing him to catch sight of one of her breasts. He then shoved his hand further up her skirt, his touch clumsy and intrusive, drunk, uncaring and unkind as he pulled her pants down. Her heart was screaming no. What is he doing to me? Why is he treating me like this? She thought herself. He took hold of her hand and forced it into his trousers, making her touch his aroused penis, and moved her hand with his. Tears rolled down her cheeks, her heart aching. She felt sick, her skin crawling. This was someone she trusted, someone that she genuinely cared about, and she didn't understand why he was treating her like this. She didn't fight, her disappointment and discomfort all-consuming, fear of what was to come next making her freeze, as he pulled her on top of him.

Just as he was doing this, Kerri's brother came in. Seeing what was happening to his sister, his face contorted and turned red. He sprang forward quickly, his rage obvious, and grabbed his father by the throat and held it so tight that his dad only took seconds to collapse unconscious on the floor, his fly still undone and his pathetic frame lying there.

Kerri was sick on the floor. Her stomach lurched, repulsed at what her dad had done and how dirty he had made her feel. Her heart was broken, and she felt something else inside, a plethora of wild emotions, an inner rage boiling deep inside her, one that had lain dormant for many years.

She stamped hard down on his genitals, and then his hands, the hands that had spoiled her innocence, destroyed the only family she knew and had become used to, not perfect, but it was her home, and she was happy enough. She then turned to his face and had stamped down three times when her brother joined in, his kicks and stamps more damaging, both young people now feral, aware of what had happened and how their dad had wronged his daughter.

By the time Kerri tried to stop her brother, who was a big lad, her adoptive father was unconscious, but still alive with horrendous facial injuries and swellings that made him look unnatural.

"Stop, stop, leave him now. He's had enough. We need to get an ambulance!" Kerri screamed at the realisation of how far they had gone, but her anger and the need for self-protection had overwhelmed her actions.

Their mother arrived home at that moment to the sight of her two blood-spattered children standing over her stricken husband. She could not believe what she was seeing. Her eyes narrowed and turned snakelike and accusatory, as she turned on Kerri and looked at her daughter with mistrust and malice, her blouse undone, her skirt short and revealing, a harlot in her mother's mind. She had already decided she was going to blame Kerri for this mess, ignoring the obvious signs of her husband's guilt.

She looked at her husband's trousers, the flies open and revealing the top of his penis. Her toes curled at the sight. Deep down, she knew what had really happened, but her misplaced jealousy of her innocent daughter would steer the way this incident would go. She stared at her husband, disgust in her eyes, his weakness stabbing her through the heart. She knew he had done wrong, actions speaking louder than words. Kerri was a mess, her clothes hanging off, but his face was a state after the attack she knew had taken place in defence against his depraved and unwanted attention.

"What the bloody hell has gone on here?" She knew that something sexual had taken place, the blame currently unknown, and she was aware of what she thought had gone on. She quickly made up her mind to cover this mess up. She needed to be able to be seen in public again and not be the talk of the town. Unfortunately for Kerri, that would not be by telling the truth.

Kerri looked distraught, and her clothes indicated that her opened blouse had not been voluntary as the majority of the buttons were missing. Her bra strap was stretched and damaged, leaving marks where it had dug into her skin as it was pulled harshly down. Kerri opened her mouth to speak, the words struggling to come out. She was still shaking and clearly upset, but when she did speak, she blurted out what had happened, truth in her tearful eyes. "He tried to touch me. He made me touch him. He was drunk and mean and angry and horrible. He forced me on top of him. It was scary, Mum; he was really frightening, rough and cruel, Mum. If Joe hadn't come in, I don't know what would have happened! Joe saw what he was doing, and even he knew it was wrong and not right, and grabbed him to save me, and he saw me kicking him, and he started copying me and it all went a bit too far!" Tears rolled down her face, sorrowful at this dreadful situation, knowing that nothing could ever be the same, and she felt sick.

"A likely story, young lady. You've been walking around here like a slut for ages, teasing and provoking, and now look what's happened. How dare you sully your father's good name like this? He's not a child molester. He's a good man, an upstanding pillar of the community!" Kerri's mother was more than aware that every word she said was not true, but her words were to protect her husband, and more so, herself. There was no way she would out her husband for what he had done, due to the shame that would come if her friends and other people knew she was married to a paedophile! She could not live with that, so made her shameful decision. It was a case of her husband over her adopted daughter, and more selfishly, herself and damage limitation. There would be no explaining away child molestation, but a damaged and challenging child going into care was most definitely the lesser of two evils, and she knew what she had to do.

Kerri couldn't hold back her words, her inner rage and hidden true self and disgust at the reality of what was actually happening boiling up here. She was young in years, but not naïve, and knew how this was playing out. She yelled at her mother, "You two-faced hypocritical bitch, you treat him like shit every day, belittle everything he does, and God knows the last time he was allowed to fucking shag your tired old body, and you fucking know what he did to me, cause he'll never get a shag from you any time soon, ya fucking stuck up pretentious, false bitch. He couldn't get near you if he tried, because you don't know how to love anyone, except yourself, ya frosty-faced old cunt. No wonder he's turned into a fucking paedo now. He wouldn't want into your crusty old knickers!"

Her mother just stood there in astonishment.

Once she had started, she couldn't stop, her loveless relationship with her mother, her upbringing all spilling out. Her start as an infant, the false love shown by her adoptive mother when they were with family and friends, the pretence of a functional family shattered by every word she said. Her mother was turning red with anger, her thoughts turning to all she claimed to have done for this waif, but all she had done was portray herself as a kind woman by taking her in. She had never really loved Kerri. She had felt a failure for her son, for not being able to bear another child, albeit it might have been that her husband couldn't create another. Kerri had been brought into the family to fill a gap, and her mother had never really taken the child into any kind of motherly bond, and once she had adopted her, there had been no going back, to save face, but now there didn't seem to be an option.

She raised her hand in a clenched fist and hit Kerri on the side of the head, over and over again, until the swelling rose, and her face looked deformed like her husband's. Joe moved forward to stop his mother, but the slap she swung directly into his face stung like a bee, and he got a fright as his mum had never hit him before. He retreated back like a scolded little boy, confused at his mum's behaviour. Why was she picking on Kerri and now him? His childlike mind couldn't understand the adult situation, because he knew it was his dad that was wrong not Kerri. Why couldn't his mum see that?

"Get out, get out now," she yelled at Joe. "And, as for you, you can't stay here with us anymore, you're too dangerous. You were and still are too much of a temptation for my weak-minded husband and his unhealthy desires, and if you utter one word of this to anyone, I will report you for assault and you'll be put away in secure, you ungrateful little bitch. You did this deliberately. You exposed yourself, teasing this weak and foolish man, and you'll have to go back into care now today. We're done here!"

Kerri couldn't believe what was happening, how quickly her life had turned upside down, everything unravelling. Although it was far from perfect, it was still home for her, sometimes loveless and cold when it came to her false mother, but she was fed, clothed and well kept. Her dad had been nice to her, up until today. She attended school and had friends there and was bright and doing okay.

There were now no tears, just a feeling of loss and resentment. She was losing everything she had known as normal, her imperfect family, and all this because her adopted father couldn't control his unnatural urges, and this had broken her heart, any trust she had gone forever, as she had been close to him and did love him. As for her false mother, who believed herself to be an upstanding member of the community, pretentious and one never to be outdone, she did not want to face the truth and do what was right for her daughter, in fear of how it would make her look. She clearly did not care how this would affect Kerri's adolescent mind. She merely wanted to save her reputation; fully aware Kerri had told her the truth.

Kerri's face was swollen and bruised, her eye now shut with the repeated assault from her mother, her inner rage momentarily suppressed through sorrow at her loss, but there was a new hostility beginning to boil inside.

Her dad started to moan from the floor. He raised his hand to his face. There was a lot of blood. His mouth, cheeks and forehead were swollen, and he was missing a couple of teeth, but he could see his wife and daughter in front of him, his daughter also injured, with his son nowhere to be seen.

He knew by his wife's face what had gone down, and he felt sick at the realisation of his fate laid bare before him. He was still drunk, his face sore, but he could remember how his daughter had made him feel. He had flashes of his grabbing at her, her confusion and scared look as he did so, and he scrunched his eyes shut hoping for it all to go away. He looked down at himself and quickly adjusted his flies. Now it was his turn to feel sick. What had he done? Regret now consumed his very being, what was left of his soul destroyed and his life broken beyond repair.

His wife's eyes narrowed, her downward and accusatory stare towards him was obvious and unsettling as she spoke, her words rasping, "She's leaving! There's no way she's staying here if she's going to make up lies and have you arrested. She's got to go, even if we have to pay for her keep. She's not welcome here anymore and, before you speak up, the decision's made, and nothing you can say or do will change that, unless you want to go to prison!"

He couldn't believe what he was hearing. He knew what he had done and that it would be obvious to his wife, but she was choosing to protect him and get rid of Kerri. He felt a huge surge of guilt. He knew what he had done was despicable, and there would be no coming back from that with her, but for his wife to want rid of Kerri was taking things to a new level of despicable. He knew how damaging this would be for his daughter, who was already insecure, due to her past. She had struggled through most of her life. Although he had acted disgracefully, he did actually love her and felt physically sick to the stomach at what he had done. He had crossed a line that was unforgiveable, and he was disgusted with himself.

She was only 15, at a certain stage in life, and now she was going into care. Kerri felt alone, panicked and desperately sad, fearful of where she would have to go. She knew her mother meant what she said, and her threat to stay silent was heard and understood loud and clear.

Eventually her dad opened his mouth to speak to his wife, but before the sentence was formed, she was quick to silence him. "Don't say a word! You disgust me, you desperate little man. She clearly can't stay. You can't be trusted around her, and you're lucky she isn't going to say a word! Are you, Kerri?" Her words were cutting and final, her lips tight and menacing, her words confirming she had believed Kerri's version of what had happened. She had already shown Kerri how vicious her aggression could be, the threat of opening her mouth was very clear. She had chosen to stand by her husband, well, herself really, regardless of the detriment to her adopted daughter, and the immeasurable damage it may cause.

Kerri's eyes narrowed as she looked straight at her adoptive mother. They darkened as their eyes met, hostile menace growing within Kerri's stare, a look that unnerved even her hard-faced cruel mother. Kerri had never looked at her like that. Kerri almost growled from within, deep and disconcerting, feral and uncontrolled, like a wild animal. Her head tilted to the side as she uttered her last words to her mother.

"I hate you for what you have done today. I'll never forgive you for this. I'd keep looking over your shoulder from now on if I were you!" Kerri felt her insides curl up in pain, with loss and fear, resentment, and now a deep-rooted desire to get revenge and a new-felt hatred and resentment growing inside.

Chapter 25

Ouch

Kay got back to her flat, the taxi rumbling loudly into the quiet street as she arrived home, the street quiet, no traffic or pedestrians about, as it was late. She had to steady herself. She had had a good night and was a little tipsy and thankful she wasn't wearing high heels. She giggled to herself as she stumbled against the gate and, once steadied a little, she struggled to get the key in the door first time, as her aim was a little skew-whiff. She was looking a little more bedraggled than she had when she left to go out, and was obviously a little worse for wear and a little more vulnerable than she'd like.

Findlay watched her silently, still as a statue, from inside his car. He had gone up town too, following the bus, watched her go into the bar and waited for her to come out. He enjoyed the thrill of what he was doing. He had left before her, to allow him to get back first, assuming she was actually going home. He had considered bundling her into his car and just kidnapping her there and then, but he came to his senses and chose to continue stalking her, for now anyway. There was more planning needed if he was to get away with what he was thinking of doing to her, which was now always on his mind. It thrilled him, the thought of having her, even just once. He too noticed that she was vulnerable, as she was a little drunk and alone, nobody around to see her home safely. No Taylor, no protector, a bonus, he thought, as his mind wandered dangerously once more.

After stumbling clumsily up the path, and after several attempts, Kay eventually managed to put her key in the lock. She was quiet when she entered the house, hoping not to wake Taylor. She hadn't seen her car in the street but assumed she would have had to park further away. But, on looking, she was a little surprised Taylor wasn't back yet. She checked the time, nearly 2am. "Mmm, must have a case that needs a little more work," she thought out loud, unperturbed by Taylor's absence.

Kay kicked off her boots, hitting one off of the wall, and continued on clumsily to the kitchen, in desperate need of some hot sweet tea. She could certainly feel that she had had a drink tonight, a few pink gins and then a couple of cocktails. Without the tea, her head might start spinning when it hit the pillow.

Findlay sensed that Taylor might not be staying there tonight, so became a little braver, stepping out from his car and closer to the flat. He felt his heart thumping through his chest, and he felt exhilarated at what he was doing, the realisation of the thrills to be had from breaking the law, embracing the excitement of the voyeurism. He felt a stirring beneath his belt, low due to the size of his protruding belly. He had wanted Kay for a long time. How long would watching be enough of a thrill for him? He had already crossed the line. The pleasure he had felt when he had stroked up her legs and touched her pants and over her pussy had been immense. He had never felt so powerful, and he had never been so hard, an arousal that he had replayed time after time since that event, wishing he had pushed his fingers inside her.

The curtains were not closed yet, Kay a little too pissed to notice or care, so this allowed him to watch from behind a thick bush in the garden. He couldn't believe his luck when Kay came through in a dressing gown, beneath it a pair of short silky pyjamas, long lithe legs, pert breasts, jiggling, now free from their restrictive bra, nipples erect with the chill in the air. He was so close he could revel in these details.

He watched, now enjoying the show, her legs opening before crossing them. He wanted to touch her. His thoughts were vile and unhealthy, and he decided he was going to have her; he was going to take her. She needed a real man to mend her ways. Just as he put his hand onto his stiff penis, he heard a car revving its engine as it turned into the quiet street and, at a glance, he knew who it would be. Taylor!

"For fuck's sake! Trust you to fucking come back now. Typical, late as usual, you butch dyke bitch," he rasped under his breath, his hatred for Taylor second to none. She was responsible for spoiling, what he believed to be, the perfect woman. Kay was his, his mind always delusional at his prowess, but now becoming unstable, his belief that Kay should be his growing stronger every day.

He was too late to get back to his car without being seen, so he squeezed between two of the densest bushes, surprisingly enough to secret his bulky frame. The door slammed loudly, and it was clear Taylor was angry, the reason unknown to Findlay, and the reason for her late arrival a mystery, but his disappointment at her returning home clear within his outward demeanour, unsure if he wanted to watch the show now, with someone he hated defiling his prize.

Taylor was clearly more adept at her key entry into the lock, and she went straight in. Kay rose up to meet her coming home. The minute she saw Taylor, she clasped her hands over her cheeks and kissed the cut above her partner's eye. "Oh my God, what the hell happened to you? Who did this to you? Did you get the little bastard, and how the hell, as inspector, did this happen?" Her slightly intoxicated approach was noticed by Taylor, but not judged, as she knew only too well how easy it was to drink a little bit too much.

"It's okay, it was just a wee arsehole that got a bit too brave, and over excited, and got lucky with his throw of a bottle. I couldn't have pretty boy Marcus's face spoiled, could I? So I put my head in the way to save him," she joked, as she had been nowhere near Marcus when she copped a bottle in the face.

Kay was relieved that Taylor could joke about it. She was clearly tense and in need of some relaxation therapy. Drink always made Kay a little hornier, so she pulled her brave girlfriend into a wild and lust-filled kiss, and was not shy in pushing Taylor's hand between her legs, Taylor enjoying what she felt, smooth and inviting. Her hand moved firmly over Kay, her free hand grasping tightly onto her breast, pulling down her top. She sucked hard on Kay's taught nipples. One by one, they stood before Taylor's mouth as she engulfed them, her fingers plunging into Kay's already wet inviting pussy. Both of them were clearly in need of sexual release, and it showed with the power of Taylor's fingers pushing deep inside Kay, not much of a build-up, as she fucked Kay where she stood, kissing and sucking her neck, lust filled desire, both needing, wanting, as Taylor pushed Kay firmly down onto the sofa and pulled her hips up to meet her mouth, hands gripping her ass, opening her wider as she adored her pussy with her mouth, her deft tongue delving deep inside Kay, swirling around and over her clitoris, as her fingers continued to fuck her, deep and powerful, Kay's moans exciting Taylor, making her want Kay more, their shared desire overwhelming. Kay bucked down hard onto Taylor's fingers, to let her get even deeper inside her, her body tensing as she ejaculated, a surprise to both of them. The relentless fucking left Kay weak at the knees. Taylor savoured this and continued pushing into her, a little slower, until Kay climaxed so hard that her body went into a full spasm, her pussy gripping tight onto Taylor's fingers. Taylor's mouth continued to lick until every pulse and shudder of Kay's body had subsided, and every swirl of her orgasm was over. Both of them were overwhelmed at this animalistic display of unbridled lovemaking, Kay now able to slip her hands over Taylor and into her too. Taylor's orgasm was quick due to the arousal she had felt whilst feverishly fucking Kay, a sudden need to release.

Findlay stood there, motionless and childlike, his mouth agape at how quickly their greeting had transcended into pure lust-filled passionate sex. He was also very aware of how much Kay had enjoyed being fucked senseless by a woman, and there was an unhealthy jealousy and desire to put these wrongs right. He would teach these ungodly dykes what God's intention was, and it wasn't two women together, one pretending to act like a predatory man. He was unhappy at what he had watched, but his body told a different story, as he adjusted his discomfort, his arousal obvious, before slipping off unnoticed.

Chapter 26

A New Day, a New Disappointment

Kerri was up early. She had a spring in her step. There was a buzz about the place today, a right hubbub about the murder, how close it was to the unit, and there was still a cordon in place and a lot of police coming and going. It was better than watching telly, and she felt a warmth from the demise of the male, and her part in the end, cruel and damaging. She wondered if the crushing of his fingers was the catalyst to his death, the final agony causing excess pressure through his body, pushing his precious blood to places it wasn't meant to go, the damage to his skull immense and life threatening prior to her assault. Her final infliction of pain might have ended it all, his organs giving way with a finality from which he could no longer survive.

She was also buzzing because she was having another visit with the social worker, the nice, kind and very handsome social worker. She smiled when she said his name aloud, and she felt a warmth in her tummy, something she had not felt before when thinking about a man. She liked the way he made her feel about herself. He didn't pressure her, judge her, or try and implement his ways. He just seemed chilled and mellow, genuinely caring about what she had to say, and he wasn't intrusive or controlling like the other staff. She liked him and felt safe around him after such a short amount of time and, to her surprise, she also felt attracted to him. But she shrugged off those thoughts, as she didn't feel ready to trust anyone enough to like them in that way.

She had a while to wait as he wasn't arriving until after 4pm, so she would have to busy herself until then. She looked out of the window and could still see the white and blue of the police tent through the trees in the distance, the cordon tape blowing gently in the breeze, the officers standing 20 metres apart. She wondered if the police would come calling again, but she thought they wouldn't be able to place her there. Nobody had seen her, and why would she be there? If anyone had seen her, she could just lie and say she had quite literally stumbled upon him, accidentally stepping on his hand when she was checking on him. She could say she had got a fright making her jump up and squish his hand and, because of that, she was too scared to say what she had done. But she quickly dismissed this thought. The police were too dumb to work that out, or so she believed.

"Happy Birthday, handsome man!" Chris brought through a lush chocolate cake, with numbered candles alight on the top, and kissed Phil full on the lips. Phil was barely awake, and only when he opened his eyes, did he see Chris was naked with a feather boa around his waist, just covering his privates and no more.

Phil laughed out loud. He loved Chris's flamboyance and humour and that he was a horny little bastard, never having enough of his lover.

"Cake first. You'll have to be the desert this time!" Phil joked, smiling at his lover cutting a slice for each of them. Chris had poured a couple of glasses of Bucks Fizz too, and they chinked their glasses together.

"Hey, remember I'm working later today. I can't have too much!" Phil protested weakly, not really giving a shit. It wasn't as if he was in the police and couldn't drink. His rules were a little more flexible and wouldn't necessarily end in dismissal.

Chris smiled and said, "You've got over six hours. It's the same as a late night out. I'll work the alcohol out of your system. Nothing better than chocolate cake and sex, lots of sex!" He meant what he said as he shoved his cake into his mouth and gulped down the glass of fizz, wiped his mouth with his hand and climbed under the duvet. Phil, still with a little morning glory, put it to good use, Chris the sub, and Phil most definitely the dom.

Two hours later, both showered and shaved, with smart clothes on, they were ready for an early lunch. Phil put on his ring as they were going out for a birthday lunch and he always wore it when they were out as a couple, as part of looking smart and ready to meet the world. They were heading into town for a while before Phil's shift. Chris was off work, so he was a little more footloose and fancy free and was wanting to enjoy some more alcohol, so they headed to All Bar One for a set lunch and cocktails for Chris. Phil had another drink with his meal and would take the bus down to Drylaw for his first meeting of the day, not risking driving.

Kerri had been out for a walk in the area and a bus ride down to the shore, and was openly impatient for her meeting with the social worker. She was building this next meeting up to be something that it clearly was not, her newfound feelings sadly misplaced.

Eventually her appointment with Phil arrived. She had showered and dried her hair, put on nice clothes, a little make-up and also a nice fragrance. She had headed down to the office where Inga was sitting completing some paperwork. Her head was down, and she didn't notice Kerri at first, but she felt her presence as she was standing in the doorway, not her usual bolshy self, patiently waiting for Inga to instigate the conversation, a first!

"Oh, hi. I never saw you there, Kerri. Can I get you something? Are you okay?" she asked as Kerri wasn't acting normally for her. It was then Inga noticed Kerri's appearance, her hair, clothes and make-up a sign that she had made an effort, even though she was naturally attractive anyway. It was obvious she had taken time to enhance her appearance and put in a little more effort. She was clearly in a different mood from the norm.

"I'm fine. I was just wondering if the social worker guy is still coming. It's twenty past four already. I've not got all day to wait around!" she said casually to make it seem like she didn't care, but Inga wasn't stupid. She knew there was something up, and she felt a wee twist inside, because if it was what she thought, she knew Phil batted for the other side, and Kerri would be disappointed.

Just then the buzzer on the secure entry system went, and the handsome face of Phil was pressed up against the window, his hand raised up to assist in peering in, trying to see if there was anyone there to let him in.

Both Inga and Kerri looked up, and Kerri's face flushed a little, which didn't go unnoticed by Inga, who shuddered inside once more, her previous thoughts confirmed. Phil was the biggest gay in any village. He just hid it really well, never camp or putting his sexuality on display, but very, very gay indeed and certainly not interested in any of the young residents in the unit, male or female. Inga also knew he was married to a copper, a double no-no for Kerri.

Kerri tried to look like she wasn't bothered that he was late or there at all and that the meeting was just something she had no choice in but, for once, she was actually looking forward to it, a pleasant surprise to her.

"I'll let him in. Where do you want the meeting today, Kerri, in the living room or up in your room?" Inga said, regretting offering her the choice straight away.

"My room please. I can't be doing with all the others here, bursting in all the time. There's no privacy!" Kerri answered, giving lame excuses for her choice to be more private.

Inga could sense what was going down and thought she would speak with Phil before he went up, but he was experienced and aware of how young adolescents of both sexes could act towards him. He was attractive but not stupid.

Kerri headed up the stair before he got into the office. Phil listened to what Inga was saying and was a little taken aback, as he felt that he hadn't really got through to this girl and that she was deep as the ocean. All that said, he'd obviously struck a chord with her and gained her trust, which for him was good, because now he could work with her to help her. Kerri's attraction to him could be a problem. This type of situation never seemed to end well. How bad Kerri's infatuation with him would be was yet to be seen.

"Is she in the living room area?" Phil asked hopefully, already knowing the answer.

"Nope, in her room I'm afraid. She doesn't want to be interrupted by the other residents!" Inga squinted her face in sympathy for him. She knew Kerri was an unknown entity and volatile to say the least. She certainly wouldn't take rejection well, but to what level was still to be experienced.

Phil found Kerri sitting on her bed. He sat in the farthest away chair possible, beside the desk, deliberately keeping a safe distance.

Kerri spoke first. "You smell like you've had a drink! The aftershave doesn't quite hide it," she said with her eyes a little narrowed, critical of him, her ability to smell alcohol almost instant, with its sweet sickly transformation on the breath a scent she would never forget, the lasting memory of her father, and his sexual assault, coming right back to the forefront of her mind. She had a hatred of what alcohol could do to a person with a weakness already present.

Phil was taken aback that she had noticed. He had not had a lot to drink and doubted he'd be over the limit, and this was not a normal thing for him. Chris was very persuasive, and he knew he shouldn't have had another drink with lunch as the scent had clearly lingered on his breath. He gave himself a metaphorical kick up the arse for being so stupid, still unaware of how Kerri's current situation had come about and that alcohol was central to the lack of restraint and behaviour of her weak father.

"I had a glass of wine when I was out for lunch today. It's my birthday, but I'm sorry you can smell it. It was just one, although, I was hoping the garlic would disguise it." This was a wee white lie, as he had had a liquid breakfast too.

"Lucky you. Is that why you were late too?" Kerri's mood had already completely changed. She had built the meeting up to be something special, with no grounds whatsoever to do so. In her mind, his arrival was going to make everything better. He was going to notice her, the way she looked, but none of this was happening. He was late and smelling of alcohol. Patience was not in her repertoire. Neither was drink, and he was clearly on the back foot, not this perfect man she had made him out to be. The feelings this was creating within her were not good.

Phil was trying to get back the favour he had once held and trying hard to get her back on side, knowing that he may have lost her already, her hostility clear. He could feel the bristling malevolence oozing from within her, her outward façade changing, and it wasn't a good change. It was unnerving, the speed of change and the ease of the U-turn within her.

Phil put his hand on the table, his ring clacking on the surface gently, loud enough for Kerri to look up, as she thought he was getting up to leave, and although she was angry and disappointed, she didn't want him to go, not yet anyway.

"Was your lunch nice? Were you with your girlfriend?!" she asked with misplaced jealousy in her voice. She felt foolish that she had thought he would be single, although she would have been amazed if he wasn't.

"It was very nice, and I was out with a friend. I don't have a girlfriend," he said in his kindest voice, hoping to alleviate her curiosity as to whether he was single or not without revealing the truth. He moved his hands onto his knees. "Enough about me, how have you been? It must've been like a circus out there with the incident the other night. It must've been a bit frightening too, no?" he asked, trying to divert the conversation.

She smiled. "Not really. These arseholes are always kicking lumps out of each other all the time, but this time they did it right. Just annoying really, but if you live that way, then you get what's coming to you!" Her disassociation and lack of empathy for the seriousness of the murder was a little shocking for him, her words, so matter of fact and openly hostile, her eyes changing to dark pools with a slight smile coming over her mouth at the thought of the guy begging for his life. Her self-protection mode was coming into play, her true colours taking over again, shutting him out, closing the door she had foolishly opened for him. She was getting angry at Phil, her inner rage surfacing because he had made her feel a short-lived happiness. She couldn't believe she had let herself feel for this man. She had been let down again, and she didn't give second chances. He had made her look like a fool. His now awkward attempts to get her onside would not be given a chance. In her mind, he was the same as the rest of them and would be treated with the disdain he deserved.

Phil was disturbed at the way she was looking at him, the previously restrained hate clearly filling her mind, and that's when she clocked his ring again, white gold, with Celtic engravings, very unique, but not so unique that she hadn't seen one similar before. It was almost identical to the one she had seen only yesterday, in fact. It was the same ring that the bent copper wore when he came to ask questions about the murder of the man at the back of the unit. She felt her breath catch in her throat, and everything fell into place. No wonder he wasn't looking at her the way most other men did. He was a bent shot too, and to think that she thought he might like her! What a fool she had allowed herself to be, and she didn't like how this was making her feel. Stupid, really fucking stupid, weak and threatened.

Kerri's face contorted with a snide stare. "Nice ring!" she said, staring at him, looking at his eyes. "Are you married? What's her name?" she asked, deliberately waiting for his deceitful reply, her trust in him well and truly gone and never to be repeated.

"I am married, and it is a lovely ring. Who I'm married to is nobody's business though!" he said truthfully, knowing trust was the most important thing between him and his clients.

"Why won't you say? Are you ashamed of who you are? The bent copper yesterday was wearing the same ring, and I haven't seen a ring like that before. A queer thing to get them specially made though, eh, don't you think? Do you think I'm a fucking daft wee lassie?" There was a newfound venom in her tone, well, new to Phil anyway.

Phil couldn't help thinking to himself that she had to have been a bit naïve to think he was interested in her in that way, even if he was straight, showing she wasn't as aware as she thought she was and had actually been that daft wee lassie she was claiming she wasn't, but he also realised she was mortified to have been wrong. He knew she was a damaged soul, but there was something sinister and nasty about her now, vengeful and unforgiving, with no conscience or thought for others.

"I'm not ashamed; I just like my personal life to remain private. I hope that isn't a problem," he said, a little wary of how she was acting and the obvious change in her demeanour.

Her response was clipped and dismissive. "Nope, not a problem, not a problem at all. I should have known you were bent, reeking like a whoor's purse, your trimmed chest hair under your shirt, immaculate really, not really a straight thing for a guy of your age!" She was deliberately trying to insult him. He clearly didn't look gay, and was still only in his thirties.

Phil was annoyed, and saddened that he had obviously lost her, not knowing what this petite unassuming person in front of him was capable of and what could happen when someone irked her or let her down.

"Listen, Kerri. I'm sorry I was late, also that I let you down. I didn't mean too. Can we start again? I want to help you; we need to discuss where you'll live once your time here's over. Please forgive me. Let me help you!" he pleaded with her, his eyes genuine and caring.

Her eyes remained dark and menacing, staring right at him, cold as ice and now filled with uncontrolled hate. "Nope, we're done here! You're just like the rest of them, not to be trusted, full of shit, have your own agenda. You don't really give a fuck about me or any of us, and we're just a means to an end, a wage. Now fuck off back to your wee bum boy and leave me the fuck alone, ya false-arsed queer. Away and fuck yourself, which I'm sure you'd like to do!" She cackled at her own joke and felt sick to the stomach at how she now felt. He would pay for making a fool out of her.

"Wow, that's a little harsh! I'm sorry I've made you feel this way. I didn't mean to. I'll get your case reassigned then, and I hope the next social worker is better placed to help with what you need." He was sad he had clearly failed.

"I don't fucking need another fucking social worker, especially not a queer one. I don't need anyone or anything. I can look after myself. I can find my own way in life without you fucking softy Walter, do-gooders burying your noses into everyone's business. Now get the fuck out of my room before I say you fucking touched me, although that wouldn't be likely, would it now, ya big bender?" Her bitter resentment was on open display.

"Okay, message received, loud and clear. I hope you find what you're looking for." Phil turned to leave.

"Oh, don't worry, I will. I always do!" Kerri sneered, with her teeth grinding together and heard by Phil as he left, the sound uncomfortable and threatening.

Phil's hair raised up off of his neck when he turned his back on this young woman, her eyes and facial expression demonic and crazed, although she sat calmly on the bed, staring right at him, a discomfort he had never felt before, and didn't like turning his back on her, in fear of what she might do.

Inga was coming up to the top of the stair, and asked, "Well, how did it go? I didn't think you'd be leaving this early. Is everything alright, you look a little stressed?" She was a little concerned, as Phil very rarely got stressed, and she certainly hadn't seen it before.

"Let's talk!" he said, as they walked back down the stair to the office, a little shaken at the sinister change in this young woman, and how it made him feel, and now felt she was truly unhinged.

Chapter 27

Coming Ready or Not

Kay was back at work following a rest day. One of her first duties was to bring Marcus the results of the sample analysis from the drowning victims, which up until now had not been tested, as there had been no dubiety raised in relation to the suspected suicides. Both drownings had been within a month of one another, but there had been numerous other deaths and suicides throughout the city over that period. Only their place of finding had been a little out of the ordinary, but there was always a first, and some odd and unexplained tide had perhaps been responsible.

No forensic samples had been taken originally, as no crime had been suspected or allegations of such made. Without an identified crime, there had been no reason to incur any unnecessary analysis costs.

Marcus listened as Kay explained there was a high quantity of fresh water in the samples taken from the lungs from both separate alleged drownings, and a much lesser quantity of sea water, as well as traces of soap and shampoo, and sperm.

"What the fuck? How is this possible? This means both had drowned, but not in the sea. We need the bloody bodies exhumed, and forensic samples taken and tests done urgently, nail scrapings, mouth and penile swabs, although there won't be a hope in hell of finding anything now after being in the sea for that long, and his corpse being allowed to rot!"

Marcus got up from his desk and went to Taylor's office. She had the phone to her ear, deep in conversation. She mouthed to him silently, "Is it important?"

"Very! It's urgent," he emphasised in a low voice, the results from the water found in both of the victim's lungs in his hand as he waved it in front of her.

Taylor mouthed, "Okay, give me a minute," and managed to politely end the call, promising another call back later in the day.

Beckoning him into the office, she asked him to pull up a chair beside her and looked up at him with concerned eyes.

"What have we got then? Your face is a picture!" Taylor smiled at him, not overly perturbed, but unaware of the news to come.

Once Marcus had told her what Kay had brought through, she was a little more concerned, and exclaimed, "I bloody well said to Findlay at the time that corpses don't get washed up where these two had. The tides either take them over to Fife or further up the coast to Long Niddrie Bents. I knew it, but he wasn't having any of it. He wrote them off as suicides straight away, even though one of the victim's wives didn't believe he'd take his own life. Findlay just wanted a quick fix, but unfortunately it was in his rights to do so and make these decisions. It would have taken some doing to get those bodies down to the beach though. They were big bloody men! What the hell are we looking at here? Surely not another serial killer?"

Marcus rubbed the back of his head and grimaced at what was going down and what he was about to say.

"Ma'am, I've been thinking. Dangerous, I know, but the other two macabre deaths in town recently were never investigated further than as suicide and accident. They've been written off as suicides. Do we open up those enquiries too? They were both within the same time frame and they didn't sit right with me at the time, neither of them!"

"Eh, why those two? There are loads of suicides all over the city, and accidental deaths, albeit these two were pretty gross," Taylor explained, trying to see what made the other two deaths worthy of reopening and the cost and resourcing of the enquiry into them. This was something her new promotion brought into the equation as she was responsible for the justification of expenditure.

Marcus paused. "It's a hunch really. They were weird; the timing is around the time of the drownings, and it was almost like a cluster of unexplained deaths, maybe a couple too many, but I think we should get a list of the witnesses, recontact them, review any CCTV that was saved and see if there's anything to link them, any bystanders that are looking not quite right or of similar appearance at both scenes."

Taylor sighed, knowing the cases had all been closed down by Findlay, who always did as little as possible within the boundaries of requirement. Without accusation or grounds for suspicion, he was within his powers to do so, and may have been right, but he was a lazy man.

"Okay, Marcus, exhume discreetly. No press, no leaks, get samples and send them off for urgent analysis, and let's see what we have here, see if there are possible crime scenes for where the men actually did drown. Get a warrant to secure their phones, laptops and any other technology that might lead to a clue as to why they died. And if there's any reluctance in handing them over, we'll deal with that at the time." Taylor's mind was already leading to possible deviance and the need to hide such evidence or information that could lead to embarrassment for the deceased's families. Both Taylor and Marcus, cynical by nature, wondering if revenge might have been a possible motive to kill a predatory male, but they couldn't put the deaths of the two women in that category.

Marcus had to head off. He was going to the mortuary with Chris, the body of the only known murder victim was another kettle of fish. Every hair, fibre, bruise, injury, illness, possible cause of death or evidential sample would be searched for and examined to the nth degree, no stone left unturned, as there was no doubt there was foul play here. This male had been murdered and, in Edinburgh, murder was not so regular that they couldn't do a very thorough examination of everything in order to find the culprit.

Chris took a deep breath and grabbed his coat. They made their way into the town, and up through the Grassmarket to the morgue, passing the usual suspects on the corner at the Salvation Army building with purple cans of super lager in their hands, but they were in good spirits and laughing and smoking sat on the edge of the steps in the morning sun. On arrival, they were led to where the male lay. He was in tray 13. How fitting, Chris thought to himself, a little superstitious.

This time he had come prepared. He had Vicks VapoRub and Airwaves chewing gum, all to prevent him throwing up or having to leave the room again. He wasn't going to be the butt of the week's jokes again.

Marcus was nonplussed about the situation. He had smelled the aroma of a corpse many times, although, when the door opened to the morgue, it still hit you like a wall of death. The fridges whirred loudly as they kept the bodies in limbo, awaiting their autopsy, or for the forgotten in society, their identification, all waiting their turn to be turned into human canoes.

Dr McKay was there waiting on time as always, known for her meticulous methodology, skilled in her field. Once the corpse was brought before her on the metal slab, she got to work efficiently. The body already photographed and all visible injuries documented, she held the formidable saw and did a practice to check the blade was working properly and secured. Chris winced and a shiver went down his back, knowing what was to come. Once checked, the circular saw ground through what was left of the skull, exposing the damaged brain to be removed and dissected. Once completed, the tongue, still attached to the oesophagus, was removed and examined. She sliced through the tongue like cutting a piece of chicken, her blade immensely sharp and adept. The pathologist worked her way through all of the internal organs one by one, weighing, measuring, taking more samples. Confirmation was made of an internal bleed, a ruptured spleen and damage to the liver, probably caused by being stamped upon. She documented the positioning and the depth and location of each injury and the severity of it. Every so often she would look up at the officers and smile, watching Chris squirm with discomfort. There were numerous visible footprints on the body, two different patterns, where he had been repeatedly stamped on. She came to his hands. One had defence wounds on it, and the other looked like it had been stood on and dragged or crushed. The doctor noticed another shoe mark, subtle markings, but definitely different to all the other prints left all over his body. Gravel stuck in his flesh, and what looked like a tiny piece of food was stuck in the damaged tissue.

Marcus and Chris were taking notes, recording the whole autopsy, the findings and all anomalies. There was curiosity regarding the possibility that there may be another assailant. When Doctor McKay had finished, she could see Chris was relieved, and she squeezed his shoulder gently in a reassuring gesture.

Elsewhere in the city, Marcus's wife Maria was picking up Wee Davy from school. She watched smiling as her little blond tousle-haired boy came skipping out from the playground, his broad smile making her heart melt with love and warmth. She was always there for her son, very rarely letting him out of her sight these days after the incident over a year ago, which had so nearly taken him from them for good.

She bent down to give David a big squishy cuddle, and

that's when her waters broke. All of a sudden there was a puddle of water beneath her. Wee Davy's face scrunched up in confusion thinking his mummy had wet herself! Maria was doubled up in pain on her hands and knees as other parents came rushing to her aid, one already on the phone for an ambulance. The contractions were coming less than two minutes apart, and Maria gripped onto another parent's hand and said, whilst panting, "The baby's coming, right now!"

David started to cry. He had never seen his mummy in pain before, and she had never wet herself either. He thought she was ill until she spoke to him through loud and heavy breaths. "David, take my phone and call Daddy please, now, quickly, my little love. Your little sister's in a hurry to meet you!"

David stopped crying and smiled in realisation of what was happening, and thinking of the baby in a rush, he visualised her running around inside his mummy's tummy, excited to be out and then they could play together.

He already knew the code to open the phone and rang his daddy, but there was no answer, and his little face saddened.

Marcus was still engrossed in the paperwork at the autopsy. He could feel the phone vibrating in his pocket, but was not in a position to answer it, as he was sterile and gloved up and the recording was still going. He assumed the call was from Taylor with more news about other enquires, stupidly not thinking about Maria and her full-term pregnancy, not initially anyway.

It was Chris that took off his glove and pushed his hand into Marcus's pocket, wincing a little as Chris's hand brushed his genitals unintentionally.

Marcus frowned at the intrusion initially, but smiled with raised eyebrows, realising what Chris was doing, as Chris mouthed, "You have to answer your phone, ya muppet! What about Maria, and the baby?"

The phone rang off just as Chris pulled it out, but he had

seen the picture of who was calling and told Marcus it was Maria.

Marcus's stomach dropped into his shoes and twisted into a tight knot, because Maria didn't usually call him at work unless it was an emergency. The last time was probably when David had been kidnapped, it was that rare for her to call.

He rang back and Wee Davy answered immediately. "Mummy has wet the ground at the school, the ambulance is coming, she is crying and shouting and said my sister is hurrying to see us now!" he said innocently, not quite grasping the enormity of what was happening.

Marcus asked where they were, and David told him, and he was in two minds as to where he should go, straight to the hospital or to the school in case there was a delay with the ambulance.

He gave his apologies to Chris and Dr McKay, and told them he had to leave as it was an emergency. He popped the blue light on the roof and jumped in the unmarked car and hit the siren, driving off like a bat out of hell, his tyres skidding off of the cobbles as he sped through the Cowgate and onto the Grassmarket, down Morrison Street, and past the Haymarket Railway Station, dodging a tram by inches as he cut in front of it, knowing he would be hindered greatly if he was caught behind it, past Murrayfield Stadium where Scotland Rugby play their games, up over Murrayfield, down Ravelston Dykes and onto Queensferry Road, arriving at Davidson's Mains primary school just as Maria was being lifted into the ambulance. His heart was pounding as he screeched to a halt. His driving had calmed a little as he approached the school, ensuring he didn't end a life whilst trying to get there to see a new life arrive.

Marcus parked badly, abandoning his protruding vehicle, and jumping from it to get to the ambulance as the doors closed. He rapped on the door loudly as the blues came on the roof, the driver clearly about to leave.

The door swung open and Wee Davy shouted out in glee that his daddy had arrived.

"Are you Maria's husband? We have to go, and the boy has the only seat in the ambulance. You'll have to follow us up in the car. Is that okay, are you able to do this?"

"No way am I going to leave her. I'm coming, seat or not!" Marcus showed his ID and climbed in and sat on the floor of the ambulance, reaching up for Maria's hand. She was distressed and wincing in pain, and Marcus felt a twist of uncertainty inside and a fear that not all was well.

"It's against our protocol, and that badge holds no jurisdiction here, but your wife needs to leave and getting you to leave we don't have time for, so hold on," the paramedic said with an understanding smile, totally agreeing that she wouldn't be leaving her loved one in this state either, rules or not.

They chose to take a route through town, lots of stopping and starting, rumbling on cobbles, traffic lights and general mayhem on the roads, harsh braking as people walked out in front of them, faces buried in their phones, lowering their life expectancy. All of this caused Maria to scream out in pain and grab Marcus so tightly she nearly broke his hand.

He squealed loudly and looked into her eyes from down where he sat, and opened his mouth to complain, when he heard her words, "She's coming; she's coming now. I have to push. I have to push now!" Maria's eyes were fiery and bright with life. "She's not waiting, aaaaahhhhh!" Maria continued to twist Marcus's hand. David was crying again and shouting out, reaching for his mummy, seeing the sweat on her forehead and her repeated cries of pain.

"Help her, Daddy, help her," David screamed.

The paramedic, Debbie Parker, knelt down and carried out a quick visual and was about to perform an internal examination, but there was no need. Both Marcus and the paramedic could see the baby's head.

"She's right, the baby's coming, right now!" Debbie knocked on the cab window and called to Scotty the driver to stop.

Scotty Casement joined her in the back of the ambulance, and their well-trained hands got on with the job at hand, albeit they had not delivered too many babies in their service.

Maria was unstrapped and quickly turned onto all fours. She pushed steadily with all her might, and it was less than a minute before Debbie had the baby in her arms and Scott was clipping the cord, carefully leaving space to offer Marcus the opportunity to cut it.

The baby screamed out loudly, and she was quickly wrapped up all cosy in a towel and handed to her dad for the first hug, while Debbie got to work making sure Maria was well and all was okay.

Marcus shuffled closer to Wee Davy, who was sitting open-mouthed and silent, sniffling, not quite sure whether to cry or not. Marcus managed to put a free arm around his little boy and cuddled him, and introduced him to his little sister. Wee Davy looked over the towel and, when he saw her for the first time, he was mesmerised and smitten with his little sister.

"We've got a bleed, Scott. Get us to that hospital now. Secure the boy and the baby first. The father will just have to hang on to something. This isn't going to be a smooth ride. Go as fast and as safely as you can; this is an emergency!" Debbie tried her best not to show the concern she felt, but it was there in her face for the well-trained eye.

Marcus held Maria's hand firmly as he watched the paramedic try and stem the flow of blood, an ever-increasing circle of red forming underneath his most precious wife.

David was crying loudly again, the baby now screaming too, alone in a drawer-like unit, both wanting their mummy. Maria was in tears as well, her fear growing, and her desire to hold her baby was crippling her, her maternal urge to comfort her little girl all-consuming. It hurt that she had not yet held her baby, and a fear that she might not ever do it niggled at the back of her mind. She shook her head to clear the thought. She was a fighter and she would meet her daughter.

Marcus was being flung all over the floor, and Debbie's expression read, 'I told you so!' Marcus nodded to her, now understanding that his car might have been a more comfortable ride, but he needed to be there, risky or not.

They soon arrived at the Edinburgh Royal Infirmary, at the A & E department, and were met by an emergency team, ready to take Maria and the baby though to the acute receiving unit, and get to work stemming the flow of blood.

Marcus and David were prevented from following and were led away to the relatives' room to wait, and to hope their loved ones were going to make it through this nightmare.

Marcus went reluctantly, knowing the doctors had a job to do to save his wife, and he was not part of that process. He also knew that his little boy was distressed and needed him, fearful and worried for his mummy.

Marcus felt his phone buzz. It was a text from Taylor asking how everyone was, never imagining there would be a problem.

He looked at his phone blankly, and just stared, not quite ready to share the delight of being a father again without knowing if his wife was going to be okay. She was his main focus.

He pulled out his phone and typed a short text. "Baby girl. Maria is in surgery. I'll let you know." There were none of the normal pleasantries, it was very matter of fact.

Taylor took a deep breath and clutched the phone to her chest, her eyes filling with tears. She knew Marcus. Everything was not okay.

She turned to Fran for assistance. "Fran, you'll have to hold the fort. I need to go to the hospital!"

"Like hell you will. I'm coming with you. He's our friend

and he needs us!" Fran stated indignantly, not willing to be sidelined.

Taylor realised her mistake. "Okay, keep your hair on. Radio Chris, and let him know where we'll be and that he's it until we're back!"

The detectives raced through town, the traffic causing them some issues, until Fran took out the blue light, flipped it onto the roof and pushed the siren on. Traffic parted like the sea.

Taylor looked at her as if to say she was being naughty, with an expression that would not have been normal for her in the past, her new role and recent warning making her fearful of bending the rules quite so readily.

Fran just shook her head. "This is life or death, possibly, and can be explained, if necessary. We can't spend an hour getting there, and I'm not prepared to do that, not for this!"

She was right. The traffic was crawling in the city centre, and they did not know how serious the situation was. Time was of the essence.

Decision made and rationalised, her foot pressed harder on the pedal as she moved out onto the opposite carriageway. Off she sped, skilled at manoeuvring through tight spaces. She was an advanced driver and had not failed in any pursuits so far.

Chapter 28

Knock, Knock

Kay had received a text from Taylor and offered to join her at the hospital, as she too liked Marcus and Maria, but this was quickly retracted when Taylor mentioned she was there with Fran.

Kay's tummy flipped and cramped a little, her fear that history may repeat itself now in the forefront of her mind, but still she didn't want to join them, knowing that it would feel awkward, even though she now trusted Taylor and had spoken with Fran, and they now got on better. They had to share an office and it was necessary to keep the peace professionally, albeit she would never let her guard down fully, once bitten twice shy.

She sat in her living room. It was already getting dark, and she was later home than the shift would have taken. Her thoughts were with Marcus. She too really liked him and his wife. They were a truly genuine and loving couple. Marcus was funny and kind and totally smitten with his wife and family. Kay prayed Maria would get through this.

She was a bit chilly, and the night was cold and dark, so she decided to get up from the couch and close the curtains.

Outside, the light beamed from within her living room. Kay's every movement was being observed. A well-chosen spot behind a bush gave him cover, a good view. He could watch undisturbed and had been doing so for the last hour. This time he was braver and had decided to move from his vehicle to the garden, when he saw that Taylor hadn't come back at her usual time.

He watched Kay's every move, her figure, her clothing, her facial expressions, her face whilst on the phone, the flush of her face and the obvious change of mood, all of which had kept him intrigued and strangely aroused. He almost felt he was living it with her.

Kay took a moment to look out of the window and up and down the street, something she had done every night and day since the incident at the hands of serial rapist John Brennan. She looked down into the garden area to check that too. She stared at the bush where Findlay stood, still as a statue, hidden by the foliage, squinting when she thought she saw it move. She looked up at the trees to see how windy it was outside, to rationalise her growing fear. To her relief, the trees were swaying, and when she looked at the bush again, this time, it lay still.

His eyes widened as he stared at hers. It was as if she was looking right at him. He thought he had been spotted but chose not to run yet. He would leave if she left the window. There was no way she could identify him, not with him being secreted in the bush.

Kay shook off her thoughts, still looking straight at the bush, checking, making sure, telling herself she hadn't actually seen anything that couldn't have been caused by the wind, but the movement was enough to keep her looking, and she felt slightly more uneasy, an unexplainable sensation, the feeling that someone had just walked over her grave, that she was being watched, but there was nothing to be seen.

One more look around the garden, and then back to the bush. It lay still as the trees continued to sway, making her feel even more tense and anxious. Her logical thinking couldn't find a reason for the previous movement if the wind wasn't moving it now. She felt sick.

She gripped the curtains, her blouse pulling tight over her body and breasts. His eyes, transfixed on her eyes initially, now lowered to enjoy the view of her breasts, while managing to remain statue still, ensuring he wasn't discovered. He revelled in the delight of her now obvious fear and unease. The thrill of watching, waiting and stalking this already vulnerable young woman was exhilarating and addictive.

Kay moved slowly away from the window, fear rippling through her, and sat back on the settee after pouring herself a glass of wine to settle her nerves. She tried to phone Taylor to alleviate her fears, to calm her down, something Taylor was very good at, but there was no answer from her partner's phone. It went straight to voicemail. Dismayed, Kay felt even more alone and vulnerable, but she rationalised it, knowing there was always a poor service in the hospital, assuring herself that was where Taylor was. Eventually, she nodded off with the TV on in the corner, her mind still darting through the visions of the past, until she came to her safe place, one that she had trained her subconscious mind to take her to when she felt frightened, even in her sleep.

They took a deep breath as they reached the door, taking time to ingest every little thing, the bright colour of the door, the flooring outside the door, the ornaments and the outwardly feminine touches made to enhance the look. Their hand rose up to knock. They knew they were not either expected nor would be welcome, but the thrill of what they were doing was too intense to worry about what may happen to them once inside.

Their hand slipped into their pocket, caressing the bottle of Rohypnol there, alongside a makeshift ligature, nondescript, easily obtained and unidentifiable if their hands remained gloved. Excitement rose in their belly and the decision was made. I need to do this now, you'll never make me feel like that again, never! Unhealthy, vile and resentful thoughts engulfed them. There was no turning back. Vengeful desires and the need to even the score were to the fore.

He jumped up as the light knock came at the door, muttering under his breath, "Who the fuck will this be at this time of night?" not really wanting to answer the door.

On peering through the peephole, he saw who it was and decided not to answer the door, but she had already heard him in the hallway, and her course was set. She wouldn't be denied her time. She took her chance and turned the handle and, to her surprise, the partner of a cop had failed to lock the door. How unlucky for him, that was his only chance to survive this visit, Kerri thought, as she pushed open the door to see Phil heading back towards what she assumed was the living room, having chosen not to answer the door.

"Hello, Phil!" she said, completely brazen and unnerved by her intrusion without invite. She knew how to play the victim, and to make him feel guilty enough to allow her in, and give her time to listen to what she had to say, to make him think he had another chance to save her damaged soul, which is what he would want to do, what he was trained to do. The thought made her laugh to the point it showed, and a very girly giggle escaped her mouth. She knew she was no match for him one on one, as he was muscular and strong.

Phil turned and just stood there looking at her. Her head was tilted slightly to the side. She was tiny, so vulnerable to look at, but within was a sinister and evil creature, her full sadistic nature yet to be displayed or visualised, and, at present, still unimaginable to him.

"Kerri, this is a wee surprise! Do you not normally wait to be invited in?" he said with angst and false calmness, attempting to feign sympathy, and alarmed she was here in his home.

Kerri was no fool and could see she had unnerved him

and made him a little on edge, but she would sort that. She began to cry, her shoulders heaving up and down, audible sobs emanating from her small frame, her act well-rehearsed and incredibly believable.

Phil was taken aback. He thought she was there to give him another volley of abuse, but perhaps that wasn't the case, going by this very outward release of emotion and weakness.

He wasn't a naïve man, but he felt sorry for her. She had clearly had a crush on him, and he had sent her immature world crashing down around her and, as his overriding aim was to save as many of these vulnerable young people as he could, he set to work on trying to put right what she thought he had done wrong. Certainly, it had not been deliberate.

"Come in, Kerri. Come through and I'll make you something to drink. Do you drink tea? I'm just going to have one," he asked in a kind voice, eyes soft and genuinely caring.

She smiled, outwardly a sweet innocent smile, inwardly a sneer of success, as getting in without trouble or disturbance was what she needed to pull off her macabre plan.

She followed him through, continuing with the lost-puppy, vulnerable façade, and sat in the seat offered to her, close to his, and his closest to the door. Perfect! She smiled.

He left the room and came back in with two big mugs of tea. "Sorry, I never asked what you took, so I brought the sugar through so you can help yourself. I'm a right sweet tooth and take two!"

She leaned forward, took a heaped spoonful of sugar, popped it in her tea and stirred and stirred, until she even began to irritate herself.

Phil's mind was racing, debating whether he should text Chris about her visit, knowing he was held on at work as Marcus was at the hospital.

"Don't be silly! She's just a little girl by nature and in her frame. She can't harm me. Hmm, unless she makes a ludicrous allegation, but that would never hold up!" he reasoned inwardly with himself about this visit, one he would try to keep short, but still do his best for her, his work ethic and integrity pushing to the forefront, and his logical reasoning blighting out any possible danger that he couldn't handle anyway. This girl was tiny in stature.

Phil sat close to her but at a safe distance from any accidental touch of hands. "Kerri, how did you know where I stay?" he asked, his eyes curious as he had never disclosed this and had not been careless with his belongings, or so he thought.

She smiled and put him right straight away. "Do you always keep your wallet in your jacket, inside pocket, when you leave it over a chair when visiting?"

Phil scratched his head. He didn't think he had lost anything, but when she flipped his driving licence onto the table, the realisation that she had been through his pockets hit his guts like a stone.

"How could she get that, I was there, I never left the room?"

He hadn't realised how adept her hands were and her speed of movement. She had also learned distraction techniques from her time in care, which kept her in money too.

Phil was taken aback. "Wow, thanks!" he said sarcastically, not offering any kudos for her untrustworthy act attempting to keep things calm. He was irked at the audacity of this girl.

"Have you got any biscuits? I'm starving," she asked, her slight frame clearly in need of more nourishment. Phil loved a biccy with his tea, so jumped up to quickly go through to the kitchen and get some to neutralise their cravings, never giving a second thought at what she might do.

Her hand shook as she twisted off the cap and poured a decent quantity of tasteless, odourless liquid into his tea, not enough to make it cold, but enough. She listened as she poured, fearful of being caught.

Phil wasn't gone long, and arrived back in the room with

three different packets of biscuits, chocolate, shortbread and cream-centred ones.

"Variety is the spice of life!" he said, smiling, liking all of what he had brought through to the living room and looking forward to having one of each.

Kerri was still sitting firmly in her seat and looking up at him, wide-eyed and unemotional.

He offered her a biscuit, and she took several, confirming her genuine hunger in his eyes as she scoffed them all, one after the other, playing into his hands, not really wanting food at all.

He settled back in his chair, already on his second mouthful of chocolate biscuit, a large cup of tea in his hand. He slurped at it, taking a big gulp, helping to swallow the biscuit down, then another and another.

"So, tell me, why are you here? Have you come to bring my driving licence back or do you need to talk about something?" He was still lucid and in control of all his faculties.

Kerri watched and chose to answer to keep him focussed on her as he slowly ingested the drug.

As she started to speak, he munched on another biscuit and gulped more tea, all heightening the chance of taking in a more incapacitating amount of the drug, with irreversible affects. The inability to move or defend himself would come in a short space of time.

He listened as she told him of her family and her loss of trust and identity, and her brother, and her father's assault on her, and her mother's denial. She blurted it out in quick succession to give him a sense of achievement at her opening up to him, her secrets laid bare, a start to her recovery in his mind. Kerri knew her secrets would remain safe, as he would soon be unable to speak or defend himself.

He finished his full cup of tea, a quick drinker once started. This allowed him to offer her his full attention. He noticed his hand tremoring as he laid down the cup, loudly clacking it on the glass table, his heavy-handed touch a worry to him. Chris would be raging if he damaged it, as it was designer and he had picked it, flamboyant by design but certainly not robust. He hadn't realised his lack of control and just thought he was being clumsy.

Kerri's eyes became fixed and dilated, pure evil filling her mind, her prey becoming weak. Soon Phil would be unable to defend himself from her final plan.

"Are you okay, Phil? Can I get you something?" she said with a hint of cruelty in her voice. She sat poised as she watched, a bit like a praying mantis about to devour her mate.

He looked at her through cloudy eyes and caught sight of her sneer. "Kerri, what have you done? What have you given me? Don't do this. Help me! Do the right thing. You can't come back from this if you take it any further!" The realisation of the situation hit him hard. He could feel his limbs falter, and there was panic in his eyes. His mind wanted him to lunge at her, but his body remained still.

"What are you talking about, Philip? I've not given you anything, although do you gay guys not take this stuff anyway? I've read about you all and what you do!" She smiled. "It won't kill you, but you won't be able to move!"

This he had already discovered.

She continued talking at him. "But you'll have to watch me when I kill you!" Her smile was cruel and filled with resentment and entitlement because, in her mind, he had wronged her, made a fool out of her, with his lies and deceit, luring her in the way he did, making her believe that he cared about her, making her like him under false pretences.

"Why? I never lied to you. I want to help you. I genuinely do. Don't do this, please!" Phil could see her demeanour had changed, her eyes fully glazed over and no longer listening to him begging her. His voice was beginning to falter, and he could feel his mouth and ability to articulate properly decreasing quickly.

She did not answer and now stood behind him. He had slumped forward, aware but unable to move, still conscious as she put her nitrile gloves on, snapping them loudly, causing his fear to deepen. She pulled a ligature out of her pocket, ready for use.

She lifted up his head and looked into his eyes and said, "You should have locked the door, Philip," as she threaded the ligature carefully under his chin and all the way around his neck. She pulled it a little and watched the terror build in his eyes, tears appearing at the realisation of his fate, his hands motionless and nonfunctional, the commands from his brain failing to ignite the movement he desperately demanded of them, his lips trying to form words in an attempt to stop her.

She looped the other end of the noose onto the door handle and lifted his head up, using the door as a kind of winch, smiling and watching as the ligature tightened it again, enjoying the fear and terror that was staring back at her. She liked how powerful it made her feel, how she drew strength from what she was capable of, growing with every soul she took. She also believed she was clever and almost invincible. Nobody had ever questioned her for anything she had done lately; no one was even looking for her. She felt like a God.

She pulled tightly and pulled the chair back, which toppled Phil forward, putting his full weight on the ligature as it started to throttle him. His eyes bulged, his face turned purple and it was clear he could no longer breathe.

Kerri's head turned in a puppet-like fashion. She licked her lips as he gurgled and slavered, drool dangling down from his mouth, as his life slowly drained away from him. He couldn't even raise a hand to stop it.

She watched with intense curiosity, admiring her work,

until there was no more movement, his weight fully forward while his knees remained on the floor.

Once she believed he was dead, she left him suspended there, no emotion shown or felt as she picked up the teacup, wrappers and anything she had touched. She wiped the driver's licence down and lifted his head up one last time to check he was dead. She was meticulous in her clear-up. She wanted her visit to be unseen and invisible to police detection. She took a last look around the room. It was time to leave, now that her body was fully charged with the thrill and power of her callous and misplaced murder of this beautiful, innocent, kind man.

She pulled her hood up before she left, closed the door, keeping her gloves on, and crept slowly and carefully through the common stair back door, praying no one was around to see her. Once outside, she hopped over a few fences and disappeared discreetly into the night, a smile creeping over her face.

As she got further away, a cackle came from beneath the hood, her eyes bright and alive, her heart pounding and tingling, exhilaration coursing through her veins.

"He got what was coming to him. That will teach him to lead me on, fucking faggot!"

She had looked over the scene. It would look plausible that he had killed himself, although there would be no obvious reason but, as she knew, there was no knowing the depths of depression and despair that can lie beneath the outwardly happy and well-looking exterior of many that the rest of the world doesn't get to see, and don't have a clue what is on their mind, until they are gone and it is too late to save them.

She started to skip, a bit like a young child, her twisted sense of self-righteousness filling her with reasoning. This man had deceived her, and she didn't let things like that happen to her, not anymore. Never again would anyone cross her, nor would she trust anyone ever again, and now if she wanted to harm someone, anyone, for no reason, then she would. She would decide, and once the person was chosen, they would succumb, without a chance given to plead their case.

Chapter 29

Who's Been Watching You?

Taylor looked at her phone and saw there was a message from Kay. Once she read it, she was torn by the need of a desperate friend, still waiting to see if his wife would survive, and her partner who was spooked at home. Just as she was mentioning it to Marcus and about to have to make the decision of what to do, a surgeon came out of Resus, having been in there for two long hours. He removed his mask and came over to Marcus, who sat with his hand in Taylor's and his arm around David.

"Hello, I'm Dr Morag Nicholson. Are you Mr Black?" Once Marcus confirmed who he was, the surgeon continued, "I've been treating you wife, and I'm pleased to inform you she's no longer in a critical condition. She lost a lot of blood and was haemorrhaging badly, but we've managed to stop the bleed and carried out a transfusion to replace the loss of blood. Her condition has improved greatly and she's now what we call stable. I'm afraid we'll have to keep her here for a few days in intensive care to monitor her closely and be there if there are any further complications. I also have other news for you, about the little one, your daughter. She's doing well, and has certainly found her voice. The nurse will bring her through to the ward where you can stay if you'd like and get to know her a little better!" She smiled kindly, before shaking Marcus's hand and squeezing his shoulders caringly, noticing that Marcus was sheet white in terror at what she might have been coming to say.

Tears of joy now filled his eyes and his heart thumped through his chest. The relief was overwhelming and Marcus began to sob openly, relief flooding through him at the news that his soulmate had been saved. His mind had gone through all sorts of scenarios, and the longer she was in there the more and more negative his thoughts had become, although he continued to hope and pray that she would pull through.

Taylor and Fran hugged him between them, nearly squashing Wee Davy in deliberate jest as they did so. Marcus just continued crying in the safety of the arms of his friends and his loving little boy.

"C'mon, Daddy. Let's go and see Mummy; we need to see Mummy and the baby. I need to introduce myself and I want to hold her," Wee Davy said, jumping up.

Marcus pulled him in even more and held him close and told him that he loved him. He cuddled him and tickled him, and smiled, something he hadn't been able to bring himself to do over the last two hours.

Taylor kissed Marcus's face and scrunched his cheeks and congratulated him. She could leave now, knowing Maria was hopefully through the worst of it and that she wouldn't be allowed in to visit anyway.

Fran said her goodbyes as well and handed Wee Davy some pennies to get himself a treat, and he instantly said he would use it for a present for his mum and sister. On hearing that, Taylor too handed the little boy more money. "There's enough for both of them now and a wee sweetie for yourself for being so brave and getting help for your mummy and sister so quickly!" She ruffled his fluffy blond hair, looked towards Fran and gestured to go.

They strode out of the hospital, thinking back to Susan and the evil monster John Brennan, and the cat-and-mouse chase that seemed to go on forever a couple of years back, and to their secret liaisons with one another, all put to the back of their minds these days, for good reason.

Taylor liked Fran, but thought they had had their time together. Exquisite as it was, she couldn't get past Kay and her feelings for her. Fran had been a divine interlude, passionate and exciting, and lovemaking that required athleticism and stamina, and for both, that had not been forgotten, merely put neatly in a box, not to be opened again.

In the car, Taylor was waffling on about Kay and her being frightened in the house when Fran put her hand on Taylor's as she changed gear. Taylor nearly jumped out of her skin, with sensation and surprise. "What the fuck, Fran? You nearly made me crash the bloody car!" She was confused as she looked at Fran and pulled the car safely into the side, as Fran's expression was unreadable.

As Taylor turned to face her and ask what was up, Fran raised up from her seat and kissed Taylor's slightly open mouth, taking full advantage. Her lips were soft and tender, moist and open as she slipped her tongue into Taylor's very surprised mouth. The kiss was tantalisingly seductive, familiar and inviting and, for a couple of seconds, Taylor allowed herself to be kissed, beginning to get carried away with the moment. She kissed Fran back, tongues meeting, and Taylor felt that surge of passion in her stomach, illicit and unfaithful, and that was enough for her to pull away from her former lover.

"You can still feel it. I know you can. I dream about you. I think about you touching me, fucking me, licking me all the time, and I even picture you fucking me when I'm with someone else. I can't get you out of my goddam head, Taylor. I can't just sit by and watch you with Kay and not tell you how I still feel!"

"You mean when you're with your partner, Lana, Fran?

She's not just someone else. I thought you loved her!" Taylor's face was flushed. She was clearly affected by what had just happened, and aware of how it felt to kiss Fran again. It was nice, too nice, as she thought back to the time they shared and their lovemaking. It had been exhilarating and passionate, to say the least. Fran was a willing receiver of as much as Taylor could give her.

"I do love her," Fran said with a sad expression. "I do truly love Lana. She's genuinely wonderful, strong, kind, dependable. The only problem is, she's not you, and all I think about these days is you, just you, you and Kay, you with Kay, you kissing Kay, you fucking Kay. All the time I'm wishing you were still with me. I've missed you so much, your touch. I see you every day at work; I can smell your scent. It drives me crazy, and I watch you loving her and it hurts me. My heart still aches for you, for what we had, and I don't know how to let go, and by God I've tried!"

"Wow, Fran. I'm so sorry. I didn't realise that you still felt that way. I thought we'd moved on, I truly did. I thought you were happy. I caught your look the other day, though, and that explains what's happening now. But you know I'm with Kay, and we're in a faithful committed relationship!" Taylor tried to be truthful. She was in love with Kay, but still thought about Fran on occasion too.

Fran put her hand high up on Taylor's thigh, knowing she would feel the pressure intimately, and she most certainly did. She squirmed away from her touch, Fran's scent, the scent that used to send Taylor's heart racing when she used to bury her face in her neck as she fucked her.

"Fran, stop this! I need to get home. We can't start this again. I can't do this to Kay, not again. She trusts me, and I love her!" Taylor explained seriously and in a definite tone of voice.

Fran looked hurt, her eyes watery and beautiful, her face so pretty, even with the burns and scars from the fire she had been trapped in last year. Taylor's heart felt heavy with the burden of Fran's despair and continued affection, and the new problem she faced, not least with her own unrelenting desire.

"I'll take you back to work and I'll see you to your car, make sure you are okay, and get you back to someone that truly loves you, adores you in fact, and that doesn't happen every day, so be thankful for how good Lana is for you!"

Fran just sat in silence. She had listened, but still couldn't help feeling the same.

Once back at Fettes the old headquarters, they walked silently to Fran's car. Taylor opened her arms to hug her, a hug between friends, holding it for longer to show she truly cared.

Taylor was really late, her head swirling with what had just happened, how Fran had felt, and how her kiss and touch had made her feel once again. She watched Fran leave and then headed home as well.

Taylor parked as close as she could to the house, not noticing a familiar car parked further up the road, just pulling out and exiting through the top road to avoid being noticed.

She skipped up the front steps, anxious to see that Kay was okay. Kay was still in the lounge, but sound asleep on the sofa, an empty bottle of wine on the table.

This made Taylor feel even more guilty for being home late, with Kay sitting in here alone, frightened that there was someone out there watching her.

Taylor left her to sleep and went through to the kitchen to get herself a beer from the fridge before slumping down beside her, the tidal wave of motion enough to wake up Kay. She jumped in surprise that there was someone beside her. The fear kicked back in and she screamed out in terror and started to crawl backwards away from Taylor. Taylor spoke to her softly, and she soon calmed down with her familiar voice, changing direction and moving towards Taylor to cuddle into her, wanting to be held in her arms and feel safe at last.

205

Her nose pressed close to Taylor's neck, her familiar scent reassuring, until she realised it was tinted with another familiar one too, one that she hoped she would never smell again, and she felt nauseous straight away.

She looked up at Taylor, searching her eyes for guilt and avoidance of eye contact, but her gaze was met with steady eyes filled with love, not deceit, and she felt herself relax a little.

Kay had explained about the bush moving in an unusual way even though it was windy. She explained how it had looked odd and not normal, and that it had stayed still the second time she looked, even when the wind was still there. Both Kay and Taylor attempted to rationalise her fear and eventually reasoned that it could have been the wind, as its movement is never the same. They looked out the window together. It was dark and the bush was completely still, with nothing untoward to see.

Later on, Taylor was lying in bed thinking of the day's events, which had been quite something. Kay came out of the ensuite, naked and inviting in her stance, and she made sure that Taylor noticed her before walking slowly towards the bed, seductive in her movement, knowing Taylor was a very visual person, and would be aroused at the view before her. Taylor reached out to touch her, and was pushed dominantly aside as Kay roughly shoved her onto her back and opened her legs firmly and with purpose. Taylor was wet, very wet, too wet.

Kay wondered why, but what she was looking at was heaven to her eyes and she took Taylor into her mouth. Taylor arched her back at Kay's touch, her mouth gentle and arousing, her fingers long and slender, their motion slow and enticing. Taylor's body was close to orgasm already. With the day's events, she needed to let go, and she wanted Kay to fuck her. She watched Kay's cat-like position, her breasts, her bottom, everything sculpted to perfection, and that was enough for Taylor to groan with the pleasure Kay was giving, and she released in a thunderous climax, curling up her thighs as the sensation curled and continued inside her, along with Kay's fingers thrusting into her.

Taylor was about to return the favour and was looking forward to it, but Kay had come up for a cuddle. She had other plans and wrapped her legs around Taylor. She shut her eyes and was asleep in seconds.

The night passed too quickly, both slept deeply, before the hideous sound of the alarm awoke Taylor from her dream-filled sleep, several of which she was glad she wasn't sharing.

They kissed, lingering and passionate, and showered quickly, a playful push and shove to get to the mirror, and Taylor was good to go first, well groomed, and smelling nice in her unisex scent, suit fitted to her athletic body, and the same with the blouse. Kay took in the sight of her lover before she left, a sight she hoped would be hers, forever.

Taylor closed the door behind her and was about to head straight for her car, when she hesitated, and looked over at the bush, smiled and was about to walk past it, shaking her head at what she hoped was just the wind, but couldn't help herself as her curiosity got the better of her. She walked over to it as she needed to make sure for herself it was all just nonsense.

As Taylor walked around the evergreen bush, she noticed a branch or two were bent over and out of place. Her expression filled with curiosity, and on looking down she saw the ground had been disturbed. To her horror, there were heavy-trodden footprints there, clear as day, and Kay had been right with what she had felt: someone had definitely been there, and most likely feasting on the view in the window.

She went back to tell Kay what she had found, and suggest they stay at Taylor's flat for a while after that discovery, which was unsettling to say the least.

Taylor called it in and stayed with Kay until the response officers arrived to take details and get SOCO down to take shoe impressions and carry out a search of where the person had been standing watching. A full enquiry would need to take place, as the intention of the stalker was yet unknown. After she was sure Kay would not be left alone, Taylor headed off to work to see what the day would bring.

Chapter 30

Too Late

Simultaneously, Chris finally left the office. An unexplained death to look over on the back shift had left him with a lot of loose ends to tie up, and he had to make sure CID were aware of their responsibility in relation to ownership of the case, both areas of expertise sharing the tasks and enquiry required into these types of crimes.

He had already sent several texts to Phil, but none of them had been answered, although the first was after 10pm and there was a possibility he would be in bed early, as he had to get up early in the morning for several planned meetings.

He was tired, but he sped through the empty streets making progress as he made haste to get home to his lover. There was hardly any traffic on the roads, and he was looking forward to snuggling into the big strong safe arms of his partner. It seemed like an age since they had said their goodbyes the morning before, too long, but absence makes the heart grow fonder.

He parked his car as close to their flat as he could and skipped up the stairs. He had his keys in his hand, wondering if Phil had taken his advice and locked the bloody door for once, but not surprisingly, he had not! Chris rolled his eyes.

It was dark in their hallway and he chose to keep the lights off, so as not to wake Phil from his well-needed slumber. He crept through and headed to the bathroom, cleaned his teeth, and all the other necessary pre-bed rituals.

He slept naked, so went through to the bedroom to undress. The room felt chillier than normal, and it was unnaturally silent. He let his eyes adjust and saw that the bed was still made. Phil was not there.

His heart skipped a beat, dropping like a stone, instantly worried where Phil might have gone. He pulled out his phone to ring him, standing rooted to the spot, when he heard Phil's ringtone. It was coming from the living room. He was a little annoyed with himself that he had worried so much about what might have happened to him, when he was probably crashed out on the sofa, having maybe had a wee drink or two pre-bedtime.

He rushed through to the living room, pushing the door with force to open it wide, deliberately noisy to wake Phil up and give him a row for falling asleep there, and get him through to the bed.

The door felt very heavy, and he hurt his wrist as he was stopped by the stiffness of the door. There was an unexpected weight behind it, preventing it opening fully.

Puzzled by the door not opening, he put his shoulder into it a bit more and it gave, but still a weight or something was behind it. He put his head around the door and vomit instantly filled his mouth as he saw Phil motionless behind it, his body in a vile and unnatural position. The discolouration in his face was something he had seen many times before at the many deaths he had attended. He knew what he was seeing and what it meant. This didn't stop Chris lifting Phil's weight off the ligature and immediately trying to revive him, hands shaking, terror in his already breaking heart, as he looked down in anguish at his lover's opaque and soulless eyes, his heart willing Phil to survive, his head telling him he was already too late. The signs of death were clear and obvious, but he hoped he was wrong and pumped ferociously down on Phil's chest.

Chris knew that he needed assistance if there was any chance of Phil surviving, and dialled 999 after the first few cycles of CPR. Tears streamed down his face, as he desperately tried to save his soulmate. His heart was sore with the reality of the situation and that he was too late.

"Why? Why would you leave me? You should have come to me. Why would you do this to yourself? You never said there was anything wrong."

His police mind began to question what he was seeing, what he knew, his head going into overdrive. He knew this man, his lover, and there had never been a sign of depression, unhappiness, low mood or suicidal thoughts. There was no way this beautiful, strong, confident man would ever take his own life. Something else had caused his death.

Within minutes, police and ambulance arrived, and they took over from Chris, quickly and efficiently fitting the defibrillator. The line was flat. It was too late to save him. There was no survivable rhythm or output. He was already gone. Chris dropped to his knees, his heart in agony, the loss all-consuming. He fell on top of Phil's motionless body, sobbing for all to see.

Officers let him hold Phil for a while, aware that this would become a crime scene and that he shouldn't touch the victim, but he had already given CPR, and his DNA was already there. They had to eventually prise Chris away. Phil's lifeless body was now cold to the touch, although there was still warmth in certain areas, which made Chris even more angry as he had been so late home from work. Maybe if he had come home on time, he would have been able to save him.

Taylor was at work earlier than normal, trying to make up time from the late shift the night before. The enquiry at Kay's house had delayed her a bit, but she was still early, and she wondered what she had missed.

The office was a hive of activity. There was a definite buzz about the place, and it was more frenzied than normal. Eyes were dropping as she looked towards them for an explanation as to what was going on.

"Has there been a Murrrderrrr?" she said trying to bring a little humour to the sullen faces she was met with.

The nightshift sergeant had only just realised Taylor was there, an hour earlier than normal, and was surprised to see her. She moved towards her swiftly, knowing she had to be told quickly before she used any more misplaced humour.

DS Liz McFarlane took Taylor's arm and beckoned her gently towards her office, away from the detectives busily phoning and arranging SOCO and resources for a crime scene, which was nothing out of the ordinary.

Taylor was a little perturbed, wondering what had happened, unsure of the mood of the others, impatient to know what was going on that would cause this much concern and oddness, until DS McFarlane started to reveal the reason for the mood and hustle and bustle in the office.

Taylor sat silently and caught her breath as she found out about Chris's partner being found dead in their apartment.

"Where's Chris? How is he? Does he know anything about how it happened?"

"He's in the interview room, speaking with the officers. He's in bits, although that's to be expected. He'd only just left here. It was a busy night, shitloads going on!" DS McFarlane said kindly.

Taylor felt her stomach knot as she realised that, because she had gone to Marcus, poor Chris had had to stay and keep an eye on things, and in turn that made him late home. She regained her focus, and asked, "What's the story? What are your thoughts?"

"No thoughts really. He was found hanging behind the door, bent forward on his knees, textbook suicide, door unlocked though, but apparently that's normal."

Taylor raised her eyebrows. "What, suicide! You're kidding me? He didn't seem unhappy, in fact the exact opposite. Surely there must be more to it. This needs looked in to."

DS McFarlane sighed. "There was nothing out of the ordinary in their flat and no defence wounds on him. SOCO are heading down. CID have been there, and even though Chris is adamant that he would never take his own life, it's all looking that way at the moment, unfortunately."

"What about toxicology? They'll be taking samples, won't they?" Taylor looked at her with concern.

"Not necessarily. Everything's pointing to suicide, I'm afraid. You know how costly samples are, and, without a reason, they're not a given."

Taylor stood in silence, digesting what had been said. She knew fine well that without evidence of a crime, they wouldn't do everything just because a partner didn't think their loved one would do that type of thing. It was how the majority of loved ones who had lost a partner to suicide reacted, always searching for a more sinister reason for their demise. It was always better than the unthinkable thought that their loved ones were so lost that there was no way out other than to take their own precious life.

Chapter 31

Family Ties

Kerri was sitting in her room, smiling at herself in the mirror. She liked her impish features, her bright eyes, filled with delight, her appearance almost angelic. Momentary happiness filled her. Her vengeance was cruel and unkind, she herself damaged and alone, needing something – trust, security – but her mind she couldn't get past the betrayal. Everyone had turned on her. She had nobody, her immature feelings unable to deal with so much loss.

Her happy mood did not last long, though, and her eyes darkened once again as she felt a shudder down her spine. She felt nauseous, rage filling every fibre of her soul. The killing of an innocent man had only quenched her vengeful mood for a short while. Her bloodlust was back. Her heart pounded almost out of her chest. She felt she couldn't breathe. She was grasping at her neck, visions of her father grabbing at her in a vile and depraved way coming at her, her cruel and disloyal mother, her awkward, but loyal brother. She gasped and gasped, but struggled to get enough air into her lungs. Whatever had caused this fit of anxiety was giving her physical symptoms, and she passed out on the bed, fully clothed, her bed still made.

Morning came and the staff, one of whom was Inga, were doing the rounds checking on the residents, making sure they were all still there. They were late because there were already two absconders, both missing since the evening before. Officers were there taking the reports for the missing persons application and checking the CCTV to see what they had been wearing and the exact time they left the unit.

At that time, Chris was still giving a statement to the police. He was going over everything Phil had been doing, his plans, his mood, his life story, who he had been dealing with in relation to his work. He mentioned the odd and fixated girl at the Drymuir young person's unit. He was aware that Phil had said she was tiny in stature and, in his mind, not capable of harming such a well-built, strong and big man. The officers took down every detail spoken, aware that this was a colleague, a very distraught one, one that was utterly convinced his partner was of sound mind and the furthest person from suicide on earth. The officer taking the statement had dealt with many suicides and many victims who said similar things. He listened to everything said, the plans made, the lack of any other background that would lead to Phil taking his life. There seemed to be nothing, nothing at all, to suggest this was on the cards, planned, or even thought of, no note, no preparations, absolutely nothing. Although this could have been so many other people's version of events, he was going to explain everything to CID, just because of the absolute negative regarding evidence of why he would take his own life. There was also no evidence to suggest otherwise, but Chris was a colleague and he had to see if this could be taken further.

Taylor was at her desk when the CID contacted her department. DS Thomson explained everything they had, or didn't have, pointing out that there may be more to it, without a shred of evidence to back up his view, which left everyone in charge with tough decisions to make.

Taylor knew it would be her decision to take things further if Phil's death was deemed suspicious, a difficult one for her, damned if you do, damned if you don't, a waste of money if it was suicide but an unknown suspect still out there if it wasn't.

Kay walked up to the glass-fronted office and smiled at Taylor. She too was upset for Chris and what he must be feeling. Taylor beckoned her into the office and asked her to take a seat. "I need a friend just now, an extra opinion. For once in my career, I've been left with a decision to put to senior officers for a final say on what should be done relating to Philip Chancellor's death, and it's down to me to say yes or no, to even argue the case for further investigation, without a bloody shred of evidence to say a crime has been committed. It's merely an opinion of a colleague that something more sinister has gone on there, as he knows the victim. Would we take this further for anyone else, who wasn't a colleague? No," Taylor sighed into her hands.

"What do you believe in your heart?" Kay reached out and held both Taylor's hands.

Taylor looked up, her eyes red and filled with emotion. "That doesn't matter, does it? My decision has to be objective. It's down to what we can prove, putting the case forward without looking like an emotional fool and being overly loyal to a colleague, a colleague that just doesn't want to accept the truth, that his partner took their own life."

Kay offered her opinion. "No evidence or not, you could investigate a little, to prove or disprove a theory, without going full hog, just negate the possibility of what Chris believes, a bit of extra CCTV work, have officers speak to all the young people he was dealing with, and keep Phil's body forensically preserved for samples later, if required. Say it how it is, what initial steps you're planning to take, just to be sure there's been nothing untoward, for your own peace of mind and for your friend, Chris. Go with your gut, practice what you preach. It's what you keep telling me. You're only asking me because you'd have already written it off as a suicide straight away if you'd been sure, and it's clearly not what you believe either."

Taylor looked up at Kay and, for the first time, she smiled, her decision made. Kay was right; she knew her partner. This suicide didn't sit right with her either. Their conversation showed how much her partner knew her, and if something happened to her, Kay would respond like Chris, who also had a deeper knowledge of his partner and a true belief that he would not have taken his own life. She would want Kay's thoughts taken seriously too.

Kay got up and smiled, having helped Taylor, who she knew very rarely reached out for help. Fran, who was at her desk, looked on at them both, her resentment getting a little unhealthier and starting to hurt, as she watched their bond and obvious affection for one another.

When Kay had left, Taylor picked up the phone and rang Superintendent Brooke Sommerville, hoping she would understand what she was going to do with her resources, with only a suspicion, not evidence, in the hope there would be something amiss.

Heartbroken, Chris was not permitted to go back to his home. It was now a secured locus for further enquiry, until a decision was made, so he headed to his mother's house, but he was okay with that. He knew she would reach out to him and understand his grief and look after him.

Philip Chancellor's body was still in situ within the house, SOCO photographing everything, standard procedure for suicides, but their brief was a little more in-depth, a search for further clues to any wrongdoing.

Bins were emptied, everything was noted, every detail photographed for further examination, looking for clues. The officer taking the photos stopped and photographed the tiniest piece of biscuit wrapper, the piece that would be torn when opening a new packet. It had been found poking out from under the cupboard. Not really thinking much about it, he clicked the camera and put the wrapper in an evidence bag.

Cupboards were opened, pictures taken of contents, everyone looking for clues of anything untoward, things missing, cups used, anything that would point to foul play.

Once the photographs and samples were taken, DNA was taken from Phil's body. Chris had already had his taken for elimination to compare against any samples found in their flat.

Officers accompanied the body to the morgue and filled out the paperwork, and the flat was sealed to prevent access.

Inga knocked on Kerri's door. There was no answer, so she unlocked it and went inside. Kerri was lying on her bed, she appeared to be sleeping, but Inga noticed that the bed was unmade. This was not normal for Kerri. She loved her bed and very rarely got out of it in time. She still had her clothes on, and that too was not normal. Inga had checked on her last night at 9pm and she had been in her room and just about to go to bed. Could she have gone out last night? Why? She didn't have friends. Inga was worried for her, due to her past and promiscuity with older men, her vulnerability and the fact she didn't care about her own welfare, frequently putting herself in harm's way. Inga believed she had turned a corner in relation to that behaviour, but maybe not. She could ask her, but she knew Kerri wouldn't tell her anything, so CCTV was the way forward.

She shook Kerri by the shoulders, and she woke up with a start, her face angry and red where she had been lying on it. "What the fuck? Get out of my room. Leave me alone, ya fuckin weirdo!"

Inga was irked at Kerri's response and was at the end or her tether with her. She would look into this. This girl was skating on thin ice, and there was something about her, something not quite right. She was no longer willing to give her the benefit of the doubt. "I need to speak to you. Were you out last night?" Inga was direct and straight to the point.

"No, why? It's none of your fucking business!" Kerri stood up and moved right into Inga's face, her thoughts dark and quickly losing control. Restraint from acting on complete impulse was starting to take over, her sense of reason and self-preservation now waning. Her fears of being caught for the crimes she had committed were catching up with her, her real feelings betraying her, sadness and loss, masked with hatred and revenge. She needed to get the ones who caused this, the ones who let her down so badly, the ones that had caused all of her loss. The noose was tightening on her. She knew everything would catch up with her, so she needed to finish this.

Chapter 32

Time to Deal With Them

Findlay paced around his house, the emptiness consuming him, his thoughts no longer clear, the divorce papers fresh out of the envelope in his pudgy hand, ruddy faced, sweat beads on his forehead, and a hateful anger building inside him.

In his mind he was surrounded by deceitful women, those that couldn't be trusted, flirts, cock teasers, gold diggers, bitches, all sluts, whores or dykes, and no match for men.

He was getting more and more disassociated with reality. He knew he had overstepped the mark that day at work. He had wanted Kay for a long time. Clouded reality had made him take what he thought she might want, enjoying the fear and power as he invaded her space, the rush he had had when he touched her. He had already relived her torment, as he had chosen to read the written statements of her ordeal, with an unhealthy interest in each and every detail relived, her inner soul tormented by her assailant. He lavished in the thought of being the perpetrator, taking this beautiful woman, having her, willing or not. His mind flicked back to the humiliating present. His mates in the police had kept him up to date, letting him know where the criminal enquiry was at and why he was being looked into, and that the items of clothing seized were being forensically examined. He felt a little sick. He knew his hand had stroked over Kay's tights, right up to her crotch, he remembered how it felt to touch her, push into her, wishing he had done more, because he wouldn't be able to explain why his hands were that high up on her thighs and further. His deviance would be proven and claims of careless touching would still leave him in hot water. He could get charged with a sexual offence, although in his mind, it would only be minor. What had he actually done? It was all a mistake; he was only trying to help her!

He shook away his thoughts. He wasn't going to let her ruin his career. He was clever enough to know what he needed to do, introduce a mistake, the element of doubt and explanation. He would try his best to get away with it. Of course, in the panic when he turned her over, he may have accidentally touched her upper leg, or higher, in the haste to move her, which could have happened by mistake quite easily, he convinced himself.

His mind filled with one problem. His mates had failed to let him know there was another investigation underway into the intruder at Kay's home, and that they believed she had a stalker, his mates not knowing to tell him, as they were unaware of the connection.

Findlay did not know his nightly presence had been discovered, and he was looking forward to watching her again, having enjoyed the delights of seeing her lithe body.

He would wait until later to revisit her and make sure Taylor wasn't around, because she was far more aware, and he couldn't risk it. He hated to admit it, but she was a fierce and capable woman, once angry.

Taylor had tainted Kay's mind in his opinion. He was now thinking that she too might have to go. Findlay was no longer thinking like a rational person. He would do what was necessary to save his skin and certainly no longer within the boundaries of the law.

Chapter 33

They Deserved It

The streets were quiet as she walked innocently along, inconspicuous as she made her way. There were only a few cars on the move at this time of night and it was easy to move virtually unnoticed, everyone just getting along with their own business.

Darkness was her friend, her faithful friend, always there, cloaking her evil frame from watching eyes, her gender and identity secreted beneath her clothing. The street lights dim and eerie, their appearance movie-like with the amber glow, most residents happily tucked up safely inside, away from the darkness outside. Five-story tenements lined one side of Lower Granton Road. On the other was a walkway leading to the sea, the street lights over in Fife visible and reflecting an orange glow off of the water, their presence watching peacefully over the Firth of Forth, the lights from the buildings in Edinburgh also mirrored on the water, a romantic scene, the opposite of the torturous light that would soon consume the night sky. The silence would soon be scarred with the screams of terror, hands raised, begging for a saviour, one that she would make sure would not come quickly enough. She stopped and stood still for a moment, taking in a deep cold breath, allowing her mind a little clarity, searching for alternatives, reasons not to do what she was thinking, but her mindset was clear, and the reasoning unchanged. They deserve this, they shouldn't have abandoned me, they are cruel and selfish, they have ruined my life, and I will make them regret their actions.

The window clicked gently, the noise light and unheard, as she gently raised it up, just enough for her tiny frame to slither silently into the room, noiseless and snakelike. She moved from room to room, stealth concealing her steps, familiar with where to place them without making any noise. She knew this house, the smells, the layout, where to hide and where to go to find her prize. She also felt her stomach twist into a painful knot, one of sadness, loss and more recently hatred and resentment. She looked at the door to her old bedroom; it was closed, probably never opened since her abrupt departure. She turned away, her eyes watering, and gently opened the door that was already ajar. She looked into the room, high ceiling, a king-sized bed in the centre, one that totally dominated the room, just like the two people in it. Her eyes narrowed as they adjusted to the dark, focussed like a hawk honing in on its prey, making sure they were both present. Her blood felt cold in her veins, but her heart was on fire, alight with the desire to harm these people, reap her revenge. In her eyes, they deserved it, her mother for not protecting her and him for being a depraved and weak pervert, who was now disgusting, needy and untrustworthy, a paedophile. He should have loved her in a different way and protected her. She looked at them, hatred creeping through her veins. She hoped that what she was about to do would free her from the pain she was suffering. Everything else she had done lately had only felt good for a short time, her emotions fighting with her.

Her heart fluttered with cruelty in anticipation of the unbridled pain and suffering that would soon come to them. With this, her thoughts warmed her inside as she pulled out the accelerant knowing that speed was of the essence, as the smell was strong and could wake them up before the fire took hold and they started to burn.

The spray was silent and slick, the contents flowing quickly from the canister onto the carpet and bedding, her nerves and impatience kicking in, fear of being discovered creeping up her spine, knowing they could overpower her together, or that she herself could get caught up in the fire.

She saw her father move. Her hair stood on end. She knew he would smell it; he always had a good sense of smell. He sat straight up, and she watched him catch his breath as he rubbed his eyes, disbelief in seeing his daughter standing in the door-way, not even thinking of what the smell was that was now invading his nostrils. His fear was only for himself, knowing what he had done to this girl and worried about what she could do to him, and knowing why she would want to.

She was glad to be looking into his eyes, silent vengeful sig-nals passing between them. Her head tilted to the side, like a broken puppet, dark shark-like eyes, dark and void of emotion, but with a smile that was sweet and childlike. He blinked and tried to focus a little more in the dark. He couldn't read her thoughts, he never really could, but the fear within him, made it nearly impossible to move. He was rooted to the spot and very wary of her.

He jumped when she started to cackle at him loudly. She flicked the lighter, and a long slim flame rose brightly into the air, the flame lighting up her eyes, dark and sinister, now with a hint of colour, a sweet smile still fixed on her face. Her head moved maniacally and quickly to the other side, and back again, the motion unnatural and odd, terrifying to watch, demon-like, as if she was possessed. Finally, her father man-aged to move and raised up from the bed towards her. Her mother was awake now and sat bolt upright. When their eyes met, her loveless resentful hostility was clear and obvious. She was quick to speak, her vile and hostile words coming with rapid fire from her venomous mouth. With her there was no fear, just a nasty barrage of words, every one of them reaching its target with force, but this did not deter Kerri, it just fuelled her already present hatred and made her even more determined. Any hesitation that there might have been, to stop her doing this, was now well and truly gone. Her mother got up quickly and sprinted towards her, her face filled with anger. She was resentful and unkind, ready to scold and assault her daughter, but before she could reach her, Kerri sprayed her with the can of accelerant, full force in the face, the pressurised liquid igniting as it passed over the naked flame. The fuel burned brightly with a whoosh, the spray of flame covering her mother who was still rapidly heading towards her, the floor and bedding also catching fire, the room instantly ablaze. Her dad, who was also moving towards her, was not quick enough, and he too was sprayed mercilessly with fire.

His words were audible and desperate. "Don't! Stop!" her dad yelled out at her, his pyjamas now on fire, the fabric assisting with the inferno, nylon melting against his skin, his screams guttural and hideous, the pain obvious as he contorted and flailed out in a feeble attempt to put out the flames.

Simultaneously, her mother, now on fire, was much quicker to get close to her, the only words uttered were, "Don't you dare you, you spiteful little bitch!"

With only a slight twist of her hips to avoid any contact and another forceful squeeze on the container, Kerri sent another rush of fiery liquid straight into her face this time. The torturous screams were like music to her ears. Her eyes gently closed and opened again quickly, not wanting to miss the show, watching her mother screaming and holding her face, frantically trying to stop the flames that were about to engulf her, but she was already burning and weeping. A waxy substance appeared as her face started to melt, and so would Kerri if she stayed there a second longer. She had achieved what she came to do. She turned on her heels and headed back to the doorway.

She slammed the door and turned her father's special key, a key that she knew only too well, allowing time and privacy, time to conceal what was going on. The door was solid and would be slow to perish in the flames. It would withstand any level of barrage from these meagre human beings within, and certainly not without tools. She took one last look at the door, listening to them inside, their futile screams loud and desperate. The child within her was terrorised at what she had just done, and there was a hesitation, a feeling of remorse. Was there a chance to reverse it? Her hand reached towards the door, but the young vengeful woman within stopped her almost instantly, redirected her thoughts back to what they had done and reminded her that they deserved her wrath. The cruel grin reappeared on her face and she sneered happily at what she had done, once again revelling in the pain and cruelty they would suffer, rationalising her reasons and putting any doubts back where they belonged. She headed for the stairs. The screams would not be as audible down there.

But her escape route was now blocked, obstructed by her oversized simpleton brother. He was smiling at her and appeared happy to see her. He had helped her out with a few things recently; the sheer weight of a dead body was something she couldn't carry herself. He was pretty strong, obedient and completely gullible, believing her lies and threats, the offer of endless treats making up his mind to do what she said if and when she needed him. He didn't have the mental capacity to think of the consequences, or wonder why there were dead men. He just knew not to tell, or he would face her wrath, cruel words and punishment. For once her thoughts betrayed her. She felt something. It was odd and not familiar, but she was having difficulty right now. She had come there to kill them all, no witnesses, no memories, no more living history. It had been easy in the planning, and she had never once thought she would hesitate, and certainly not twice. She actually felt something for this big dummy standing in front of her.

He reached out his arms to hug her. He clearly loved his sister, but she feared that he couldn't survive without his parents. He'd be sent to some shitty home just like her and would be bullied half to death, and she couldn't have that. But she went to his arms anyway and let him swallow her up in a bear hug. She loved him, but could not protect him from life, and now that she had reaped her revenge on her despicable parents, she had deprived him of his providers. She felt sorry for him as her emotions continued to battle against what she needed to do.

As he hugged her, he asked, "What are you doing here? Do Mum and Dad know you're here? They will not like it if they find out!" As he said the words, he started to sniff the air, unhurried and cartoonlike in his appearance, his reactions and thought process all in slow motion, but he knew what fire smelt like and raised his hands in exclamation. "Oh no, there's a fire, Kerri! Help me get Mum and Dad awake and get them out," he cried, his innocence and sense of reality as to what was happening clouded by his impairment. His desperate eyes staring right at Kerri to help him.

She came to the conclusion that she couldn't kill him, not directly anyway.

"Quick, take this key. I think they're up in the bedroom sleeping. Hurry, you'll need to save them!" she said with her fake concerned face, assisting in his decision.

He grabbed the key from her, doing what she said as usual, and started to run up the stairs with a sense of purpose, his thick and chunky legs moving as quickly as they could. He could see smoke coming from under the door of his parents' room and could hear their screams, blood curdling, with a sense of finality about them, which made him even more terrified, but he knew he had to get in and help them.

Kerri turned and ran out of the door. She knew that her parents would not survive the burns they had already received, and her big daft brother would open the door and increase the oxygen even more. He would be blasted back with the flames as he did so. In her twisted mind he had gone up there through choice, her conscience now devoid of any guilt. He too would now be free of his troubles.

She left through the communal stair back door, and as she was making her way to the back of the garden, she heard a crash and glass tinkling as her mother came flying out of the window like a comet, alight with flames pouring off her body behind as she fell. When she landed, there was a sickening snap as she landed full force onto her head, her neck giving way on impact.

Her brother had reached the door, turned the key, and put his shoulder into it to shove the weight that seemed to be stopping the door from opening. It finally pushed inwards and the unlit smoke swirling around the ceiling lit, and the flames gathered momentum and flashed out of the door straight into his face. His final view was that of his dad's body curled up behind the door, gnarled in appearance and smelling like a roast pork dinner. He screamed at the sight, before his body felt the searing pain of the flames. The scene was unfathomable, for all that would see it, and those now coming to assist would also stand in disbelief at the sight of what lay before them.

Kerri stopped for a moment to look at her mother's deformed and burning corpse. "Oh well, that will teach you to side with the devil and capitulate his crimes just to save your precious reputation. Now you'll burn in hell where you belong, by his side, no longer shielding him from the truth that would have ruined your outwardly perfect little world, you fucking twisted, uncaring bitch, the demon's whore." Kerri sighed and smiled in a resigned manner. "That depraved bastard came to me for what you wouldn't give him, and you knew it, and didn't stop it. What mother does that?"

She looked up at the open window, flames licking out and upwards to the window of the next flat.

She started to move off as the sirens came roaring into the night, too late to save those within. Maybe they could save some of the other tenants in the block, not that she cared that much about anyone anymore. Her past had been pleasurably erased, her dopey brother safe with his parents, where nobody could harm him.

Faces began to appear in their windows, but they were watching the burning building and those trapped inside, not noticing her, her stealthy motion and dark clothing shielding her from view as the fire brigade arrived.

Lana stepped out of one of the fire appliances and started to unreel a massive thick pressure hose, instructing other fire fighters to look for hydrants to link their hoses to. There was only so much water in these units. The crew got to work quickly, their breathing apparatus on, and moved to where the seat of the fire appeared to be.

Police and ambulance crews arrived moments later, the response officers there to close off the streets initially, make enquiries as to what might have happened and assist with those that had already evacuated the building prior to their arrival.

People were told to stay in their homes. The stairway was now a funnel of smoke and acrid fumes, not conducive to life. Lana's team, kitted up with breathing apparatus, moved up the stairs within the two-levelled flat. On reaching the upper landing, they saw a lump of something fuelling the fire and started to douse the flames that were licking the ceiling, the power and intensity forcing them back initially. They directed their hoses together, tackling the flames, their worst fears confirmed. The fuel source was human, and the fat from his flesh had acted like another accelerant and spread the fire on the landing. Lana knew there would be no survivors in here. The intensity of the heat and flames would have killed anyone in there, but they pushed forward, in hope there was a miracle to be had and to prevent further spread of the fire and save the other houses and those trapped within.

Chapter 34

Restless

Findlay sat watching television. He was restless, bored sitting there helplessly doing nothing, his frustration at how he had ended up eating away at him. Why him? Why did these namby pamby politically correct, office-dwelling do-gooders believe these conniving women, their incestuous behaviour, their lies, the way they swan about the office? Had the world turned upside down? Had everything that was normal just disappeared, lost in a new world of infinite freedom? "It shouldn't be happening, it's not right, and not in my fucking lifetime if I can help it," he thought.

He hadn't realised he was gritting his teeth, his hands balling into fists. The desire to watch Kay again was getting more powerful, even if the risks were getting higher. He couldn't find the will or sense to stop himself, and grabbed his keys, forgetting his black jacket, and marched off towards his car, ready to feast his eyes on Kay's beautiful body, or maybe just feast on her, his desire moving from voyeur to the physical. His mind stirred unhealthily, moving onto a more sinister track, to what he wanted to do to her, what he would take from her, and what she as a submissive woman would do for him. His depravity had become boundless since his wife left. He was out of control, filled with hate and resentment. He could no longer demand conjugal rights from her to suppress his unhealthy appetite for sex, selfish self-satisfying sex, and he hadn't had any since that day, except from a screen and the love of his pudgy little hand.

It wasn't dark yet, and he soon realised that his light-coloured top would stick out like a sore thumb. He would be seen if he wasn't careful, but he was agitated and impatient, filled with unhealthy desire and a discomfort down below, his needs unfulfilled, his mind broken, and he was starting to fantasise about hurting her, as she had been hurt before. He had relived her previous ordeal at the hands of Brennan in his thoughts and dreams more than once, reading the files repeatedly, and getting off on them. The arousal from her pain was a powerful draw, and the brutal power and control intrigued him, the ability to take such beautiful treasure without permission becoming more enticing each day. In his day dreams, he would re-enact the scenes over and over. He would play the role of Brennan, and it turned him on. The dominance and control forced upon Kay was now driving him, and he now thought that if she was not willing to give it to him, he would take it anyway. The restraint of being an officer had become a burden, and he knew it, although he didn't want to admit his policing career was over. There was no going back and there was now very little to lose to take that ultimate prize. In his sick mind he wanted her to enjoy him, enjoy him taking her, a fantasy he would make real, his thinking totally deranged, still believing that whatever he did to her must be enjoyable, because it would be for him. He was an overconfident, arrogant, unkind man, who in his life had controlled everything, and he wasn't ready to stop just yet.

Findlay was now a loose cannon and becoming very dangerous, his self-control lost in his fantasy world, his reasoning gone, and no longer restricted by rules. These dyke bitches had seen to that and had ruined everything he had. He was ready to show them who was in charge and that he was their master, ready to take back control at whatever cost. Although his judgement was clouded, he knew he was finished and may ultimately end up in prison, but in his mind for virtually fuck all, so now he was going to sample things that were previously out of reach and go out with a bang. If he was going down, it would be for a very good reason.

He hurtled his car recklessly around the streets. The cobbles were slippery, his tyres bouncing as he sped through the city centre. He was reckless, impatient now with a sense of reasoning, totally out of control as he headed towards Kay's house, his actions drawing attention from passers-by, crazy really, but he wanted Kay. He could almost taste her, and in his desires, he would certainly experience that pleasure, without permission or consent, making sure she would be watching, totally aware and unable to stop him.

His driving was bordering on the ridiculous, the speed increasing, and his foolhardy moves were not going unnoticed. A response car was sitting at a junction when Findlay's car whizzed by. Officers Vicky Horne and Davina Clark were parked up, chatting away, talking fashion, holidays and dogs, when his car whizzed by.

"Did you see that dickhead? He's certainly getting pulled!" Davina said in her South London accent, a transferee from the Met. She was a wise old gal that took no shit from anybody, and could handle herself, a black belt in Judo, and a mouth with similar qualifications.

The air turned blue with his vicious language, his newfound hatred for the police flowing from every vein. The blue lights, gaining from behind, shone brightly in his rear-view mirror, matching the colourful choice of words directed at the feds following him. More venomous words rolled off his tongue towards the cops behind him, the importance and enormity of their stop would never be known by them, his depraved and murderous plans thwarted without being known or provable.

Findlay finally pulled his car into the side abruptly, knowing if he did not, they would just get more assistance to help them, and he would be forced off the road. He got out straight away, his posture defiant and intimidating, and strode aggressively towards the set pulling in behind, something officers didn't like because it puts them at risk, a hostile approach was not acceptable and taken by officers as an aggressive gesture.

"What? What did you stop me for? Speeding? How do you work that out? Your motors don't have the gear to fix speeders. So, tell me, why did you pull me over, eh? Cat got your tongue!" His sarcasm and belittling tone were blatant and unreserved, his attitude stunk and he barely gave the officers a chance to speak to him.

His aggression was boiling over. He was a rude man, abusive and his general behaviour a disgrace, with total disrespect to women.

"Fucking split arses too, just my fucking luck, prick-teasing sluts!" He smirked as he looked down at his feet, his words said in a whispered rasp, but he thought it was not quite loud enough to be audible, because that term was an absolute no-no these days, like a red rag to a bull.

Both officers were now out of their vehicle, and thankfully out of earshot. They moved around and stood in front of him, both small in stature, similar in height to Findlay as he was not tall, their posture was that of control and confidence as they observed this rather dishevelled rotund man, both thinking he wouldn't be too much of an issue to handle, if it came to that.

"Sorry, I didn't quite catch what you said there, sir, the last bit, when you whispered at your feet?" Officer Clark asked in a sarcastic tone, as she had heard quite clearly what the obnoxious little prick had said about them and, with that statement, she knew he must be a cop, as that derogatory term for a female officer was often used by male cops about their genitalia.

Vicky stepped in. She was slightly less experienced and a little less robust, but spoke in a clear and controlled tone. "Calm down, sir! You're indeed right that we don't have the equipment in our car to record your speed, but we do have eyes, two sets of them in fact, which means corroboration that you were indeed speeding, driving carelessly, and that's why we have selected you to stop and warn you about your speed and manner of driving!" Her voice was slightly heightened and clipped, a little unnerved by the boiling hatred oozing from this angry little man.

"Listen, you wet-nosed snotty little bitch! Wind your fucking pretty little neck in. I've done fuck all wrong and I know you can prove fuck all, so stop talking shit. Now why am I still here? You've said your piece. What are you keeping me here for? This is illegal!" His voice was raised, eyes narrowed and confrontational, as he stepped forwards, moving into PC Horne's reactionary gap, closing down her safe space, deliberately, his actions intentional and intimidating.

The more experienced cop moved forward, her presence more formidable. "Sir, step back from my colleague, watch your language and calm down. The way you're acting is not acceptable. This is your last chance to change your behaviour, or you're getting arrested!" She moved right into his space, her intentions clear, with her face right next to his, her tone also threatening, unnerved by his attempts to intimidate them and with the knowledge of her abilities to back it up.

This was a direct challenge to his masculinity. Findlay's face was puce, mottled purple, and he looked like he was going to explode. He was certainly not going to obey these women, and he responded aggressively.

"Eh, and who the fuck do you think you are, Billy big baws? You don't frighten me. Do you know who the fuck you're talking too? I'm Inspector Findlay from the Major Investigation Team, and I'll need your collar numbers cuntstubbles!" he said, deliberately mispronouncing the word, to belittle the officers and undermine their authority.

Unfortunately for him, the cops were not perturbed by this rotund, little man, and even smirked a bit when Findlay came out with the, 'do you know who I am' statement, something they faced with regularity, especially from those who thought they were above the law through either status or misplaced importance, which was clearly not the case here.

PC Clark spoke right into his face, "I don't care if you're the Prime Minister! You'll listen to what we're telling you, and desist from your behaviour, or you will be arrested. Do you understand that?" she said in a forceful, but controlled voice, deliberately invading his personal space.

This infuriated Findlay. "You insubordinate little cow, I'll fucking have your badge." He moved aggressively towards PC Clark, with his fist closed, and motioned to punch her, only to have his legs swept from beneath him, the two officers taking swift and robust action. They pinned him down, securing his arms to get the cuffs on, PC Clark holding him face down and twisting his arms out from beneath him with the help of her baton, with PC Horne clicking the cuffs on with skilled precision and sufficient force for Findlay to feel their application. He was a little stunned at how proficient these pretty little girls were at their job, his thoughts still belittling and condescending.

Vicky Horne stepped forwards and spoke to him, barely out of breath from their swift and controlled encounter. "You're under arrest for assault. I must caution you, you're not obliged to say anything, but anything you do say will be noted and may be used as evidence. Do you understand?" Findlay just growled. She looked at him with disdain and carried on. "Would you like to make a reply to your arrest?" She stared at him, waiting for him to speak, and it was worth waiting for.

Findlay's face was almost purple. "You fucking cock-teasing

sluts, fucking bitches, you're all the same. I'll fucking have you for this, and if these cuffs weren't on, I'd fuck you right up, you fucking useless jobsworth wet-nosed little cows. Where are your husbands? You should be home looking after them." He looked up at their nonplussed expressions. They had heard it all before. Then he stopped, and they could see him thinking of what to say next to try and get a reaction from them.

The pause was long enough for Vicky to continue. "Is that your reply?" she said, before he sneered right at her.

"Aaahh, I get it! Who'd marry a couple of dyke bitches like you pair? You're far too manly to get a fucking man!" His rants were totally unfounded, of course, as both women were far from manly. They were simply strong and confident, and, to the contrary, both straight.

Both women had loving partners, that were not sexist and misogynistic pigs like him and did not feel threatened by having strong, capable independent females in their lives.

PC Clark had had enough of his shit and moved him firmly towards their vehicle, calling in their arrest to control and restrict the incident, as it was an officer that was being arrested. He resisted her push, but she equalled his strength and lifted his cuffed arms higher up his back, which pushed his face forwards, and, due to his belly and lack of flexibility, this proved a little uncomfortable for him, and he stopped resisting and got in the vehicle.

Kay walked into her living room and looked out into the garden. Now back at her apartment, she shivered as she looked at where the stalker had stood. Her hair bristled with tension. She pulled the curtains closed, unknowing of what had been planned for her that evening.

Chapter 35

Revelations

CCTV had been viewed, thousands of hours interrogated by the same poor officers selected for the task for days, and they had found something that could also be nothing. There was a person of similar description, could be male or female, in the town near to both incidents, both classed as suicides at present, but meriting a more in-depth review and, with this new lead, it certainly required more investigation. These incidents may be as they initially seemed, albeit there was only proximity and nothing conclusive to say that the same person had been involved in the two deaths. But it was a massive coincidence to be there on both days, far less at the times and locations of both incidents.

They tried to follow where they had gone after the events, but there were too many black spots not covered by CCTV. They had left town somehow and had not been retraced since their last sighting. Bus CCTV had not been collected at the time and would have been wiped by now.

Marcus was more interested in this than Taylor, as she was still getting heat in relation to Phil Chancellor's death and her not investigating further. Chris was not accepting that it was suicide and was demanding a full PolSa search of his property, to have expert searchers systematically go through every single item in their flat, as this hadn't been done yet. Hopefully there would be something, anything, out of place that would at least throw suspicion into the mix and make them believe him that his partner would never have killed himself and had been murdered.

Chris was on the phone to Taylor, as he was most days, since he was now on special leave due to the bereavement, which was meant to be giving him time to grieve properly. Instead, he was ranting, sobbing, shouting, being calm, a full mixture of emotions, nothing ever the same or settled, and it all stemmed from the fact that he knew his partner better than anyone, but no one was doing anything about it.

Taylor was listening and understood how he felt. She had dealt with many situations like this, when everything pointed to suicide. Unfortunately, it usually was, either by misadventure, or possible accidental or deliberate overuse of substances, nothing she hadn't experienced before, even the denial of loved ones not believing that this could actually be the case, always holding on for something that just wasn't, and not wanting to believe a decision like that.

"What about the girl, the crazy girl, the one he was assigned to at the Drymuir unit? Have you checked her? He said that she liked him," he shrieked down the phone. Even he knew he was clutching at straws, as there had been many young girls that had had a crush on Phil, and deep down he didn't really think it could be Kerri, so how could he convince Taylor, if he wasn't convinced himself?

Taylor, however, had listened, but quickly rationalised it.

"Which girl? He must have worked with numerous young people," Taylor said, with impatience in her tone, not thinking for a minute a juvenile was capable of such a contrived and cruel act. Chris had been on the phone five times already just that day. Her long back shift was nearly over, and she was tired and losing patience. Although he was a colleague and she was trying to see it from his point of view, at the moment there was nothing to substantiate his pleas.

Marcus was listening to their conversation, as Taylor had taken the call in the open plan office, and he was all ears and wondering who they were talking about. She might meet the physical description of the unknown person from the town they had just watched. It was a long shot and still wouldn't be conclusive even if she did meet the description, but if it was her, she would still be classed as a juvenile.

Taylor sighed heavily down the phone. It was unintentional but noticed by Chris. "Sorry boss, am I boring you?" he said with sarcastic venom in his tone, his anger spilling over. "It's only a matter of murder I'm talking about. I know you think I'm bat shit crazy, but I knew him, just like you know Kay. Put yourself in my position. There's no fucking way he killed himself, and he wasn't into any of that kinky choking shit either. He just wouldn't do this, Taylor!" Chris was livid and crying. He couldn't take any more and slammed down the phone.

Taylor stood, mouth agape, still holding the phone just away from her ear, her expression one of disbelief, but he had struck a chord with her. He was right. If the shoe was on the other foot, she would never accept the decision without a fight or proof that she was wrong. She tapped her foot, rubbed her chin, and chose common sense over the budget. She chose to give him that, that doubt of how things looked, or were meant to look, and would take it a couple of steps further to ensure there wasn't something amiss. She would argue the case for further investigation to the powers that be. She started to put the wheels in motion for a full forensic and PolSa search of the property and would send Marcus down to speak with the girl Chris was ranting on about, to put his unfounded theory to the test, but also to visit all of the other young people he was open to as well, to avoid missing any other opportunities.

Marcus looked up at her, meeting her eyes, and gesturing to her "What?"

"Are you able to go and see that girl Phil was assigned to

tomorrow? We at least need to talk to her, see what we can find out about her, see how she is with us, and her reaction to his death, and make sure you mention that he was gay to see what her reaction is, will you?" she said with a pleading smile, knowing he too may cause a certain reaction with her, if Phil had.

Marcus looked keen, also wanting to check on his little theory from the CCTV, choosing not to mention it to Taylor, not just yet, just in case she thought he was stupid too, and she was clearly not in the mood right now. Tomorrow would be better for everyone and if they were similar, only then would he let her know. He was pleased they were going the extra mile for Chris.

"Are you up for that, Marcus? It means you can leave early tonight and change your shift around tomorrow. We can't go there at this time of night without evidence anyway, and she's in care, so we need to respect that she's still treated as a young person, a child, literally, but we have to speak with her, you never know!" Taylor didn't like being press-ganged into doing things she wasn't sure were relevant, but Chris was a colleague and he was relentless in his pursuit of the truth, even though the truth may not be what he wanted to hear.

Marcus was happy with that. He hadn't seen Maria properly all week and it would be nice to surprise her and have time to sit down and talk instead of just climbing into bed in the dark.

He hadn't cuddled the baby recently either, not wanting to wake her, but if there was a night feed required tonight, he would make sure it was his turn, and get his much-needed cuddles that way.

He didn't need to be asked twice, and grabbed his jacket and headed for the door, looking back and saying goodnight to the back shift, and Taylor.

She had a few things to tidy up herself and had to plan for

the next day, still blissfully unaware of the fire and Findlay. These would be treats to savour the next day. CID were currently looking into the fire, and at that time there was no need for the MIT to be informed or involved, those in attendance not quite sure what they were dealing with. The fire service was still there, and the building deemed too unsafe for the officers to enter. They were still venting the building and accounting for all of the other residents. Three melted bodies lay in situ, unidentified. Officers were looking into the voters' roll and housing records to identify the possible occupants.

Fran was still in the office, typing furiously. She had a report to finish, and it had to be in by the following day. She hated unnecessary pressure, but she was nearly there, just filling in the analysis of evidence section and then it would be complete.

As always, she watched Taylor while at work, but tried not to do it too often, as she was still hurting and angry with her boss and she was still in love with her, which she knew was unhealthy and a little unfair. She knew Taylor was under pressure, at one time Fran would have been the person she turned to for comfort, reassurance and stress relief. She coughed falsely to get Taylor's attention, with no response but, the second time, it was successful.

Taylor turned and said, "Would you like some water? That's a nasty cough," her expression sarcastic but kind, knowing that it was deliberate to get her attention.

Fran just smiled, heavy hearted.

"I'm okay, are you?" It was a loaded question. Fran knew full well that Taylor was under the cosh, her new role as acting inspector certainly offering up more stress and responsibility.

"You know me; I'm all good!" This was a blatant lie of course. She knew Fran knew her better than that and could see the signs of stress building up. People were dying, and how was still a mystery. The evidence and sheer volume of it was pointing to foul play, but with no obvious pattern or suspect yet.

"Honestly, I'm okay. There's just a lot going on, here and at home. Nothing's ever simple in my life, as you know. What about you, how's Lana?" Taylor changed the subject back to Fran deliberately.

"Lana's fine, lovely, strong beautiful, and I love you!" she sighed heavily. "I fucking love you! You! You crazy two-timing, heart-tearing addictive woman, but also so tender and caring. You're a fucking gorgeous woman, and I hate you for it!" Fran's eyes were tearful, and her heart was pounding.

She put her head down and spoke sadly, "I need to transfer out of this unit. I can't stand this. You're driving me crazy and you don't even mean it!" Fran was being torn apart inside, just by her proximity to Taylor.

"What? No way! I'm sorry you feel that way, but I'm, I'm with Kay, and, believe me, right now she needs me!" Taylor stared at Fran, her words a little forceful, but Fran was astute, and sensed a little uncertainty in Taylor's voice, and that's all that she needed to know that Taylor was Taylor and would never truly be happy being tied down to anyone, not yet anyway.

"Do you need her though?" Fran's words took Taylor by surprise, the question making her pause. She didn't answer straight away.

"Of course I do, I love her!" Taylor expressed with as much honesty as she could.

"I know you love her? I asked if you need her. You're you, and I don't think you've ever needed anyone." Fran's words were harsh, but Taylor knew they had an element of truth in them.

"You need to get home, Fran. You can send that report to the nightshift sergeant and get it sent away. I need to head now. Kay's alone, and I need to be back in in the morning with Marcus. I'm interested in where this goes, but not convinced this young girl can have anything to do with any of it."

Marcus arrived home. To his surprise the lights were on, and Maria and his lovely daughter were up. The baby was suckling, which spread warmth through his heart, two of the loves of his life sitting there on the sofa, peaceful and precious. He took time to enjoy the view, and then excused himself to quickly head upstairs to peek in at Wee Davy to check on him before going back to join his girls on the sofa. He stood in the doorway, looking over at his little blond angel, and his heart still skipped a beat, one of love, anxiety, and an ever-present fear of losing him again, a swirl of mixed emotions ever since the boy had been abducted and the world had fallen at his feet. It had also shown him that family were the reason to live. He was more protective than ever, but careful not to smother them. His heart filled with love, he headed down the stairs to get his cuddles from the female side of the family.

Marcus sat carefully beside Maria, offering his stubbled face for a kiss, and then leaned in to kiss the baby's forehead, her name finally chosen after a lot of discussion. Her name was Lily. He put a gentle arm around Maria and leaned in to watch the mothering of the child, and he beamed with love.

"I'm a lucky man, and I know it. You are all so beautiful," he said as he looked into her eyes.

Maria, aware that she hadn't showered, had milk in her hair, and that her t-shirt had an aroma that she didn't like too much, looked at him with her lip curled in humour. "Are you blind? Do you have a nose? In fact, once she's fed, can you take her and I will have a quick shower, to let you look again and maybe the view will be better after that?" She smiled at him and kissed him, deliberately leaning in closer, to allow him a wee sniff at her cheesy t-shirt and milky hair.

He laughed and said, "Okay, I'll take the baby, but you're still beautiful, and I really like cheese, so you're still a winner to me. I just need a wee selection of biscuits now!" He laughed at himself.

Maria came back and kissed him full on the lips, and then pulled away and scrunched her t-shirt in his face. She could smell it, so he definitely would, and it was totally rank.

It was her turn to laugh as she walked out of the room, looking over her shoulder, with a little minxiness about her, a look Marcus hadn't seen for a while.

This caused a stir in his tummy. He looked down at little Lily and smiled at the wee tot, happily fed and falling asleep in his arms. "I'm blessed, truly blessed."

He gave his sleeping angel another five minutes, and then headed up the stairs to put her down, as Maria had not yet returned. As he reached the top of the stairs, he saw Maria's naked little bottom disappear into the shower, and he couldn't help but smile, as he too needed a shower, and why waste water? he thought. He quickly but carefully put his daughter into the cot and tucked her in, not a stir, just little angel puffs of breath, and he kissed her head. "Good girl," he whispered knowing that if she had awoken, his next hopeful plan was not to be.

He went out into the hall and naughtily stripped, before gently knocking on the door. Maria looked up from washing herself and beckoned him in with a smile on her face. He looked quite funny standing there, acting all innocently, stark bollock naked. He was clearly pleased to see Maria naked in the shower. She had just put shampoo in her hair. The soap was cascading down over her breasts, and she was using her soaped hands to wash between her legs. This was indeed a great pleasure to watch. Marcus could feel the strain of torment in his groin, from the test of time, but he knew not to push things.

"Well don't just stand there, come in and wash my back, and wherever else you think needs a wash."

Marcus felt like a kid in a sweety shop. Their lovemaking had been sparse, and quite rightly so, but it appeared that Maria was now ready, and so was Marcus.

He stepped into the shower, moved in behind Maria and kissed her neck, sucking gently and gripping a little with his teeth, his hands slipping over her beautiful curvaceous body and enjoying the lubricant of the soap to enhance the sensuality of his touch. Maria obviously liked his touch as she leaned back into him and moaned a little as she opened her luscious mouth to kiss his more rugged one, albeit his lips were soft and tender with his reply. She gripped the outside of his hands and pulled them further around her waist and between her legs and moved them in a rhythmic motion for him, gliding easily with the help of the soap. He knew not to enter her, letting the stingy soap slowly rinse away, leaving her own moisture behind, smooth and inviting. Only then did he let his fingers slip into her a little more, gentle, but strong enough for the sensation to rush through Maria's love-starved body. She let out a moan, loud and needy, her legs parting a little to let him in further, the motion of his hands working together, the stroking over her giving way to the intrusion of his fingers of the other hand and, together, they were irresistible. His fingers delved inside her as the other hand rubbed over her pussy in time. She stopped his fingers, and he thought he had hurt her.

"Are you okay? Sorry, is that sore?" Marcus's face was full of concern.

But Maria's was not, hers was filled with lust and unfulfilled desire. She wanted him inside her.

She pulled his neck forward and whispered in his ears, "Fuck me, Marcus, and stay where you are. I want you behind me!"

Marcus was a big man, and he was cautious as he entered her. Maria, however, was not and put a stop to his misplaced caution as she pushed right back onto him, her natural lubricant easing his entry, taking his full length deep inside her. She pulled his hand back around to her pussy, and motioned his fingers back to the rhythm he had before, and started pushing back on him letting him know he could take her, and he began to thrust into her. Water was going everywhere, his thrusts more frenzied, but trying his hardest to keep going without coming, trying to let Maria reach her climax before his.

Maria had been with Marcus a long time and she knew he would be close, so she took his hand at the front and rubbed more intensely right where she needed it, with her hips thrusting backwards onto him, deliberately pushing her buttocks right back onto Marcus, his eyes feasting on this glistening spectacle, his moans loud. He couldn't stop himself coming but kept thrusting into her as he climaxed, his hands trying not to give way to the euphoric sensation rippling through his groin and body. Maria was also there, and her pussy gripped him tight and the swirls and pulsations of her orgasm joined his and their bodies swayed and rocked until they were both spent, his kisses still heated on her neck and her mouth, she, twisting around to receive him, the water still running fast over their bodies and the spillage obvious on the floor opposite the shower.

"Wow, I needed that," Maria laughed, as poor Marcus set himself free from her grip, his legs a little shaky after that unexpected effort.

Marcus just smiled and brought her around and held her in his arms, the love obvious in his eyes, and his kiss, tender and loving, showing her how much he cared for her.

"Mrs Black, you are so naughty," he said, still smiling.

"Eh no, you, Mr Black, are the naughty one, coming in here in your birthday suit, and certainly showing a little interest!" She giggled into his mouth, as they pulled away to get dry.

"Mummy, Mummy!" came a sweet little voice from the other room as both turned around guiltily, like a couple of naughty school kids caught kissing in the playground.

"Coming, honey," Maria said caringly, wrapping the towel around her tightly.

Marcus was still drying himself when their little tufty-headed, blond imp came through, bleary-eyed and sleepy, tousled mop of hair, not a strand in place, rubbing his eyes.

"Hi, Daddy! What are you doing in the bathroom?" His question was innocent, but made Marcus blush at what had just gone before, delighted that Wee Davy still called through to be taken to the toilet and hadn't just wandered in, as that would have meant a lot more explaining.

"OOO, the floor's wet, Daddy. It's horrid on my feet. Why's it so wet? It's not normally wet," he continued, as if he knew something naughty had just gone on, but that was just Marcus's mind overthinking things.

"Oh, sorry that was me. I got out of the shower and forgot to put the towel down. I'll wipe it up quickly." He bent down and kissed the little lad on the head, and Wee David cuddled into Marcus's leg, his head resting on his thigh, his eyes still half-closed, as Marcus ruffled his hair even more.

"C'mon you, back to bed now!" Marcus lifted his son high into his loving arms, and he snuggled in.

"Daddy, can I say night night to Lily before I go, please?" His voice was sweet and pleading, so there was no way the answer would be no.

"Of course you can. She's all snuggled up and cosy, because Mummy had just fed her when I got home!"

"Aw, she's so cute, so teeny tiny," Wee David said as if he was some sort of giant.

He already really loved his little sister. He'd taken to helping Maria and getting things for her when she needed them.

Once everyone was tucked up in bed, Maria came through

and was up for a little more intimate care, as she was a lady that, when her fire was lit, it took a fair bit of extinguishing, but, to her disappointment, Marcus was flat out on his back half-covered and clearly already sleeping.

"Typical!" Maria smiled, but knew he had an early start and it could wait. She knew she wasn't quite ready for one of their marathon sessions yet.

Chapter 36

Don't Make Me Hate You

The alarm seemed to go off a minute after his head had hit the pillow, but the spoils of their lovemaking had clearly taken him into a far deeper sleep than he had expected.

He skipped the shower, as he decided he was clean enough, sprayed some aftershave on, fixed his hair, and popped on his suit and bright coloured tie. He smiled at himself in the mirror, a happy man after the events of the night before.

He went into the office, briefly, and phoned ahead to the young person's unit to check that Kerri was in to avoid a wasted visit.

Inga answered and said that Kerri hadn't been out at all since the night before, which for her was pretty unusual.

He swapped his nice motor for a work one, which was no comparison, other officers not quite as clean as him. There were a few scented treasures left behind like banana skins, chippy wrappers and coffee cups.

Marcus hated how messy others could be. He knew folk were busy and, in a hurry, but there were those that left everything at their arse, just through sheer laziness, clearly spoiled wee bastards in life, wee mummies' boys, or just selfish and slobbish gits.

He threw some things on the floor and made the short trip from Fettes to the Drymuir YPU. He noticed a few well-known faces out and about, some aware of the fed car straight away, which made them move off quickly, their belief that all police were after them at all times, which was amusing to him.

He drove carefully up Easter Drylaw, as the streets were narrow and cars parked on both sides in places.

He got out and straightened his suit, his scent Sauvage by Dior, a gift from Maria, and he liked the way it smelled on him.

He rang the entrance buzzer and Inga appeared, her brows down, a go-to when she did not know who it was and a deterrent to those that shouldn't be there.

"Hi, I'm Detective Constable, oh sorry, Acting Detective Sergeant Black. I called about Kerri, for a wee chat. It's about Phil Chancellor, her social worker!"

"What about him? He's not been here since the end of the week. Is he okay?" Her question was honest and unknowing. "I've been on leave over the weekend. I take it he's off sick or something?" She clearly hadn't been informed of Phil's death, and it wasn't something you leave on a Post-it note.

"What, nobody's told you?" Marcus knew this was going to sting a bit. "He's passed away, Inga. He died on Friday," Marcus said in a sympathetic tone.

"No! How? That man was fit as a fiddle. Was it an accident?" She quizzed Marcus a little forcefully, disbelieving of the news.

"I can't say. There's an investigation ongoing, so until that's concluded, we won't know what caused his death," he stated, feeling a little unkind at not telling her the truth, but rules were rules.

Her eyes welled up with tears. She had known Phil for a while now, and he was one of the most kind and genuine people she had ever met. He had really cared for the young people, including Kerri.

Kerri was at the top of the stairs and heard what was being said. The only perturbing thing to her was that there was now an investigation, which she hadn't thought would be happening for a suicide. She thought her cover-up had been pretty thorough, as it was not her first, and, like with the others, she would be in the clear.

Inga looked up, catching Kerri's movement in her peripheral vision.

"Oh, Kerri, there you are! Lucky you're here. This detective sergeant wants to have a wee word." She stopped there, because if she hadn't known, then Kerri may not have known about Phil's death, and she was a bit worried she would freak out, as she knew Kerri had liked him.

"Come down a minute will you please?" Her words were kind, but the tearful sadness could still be heard in her voice.

Kerri made her way down the stairs and asked why Inga was crying, her words filled with falseness, knowing full well why there were tears. She couldn't help but enjoy that she had caused them.

"Come and have a seat, Kerri. I have some bad news for you, and I knew you liked him very much." Inga paused and let her sit.

Kerri sat motionless, and thought to herself, "Good choice of words, Inga, in the past tense. I did like him, but not now. The shirt-lifting liar got what was coming to him, leading me on like that." Her thoughts were cruel and matter of fact. She truly believed he had deserved it in her twisted corrupt little mind, making her feel hurt like that, let down again once she had opened up to him, her underdeveloped childlike mind not realising the difference between kind affection and adult desire, and a kind and caring man that truly had cared for her.

When Inga's words came out, she wasn't quite sure how to act, and she wasn't capable of false emotion, so she just sat there blankly staring at her feet, with not a word said.

Marcus watched this girl with intrigue. She was emotionless, which he thought was odd. He had no background information on her and did not know what to expect, but he certainly had not expected this, nothing at all, a person who appeared totally void of any emotion.

Inga looked at Kerri. "I thought you liked Phil? You said you did; you liked him coming here. I'd say you even looked forward to his visits. You got on really well." She paused. "Didn't you?" She frowned again. She was losing patience with Kerri's oddness, albeit she could be odd, but mostly abrasive and aggressive, with a large dose of intimidation.

Kerri looked up at Inga and, if looks could kill, Inga would be dead. Marcus didn't know whether to step in front of her or not, the look was so evil and brutally directed, a look that if directed at him, he'd be expecting a punch in the face, or worse. Even with his experience, he was taken aback by the look. It was as if Satan was sitting in behind her eyes, pure darkness there, an emptiness that was unnerving, and showing such open aggressiveness from a look, and from such a sylph-like and harmless-looking little girl.

Kerri got up abruptly and turned to leave. She was about to climb the stairs when Marcus spoke in a deep and police-like tone, "Kerri, I need to speak to you. Where would you like to do that?" His stance was firm and commanding, even though he had been taken aback by this girl.

Her eyes bored into him. "What if I don't want to speak to you? I hate the police! Why would I speak to you? People who speak to you lot are called grasses, and do I look like a fucking grass to you?" There was a rude pause. "Do I look like one of them, do I, fancy boy?" Her eyes challenged him, directly threatening his authority, her tone aggressive and mocking.

She had noticed he was good looking. The last good-looking male she had known was no longer here, and she started to smile. His tone needed to be taken down a peg or two, her invincibility complex now in full swing. She thought the police were daft and had no thoughts of them ever catching up with her. She knew they would ask about Phil, and her parents, but she was quite convinced she had not been noticed, and would not be linked to their deaths.

Certainly, she couldn't be seen as doing anything wrong enough for anything to be pinned on her. Nobody was alive that had seen her; the rest was all circumstantial at best and unprovable.

"What do you want to know then? Phil's dead, oh well, one less queer to worry about!" Her words were cruel and intentionally sadistic, and deliberately teasing the cop guy to bite at her hateful words, and he did.

"Listen, Kerri, you can't just be so openly homophobic like that. It's actually against the law for one, and it's bloody disrespectful to Phil. The man's dead for God's sake." Marcus was raging at the disrespect, and it was obvious to see. He wasn't used to young girls like that being quite as sick. Rude, yes, but vile and uncaring was not as common or the norm.

"Don't swear. You're not allowed to swear!" Kerri said in a petulant and antagonistic tone, knowing how much of a little shit she was being and that there was fuck all they could do about it. The rules were definitely weighted against the police, and little shits like Kerri used this to full advantage. She didn't want to speak to him, especially about Phil. She wasn't ready for it and she hadn't prepared. She hadn't thought for a second that they would have pulled her into the picture quite so quickly, so all credit to the feds.

Marcus knew he couldn't force her, but he had to speak with her at some time. He calmed down and completely changed his tack. Ignoring her hostility and essence of evil, he said politely, "Please, Kerri, I need to speak to you some time, and maybe now would make you feel better. It must be a bit of a shock about Phil!" His words were kinder. He hadn't gone there thinking she really did have anything to do with Phil's death. He was just ticking a box, or so he thought, but this girl was something else, and what he had seen so far had not been nice.

"Say please again, and I'll consider it, but I have nothing to say to you. He was my social worker, and now he's not. Next!" she said callously, uncaring, flippant, and showed just what a horrible creature she was, and he hoped that she was just playing up and not really as bad as she was portraying, but, as policing goes, he had met worse, but not usually as young as her.

Marcus could feel his stomach twist, and it took every ounce of his very being to say "Please!" again, because he had a job to do, and if that's what it took, then he had to do it.

"In my room then!" She stomped up the stair, not waiting for him.

Inga was still trying to process the death of Phil, but Kerri's behaviour was preventing any grief. She was incredulous in her attitude and change of heart, with her hideous attitude, unusual, even for her standards.

Inga motioned to Marcus. "It's now or never. If you take too long, she'll lock you out or jump out of the window and run away or something!" She wasn't joking. "I'll come up with you to check that all is okay, and that there's a safe place for you to sit, without her getting too close!"

"Too close? Why would she do that sort of thing?" he asked quizzically.

"Yeah, she would. She did with Phil. He really hit a note with her, and she was responding really well. I can't believe she's being so flippant about his death and so hostile about his sexuality!" Inga stated.

They went up the stairs and headed to Kerri's room, as Marcus was processing what Inga had just said. The thought that Phil and Kerri were close was a surprise to him, especially the hatred shown towards his sexuality, which had seemed to strike an unhealthy vibe with Kerri.

Once in the room, Marcus was aware of how bare it was, nothing homely, and there was a smell of lighter fuel in the room, but he noted that her lighter was on the table, and beside it a can of lighter fuel, so that could explain it.

"Well, where do you work from then? What department? And why do you want to talk to me, plain clothes, why me? I don't get it. CID don't usually deal with kids like us. It must be something pretty important then," she said in her most childlike voice shrugging her shoulders innocently, a total U-turn from what she had been like down the stairs just five minutes before.

"I'm from the Major Investigation Team, not CID, but we do similar things. We deal with suspicious deaths and murders and I have to speak to you about Phil," Marcus said, quite bluntly and straight to the point to see what kind of reaction he would get.

She was smart though, not easily fooled, and was full-on with her questions, which Marcus set about trying to answer, not thinking he would be giving anything useful away. He didn't see any reason not to answer her at this point, as he still couldn't see Kerri as capable of murder, albeit she had a very odd persona, almost a split personality.

Kerri already did not like this man and was uncomfortable with him being there. She felt a danger that he brought with him, and she perceived his presence as oppressive, matter of fact and mean. She would get as much information as she could, look weak and innocent, and do her best to ensure her tracks were covered, so that there was nothing that could tie her to Phil's death and keep them believing it had been suicide. She would offer false information that the last time they met he had seemed upset about something.

Chapter 37

Connection

Taylor was back in the office early doors, hoping there would be no more emotional scenes today, and that Fran had said her piece and would let things go. She was on the phone to the superintendent of the MIT. Scarlet Trainer was pretty new to the role, a slight woman, small in stature, but she made up for it in character, a woman not to be messed with if you knew what was good for you. She had rung the main office to speak with ADI Taylor Nicks and talk about the recent happenings within the city to get a full measure of what was on the agenda. There was also the fatal fire to be discussed. The fire service had deemed the cause deliberate and there were three confirmed fatalities. The MIT were to take the lead on the enquiry and not the CID, as the culprit was unknown and as yet there were no suspects.

There was an anomaly in relation to the checks on occupants at that address. On searching all police systems, and digging deep into social work records, the occupants of the flat with the fire were the estranged parents of the girl Kerri Armstrong, who Taylor realised was the one Marcus was interviewing as they spoke. DNA samples had been taken from the unidentifiable melted corpses, but there would be no similarities to Kerri, because the records stated she was an adopted child. Her biological parents had been alcoholic drug users, causing her to suffer from foetal alcohol syndrome as a baby.

"You're kidding me. What are the witnesses saying?" Taylor was a little shocked. She quizzed her boss, hoping for a little more and that someone had seen something.

"Not a lot I'm afraid. There aren't any. People only looked out their windows when the sirens were heard. There were no witnesses to the cause of the fire or the person responsible," Superintendent Trainer stated with a disappointment in her voice.

"Surely we can bring Kerri Armstrong in to speak to, as this is a bit of a coincidence?" Taylor enquired in an exasperated tone.

"On what grounds? I believe we're already speaking to her. Marcus will ask all the right questions, won't he?" Trainer quizzed.

"How can he ask the right questions? I don't even think he was here when the fire was briefed out. It wasn't ours yet at that point. CID had the lead, and he certainly doesn't know who was in that fire!" Taylor nearly shouted.

"Shit, call him now and let him know. Ask him to run it by her to see her reaction, then we maybe do it formally later if there's enough evidence to point the finger!" The Super was getting exasperated now too and was a lot less patient.

"I'll call him right now!" Taylor was a little apprehensive that it might be too late, but she acted quickly and obediently. She excused herself from the call, or so she thought, Trainer practically dismissing her as she tried to get Marcus on his personal radio.

He had already finished talking with Kerri, one of the oddest and most uncomfortable experiences in his whole policing career, and he was glad it was over, physically shivering inside as he left.

He was saying goodbye to Inga when he heard his radio

call his name. He had it turned down when he was talking to Kerri to avoid annoying her any more than she was already.

Once Marcus heard Kerri's parents had been killed, his heart sank almost to his feet. He didn't want to think someone so young, outwardly vulnerable and tiny could be responsible for such atrocities, but deep down in his heart he knew she could. She was odd and uncomfortable, filled with hostility, and could quite easily be capable of bad things, but this was three people they were talking about, all burned alive, her family, and, he believed, her own flesh and blood, not knowing all the details yet.

He explained to Inga quickly that he needed to go back up to speak with Kerri, and both of them made for the stairs, racing up them in threes, but on arrival at her room, it was locked. Marcus knocked, exasperated, as Inga used her keys to get in. Marcus instinctively wanted to kick it in, but, as Taylor had told him, there was no evidence yet to link her to the crime, so it was just a chat at this stage.

Once unlocked, the door swung open, and they were met with a sucking breeze from the open window. She was already gone.

Kerri had been halfway down the stairs when the message came over the radio as they were in the main office. Hearing it, she had bolted back up the stairs and made her way out of the window, as she had done many times before. She knew how to get away unnoticed and avoid police attention, knowing the best gardens to use and where to hide when necessary.

She checked her pocket for her new treasure. It was still there, and she made sure it could not fall out on her travels. She felt sick. The police didn't seem as dumb as all of the other residents had made them out to be. They were already on to her from last night, and she knew that the cop guy had seen her lighter fuel, but that didn't prove anything. She had a Clipper lighter that needed fuelled up and could prove that.

She wasn't sure what she was going to do, although she still thought she was in the clear for everything else she had done. She hadn't meant to do any of it initially, but the first man had been frightening and aggressive, vile, depraved and disgusting with what he had wanted from her, for her to do, and all taken unwillingly. Everything had just happened after that. Once she had killed once, there was no going back. The next time, it was very different, and she had never known such an invigorating feeling, an overwhelming sensation of power and invincibility. It was indescribable, and with it a surge of desire to do it again, to feel that way again. The feeling was impossible to ignore, and once she had got away with it, with not even a sniff of interest in her direction, she thought and truly believed that she was untouchable and the police weren't even looking for her and, even if they were, they couldn't prove anything anyway.

Chapter 38

Findlay Walks Free

Findlay had been an outrage from the minute he arrived at the cells. PCs Clark and Horne were at the end of their tether with his continual tirade of vitriol, his revilement and insults were never-ending, sexist, homophobic, degrading and more, so much so that he was taken straight through to the cells. Bored of his shit, and no matter who he thought he was, the officers were not taking any more crap from this vile little man.

As always, there were a few sweaty palms in the cells management team for keeping an inspector in the cells for such minor offences. However, the sergeant was a woman who took no shit from anybody and was all for keeping him in even longer, as she had witnessed his behaviour first hand, and if it had been anyone else, they would be visiting court in the morning. She, along with Lors, Al, Alex, Willie, Jen and the rest of the team, had seen many complete wankers in their time, but this guy was something else, a total knob, pompous, arrogant and up there with the worst of them. At least there were reasons for other inmates' behaviour, but no such back story for him. He was just a complete dickhead of the first order.

Unfortunately, Findlay had a few old school friends on the force, and strings were pulled by his mates to get him out of there with minimal charges. It was unjust and unfair. If you do the crime, you should do the time, but not everything in life is fair.

Findlay stepped out of St Leonard's front door, a wry smile on his face, his rotund frame stiffened with inner rage, though, rage at everyone he believed had wronged him, never a thought that he had brought everything upon himself, totally blind to his behaviour and others' actions in response to his.

He knew he was fucked though; his job was hanging by a thread. His pension would go too if he was found guilty. He knew his DNA was on Kay if they were checking and, even if he could try and explain it away through helping her, his DNA along with Kay's testimony would nail him and there was nothing he could do about that. Even if he skipped jail, which he might well do in today's climate of leniency, he would definitely be sacked with the loss of all benefits.

He shook his head, the madness taking over, as he walked off, head face down, muttering loudly towards his feet.

"Nothing to lose, nothing to lose, nothing to lose," he repeated in a whisper. He had been about to do something really bad before he was arrested, and now his situation was even worse, even though he had only received a written warning. He didn't realise he had started to shout in the street. People around him were staring and moving away to avoid going past him. Only once he realised what he was doing did he shut up. The last thing he wanted was to be arrested again. He couldn't risk that, not just yet. He had unfinished business. He turned and kept walking, muttering, "Nothing to lose. I will make them suffer, and if I go down for it, at least it will be for something worthwhile."

He quickened his pace, realising his car would still be where he had been arrested and he would have to either walk there or get a bus. This just heightened his anger. Those cops in the cells had been unaware of just how close to the edge he was. He had known how to answer the prerelease questions, hiding his rage and unhinged behaviour, and had passed with flying colours. Questions whether he was mad or suicidal, he would never have answered truthfully anyway.

Chapter 39

Someone Similar

Taylor was in the middle of reporting Kerri missing to response officers, so they would look out for her, leaving them unaware of the possible depth of her offending, as nothing to date had been proven, nothing at all. Everything at present was purely circumstantial. She was only a person of concern currently and needed to be traced, to check on her welfare. She was being treated as a missing person, ostensibly so she could be informed about the deaths of her family.

Marcus arrived back in the office. All heads turned to stare. He was a little unnerved at this, unaware of all that had just been reported to them.

Taylor turned and looked over at him, her eyes meeting his, her expression quizzical and a little worried.

He gestured 'what?' and shrugged his shoulders, unknowing of the magnitude of his very recent but now lost opportunity.

Taylor explained to Marcus what circumstantial evidence they could have in relation to some of the unexplained deaths in the city over the last few months, and that Kerri might be in the frame for some of them, if not all of them. He was flabbergasted at what Taylor was saying and also gutted at the lost chance to get hold of her. He had felt the essence of evil oozing out from this petite young female he had just been speaking to and, deep down in his gut, he knew that, with her presentation, she could be perfectly capable of something bad, but, due to her stature, still found it hard to imagine. He too was excited at the prospect of uncovering the slight suspect figure captured on CCTV at both scenes and the possibility that the two drownings were murders too. The city of Edinburgh had been turned on its head lately with the sheer volume of murders, which was unprecedented. Usually they would have been solved, as Edinburgh Police were good at one thing, their murder solvency rate, it still being just a small "toon" to many. Marcus sat listening, knowing it could have been Kerri.

"Wow! She was really strange, but she's tiny and it seems physically impossible that she could have done everything you're suggesting. She is weird though, aggressive, and I was uncomfortable to be alone with her. I felt my hair standing on end and my adrenaline flowing!"

He stopped talking for a moment, rubbed his stubbly chin, and gave it a little more thought. "She gave me shivers down my spine, and it was really unsettling the way she talked about Phil. She was so full of hate and malice for him, so hostile it made me and the social worker uncomfortable. She was oozing hatred, but Inga said she really liked him before, which is odd in itself!"

Taylor listened intently and asked him to watch the footage of the figure near to the two suspicious deaths in the town centre. He had seen Kerri in the flesh, how she walked, and she wanted to know his thoughts in relation to the possibility of it being her in the footage.

"Why though? Why would she do it? These were just random people, nobodies to her. Who would do that to a stranger? Why? This is movie stuff, not reality!" Marcus stated with an assured tone. "We need to be sure about this. This is some very fucked-up shit. She's just a wee lassie, broken and trying to find her way, and bloody tiny too. She's odd and evil, but she's not physically capable of what you're accusing her of, even the logistics of these crimes. The first suspicious deaths were big fucking men. They didn't just fly into the water all by themselves!"

Taylor listened patiently, waiting for her moment to share the most recent incident and the connection to that, which for her cemented her theory just that little bit more. "Marcus." Her gaze dropped. "There's more." Taylor paused again, knowing how Marcus would feel. "There was a fatal fire last night, at the home of Kerri's estranged adoptive parents. They're assuming the three dead bodies found within the house are family, parents and sibling. DNA can only confirm this. The fire service also believes the fire was set deliberately. Does that change how you feel about her capability?" Taylor herself was still struggling to comprehend that the sylph-like girl could commit such heinous crimes, but everything was certainly pointing in that direction. Her stature and the apparent inability to commit these crimes was most likely what had kept everyone from even considering someone like her for these crimes.

Marcus's mouth was agape, his heart nearly pumping through his chest. "You're fucking kidding me! You're not going to like this then. There was a bloody can of lighter fuel in her room, but to her defence it was sitting beside her lighter on her desk, and the room was reeking of the stuff. I rationalised it away. Who wouldn't? She said she was filling her lighter, which is plausible," he said, trying to defend himself. "How was I to know this had happened?" His thoughts went back to her demeanour and the coldness of her eyes, trying hard to imagine the atrocity of what he had just been told and that she could be responsible.

Taylor's face drained of any colour. "For fuck's sake, Marcus, that changes everything. She's now a fucking high-risk missing person, with a very large hint of dangerous fugitive thrown in for good measure. I bet that little fucker knows her number's up, and that makes her even more of a threat. She doesn't seem to be too choosy," Taylor said loudly and dramatically, as she slammed her fist down on the desk, making everyone near them jump, with the force of it.

She looked around the room, emotion filling her eyes, pleading with her captive audience. "Just fucking find her, folks. Tick tock, the forensic window is closing, and who knows what she'll do next now we're onto her?" Taylor's face was bright red, and she was angry and a little worried that there was more to come, because if it was Kerri, and knowing that the police were on to her, she now had nothing to lose. The actions of a desperate person, filled with hate, could be catastrophic.

She slammed the desk again, totally exasperated, her fists sore with the force she had used from the first strike of the desk, the second attempt nearly damaging it. "How the fuck did we miss all of this? We've such preconceived ideas of what has to be, what we're meant to think, programmed to think even, and just accepting what has been presented to us by the perpetrator, deliberately leading the police down the wrong path, instead of us looking that little bit further for what might have been. I know all the evidence up until the water results came back pointed to suicides and misadventure, but if this turns out to be what we think it is, we'll be crucified. Everybody loves to hate on the police and will jump on the bandwagon to blame us for everything!" Taylor was totally incensed, totally infuriated that she had been misled. Knowing she was normally more on it than she had been on this occasion, she felt like a total failure for not having looked that little bit harder.

It was all hands-on deck to find Kerri now. She was even more dangerous than before, if that was possible, and on the run too. She had proved that she was already good at hiding in plain sight and had left for a reason. She knew her days were numbered and that the police and everyone else would be hunting for her.

Kerri had gone into town. It was easier to hide there. The hustle and bustle of the busy streets allowed anyone who wanted to disappear to do just that.

She chose to sit beside a homeless man. He welcomed her onto his blanket and they sat there watching the world go by, passers-by too wrapped up in their own lives to notice the two homeless people, ignoring their plight, the invisible in society, which was perfect for Kerri just now.

She reached into her pocket and smiled, her fingers wrapping tightly around the recently acquired prize, a small plastic gift of information. She just hoped the driver's licence was up to date, and he wasn't a naughty little law-breaker. Her smile was broad and covered her whole face. The guy beside her noticed it and asked why she seemed so happy. He received no reply, only an odd look, a cold stare, blankness. A trance-like presence came over her. She turned to him, and he felt his blood run cold as she squeezed his arm, got up and started to walk away. He watched her leave, and felt unnerved and uncomfortable inside, chilled to the bone, made nervous by this young girl. He was totally creeped out by the way she had looked deep into him and was glad she had chosen to leave after that oddly surreal encounter. He had seen a lot in his time, but nothing quite like this.

Chapter 40

Vulnerable

Taylor was working, and Kay had the weekend off, so was free to relax, get out and about and get some fresh air. She was actually quite excited to get away from her house and not feel trapped in Taylor's flat, because she didn't feel safe at home anymore. Although very welcome at Taylor's, she felt she was having to be there, rather than choosing to, because of the stalker situation.

Her friend Denise Smith, one of the professional trainers at St Leonard's Police Station, was out for the day and had asked Kay to look after her dog, a beautiful female golden retriever, three years old, exuberant and bouncy, and certainly in need of a long walk. Kay decided that Arthur's Seat would be perfect for a long walk. The scenic views from the top of Edinburgh's extinct volcano were spectacular, a 360-degree panoramic view of the city. The view, stretched out to North Berwick, with Berwick Law lifting high up into the sky to the east, a full-size whale jawbone on the top when you climb it. Edinburgh Castle was a spectacular sight from there, the cliff walls leading up to the ramparts, watching quietly over the city, protecting her, every high-rise in the less salubrious areas of Edinburgh standing tall as if on parade. The views reached out to the sea and Fife, even Easter Road, the Hibernian Football stadium, and so much more. You could also see the other hills spread over the city from this amazing vantage point, all taking their rightful place on the skyline. Kay had a wry smile to herself when thinking of the Hibs stadium, thinking of her friend Christine Hoopy Collins, an avid Celtic supporter, always teasing her about how bad the Edinburgh clubs were compared to her beloved Celtic, one of the Old Firm Glasgow-based teams, currently the top of the Scottish Premier League and rarely beaten by Hibs. Unlike Kay, her life revolved around her precious team and not a bad word could be said about them, not without a protective onslaught of defence from her pal, and many a statement to promote their brilliance and their importance to her. Kay respected that, loyalty in abundance, regardless of what it related to, and this was a trait she commended.

She tugged gently on the lead, and the dog bounced up on the front seat of the car before being guided onto the floor, where she sat quite happily panting and looking lovingly towards Kay, her new best friend for the day.

She had left Taylor's house earlier, looking over her shoulder as always, these days. To her relief, as she looked up and down the street, it was virtually empty other than a few elderly women shuffling along with their messages. She was becoming a bit more relaxed, her confidence growing again, and she felt safer staying at Taylor's flat, thinking that whoever had been watching her, that random pervy weirdo, would not know where her lover's home was, and that she was safe there. There hadn't been any issues since she moved in nearly a week ago, and she still felt reluctant to go back home until the person who had been watching her had been caught, or stopped, but she couldn't really know if they had been back, not being there 24/7. There could have been further visits from her stalker in her absence.

Kay drove carefully through the city, a feeling of extra responsibility having someone else's precious pet to care for.

She kept looking at the dog Kimmy, making sure it was okay, instead of her normal routine of looking in her rear-view mirror to check if she was being followed. She was distracted. Her thoughts were with this very cute and boisterous pup, which had temporarily stopped her feeling as vulnerable or being as cautious as she normally would be. It was nice to feel that way, so she failed to see him, and he was now right behind her, his eyes wide and fixed on her, maniacal in their appearance. Findlay had finally lost it.

She drove into Queen's Park, soon to be King's Park after the recent death of her Majesty Queen Elizabeth the second. The road led down past Holyrood Palace and St Margaret's Loch and then up to the junction with the Radical Road, which curled halfway up Arthur's Seat, her chosen destination. She would park beside the small loch there. Dunsapie Loch was a popular spot for picnics and families, and there were a few there already, enjoying the idyllic spot. This helped put her mind further at ease. More people, more witnesses, more safety, she thought to herself. She pulled into the parking area, where she foolishly opened the door, and the dog jumped enthusiastically over her. She accidentally let it run away and it headed straight towards the loch, lead and all. Kay panicked; she was not used to dogs and didn't realise retrievers are land seals who love the water, and would want to get in there whatever the cost or obstacle, she being the obstacle. The dog's big fluffy feathered tail swatted Kay in the face as it leapt out. Her fears that the dog was going to bolt were short lived, as it bounded through the water and then casually into the loch, where it lay down, lapping up the water and barking happily, like a pig in mud.

Kay walked quickly over, and her frown soon became a smile, her fear that she had lost Denise's dog fading quickly. She smiled over at the stupid mutt, now nearly fully submerged, scrabbling, face in the water, searching for a rock to retrieve.

There were several cars parked there already and a pretty constant flow of other cars passing, one moving slowly and paying particular attention to her, but she was none the wiser, facing the other way, trying to coax her friend's stupid dog out of the water, but without much luck.

With the dog being disobedient, she now took the time to take a look around, as she had just realised she hadn't followed her normally rigorous ritual, temporarily forgotten due to the much-needed, happy distraction of the dog. Her gaze eventually floated around in all directions, but she had just missed him, and, in her mind, all appeared okay, with no one following her, and the sudden but momentary tension left her. She turned back to the silly dog in the water, now totally soaked. She reached into her pocket for the rescue packet of dog biscuits that had been left for an occasion just like this one.

The dog was torn between its two favourite things, the water and a treat, a dilemma indeed for that breed of dog, tummy or swim, but eventually, after another couple of minutes and dunking for a few more rocks, Kimmy decided a wee snack was the way forward, as she had now had enough time in the water. She walked innocently back to Kay, as if she hadn't done anything wrong, her tail wagging happily, quickly changing the frustration Kay had felt into warmth with a smile, because the dog seemed to know how she was feeling. Kimmy also appeared to be smiling back at Kay.

"C'mon, ya daft dog. Let's do this!" They turned to the hill and headed towards the summit, the dog now bounding in front, stopping briefly to shake and sniff here and there. Kay walked happily some metres behind the dog, blissfully unaware of Findlay parking his car in the next parking lane, between two cars, his messy motor nondescript, with nothing that would stand out. Although he was dishevelled and unkempt, he was not someone that would stand out either, sporting a flat cap and big glasses and a well-placed scarf that covered his face, a face Kay would never forget. The lenses in the glasses were dark, hiding his evil little piggy eyes. He hoped that would be enough to hide his identity until he was close enough for it not to matter anymore.

Findlay couldn't believe his luck. Kay had chosen an area that could be remote as well as busy, which offered him an opportunity to harm her, have her, or both, the order of which still to be decided. He started to mutter to himself, his pulse speeding up with his mind racing and also the effort of walking up the hill, with his big belly clearly weighing heavily on his legs and definitely slowing his pace. Athletic Kay was the exact opposite. She was lithe and very fit, and her strides were much longer than his chubby little legs could keep up with. In his favour though, she kept stopping for the dog, as it kept sniffing and chasing other dogs, and she spoke to a few people that were already on their way back down from the summit. He walked inconspicuously along with other dog walkers, and a small party that had come off a bus, allowing him to walk unnoticed by Kay.

Kay stopped and took in the views. She looked up and down the hill, taking note of those above her and below, but not recognising anyone, and not fearful of any of them, as they were all far enough away and offering nothing untoward that stood out to her. She did think the little fat guy might have a heart attack with the amount of weight he was carrying, but did not realise it was her nemesis, Findlay, and that he was actually her stalker. With a little mirth in her eyes about his plight, she turned and started to stride up the hill, even faster than before. The dog was now having to bound after her, as this meant a treat, for recall, which Kimmy had already sussed out, food obedience, go a bit further away, wait for the call, doddle a bit and then return to be rewarded, a simple game really, and she liked treats.

Findlay cursed to himself as he noticed the pace increase.

He worried that she would be on her way down before he even got to the top, and then she would have the opportunity to recognise him. He had no plan as to what he was going to do, but he had known as soon as he saw that treacherous bitch's face that he wouldn't need a plan. He was filled with hate and wanted to teach her a lesson for messing with him. How dare she ruin him? And so fucking close to his pension as well, because if he was fixed with this crime, he would be disqualified from the benefits that would bring. He knew he might not get away with what he was thinking, but, in his mind, he was burst anyway, in for a penny, in for a pound. He wanted her, willing or not, the thought of her aroused him, and he felt that she was a waste of a woman, to all good men, choosing to shack up with a dyke like Taylor, the cock-teasing bitch.

He felt his heart pounding, both from exertion and being driven forward through spite and desire, his thoughts unhealthy, matching his unhealthy figure.

Taylor was busy at her work, but always made the effort to keep in touch with Kay, especially now she had an unwanted admirer. She chose a video call, which was much more personal, but knew she had to keep it brief, as there were numerous outstanding actions still needed to try and trace Kerri. The picture came up with the sound of wind in the background, a dog barking and Kay's kind voice, a little out of breath.

"Where are you? It sounds windy, wherever it is," Taylor asked, a bit surprised Kay would take herself somewhere remote.

"I'm up Arthur's Seat with Denise's mad dog, Kimberly. She's nuts and is expecting me to throw her the ball every second!" With a grunt of effort, Kay heaved the ball down the hill, and the dog went rampaging after it, clearly excited once again at the ball bumbling down the hill.

"How is it up there? Are there lots of people about?" Taylor quizzed without trying to alarm Kay with the reason for her question.

"Yeh, lots of groups, dog walkers and the like. It's beautiful up here. You should come up now and skip your work," she said, ever hopeful it might happen.

Taylor was tempted, but knew it was impossible at this time. "Sorry, no can do, I'm afraid. There are a couple of supers coming down for a Gold Meeting, for the next plan of action, but I'd love to. Next week, I promise. I'll be off at least one day and we can take a bottle of fizz with us."

Kay appreciated the consideration of the thought, and the rain check for the following week. Just then, the dog came bounding up to her and flopped at her feet, panting and reluctant to let go of the ball.

"I'd better let you go then, but I'll take a video of this crazy mutt and send it to you. She's just too funny, especially when she races down the hill and can't stop. She practically somersaulted the last time, with her helicopter tail. I love you and I'll make something nice for when you get in tonight, and maybe some dessert," Kay said, licking her lips, wishing Taylor was there with her.

Taylor smiled at the thought of both food and Kay's idea of dessert. "I love you too. Don't stay out there too long, and make sure you stay where there are other people, please," she said with a firm tone, just wanting her back to the safety of the house.

Kay got the message, but was enjoying how she was feeling today, and she really liked the dog. "I'll be a bit longer, stop for a bit and enjoy the view at the top, circle around and head back down, is that okay?" she replied in a slightly childish tone.

Both phones now disconnected, Kay looked down at the dog, ever ready for the next throw, which Kay was ready for too. She put her phone into her other hand to try and film this calamity of a dog chasing the ball.

Kay heaved the ball as far as she could, the camera on and

shoogling around as she tried to film the mutt in full motion. This time the dog couldn't stop on the really steep part of the hill, and went bundling head over heels, to Kay's delight, albeit she felt a bit cruel, as this is what she had hoped would happen so she could show Taylor how crazy the dog really was.

She then took a bit of time to take a panoramic of the view to help Taylor experience the beauty of this glorious day.

Once finished, she hoped the file wouldn't be too big to send, and off it went. She then turned on her heels and kept on up towards the summit.

Findlay was delighted at her delay on the phone. He'd caught his breath and was a lot closer, popping in and out from behind the party that was concealing him.

Kay reached the top and stood admiring the view, the dog lying at her feet, finally tired out after chasing the ball like a big dafty. The wind was blowing in her hair, the air cooler at the top, with lots of sightseers jostling for position for the best view. Kay had seen what she came to see and started moving off to the left for some peace and quiet, fearing the dog may get trampled.

She ambled around and could feel the slope under her feet putting a strain on her ankles. There were patches of gravel, and she gasped as she realised there was an edge with a drop on that side of the hill. "Flipping heck, I never knew that was like that! Shit, where's that daft dog?"

Kay spun round in a panic, fearing she had lost the dog, or, worse, Kimberly had fallen over the edge. Her eyes widened in terror, and her voice disappeared.

Taylor was sorting out the missing person application and adding a few more actions when she felt the phone vibrate in her pocket, which made her smile. She didn't stop what she was doing straight away as there were only a few more to go, and she didn't want to miss any by taking her mind off the job, but she was amused thinking of Kay and that daft dog, wishing she was up there with them.

Kerri twiddled the plastic driving licence in her hand, and she too was smiling. Google maps had been a great help, even showing where she could hide, it was so clear and accurate. She knew she was in the right place, as she had seen him drive the car away first thing that morning, leaving them all alone. Perfect, she thought to herself. She liked him and hated him at the same time as her mind tried to process everything she had done in the recent months, and why, also how it now felt, both good and bad. She thought it weird that she liked both of those feelings and was drawn to feel those extreme sensations again, ones that offered up a sense of fear-crushing power and control.

Taylor tapped the computer with a little celebratory vigour and a feeling of short-lived satisfaction. As she rocked back in her chair, she looked out at the others in the office beavering away, Marcus a little worse for wear with the night feeds he was doing with his beautiful little daughter, his stubbled chin a little less neat than normal. Fran was chatting away with a few of the others. She had a vibrant nature, kind eyes and great sense of humour. "Shit, I forgot about the bloody text I wish I was there. I need some time off," she thought.

She pulled out her phone and clicked into the video message, and she had to turn the volume down a bit because of the wind, but she could hear Kay's lovely voice and her laughter, carefree and happy. The footage was shaky, as she tried to capture the essence of the crazy dog bounding down the hill, its feathered tail rotating as it tried to slow itself down. The dog's delight was obvious as it pounced clumsily onto the ball, its mouth like it was smiling as it began to take itself back up the hill. Taylor was smiling and enjoying the outing remotely, and the joy on Kay's face. The video showed the group of Chinese tourists chatting away as they made their way to the summit, all of them wearing light blue face coverings, unaware of how wonderful the air was in Scotland. The video went back onto the dog, and focussed in on Kimmy as she came up to Kay's feet, tail wagging and reluctant to give the ball back, so Kay chose to ignore her and take in the scenery. She took a full panoramic of 360 degrees, finishing up on the slope heading down the hill. Taylor's stomach lurched, as her eyes took in the sight of the overweight man, behind the group of tourists, who had come half into view. She would know that walk anywhere, the unmistakeable shuffling waddle of her overweight boss. "Why the fuck is that fat little bastard taking a walk up a hill? He's the most unfit lazy bastard I've ever known."

"Marcus, Marcus, Fran, get in here, and get some units up Arthur's Seat, NOW!" she shouted. She could barely breathe. Everything was falling into place. "Findlay's the fucking stalker! We need to get there right away!"

She dialled Kay's number. It rang repeatedly as she scurried around the office putting on her PPE, but the phone did not answer, and she felt sick.

Chapter 41

Fallen

Eyes wide, mouth agape as he took hold of her, his sweaty little pudgy hands offering more strength than she had ever imagined, Kay couldn't believe what she was seeing. Findlay's face was right beside hers, contorted, unhinged, and he was trying to force his kiss upon her, his mouth wet and his hand pulling her face roughly closer to his. She cursed herself for walking away from the throng of people, the wind blowing a gale up here, totally open to all the elements and noisy.

She was about to scream, when he gripped her throat tightly, his wet and desperate mouth upon her. She could barely breathe, silenced by his grip and his desperate mouth, her heart filled with terror.

That's when she felt his depraved hand groping at her jeans. He managed to get his fingers in the top of them, fumbling around at the button, which gave way and popped with the force of his meaty but powerful little hand. His mouth now totally engulfed hers, his kisses not soft and kind, but forceful and brutish, her head now getting dizzy with the lack of oxygen.

Her legs gave way, and she dropped to the ground, there was long grass to the side of the path, and Findlay smiled as he dragged her into it, secreting them from view. He had forgotten just how easy it was to choke someone out, a wee trick he had used in the olden days of policing with force, a far cry from today's rules.

He knew what he wanted and had done for several years. Kay was stunning, naturally beautiful, and wouldn't allow him into her sanctuary, so he was going to take it by force, like he had with his own wife for many years, a long-suffering woman. When once she had fallen out of love with him, the change he displayed was not a good one.

He heaved Kay further out of sight, licking his lips as he pulled her jeans open and roughly pulled them down, along with her pants. He pulled both her tops up too, to reveal her perfectly formed breasts as he knelt over her, hard as a rock, hesitating just to look at her, a few scars, left by her previous attacker, fully aware of how she got them, those files he had read repeatedly with an unhealthy eye, he himself wishing he had been that perpetrator. He looked at her body, exposed and vulnerable, and in his sick entitled perverse mind she was ready for him.

He lowered his head, leaning in to taste her, his face ruddy and sweating profusely with the effort used to get her where he wanted her, his heart pulsing heavily. In his mind, whatever happened after this, it was going to be worth it. Not caring for her for one second, just himself, stealing her intimate treasure.

Suddenly his head jolted forward, bursting his lip on her pelvic bone, as the full weight of the boisterous retriever landed heavily on him in her delightfully ungainly manner. Kimberly leapt onto his head in an effort to bring the ball back to Kay, not knowing what sinister event was taking place, the ball having rolled much further down the slope than planned. Kimberly was wagging her tail, thinking this was a game, but when Findlay pulled himself up, bloodied and raging, and swiped viciously at her head, her demeanour instantly changed to an uncharacteristic snarl. She lunged at him, snapping dangerously close to his face, catching his cheek, then she took hold of his wrist, preventing him throwing another punch at her, clamping her jaws tightly and shaking her head ferociously.

Kay took in a massive gulp of air, her gasps desperate and frantic, a reflex breath, drawing precious life-giving air into her lungs, desperate to survive. She was totally disorientated but quickly became aware of how exposed she was. Fear gripped her, hearing the loud growls, terrifying snarls, screams and yelps of pain from a very familiar voice, only feet away from where she lay. Her mind was racing, as she quickly sorted her clothes, the harsh realisation of what had been about to happen making her head spin into a rage, her emotions sending a sharp prickling sensation all over her body, fear crawling up her spine, terror surging, the urge to run and escape him powerful, but rage took over, as she saw him strike Kimberly with brutal force to try and free his arm from her jaws. This just made the dog angrier, and she gripped him tighter, as Kay's rage boiled over. She watched as Findlay managed to raise the dog over his head, her grip on him still there but no longer in control of him, as he walked closer to the steep and jaggy edge. The dog foolishly released her grip, allowing Findlay more freedom and less pain to dispatch the intrusive and troublesome creature.

Kay saw what was about to happen, as she scrambled desperately to her feet to save this brave and beautiful dog. She was aware of the cliff edge, trying to change the trajectory of her run to avoid all three of them plummeting over the cliff. She ran at Findlay, her shoulder thumping into him with enough force to knock him and the dog onto their sides. Findlay looked up at her in amazement, flabbergasted to see that it had been Kay, slight and feminine, that had decked him. Wow did she pack a punch! The dog rolled for a bit, but got back up. Kay took a brutal swipe at Findlay's head with her foot, but he moved quickly enough to avoid its full force, and it just skiffed off his head, and when she went in for another kick, he took hold of her leg and whisked her off her feet. He was raging. His hand was bleeding, with some pretty grotesque lacerations and puncture wounds, but adrenaline was swirling through him and he did not feel the pain. He was now in a blind rage, his focus fully on Kay. He no longer cared about any consequence for what he was about to do.

He rushed towards her once again, but the dog managed to get between them. Findlay pushed her down and used her to lever his way back onto his feet. He kicked her as she tried to bite his leg. His second kick was more of a push, and the dog's face changed, yelping as it slipped over the edge. Kay let out a scream as she saw the dog disappear out of sight. She ran towards the cliff edge it in an effort to save her. Her move was quickly blocked, and she was once again in the grip of Findlay, but she had chosen not to run. Her fight-or-flight reflexes had clearly made their choice, and it was to fight this hideous man.

Kay scratched viciously at Findlay's face, her nails cutting into his flesh, damaging his eye. He squeezed her ribs tightly, taking her breath away, as she kicked and squirmed viciously, managing to get her feet back on the ground, fighting for her life. To her last breath, she would fight him. She was never going to let him have her. Nobody would ever do that to her again. Their fight was barbaric, cruel and desperate, both fighting for their lives now. He was going to kill her. She could feel it in the way he seemed not to care about the brutality of his fists, but she was tougher than he thought, and she kicked out at him, stamped down hard on his shins, his feet, and swung around and kneed him in the balls with as much force as she could muster. He doubled over, but still had hold of her hair, twisting it around his fist, pulling it away from her scalp. Through searing pain, she never stopped struggling. She was now weakening but so was Findlay. Even though he was stronger than her, she was much fitter. In her mind she knew this was it, so, with one last effort, she mustered up everything she had, and she managed to sweep his legs, causing him to fall, backwards, and he was so close to the edge that his weight started to pull him over it, still holding onto Kay's hair, screaming as they both tumbled helplessly over the edge.

Their bodies bumped, bounced and twirled down the steep stoney slope, whacking off the rocks on the way down, damaging each of them as they rotated at speed towards an even bigger cliff, one that would not be survivable if they fell over it.

Sirens rang out all over the city as police officers from throughout Edinburgh made their way to Arthur's Seat, along with the fire service and the Specialist Operation Response team from the ambulance service, all converging on one place, based on nothing more than their sighting of their former colleague having a walk up a hill. Where was the danger? Nothing had been confirmed, no incident reported, yet they all came from far and wide to the same spot on the hill.

Some of the bosses had been a bit hesitant to send out a full multi-agency response without confirmation of an incident or event. This was short lived though, when the first of a multitude of calls started coming in about two people having fallen from the east side of the summit, the craggy dangerous bit, a place that all officers were all too familiar with. And as Taylor's pulse raised, the bosses' lowered, with the avoidance of an embarrassing situation hitting the papers, the headline something like: misuse of public money, as police respond to colleague walking in a park!

The police helicopter was in flight from Glasgow, their ETA still some time away.

The first sets arrived at the loch halfway up the hill. Kay's phone had pinged, from comms work carried out, at the other side of the cliff, where the fire service was busy setting up a cordon and closing off the road beneath the fallen persons. Findlay's phone had also pinged, close to where Kay's had shown. When that information was passed on, Taylor actually threw up as she marched up the steep hill, sweat already rolling down her back.

Marcus was at her side, Fran not far behind, her legs shorter, but she was still pacing forwards, desperately trying not to be left too far back. It wasn't in her nature to be a slouch; Marcus and Taylor were just fitter and taller. The uniformed officers were even further behind, due to the amount of heavy kit they had to wear, but the dog handler was catching up on them, as he was being pulled up by his rather large German Shepard.

The radio messages were frantic, and the fire service already had their sixty-foot-high cherry picker on site with two officers aboard trying to see if they could get sight of the injured parties and pass a more accurate location for those attending. Lana was also there with her team. She wondered if Fran would be there, although she didn't usually attend this type of incident.

As they marched, a very welcome message was passed over their personal radios. The What Three Words app on Kay's phone had been used to find her position. Simultaneously, the loud sounds of a chopper were heard overhead, not the police chopper, but an RAF rescue crew, one that had been carrying out a beach search for a body at the nearby Niddrie Bents for a body, but this incident took precedence, as the cliff casualties were hopefully still alive.

Taylor looked up and muttered, "A lift wouldn't go amiss," as she panted heavily, now sweating ever more profusely.

At the summit, the group of Chinese tourists were looking down the steep slope, and some were taking photos. There were a few locals at the top too, regular dog walkers and runners, some of which were starting to clamber down in the direction of the focus of all the attention. Kay and Findlay's bodies were not visible from the top, but one of the people that had been on the summit had seen the scuffle from a distance, and then nothing after that. She had made the assumption they must have gone over the edge. Her name was Kat Pence, a singer and entertainer, originally from Scotland but had moved overseas to Gran Canaria to make a career for herself in warmer climes. She was a step-forward type of girl and made haste towards what she believed was a stricken couple. Her dog Sophie bounded after her, her wee legs moving as quickly as possible. When she got there, Kat had to shove her way past the throng of bystanders, all vying for the best view, the modern way, look and film, and not help. But not Kat, she was already making her way down the slope, scrabbling her way to where she had seen the couple topple over the edge. In her eyes, it looked like the woman had judo thrown the man over the edge, and he had held on and deliberately dragged her behind, and then they were gone, vanished, nowhere to be seen. She had noticed the woman on the way up, and she was sure a big retriever had been with her.

Kay had landed heavily. She was winded and could feel movement in one of her leg bones. She also felt pain everywhere, her head, her ribs, all over. She wondered where she was and whether anyone had seen what had happened. She tried to raise her head, but she couldn't. It was as if there was a heavy weight holding her down or, worse, she had broken her back or neck. She was a logical person though, and if she had broken her neck, then she wouldn't be feeling the pain all over herself. She twisted herself around, the pain in her ribs excruciating, and could feel her hair twist and her scalp ache. She looked around as far as she could manage and, to her horror, Findlay's fat torso was partly pinning her down, her inability to move explained. She could see his arm outstretched and deformed, and it looked like his hand was still twisted into her hair, pulling it tight. She pushed away the parts of him that were on her, raised up her least painful arm and started wiggling his hand to try and dislodge it from her. It was not an easy task with the weight of even one of his arms. He grunted, as she moved him more roughly the second time. On the third shake, Kay winced in pain but seemed to have freed his hand, along with a clump of her hair. She groaned, thinking of the missing patch of hair she had already. In the bigger picture, this seemed trivial, but the memories and terror it evoked certainly were not.

She tried to call out but, on breathing in to do so, she felt pain in her ribs. Her lungs burned, and she was finding it hard to breathe. She felt dampness on her top. It was blood. "Bad idea," she thought and whispered, "Someone will come. Please come!"

Just as she said the words, she heard another grunt coming from Findlay, and then movement. He rose up, his face covered in blood, his head swollen and deformed and his eyes focussed on Kay. They were pure evil. His lip started to curl up at the side. He suddenly lurched forward, his ability to move like that astonishing Kay. She was too astounded to roll away, a searing damaging pain taking her breath away. She was on her back little more than a metre from him. His face contorted and she knew he was going to attack her again. She felt faint, and she could feel the blood leaving her body, her strength dwindling away, but as he raised up above her once again, her heart screamed out to her, "NOOOOOO!!!" The words came into her mouth and out, the pitch high and desperate, and with them came the will to fight. She thrust her unbroken leg into his belly with as much force as she could muster. Gripping the grass beside her, she pushed him with all her might. His facial expression changed, as he started to fall backwards uncontrollably. His hands were flailing and grabbing out at anything, a rock, then a foot. Kay's body lifted off the ground, her fracture grinding, the crepitus deafening, as she was pulled with him towards the cliff edge.

Eyes wide, she frantically scrabbled with her good arm to get purchase on anything, as her pace quickened, her life hanging in the balance.

"I said, fucking NO, you fucking useless fat prick. Let the fuck go of my leg, you lechy creep. Never again will your hideous desperate little hands touch me. Let me fucking GO!" Her words were aggressive, spittle escaping from her normally polite and gentle mouth.

Her leg raised up again, her body totally broken but her will intact and defiant.

Kay could feel his face crumple under the force of her walking shoe, her face one of unbridled rage and defiance as his hand lost the grip on her foot. His face, ruddy with effort and blood, disappeared over the edge as she came to a halt, too close for comfort, at the edge of the cliff. She was amazed to still be there, and alive, her will to survive palpable. Her self-defence skills and weights training had certainly helped. She allowed herself a wry smile, before the blood loss and exertion finally overwhelmed her system, and she flopped lifelessly backwards, unconscious. Blood oozed from her, a sucking chest wound threatening her life, and her ability to breathe.

Findlay could feel himself falling. Terror gripped him at the realisation of his fate, his mind still awash with hatred and spite, and still not an ounce of remorse.

THUD! His weight and the fall left his body contorted and deformed, limbs jutting out in impossible directions, his skull cracked open like an egg, an expression of incredulous surprise etched over his face. His eyes were wide open, staring up to where he had come from.

Kay's face filled with of defiance an image etched in his memory forever, before everything went black.

On the way down the slope, Kat Pence's feet were taken from under her when the gravel beneath started to roll away, and she let out a few expletives as she tumbled down hard onto her arse, but she was up again quickly, a little more cautious as she continued towards the stricken people. She was familiar with the dangerous crags and didn't want to inadvertently go over the edge. They couldn't be too far away from where she now stood, making sure her feet were safely planted and not on the rolling gravel, and listened.

That's when she heard a faint whine over to her right. Her dog Sophie was already racing towards the haunting sound. Kat scrambled over to the stricken animal, now immobile with at least one broken leg, and possibly other injuries, because a dog would have got up if it could have. She was aware she couldn't do anything for it at that moment, apart from note exactly where it was to allow others to go to the rescue. She told her own dog to stay, which it had already decided to do. Sophie was licking her new canine friend to comfort her. Kat wished humans were as naturally kind. She edged further forward, and again she stumbled, sliding and struggling to stop herself. She cursed loudly, believing this was it, but, as she got closer to the edge, she managed to dig her heels in, stopping her motion not more than a metre away from the drop below. She began to tremble when she looked down, thankful for her small frame, otherwise she may not have stopped in time, and boy was it a long way down. She decided she had gone far enough, maybe even a bit too far, and she tried to scrabble back up, but her feet would not hold. She sat down and leaned cautiously over the edge, taking a sharp breath when she saw the woman on the ledge that jutted out below. She was in a very precarious position and appeared to be unconscious, which was a good thing. She might wake up and fall to her death, unknowing of the peril she was in, that's if she wasn't dead already. Kat was totally oblivious of the struggle that had ensued minutes before.

She carefully pulled her phone out of her pocket and called 999. She was now stuck herself, but she also had eyes on the injured female and was able to give an exact location. She just had to sit tight, not move and hope she didn't slip again, or she would be joining the woman below.

She wondered where the man she had been fighting with had gone. Had he fallen further?

It didn't take long for the sound of the powerful whirl of the chopper blades to come into range. Rescue was on the way. She looked up hopefully, but also tentatively due to her now more precarious position. Seconds later the chopper was hovering high above them, keeping their height, avoiding the downdraft that could potentially blast the two females they now had eyes on off the rock face.

Taylor and Marcus reached the top just as the chopper held its position, hovering over the spot where Kay must be. They moved quickly through the gathering of tourists and locals and looked down the steep slope and craggy cliff edges. More onlookers had started to make their way down to try and help, and they assumed the one furthest away must be the one that had sight of Kay. Unfortunately, helpers could be more of a hindrance than help at times. Without the skills and equipment of the professional services, they could also become victims but, on this occasion, Taylor and Marcus were happy with their efforts to save their friend.

Chapter 42

Rock a Bye Baby

Kerri watched her take the little blond tousle-haired wee boy off to school, with the pram. She looked like a nice lady, very beautiful, slim, and slight in her figure. Kerri smiled to herself, thinking, "She shouldn't be too much trouble if I have to deal with her." She now had the time to walk around the house, then the garden, looking to see how these people lived, and also to see if they had left anything open to allow her inside, and find a good place to hide herself, and wait. She was good at that, and she didn't have anything better to do anyway.

She smiled when she saw the hopper window of what must be the bathroom wide open, to let the steam come out. Perfect. She giggled impishly, thinking it funny. These coppers should practise what they preached when it came to home security.

She nimbly climbed up the drainpipe, shuffled along the window ledge and wriggled through the window, nearly falling flat on her face and into the sink once inside, but she managed to right herself at the last moment, knocking a few things over as she did so.

She swore under her breath, because she had cut herself on a ceramic cup that cracked and split when she landed, a smear of blood now on the underside of the sink.

She took some toilet roll and wrapped it around her hand to stop the bleeding and wiped round the sink to hide her presence, scooping up the pieces of cup and tipping them into the bin, hoping that by the time anyone noticed it would be too late anyway.

She walked around the top landing, in and out of all of the bedrooms, and then into what she assumed was the nursery for a little baby.

She smiled, as she had always liked babies, then went through and sat in the corner of the room, where there was a rocking chair for nursing the newborn. She loved rockers, never having had one herself, although there had been one in the school library, school now sadly a distant memory. She sat down happily and rocked back and forward, and her heart felt heavy, as she leaned back and started to cry. Her shoulders heaved up and down. She cried so hard that her chest began to hurt. It ached for many reasons, sad for her own miserable life, sad at the loss of the life she never had. It was clear from this little room alone that the children in this family were loved and cared for in the way that children should be. She could not believe her life now, what she had done, what she had become since that fateful day, what she was now capable of, her need for vengeance and her misguided immature feelings of resentment and revenge, served on so many people, most of them undeserving and innocent, not worthy of her evil desire. After those first two sleazy men had used her and scared her, she had taken the ultimate revenge, and avenged herself by taking their lives. Granted, death was maybe not the correct punishment for their crimes, but she felt they had deserved it. She wanted to teach that type of person a lesson. But once she had a taste for it, taking their lives didn't mean a lot to her, especially once she knew she had got away with it. She felt invincible. It made her feel strong and powerful. It had been thrilling and, with the help of her easily led, controllable, strong, older brother, she had been able to make them look like suicides. The police were too thick to catch her, her brother assisting with the dumping of their bodies into the water near to Gypsy Brae. She had it made it look like they had drowned, which of course they had, just not there. This had given her a feeling of superiority. She was untouchable and, with the way she looked and how she was perceived, who would ever suspect her?

Kerri, however, was unaware that the bodies didn't wash up where she and her brother had dumped them. Tidal currents normally move the stricken bodies further up the coast to Niddrie Bents, or over to Fife. She was also unaware that there had been further investigations into their position of discovery. One washed-up body in an abnormal location may have been an unexplained anomaly, some kind of tidal surge at the right time to skip the normal current pattern, but two had to be investigated further. The oceanographer had explained to the police that this should not happen at all and that there was most likely something untoward and a very different reason for their discovery there. Thus, on their expert advice, the first body had been exhumed and a further examination of the content of the lungs carried out, leading to the discovery that the water in the lungs was not sea water, but fresh water, with the remnants of some soap, skin cells, hair, oils, disinfectant and other substances found in bath water.

Kerri sat thinking. Originally, she hadn't given the police much credit. She had been naïve and arrogant. She still thought they weren't much use, but she knew her time would be up soon. The lighter fuel in her room, the fire with an accelerant, it wouldn't take a rocket scientist to be looking at her as a suspect for her parents' demise. They would all be out looking for her.

Kerri had no idea that the police she dissed at every opportunity were also busy looking into a series of unexplained deaths in the city centre, and they were linking them all together now that a figure matching her size and frame had been seen at or near to them all. DNA from the clothing of the deceased was being examined, as well as saliva from a straw at the scene of the now deceased man at Drylaw. That was being included because his death was so close to where she lived. The locals there usually only seriously injured one another. Murder was not a common event. Finally, the officers who were eventually detailed to look further into the suspected suicide of Phil Chancellor had found a tiny piece of biscuit wrapper under his cooker in the kitchen, and it too had had saliva traces on it, most likely from being bitten open and carelessly dropped, unnoticed at the time, and missed when Kerri had cleaned up.

She was tired, tired of running, tired of everything her life had become. She just wanted to turn back the clock and wished none of this had ever started, wishing that she had been born into a different life, a life like that of the baby who lived here. A life filled with love and kindness, one that she had longed for and would now never have. She thought of what would happen to her and from the floaty warmth she had just been feeling came a darker more sinister sensation, one of hatred and resentment, one of unfairness and menacing jealous thoughts, a feeling that had overpowered her many times recently, an insatiable urge to hurt people. It was unexplainable, almost impossible to imagine, but she had now killed nine people and, to her astonishment, she was still free and able to see how far she could go. She wondered just how many other deaths were treated as accidental, suicide or unexplained. How many others were like her, cleverly murdering and disguising a death as something else, without any investigation, far less what a murder enquiry would demand?

She rocked harder on the seat. She could feel it scraping the floor but didn't care. Her tears had dried on her face, her mood now much darker and unwholesome, a spiteful sensation circling within her, overwhelming jealousy at how things could have been for her and how unfair life was. "Why me? Why have I suffered so much injustice?" Why had these men picked her? Why were they so cruel? Their dark desires ugly and intimidating, their touch seeming to have tainted her skin, their needy hands all over her, rough and unkind, their own desire was all that they had cared for, lust-filled careless groping, unhealthy reasoning in their minds that this was alright. She was an adult, she wanted it, so much pain as they took her, and the deep-rooted, terrorised, revulsion at their cruelty, their lack of care and thought for her, for what she must be feeling. They didn't care. She questioned within herself, "Do they not have partners, daughters, female family members?" She felt disgusted inside and out and was glad they wouldn't get away with it anymore.

"CLICK!" The front door was being opened. The noise startled Kerri, a prickling sensation lifted her hair up from her neck, her spine now tingling with fear and apprehension, her darkest sensations overwhelmed, a mix of fear for herself and bottled-up resentment now taking over her previous conscious thoughts. A surge of rage and jealousy took hold of her. She thought of Marcus as another smug cop and had not looked any deeper into what he actually was, a kind and loving person, a committed father, and one of the many officers that really did care and want to make a difference.

Maria was happy, sitting close to the wee one. She was talking away, nattering about nothing in particular to the baby in the pram, little Lily gurgling happily, not understanding a thing being said, but it sounded nice to her coming from her mummy.

Maria made herself a well-deserved cup of coffee, making sure to be safe where she carried it and laid it down. She was so careful around the little one, so protective and caring, her heart bursting with love for the new arrival. Lily was just a little bundle of loveliness.

Maria nursed her, because she had started to grumble due to her hungry little belly telling her so. After feeding, Maria played and fussed around with her and cuddled her, and then it was time for her daughter to have a nap. Maria sang to her as she walked up the stairs, the little one nearly asleep now anyway. She entered her room, her nursery, her special haven, a room filled with love, many nice things surrounding her, a couple of paintings, vibrant oils, filled with life and beauty, beautiful scenery of the Isle of Arran, Goatfell high on the skyline, the heather purple on the hillside. Maria smiled to herself, knowing the choice of pictures was a little selfish and that Disney may have been more appropriate, but she knew that one day little Lily would come to love that place as much she and Marcus did. The island to them was like a little miniature Scotland, but one with a lot less crime, and a place they both held dear in their hearts. Wee David had already been over every year since he was born and loved it there too, the beaches, the scenery, the swimming pool at Auchrannie resort, and of course the ice cream, Arran ice cream, Scottish tablet flavour, yum. Maria thought to herself.

She leaned over the crib and placed Lily down gently. She was so careful as she laid her down, almost fearful that she might break her, she was so tiny and vulnerable, although, when she cried, she cried with vigour. Her little lungs were certainly not weak, and her character already one of strength.

Lily gurgled and cooed, as her eyelids flickered, and then she was asleep. Gentle snuffling could be heard, with the occasional little squeaky sound as she wriggled.

Maria looked at her sweet daughter, her own heart sore with the pain of love and the desire to protect her with every fibre of her very being, a fierce burning fire within every parent. She switched on the listener and took it with her. It went almost everywhere she went, and she would jump and rush to Lily's side whenever she heard anything out of the ordinary.

She went through into her own bedroom and lay down on her bed. She was tired and needed a rest, wishing she had the crib in beside her, but they had agreed with Marcus's shift patterns that his comings and goings would wake her up, and then there would be more disruption to what little sleep they got of a night. She hated being apart from Lily, even for an hour or two. Some evenings she would go through to the nursery with a blanket and sit on the rocker and watch one of her most precious beings sleep soundly, the motherly strings pulling her towards Lily, drawing her to her side, seeking comfort from the little one and vice versa.

Maria was a little worn out, and she drifted off to sleep, the listener on her pillow and her heart pulsing with love for her life, her children and Marcus. She was blessed, as sleep took over her.

Chapter 43

Accident or Not

Taylor and Marcus watched, their hearts in their mouths as the fire crews and SORT team scaled down the slope and onto the ledge. The first person brought up was Kay. Her face was a mess, her hair matted with blood, her legs splinted together, and the medics fussing around her, all of them having to be winched to safety. Taylor's heart was sore, aching with that sense of fear, one she had sadly felt before, and not that long ago. She feared for Kay, both physically and mentally. Would she be able to survive this again?

Taylor ran over to them the minute they were brought up to a safer place, and she gently took hold of Kay's hand. It was cold and unresponsive, which made Taylor recoil a little, as it didn't feel normal. Kay was showing no signs of life. Marcus stood there speechless. He could not believe that, once again, Kay was in a critical condition, again at the hands of a violent sexual predator, this time a colleague. Marcus had surmised from the video of Findlay, on the hill at the same time, that he had been responsible, a man on the edge recently with nothing to lose.

But they still had no idea what had taken place. No one at the summit had seen what happened, although they were aware there was another person down there who might have. According to one of the regular dog walkers, another female dog walker had been seen making her way down the steep slope.

The next person hauled up with a harness around her was Kat Pence, the woman who had raced to Kay's assistance and nearly got herself into trouble doing so. She had been close to heading over the cliff edge herself in her haste to try and rescue the stricken female.

Once up at the top, Taylor, who was watching Kay being loaded onto the chopper, turned and headed to speak to the woman who called the police and helped find Kay.

Taylor held out her hand in a greeting to Kat, who was being unstrapped. "Hi there. I'm Acting Inspector Nicks. Are you okay to answer a few questions?" she said with a smile, albeit she was tense and worried for Kay.

"Sure. Are you okay? Do you know her? You seem a little upset for a copper. You must deal with this type of thing all the time," Kat quizzed.

Taylor was nearly in tears at the realisation her emotions were there for everyone to see. "She's actually my partner, and she doesn't look too well at the moment. Thank you for helping us get to her and give her the best chance of survival. Did you see what happened to her?"

Kat winced a little as she stepped forward, and Taylor asked if she was okay. Kat smiled contagiously up at her, as Taylor was much taller, and stated quite comically, "I have a sore arse. I fell right on it on the way down, full weight too, and I nearly went arse over tit, nearly over the edge, in my haste to get to the injured lady, your partner!"

Taylor smiled back at her. She found it hard not to, as this lady was vivacious in character, and a genuine salt of the earth, brave and unselfish too. She had clearly risked her own life and safety to help another.

"I saw the lady in the stretcher from where we are. She was on the ledge. She seemed to be fighting with a fat guy who took hold of her. He had her on the ground, but your lady was able to fight back, and they both went over the edge together!"

"Where's the man then?" Taylor asked. "Did you see him? Is he alive? Can you describe him?"

"Nope, I never saw him. He must've fallen further down the cliff. He wasn't where your friend was lying. Has he been rescued yet?"

"We'll get to him soon, but you found Kay, which is the most important thing!" She saw Kat rubbing her sides. "Are you okay? You'll need to be checked over too, you know. You've clearly hurt yourself more than you're letting on," Taylor said as she ushered her over to one of the paramedics.

Taylor stuck around while they checked over Kat. They had to lift her top and lower her trousers a bit, making Taylor feel a little uncomfortable watching, but she did take in Kat's well-formed frame, which revealed a huge haematoma from the top of her pelvis down past her buttocks. It looked nasty, and there were bits of gravel embedded in it.

Kat winced when they pressed around it and stated that it would need scrubbed out, not overly happy about the scrubbing nonsense.

Taylor's attention was drawn away from Kat when there were shouts from the fire and SORT crews, who were winching another stretcher up.

This one took a little more strength and effort to get up there, as the frame of the man on it was weighty to the eye. He was clearly in a complete mess, and Taylor could not tell if he was alive. In her heart of hearts, she wished he wasn't. She hated him for what he had done to Kay over the time she had known her, how his gaze had made her skin crawl almost daily with his vile stare and hideous thoughts that she knew he was thinking about her partner. She had seen him, his eyes undressing Kay, as he watched her constantly.

She smiled at Kat, excused herself and moved over to where

they were bringing up Findlay. One glance and she knew it was him, his pudgy hands, his piggy little face, although it was pretty damaged.

She asked the two paramedics if he was alive, and they looked at each other, before one responded, "Barely, he needs airlifted immediately!"

Taylor could feel the bile rise up in her mouth. He was alive but there was only one chopper and her precious Kay was already in it! "No! No way! She can't be in the same place as him. He did this to her. This isn't right! I'm going too. This isn't right!"

Taylor was raging, her stomach twisting with hate-filled thoughts, as she climbed into the chopper. Even so badly injured, she would not be taking any chances with that vile little prick.

She took Kay's hand as the chopper rose, fear deep in her stomach, as the chilled touch was not comforting. it just built more fear, fear that Kay might not make it.

She looked over at Findlay. The medics were still working on him, and all she wanted to do was shove him out mid-air.

Chapter 44

The Net Is Closing In

Kerri stood over the crib, her heart racing at her situation, how much love the woman had shown this little baby. She wished it was her receiving this unconditional love. She didn't really want to hurt the baby, but she did want to show the smug cop that he should not underestimate her with his air of superiority that she believed he had shown to her. He wasn't like that at all; he had just been overwhelmed at how hostile and disconnected to reality she had been. It was her that had a misplaced air of superiority. Kerri hadn't liked to be put on the spot like that, which was Marcus's job. Her problem was that he was handsome like Phil had been, and what a liar he had turned out to be in her eyes. Her judgement had been so wrong before and was miles off the mark once again, her immaturity on full display. Her conviction that her thoughts were right had led her down a hideous path of revenge and hatred. She had dispatched so many people in such a short time, with not too many questions asked, the ease of escape hard to believe. It now fuelled her desire to continue. Their failure to capture her, to stop her, it was actually their fault in her mind, because they had not caught her sooner, which would have prevented her from hurting so many people. Her insane thoughts just made her keep doing it. The acts made her feel good, and she now did it because she could.

She felt trapped, trapped by her twisted sense of vengeance, but she was here. She had come to show Marcus how clever and powerful she could be.

"I'll teach him, and show him what loss feels like, intense sadness, loneliness, fear and insecurity, and this little baby is the key to all of that!" Her words were in whispers, but her face was contorted and unfeeling once again, her more human emotions now gone.

She reached into the crib, moving carefully so as not to wake the little one when she lifted her. She cradled Lily gently in her arms. She knew the woman she presumed was Marcus's wife would follow her. Her love for this tiny little child would drive the woman to the conflict Kerri desired. Kerri would let the fear and panic set in, and she knew the fight in the woman would be greater due to this. With a misplaced sense of power, she believed that the slight woman would be weak and defenceless against her.

There was not even a whimper as the little tot continued to sleep in her arms.

Kerri turned. There was a quiet squeak from her trainer on the floor, and she froze to the spot, her heart nearly beating out of her chest, fearful she would be discovered before she had even done what she had planned!

After that mistake, her senses heightened. She was more careful. She moved quickly. Silently opening the door, she left like a ghost, the baby undisturbed in her arms, lying there contentedly with a false sense of comfort and safety.

Marcus stood at the top of the hill and watched as the chopper took off. Taylor had accompanied it. Even with all the assurance and advice offered to her, she would never let that vile man lie beside her beloved Kay unsupervised, not even if he had been decapitated. His injuries looked pretty catastrophic, but, still, she was not taking any chances. If he was breathing, he was capable of his perverse thoughts and desires.

Marcus knew that this was going to be a long day for everyone involved and, being the type of man he was, he thought of his wife and family first and wanted to check in with them to make sure all was okay with the ones he loved. He had a niggling feeling in his guts. There was no reason for it, but it was definitely there.

Marcus's phone was ringing. It rang several times with no response. The sensation in Marcus's stomach now ignited, stirring a sensation of instant nausea, tinged with fear.

Maria had left her phone downstairs, and on silent because the baby was down for her nap. This was not normal for her. She would usually have it beside her on vibrate in case the school called about Wee Davy.

Kerri moved swiftly out the back door. The houses there led down to the river Almond, a place that could be really busy or quite pleasantly tranquil, depending on the time of day, and when you walked into the nearby Dalmeny Estate, there were steep banks where nobody walked. One led to the water's edge, and she chose that way to avoid any unwanted questioning eyes.

Marcus phoned home again, and then again. His human instincts were causing his hair to bristle and blood to rush through his veins, with no real reason, just a huge surge of adrenaline, which made him feel sick. He had work to do at the station, but his heart was summoning him home, NOW!

Maria must have been really tired. She didn't normally sleep so long. Little Lily would be demanding food and a cuddle, but clearly not today, Maria thought. She smiled at the thought of the wee one having a wee lie in to herself too.

Then her motherly instincts kicked in, NO! It was too quiet, not normal, causing painful pins and needles to stab cruelly into her face. She sat bolt upright and rushed through to the nursery. Lily was gone, missing, and she fell to her knees screaming, screams that cut through the air like a knife.

Terror once again ripped through her heart as she remembered David being kidnapped. But this time her fear turned to rage. Fierce predatory instincts, that of a wild animal, rose within her. At this point she was capable of murder to get her child back.

Marcus was really worried and was speeding through the city, his phone on constant redial still with no response, but, just as he was about to give up, Maria finally answered. Relieved, he was about to ask about her day, when a guttural roar exploded out of the phone.

"She's gone. The baby's gone. She's been taken. Why? Who would have done this? WHY ME? WHY HER? NOT AGAIN, MARCUS! I can't feel like that again. I can't take this anymore, not again! I'm going to search for her and when you get here, you'll hope that you find whoever did this before me, because I don't know what I'll do!"

Marcus was sick in his mouth, his heart sank to a new level with the pain of fear and sadness, but he too was now filled with rage, his mind circling around all the possibilities. What he had just witnessed, the current investigation, everything swirled around like wasps in his brain, trying to take in the magnitude of today. But his mind came quickly back to the girl, that girl. She would have had access to his wallet, his driving licence and his address. His mind wanted her to be just a mixed-up kid, but his heart told him from their very first meeting that she was unusual and, with what they had discovered this week, she was truly evil and capable of anything right now, because she was close to being trapped and caught. That would make anyone act differently, with nothing to lose, go out with a bang, teach people more lessons, and he could sense that she didn't like him. But, holy fuck, he thought, this is taking things too far, and he knew Maria. She was like a feral cat when it came to her children.

"Maria, listen! I'll call for help, get some officers down

there. Wait for me, I'll be there in five minutes!" Marcus pleaded. He didn't want Maria to do something she may live to regret, no matter what the circumstances were. He knew the law, and no matter how far you were pushed, things didn't always go in your favour in court when the good fought back rightfully against the bad.

CLICK! The sound, though quiet, was like an explosion in his ears. She had ended the call.

Maria ran frantically from her house, asking every person she met if they had seen someone with a baby. She had no idea who she was looking for, as she had cut Marcus off before he could say anything more about who Lily's kidnapper might be. She had assumed it would be a man that had taken her baby, just like they had done with David two years before. But she was wrong. It was a small-framed, pleasant-looking girl, with features that everyone's unconscious bias would not instantly judge. And, as Kerri had discovered, she could get away with murder with her impish, nonthreatening features, and she had done, repeatedly over the last few months, now more aware than ever that she had an advantage in life because people thought of her as harmless and weak.

Maria raced up the side of the river, her breath rasping. She was not as fit as she used to be, especially after giving birth recently. She could feel the burning sensation in her lungs. She was now crying. Those watching her run by were concerned for her, and at least two of them phoned the police, not knowing there were officers already on their way.

Kerri didn't know where she was going. She was not familiar with the area, so she kept close to the water and under the trees. The baby was awake and grumbling, which annoyed her a bit. She didn't realise that babies didn't do what you wanted them to do, when you wanted them to, and what she needed was for the baby to be quiet. She didn't know that babies can feel your emotions, your tension, and respond accordingly.

Suddenly, Lily's shrill and piercing cry was deafening. It would certainly draw attention to them. Kerri held the baby tighter, crushing her into her body to muffle the cries, as she kept on moving, to where she did not know. Then, to her surprise, the cries stopped, and the baby was silent.

Kerri released Lily from her grip and looked down at her. Lily's complexion had changed. There was a pallor to it. She didn't look the same.

Kerri panicked and quickly put the child down in the high grass by the river. This had not been her intention. Believing she had killed the baby, she felt odd, and a little scared.

Her mind was scrambled. She hadn't meant to harm the baby, just teach Marcus a lesson, make him feel small and helpless, like she had felt when he spoke to her, when all he had done was search for the truth and try and be kind, reining her in when she was challenging and hostile to Inga.

Kerri ran and ran, trying to get as much distance between her and the baby, tears streaming down her face, her mind regressing to that of a guilty child, fleeing from the telling-off she was about to get. For the first time, she felt remorse, guilt, regret. "What have I done? What was I thinking? Why, why a baby? Why anyone? Why me? I'm sorry, so sorry. Please forgive me, please." She reached the sea. The tide was coming in quickly. It was close to high tide.

Marcus called Maria again. She answered but didn't speak, as he told her his thoughts. She was running. Marcus explained about Kerri and described her, stressing that Maria should not approach her, as there was more to her than met the eye. Kerri was dangerous and capable of murder.

Kerri could hear the chopper in the distance, coming from Glasgow, as Edinburgh did not have its own. It had already been called earlier for the incident at Arthur's Seat, refuelling at Fettes, and that's why it was on the scene in minutes. Then she heard sirens and, to her surprise, footsteps fast approaching, and panting and rasping as a woman came into view, the same woman she had watched earlier, the lady she thought was Marcus's wife. She was sweating, her hair tousled as she had clearly been running off the beaten track, just as Kerri had done. Nobody Maria had spoken to had seen anyone with a baby, so common sense had told her to do what the hunted person would do, take cover and hide yourself.

Maria saw the young girl on the beach, just as Marcus had described her. Her heart sank as she realised she did not have Lily with her. Where was her sweet innocent little daughter?

Kerri froze, her mouth agape at Maria's appearance. She looked a little mad, feral, her eyes totally fixed on hers, her head tilted to one side in a maniacal stare.

"Kerri! It's Kerri, isn't it?" Maria quizzed the young woman on the beach, her tone of voice calm and demanding, unwavering and certainly not scared. Marcus had described Kerri to a tee.

Kerri was taken aback when Maria said her name. She couldn't understand how the woman had caught up with her so quickly. She looked mad, but oddly calm.

"Yes, I'm Kerri. Who's asking like?" she replied, a tone of insolence in her voice, which she quickly realised was a mistake.

It only enraged Maria more, her heart screaming out from inside her, her fears for her daughter rising up like molten lava, as she faced this insolent pup of a girl, who was now taking the piss out of her.

"Where is my baby, my daughter?" she began in a quiet and menacing voice.

There was an uncomfortable silence. Kerri squirmed where she stood, thinking she had killed the baby. She was actually frightened of this lunatic woman.

Maria moved closer and began screaming at the top of her lungs, "WHERE'S MY BABY? YOU BETTER NOT HAVE

HURT HER, OR I SWEAR TO GOD I'LL FUCKING KILL YOU WITH MY BARE HANDS, SO HELP ME!" Her face twisted into an ugly and threatening expression.

Kerri just stood still, not answering. She did not want to tell this woman about her now silent baby, fearing she would actually kill her. Maria looked deranged.

Maria moved quickly towards Kerri, her eyes never leaving hers. Her repeated pleas about the child came in rapid fire, but none were answered.

Kerri thought about fighting the woman, but she knew her rage would give her the edge, so she turned on her heels and started to run, but she had underestimated the softness of the sand. She had never run on sand before, but Maria had. She regularly used it for fitness training with its extra level of difficulty.

Maria was already tired from running and searching, but her motherly instinct was driving her, her insatiable love for her child and the relentless need to find her.

She closed down the space quicker than Kerri thought possible, and the girl soon found herself face down in the sand with Maria's body on top of her. Maria wrenched her head back with a brutal damaging grip of her hair and screamed right into the side of her face, spittle landing on Kerri's cheek, "WHERE'S MY FUCKING BABY? YOU BETTER NOT HAVE HURT HER OR I'LL RIP YOUR FUCKING FACE OFF."

Maria's grip tightened on Kerri's hair and she twisted it even more as she started violently shaking her head from side to side.

"WHERE THE FUCK'S MY BABY? THIS IS YOUR LAST CHANCE, YOU LITTLE FREAK." Maria's words were now slower and more menacing, as her temper rose to a height she had never experienced before, her fear for her child terrorising her. "TELL ME, OR I SWEAR TO YOU I'LL KILL YOU WITH MY BARE HANDS!"

Maria turned Kerri over onto her back, so she was now facing her, their eyes meeting, one's in fear and the other's filled with pure rage and madness. She brought her face right up to Kerri's, so close their noses touched. "THIS IS THE LAST TIME I'LL ASK YOU, WHERE IS SHE?" Tears were rolling down Maria's face now, her hope of seeing her baby alive fading, and her heart crumpled as she thought of the loss of her new love, her son, her husband and of what she was about to do.

She punched Kerri in the face, bursting her nose and lip, and repeated the question, Kerri not answering, because that could seal her fate. The baby had stopped crying and was still as a stone when she laid her down.

Maria wrapped her hands around Kerri's throat and started to squeeze, and squeeze, until her grip was ferociously tight. Kerri's eyes bulged hideously. She tried to grab at Maria and move her off her, but Maria was wiry and strong and knew how to fight, unlike Kerri, a cowardly monster that killed when her victims could not fight back.

Her vision was blurring, and she was drifting away, Kerri's life slowly ending, and with it came a sense of peaceful serenity, a feeling she had not felt in her entire life.

The force of Marcus's body shocked her, as he pushed his wife off the girl. It had an immediate effect, Maria's grip now released, but Kerri still lay there motionless. He had started on his journey way before any other officers were summoned, but they weren't far behind.

Maria was winded and lying on her side. Marcus helped heave her upright, not intentionally hurting her, and held her, tears running down her face, as she looked down at the lifeless body of Kerri, her lungs starved of oxygen long enough to kill her, her face drained of colour and her chest not rising and falling anymore.

Both sat there stunned, but Marcus sprang to life and

started CPR, refilling her lungs with oxygen, giving her another chance. She was young. Her heart was not the problem here and he could save her, her chances of survival higher than many of those he had tried to save in his time.

Maria sat and stared. "What the fuck do you think you're doing? Stop, STOP! Let that monster die. She deserves to die. She's a deranged bitch." The venom and demanding tone in which she spoke unsettled Marcus, and frightened him too.

Still giving compressions, he said calmly, "I'm not saving her; I'm saving you, because if she's dead, then you'll go to jail!" His eyes were kind, but desperate too.

Officers started to appear on the beach, along with medical assistance.

As they approached them on the beach, Cramond Island visible in front of them, Kerri moved slightly, a visible sign of life, then gulped in the biggest breath. Her eyes opened. They were doll-like, terrified and still, appearing to bulge from her face. There was petechial haemorrhaging in the whites of her eyes, and Marcus knew what had caused this, as he had witnessed it, and his morals were now being tested.

She looked at Marcus, and then at Maria, and started to cry, her tears genuine. She guessed that he had saved her and knew what Maria had tried to do. She rubbed her painful throat, as the numerous responders watched on, the paramedics now crouching down to help her, unaware of who and what she was, and what had happened there. They were all none the wiser, as no one was saying anything. The situation was surreal.

Kerri put her hand up to stop them and tried to speak. The words were not clear. "Sorry" was the only audible word, then more tears, then "I didn't mean it." Then Maria pounced on her again and slapped her face so hard that the others winced at the force.

"WHERE DID YOU PUT THE BABY? STOP FUCKING

FEELING SORRY FOR YOURSELF, YOU DERANGED LITTLE BITCH, AND TELL ME!" Maria had hold of Kerri's shoulders and was pleading with all her heart could offer.

"I left her further up the river in the brush near to the water. I didn't mean to hold her that tight!" Her words were coming out firm and truthful for the first time in a long time. They felt different to her, as if they were releasing some of her badness.

Maria began to sob, her shoulders slumped with the words that had been said. She seemed to visibly sink into herself, as if her hope had disappeared, and she cried uncontrollably. Marcus passed Kerri's message on to those responding, and to the dog handler who was already making her way along the riverbank from the other direction, aware that the river was tidal and the water was rising quickly. Marcus had not taken these words as his daughter's finality, and got up straight away and sprinted in the direction of the river upstream. Maria did not move, her sadness immense and for all to see, as she feared the worst. She did not follow Marcus, as she did not want to see her beautiful lifeless daughter. Tears flowed uncontrollably down her face.

The paramedics, put off by Kerri's fierce refusal for their offered assistance, had taken a wise step back, as the girl gave off vibes of violent anger. Arriving police officers were unsure who was who, as nobody was telling anyone anything. Kerri suddenly jumped up and ran towards the water, her pace quick on the wet sand. She leapt over the waves, knee high, and before anyone could respond she was more than waist deep and 30 metres out from shore. Her clothes were weighing her down now. Two officers started to remove their kit and stab vests, but their boots took longer, neither one of them wanting to drown with the weight of them.

By the time they entered the sea, Kerri was neck deep and treading water. Kerri's head was filled with mixed emotions, sadness, regret and now remorse. She felt she had no other option but to end her life. She was a lost soul with nobody there to love her. She wished she could turn back time and undo all she had done over the last few months and make different choices, but life doesn't work that way.

The sea was freezing cold, and she wouldn't last long. Other officers had been passing updates about the position of the female, and the helicopter was now hovering high above.

"She's neck deep, officers 20 metres back from where she is, shit! She's gone under; she's under." The slightly panicked officer watching the tragedy unfold couldn't believe how quickly she had disappeared.

Eyes fixed on where she had last been seen, the officer saw a hand and her angelic face appear one more time, before it tilted slowly backwards, enough to take her final breath, fear in her eyes, before the weight of her clothes pulled her down.

The sea was covered in windy squalls, the water being driven sideways by the winds, and the undercurrents were pulling in all directions, with the river also flowing into the area where she had gone under. The officers swimming out to her could feel the pull as they tried to keep on course, but the sea had a different idea, and was causing them to drift off course.

They arrived where they thought the girl should be and started to dive under in hope that they would touch a piece of her and bring her to the surface. Time was ticking and those on the shore knew it had been several minutes since the last sighting. If she wasn't found soon, her rescue was becoming less likely.

Taylor was listening to the transmissions. "How the fuck did they not have hands on her? Why was she able to get in the water, for fuck's sake? Whoever's down there will be in trouble." She knew fine well that the bosses, and the public too, would be looking to blame some poor officer. Nothing was ever the fault of the perpetrator, always the police, even though they risked their lives daily and were brought down by the constant negative, untruthful press.

Marcus was moving quickly, the water rising just as fast, his legs tiring, his pulse racing at the effort he was giving.

The baby lay less than a foot away from the river's edge, still silent and motionless. Her cheeks were a little pinker than before. Water began to swirl under her, and it was freezing. Little Lily didn't like a warm bath, far less an ice-cold one, and let out an incredible wail of annoyance, a clear signal of displeasure at her predicament.

Kerri gulped in another mouthful of sea water. Terror ripped through her, now regretting her decision to end her life, her instinctual efforts to get back to the surface and stay afloat were to no avail. She stopped moving in the darkness, life leaving her young body, her twisted life laid before her, the fear of dying was now gone. All that remained was deep sadness at what she had become, her loss, the betrayal, and the vengeance that had overwhelmed her, overawed by its power. Death was now upon her, unaware that she had not killed the baby. In her mind, she had given her life for the life of that little baby girl she had accidentally killed, guilt and repentance her final emotions.

Marcus ran wildly up the river, his heart skipping a beat as he heard the familiar sound of his daughter's healthy lungs, but he knew she was still quite far away. He could see the water creeping up at the river's edge. His heart was in his mouth, with the thought that she had survived, only to drown helplessly waiting on her daddy getting there to save her.

The dog heard the sound too, its hunter instincts unleashed as its pace quickened in the direction of the baby. It was free of the handler and now heading at full pace towards the squealing sounds.

The general-purpose dogs were powerful and dominant animals, able to confront the worst in society with controlled aggression. The handler raced after her charge. It had never tracked a baby before, a fact that dominated her thoughts. What would the dog do to a squealing baby? She hoped her worst fears would not become reality.

The dog raced through the water and onto the bank, stopping dead as it nearly stood on the child, now lying in two inches of water, and screaming!

The dog barked loudly and appeared aggressive as it looked upon the bawling child. It opened its jaws, baring its teeth close to her chest.

Lily's screams changed to coos and gurgling as she put her hand up to touch the dog. The dog snuffled her, taking in her scent, then decided to nuzzle the baby with its nose, and once again opened its mouth wide. Seeming to know the danger she was in, it gripped Lily's baby suit tightly, lifting her clean out of the water, and carried her away from the river and lay the baby gently down in the long grass. It wagged its tail and started barking louder and louder, summoning help, whilst it remained on guard of the helpless little mite, who was now crying again and very cold, the dog not bothered now at the squealing infant, having decided it was no danger to him. It lay down and curled itself around Lily, instinctive behaviour to warm and protect her.

Marcus raced into sight, a little too quick for Jet. The dog rose back up to its feet, hackles up, his snarl fierce and threatening, unknowing whether Marcus was friend or foe. All officers are trained to know when the GP dog is loose and to keep still as a statue in its sight, otherwise they are fair game for a chase or a bite and grip, neither of which would be very pleasant. Police officers call them land sharks.

Marcus slowed down but did not stop. He just wanted to hold his daughter, an error as the dog saw this as a threat and bounded aggressively towards him, barking and growling fiercely.

"STOP, STAY STILL. DON'T MOVE, OR HE WILL BITE YOU," the dog handler Lesley Laidler yelled, her voice loud and bracing. "JET, NO, STAY!" she commanded. But the dog kept bouncing forward, his tail starting to wag a little at his defiance, but the next command, "JET, HEAL, BALL," made him change course and start heading back, not to the handler, but to guard the helpless little baby.

Marcus, a little unnerved and knowing he was lucky not to have been nipped, asked if he could move. Lesley grinned at him, knowing he had so nearly shit himself there, and did like to tease the officers in suits. Lesley had been a handler for the last eight years. Jet was her second dog and he was a testing lad. She herself was a cheerful, playful soul, with a cheeky smile and a minxy nature, and scenarios like this were right up her street. She knew the dog wouldn't have bitten him as it would posture first, and only if he ran or threatened it would he bite, or on command of course. She stood there with mirth in her eyes at Marcus.

"Yeah, sure you can, but I don't think he'll let you have the baby yet!" She smiled as she watched the dog wagging his tail sitting next to the baby. Jet looked like he too was smiling, wide mouthed, very pleased with himself.

Lesley tethered the dog, praised him and threw him the ball, to his delight. "You're safe now," she said to Marcus with a broad smile on her face.

Marcus straightened his trousers and hoped he hadn't wet himself. He smiled at Lesley. "Thank you so much for finding her!" He had tears in his eyes, the stress of the whole situation, laced with the fear of being turned into a tea bag by a police dog, was all a little too much for him.

He moved quickly to where little Lily lay, and called in the exact position, before gently lifting her up into his arms and holding her close to him. He felt the cold clothing on her and snuggled her into him for warmth until the paramedics arrived with dry blankets.

Marcus sat down, his legs turning to jelly with the massive release of adrenaline and relief from the traumatic situation.

Chapter 45

Til Death Do Us Part

The beeps sounded loudly, as the wires and drips and other equipment worked to keep Findlay alive. His wife, Annette, looked down on him, surrounded by all this noise and chaos. Taylor had just left the single room in which her husband lay.

She had explained to Annette how he had come to be in this position, ensuring her words were loud and clear, ever hopeful that Findlay could hear her. And, to her delight and surprise, she did note the pulse monitor speed up momentarily.

Taylor had hugged her and apologised for the predicament she now found herself in, and she genuinely felt for the woman.

If Findlay had survived, he could face trial and lose all his pension benefits. If he died, then the pension would survive. Annette knew all of this and had been reeling for months as her husband awaited trial. He had made her life hell for the last 15 years. He owed her a decent life, without him, she thought to herself.

She looked at Findlay, his injuries, which would now require constant care, his physique, which had recently been ever growing, and her body shivered at the way he had behaved towards her, his demands, and the way he took them, and how that had belittled her and made her feel suicidal and depressed. She stood there with a feeling of helpless emptiness, regret that she had not divorced him and taken her life back, and half of everything, only now realising she was strong enough.

She leaned into him and whispered in his ear, her words cruel and unforgiving. She let him have it, everything she had ever thought about him or felt when he took her without consent. Now that he wasn't in a position to physically hurt her, she too would be pressing charges, and she would make sure he went to jail for more than a minor offence. She reinforced what the other prisoners would do to him, and she went on and on, and then, at the end of everything she had said, she changed her tone and got as close as she could. "You'd be better off dead, you know. It would be safer. Yes, that's the best thing for all of us. Your reputation, however low it might have been, will be gone; my reputation would go down with yours and my life as I know it would be over. Mud sticks!" she rasped in his ear with intent. "I think it's best for everyone if you were gone!"

She bent over and kissed him, her mouth fully covering his. Yes, her DNA would be on him, but totally explainable, no pillow fibres. She pinched his nose, her kiss similar to what he had forced on her repeatedly, wide mouthed and vile.

She switched off the heart monitor and anything else that would beep for the time being. She saw one of his hands tighten a little, but he couldn't use it. His eyes popped open. He could not believe what he was seeing, his wife suffocating him. He started to panic as the lack of oxygen took effect, but something else was happening. He was starting to fit, his convulsions breaking the seal and, unknown to Annette, he was going into cardiac arrest due to the panic and raised heart rate that his body was no longer able to tolerate so was choosing to shut down.

Annette panicked as he convulsed so violently. She pulled away and switched everything back on and wiped his mouth with her hand. The monitors sprang back to life, beeping and wailing, calling for assistance along with Annette, as she screamed out convincingly for help. There were sounds of trolleys, footsteps and chatter in the corridors, as the team came to her assistance.

They went to work, subduing the seizure and starting CPR. Findlay no longer had a pulse. They asked her to step aside and wait outside, which she obliged without issue, reaching out to a nurse, asking her to save her husband.

The nurse patted Annette's hand and said, "We'll do everything we can, but he's in pretty bad shape!" She apologised before leaving her and rushing into the room.

Minutes went by. They seemed to take an age, but Annette could hear a long continuous beep, and she had watched enough television programmes to know what a flat line meant.

She sat with her hands cupped to her face and cried, a mixture of relief, guilt, fear, and the unknown, her actions and whether she would be found out for speeding up his demise.

She looked up the corridor, searching for CCTV cameras, and her heart sank as she saw a camera in the corridor outside her husband's room. She wondered what it could reveal.

Chapter 46

DNA Confirmed

Chris Steele was in floods of tears when Taylor confirmed Kerri had been in the flat of his beloved partner Philip Chancellor and that there were paralysing drugs in Phil's system, some known to be used consensually, but, when combined with Kerri's DNA on the biscuit wrapper, this had been recorded as a murder. Chris was sad but relieved to know Phil had not killed himself, and not chosen to leave him. He took solace in the fact that his perseverance had allowed the investigation to take place and reveal the truth.

Investigations into the two drowned men were still ongoing, as where they were actually killed had still not been confirmed.

With regard to the two accidents/suicides in town, minute traces of Kerri's DNA had been found on the clothing of the victims, and CCTV showed her in the location of both of these deaths wearing clothing she was confirmed as owning, and they too were now being classed as murder.

Kerri's DNA had also been found on the cycle track where the brutal assault had taken place on a young man, but it was proving difficult to link her to having been involved in any crimes there, as there had not been any witnesses to the attack.

There was an abundance of circumstantial evidence in relation to her brother and her parents' deaths, and everything was being taken to the Crown Prosecution Service for decision and instruction. This was all in case Kerri was traced alive. She was still currently missing, and now being treated as a high-risk missing person.

Then there was the abduction charge for Marcus's daughter as well as many, lesser charges that paled into insignificance compared to her list of other serious offences.

Taylor and her team were astounded that a girl like this could be capable of this level of contempt and hatred and to think so little of other's lives. But they were more taken aback at the fact she was clever enough to cover up her behaviour and get away with so many killings without any investigation even beginning until it was too late.

The bosses were having a field day, blaming everyone but themselves. The knives were out, and the Kevlar vests were secured to the MIT officers' backs as the shit hit the fan. The press were sensationalising everything and belittling the police as usual. Negative press sold papers, and shit was always known to roll downwards.

Even looking back at everything they had, there had to be suspicion to proceed with further investigations in relation to any of these events, and there had certainly been no obvious link between them. If it hadn't been for the persistence of their colleague, Chris, and his knowledge of his partner and disbelief at him taking his own life, that too would have been written off as suicide.

Without a crystal ball into what had gone on, evidence to prove any foul play had to be searched for, as it hadn't been obvious. Only after they found reason for suspicion that a crime had been committed, could they justify the time, resources and expense to investigate fully. Unfortunately, the bosses wouldn't see it that way, even though they were privy to all the information available to the MIT, and they themselves had taken all of the incidents at face value with little or no concern or interest, and certainly no instruction to delve any deeper.

Chapter 47

Kay, Maria, Fran, Findlay, and Kerri

Taylor was visiting Kay. She was conscious and talking, but had some pretty damaging injuries. She was relieved Findlay had passed away, as she would never stop looking over her shoulder. She was very emotional. Everything she had worked towards over the last two years had taken a mammoth step backwards in relation to her mental health and, now that she was physically damaged, the hill to climb would be even steeper. Taylor sat up beside her and held her carefully, reassuring her she would be there for her and help her get through it once again.

Superintendents Brooke Sommerville and Lara Blantyre were reading over all of the documentation, where things could have been detected earlier, but without linking the full chain of events, maybe not. Everything appeared initially to be a list of tragic accidents, with no clear link to criminality until things had gone too far, but they were fair women, not everyone was like them.

Maria and Marcus were back home after the baby had been checked out and given the all clear. Even after what she had been through, she was fine and fit to go home. Marcus sat silently at first, but he felt the need to mention to Maria, what he had seen her do to Kerri at the beach. He knew if Kerri's body was traced, there would be damaging physical signs on her neck, and they would have to be explained, but he believed nobody else had seen anything, except the slap. They would cross that bridge when they came to it, and who knew what state Kerri's body would be in if it was ever found? Many people that had gone into the Forth had never resurfaced again due to the currents.

Fran cuddled into Lana. She felt safe there. She knew Lana truly loved her, but her heart and mind still wandered back to Taylor a little too often, and to Kay, and their situation. She had been Taylor's shoulder to cry on the last time Kay was recovering. She wondered if history would repeat itself and allowed herself to dream of this possibility.

Findlay's body was moved to the morgue, his eyes still frozen in a constant stare and his expression of surprise and betrayal etched on it, to be there forever more. There had been no suspicion of foul play in relation to his death in the hospital, and statements and evidence were still being gathered in relation to what happened with Kay up on Arthur's Seat.

A week later, Kerri's body popped up, slightly bloated, and now visibly floating on the surface. The tide was taking her to the shores of Niddrie Bents, her neck bruised and her nose clearly broken. The irony of where her body was going to wash up proved that where she had chosen to dump the bodies of her first victims was not where the sea normally likes to take them.

THE END

Previous Novels by Lee Cockburn

Devil's Demise
Book one in the series
published 2014

A cruel and sinister killer is targeting Edinburgh's most powerful women, his twisted sense of superiority driving him to satisfy his depraved sexual appetite. He reveals in the pain and suffering he inflicts on his unsuspecting victims, but a twist of fate and an overwhelming will to survive by one victim ruins his plans for a reign of terror. His tormented prey will need all her courage if she is to survive the hunt. DS Taylor Nicks, DC Marcus Black and the team are failing to get a positive lead as this unlikely monster wreaks havoc on the city, always managing to keep one step ahead of them. DS Nicks, a strong, intelligent and striking woman, is now under mounting pressure both at work and in her eventful private life. Can she stop the evil beast before he takes his ultimate revenge.

Porcelain Flesh of Innocents
Book two
published 2017

Detective Sergeant Taylor Nicks is back and in charge of tracking down a sadistic vigilante, with a penchant for torturing paedophiles, in this unsettling crime thriller by a real-life police Sergeant. Vivid, dark and deeply disconcerting, the perfect read for serious crime and police thriller fans.

High-powered businessmen are turning up tortured around the City of Edinburgh with one specific thing in common – a sinister double life involving paedophilia. Leaving his 'victims' in a disturbing state, the individual responsible calls the police and lays bare the evidence of their targets' twisted misdemeanours to discover, along with a special memento of their own troubled past – a chilling calling card. Once again heading the investigation team is Detective Sergeant Nicks, along with her partner Detective Constable Black, who are tasked not only with tracking the perpetrator down, but also dealing with the unusual scenario of having to arrest the victims for their own barbarous crimes. But with the wounded piling up the predator's thirst for revenge intensifies and soon Nicks discovers that she is no longer chasing down a sinister attacker but a deadly serial killer.

Demon's Fire
Book three
published 2019

The third instalment in the crime thriller series featuring DS Taylor Nicks and DC Marcus Black. The city had barely settled back to normal when the sky turned orange as flames licked upwards and smoke billowed out from a quiet industrial estate in Edinburgh. Blood curdling screams of those trapped within were muffled by the sound proofed room as the women climbed desperately over one another to try and escape, their efforts futile against their prison walls, their captors slain where they sat, bullet holes in their heads. Human trafficking, prostitution, drug dealing, kidnapping, violence and murder hidden in plain sight in Edinburgh City Centre. Drug dealer Burnett's grip on the city has no limits, and he will stop at nothing to ensure that remains the case. Nicks and Black struggle to secure evidence against him within the confines of the law, but an enemy of Burnett, hell bent on revenge, doesn't have to play by their rules. A thrilling story of crime and retribution, good versus evil, this novel will have you on the edge of your seat as the tentacles of despair take hold of your emotions. Hearts are broken and others mended as the tale gathers momentum, the lives of the officers forever entwined by fate.

Sylph or Satan is the fourth book in the series, where the two main characters Detective Sergeant Taylor Nicks and Detective Constable Marcus Black both detectives within the Major Investigation team continue their investigations into serious crimes within Edinburgh City, along with the continuation of their personal lives.

I apologise for the delay in the completion and publication of this novel. This was due to the Covid virus interrupting all normal life and several hundred hours of home schooling.